"Warren once again delivers a **high-acti[on]**"
—*Publishers Weekly* on *The Heart of a [Hero]*

"**Fast, intense,** adventurous read with all the feels."
—*Write-Read-Life* on *The Heart of a Hero*

"**Action-packed suspense**."
—*Life Is Story* on *The Way of the Brave*

"The **danger, risks, and romance**
all in one action-packed read."
—*Urban Lit Magazine* on *The Way of the Brave*

Books by Susan May Warren

MONTANA RESCUE

Wild Montana Skies

Rescue Me

A Matter of Trust

Troubled Waters

Storm Front

Wait for Me

GLOBAL SEARCH AND RESCUE

The Way of the Brave

The Heart of a Hero

The Price of Valor

THE PRICE OF
VALOR

SUSAN MAY WARREN

Revell

a division of Baker Publishing Group
Grand Rapids, Michigan

© 2020 by Susan May Warren

Published by Revell
a division of Baker Publishing Group
PO Box 6287, Grand Rapids, MI 49516-6287
www.revellbooks.com

Printed in the United States of America

Library of Congress Cataloging-in-Publication Data
Names: Warren, Susan May, 1966– author.
Title: The price of valor / Susan May Warren.
Description: Grand Rapids, Michigan : Revell, a division of Baker Publishing
    Group, [2020] | Series: Global search and rescue; 3
Identifiers: LCCN 2020003609 | ISBN 9780800735869 (paperback) | ISBN
    9780800739225 (hardcover)
Subjects: GSAFD: Love stories.
Classification: LCC PS3623.A865 P75 2020 | DDC 813/.6—dc23
LC record available at https://lccn.loc.gov/2020003609

20　21　22　23　24　25　26　　　7　6　5　4　3　2　1

CHAPTER ONE

AS LONG AS HAMILTON JONES had breath in his body, nothing, not even tooth decay, would hurt his little girl.

"Seriously, Ham? It's cotton candy, not meth. Let the poor girl taste a cloud of pure sugar." Jenny Calhoun looked at him with one eyebrow raised, amusement in her expression.

He couldn't look at Aggie staring up at him with those pretty blue ten-year-old eyes. "Please, Daddy?"

Shoot. Agatha Jones had employed the lethal *Daddy* kryptonite, a name she'd been using with devastating regularity for the past month.

Ham dug into his pocket for a couple George Washingtons.

Aggie jumped up and down, clapping, her blonde braids whipping around her head. She'd lost a tooth just last week—one of her primary molars—and it had completely freaked him out.

He'd googled it, taken her to a dentist, and discovered that apparently kids lost teeth until they were twelve. So maybe getting a little sugar decay wasn't the end of the world, but . . .

"Just this once," he said as he slapped the dollars into her hand. She grinned, a gap in her gums, and took off for the cotton candy stand.

Next to him, Orion laughed. "Ham. You've said that five times today."

He glanced at his teammate, and especially at the oversized stuffed moose Ry carried under his arm. Ham had won it for Aggie at a sharpshooting booth. Ham would be carrying it, but he already carried the dolphin he scored for her at the balloon-dart booth.

So he turned into a pansy when his amazing, beautiful little girl smiled. But sheesh, he'd only recently discovered that he was a father. He had ten years to make up for.

The night was cool, the crispness of early autumn spicing the air. Overhead, stars fell across the horizon, but the bright lights of the county fair and carnival blurred them out. Ham and Aggie had spent the day watching piglets, petting lambs, climbing on pretty green tractors, eating mini donuts—another of his fatherly fails—listening to country music, and figuring their way through a hay maze.

All that remained was the midway.

No. As in all caps. N.O.

The last thing he wanted was his daughter losing her gray matter on one of those spinny rides gone wild. He'd heard horror stories of seat belts failing and kids launching from the twirling cups of poorly maintained traveling carnival rides.

Besides, he'd made promises to . . .

Nope. Not thinking about *her*. Except, shoot. Signe was always with him, there, in the back of his head, haunting him. *"Don't try to find me."* Her last words to him, right after she'd left Aggie in his care.

Right. Ham had been struggling with his response for three months now. He didn't do "sit around and wait" easily. Not when someone he loved needed him.

Except, maybe Signe didn't need him. Had never, really, needed him.

Yeah, he'd been all kinds of foolish when he married a woman who so easily walked away from him.

"I want to go on the Ferris wheel," Jenny said as she looped her arm through Orion's. She wore her blonde hair pulled back into a long braid, a jean shirt, and a pair of leggings. Orion found her hand and braided his fingers through hers. He barely limped anymore from his recent knee surgery, and just last week, he'd started instructing a new ice-climbing class at Ham's GoSports Minnetonka location. He wore a T-shirt and a pair of cargo pants, his Alaskan blood always hot down here in the Lower 48.

Ham followed Orion's glance at the Ferris wheel. The ride had romance written all over it, lights glittering against the Minnesota night sky.

Ham knew that on this weekend's agenda, this little getaway to Jenny's former foster family's winery in midwestern Minnesota, was Orion's hope of proposing.

"Hand me the moose," Ham said, and Orion grinned at him.

Ham stood there, one animal under each arm as Orion and Jenny left to get on the ride. It looked safe enough—each seat formed to look like a balloon with a basket and an arched roof.

"You must be a sharpshooter to nab such big prizes." A man stood nearby, looking up at the Ferris wheel, then at Ham. Dark complexion, dark hair. He had a hint of an accent. His face was reddened with a fresh scar on one side, as if he'd been in a terrible accident.

"Naw. Lucky shots," Ham said.

The man looked back at the Ferris wheel and waved. A number of children in the array of baskets waved back, so he couldn't be sure which kids were his, but the man turned to him. "We'll do anything for our kids, won't we?" Then he walked away. Yes, actually, he would.

"Daddy, do you want some?"

7

He looked down and found Aggie looking up at him, grinning, holding out a fluffy piece of blue cotton candy.

For a second, he was back in time, Signe grinning at him as they sat on a picnic table near the blue waters of the community pool, her blonde hair a mess, her face grimy as she held out a melting ice-cream cone. *"Want some?"*

He drew in a breath.

Aggie's eyes widened. "Daddy?"

He wasn't sure if he saw fear or just confusion in her pretty blue eyes, but whatever it was, it snapped him back to now, and he crouched before her. "Yeah, I'd love some, honey." He opened his mouth.

She smiled and fed him the cottony sugar.

Oh my. He hadn't had cotton candy since . . . well, maybe that was another memory he should tuck away. It seemed that every good childhood memory contained a shadow of Signe.

He really didn't know how he'd survive knowing she was out there . . .

"Don't try to find me."

Right.

"Ooh, look. Orion and Jenny are on the big Ferris wheel!" Aggie's gaze had turned past him. He noticed that she wore ketchup from today's hot dog on her teal Frozen-themed sweatshirt. And a hint of chocolate ice cream on her sleeve.

Apparently Orion was right, he had problems saying no. But how was he supposed to deny anything to this pint-size version of the woman he'd never stopped loving?

"I wanna ride!" Aggie grabbed his hand and pulled him with her. Ham nearly fell, still crouched, but managed to scramble up and pull her back.

"No, Aggie. We're not riding—"

"Please?"

From high above, Jenny was calling to them, waving. Aggie waved back wildly. "Please, Daddy? I've never been on one."

Really? He knew so little about her past ten years. Aggie had shown up three months ago on a seashore in southern Sicily after the yacht she'd been a passenger on, with her mother, had exploded in the Mediterranean. The US Air Force base took her in after she identified herself as an American . . . and former SEAL Hamilton Jones as her father.

He'd gotten on a plane, not sure what to believe. After all, he'd watched Signe die ten plus years ago in Chechnya, during an op-gone-wrong.

"I don't think so, pumpkin."

"Please?" Her cheeks were stained blue. He pulled out a napkin from his pocket and tried to wipe her face. She jerked away.

Yes, sometimes he'd really like to know what happened to his child over the past ten years to put that hue of fear into her eyes.

Except, just thinking about it gnawed a hole through him. Maybe he didn't want to know the details.

He handed her the napkin and she wiped her face.

Around them, the midway was a cacophony of screams and laughter, music and the smells of fried cheese curds and hot dogs. People milled everywhere, crowds ever moving through the narrow thoroughfares. The perfect place for someone to sneak out and grab her when he wasn't looking. Only a couple months ago, that very thing had happened at the Mall of America. Someone from Signe's past.

A Russian.

Probably in league with the man who had held her hostage for ten years—Chechen warlord Pavel Tsarnaev. That much Ham had gotten out of Aggie.

Yes, better that he didn't know the details of Aggie's past, or he might never sleep again.

Might, in fact, completely ignore Signe's request and find her anyway.

Because deep in his gut, he knew she was in trouble.

Needed him.

The Ferris wheel was slowing to let people out, and Aggie ran over to Jenny as she got off.

Ham followed. Raised an eyebrow to Orion.

Orion shook his head.

Yes, well, pulling your heart from your chest and offering it to a woman with a proposal just might be the most terrifying act a man did. He well remembered when he proposed to Signe.

He'd meant forever.

Apparently, she thought their marriage should just last the weekend.

No, that wasn't fair. He shook the thought away as Aggie ran back to him. "Jenny said it was amazing. You can see for miles."

Ham gave Jenny a look. She shrugged. "It is. You can."

"Please, *please*? I won't ask for another thing tonight, I promise."

Oh kiddo. "Honey, it's not . . ."

"Go with her, Ham. I'll hold the zoo." Orion stepped up to him and reached out for the stuffed prizes.

"Yay!" Aggie said and shot up the ramp.

"What—wait!" He dumped the animals in Orion's arms, about to follow, when his phone buzzed in his back pocket.

He pulled it out.

Seriously?

"Aggie! Wait for me—hello?" Maybe he shouldn't be quite so abrupt when he answered the call of a US senator and presidential candidate.

"Are you okay, Ham?" Former SEAL Isaac White's low, calm voice came through the line.

"Yes, sir," Ham said, frowning at his daughter as she gestured to him to join her. He shook his head. Mouthed a very clear *Wait for me.*

Then he turned away to keep her from distracting him and put his other hand to his ear. "Just at a fair with my daughter."

"I hope this isn't a bad time, but I need to talk to you."

"Absolutely. What can I do for you?" White had ferried his team back from Alaska after a near-bombing three months ago, and besides that, he and Ham went way back to when they served together on Team Three.

"Can you come to DC? I need a favor, but . . . well, I need to talk to you face-to-face."

"This about our mutual friend the Prince? And the rumors that the CIA NOC list is—"

"There's a fundraising event Tuesday night for the Red Cross. Maybe you and your team would like to join us?"

Ham could hear the unspoken plan—White was suggesting a cover story for Ham's trip.

Which meant their meeting was something he didn't want the media, or maybe even Ham's people, knowing about.

"I can make that happen," he said, watching a mom and dad pick up their young son and swing him between them. The kid laughed, kicking his legs.

"So, I'll put you down for how many tickets? Eight?"

"Seven." Orion, Jenny, Jake, Aria, North, and he'd ask Scarlett, his newest addition, to join them.

"Perfect. Thanks, Ham. Text me when you get in."

"Aggie!" Jenny's shout behind him made him turn.

Everything inside him went cold. She'd gotten on the ride without him.

But that wasn't the worst.

His brave, headstrong, curious daughter—and she got those

11

genes directly from her mother—had boarded one of the rusty, ancient balloon chairs and risen to the apex of the Ferris wheel. But, as the ride came down the back side, the basket had swung and somehow latched on to the basket next to hers.

As the ride moved toward the far side, her basket had begun to tip.

If it kept going, it would invert, dumping her right out.

"Stop the ride!" He took off up the ramp toward the operator who was frantically trying to slow it down without jerking it to a violent stop. Ham pushed him away and slammed his thumb into the emergency stop.

The entire ride shuddered, screeching and groaning as it halted.

Screaming. Not just the spectators, but Aggie, high above, maybe fifty feet, clinging to the basket.

It had inverted to nearly a forty-five-degree angle, and she clung to the bars, her legs dangling over the edge.

Ham's heart stopped, a rock right in the middle of his chest.

"Help! Help me, Daddy!"

She might not have said it, but Ham heard it, deep in his bones.

"Hold on, Aggie!"

While every shred of common sense told him to wait for the emergency help, the father inside him wasn't listening.

It wasn't a difficult climb. Up the center spokes to where they connected at the center, maybe six feet apart. Then a climb up each one until he came to Aggie's.

"Hang on!"

Except she was kicking, screaming, and using up all her energy. "Calm down! I'm on my way!"

"I'm falling!"

"No you're not! You're going to hold on until I get there. Hold on!"

He hit his hands and knees, scrambling along the edge to her balloon. But the way the carriage had stuck, the back of the basket blocked his entrance.

"I'm almost there, honey." He swung down, dangling as he started to work his way the last few feet.

The Ferris wheel began to move.

"Stop the ride!" Maybe the emergency stop had malfunctioned on this decrepit ride.

"Hold on, Aggie!" The basket inverted and now Aggie, too, dangled from just her grip on the pole.

"I can't!"

He reached for her, missed. Her fingers began to loosen.

Nope. Not on his watch. He'd made promises to Signe. To himself.

To God, long ago, when he said, "I do."

He swung and wrapped his legs around her body. "Grab onto my waist!"

She looked at him, wild-eyed, then lunged for him.

"Lock your arms around me," he said. Sweat slicked his hands. He just had to work them back to the jutting arm—

The ride stopped, a violent jerk that nearly dislodged Ham's grip.

Aggie slid down to his hips, then his thighs. He clamped them tight. "Aggie, hold on to me!"

She looked up at him, tears staining her face. "I can't!"

"You can and you will," he said, finding a voice that he'd used for years commanding his SEAL teams. "You are my daughter, and I know you can do this."

She swallowed, nodded.

He worked them over to the arm, his body trembling. Now to get her up—

A hand snaked down over his shoulder. "Reach up and grab my hand, Aggie."

Orion. Ham looked up and his buddy was leaning down over him, his legs hooked into the girder.

"I . . ." Aggie met Ham's eyes, hers pleading.

"I got ya," Ham said and pulled his legs up.

Orion grabbed her wrist, then the other. Suddenly she was swinging free, being hauled up by Orion to the metal arm of the wheel.

Ham hooked his leg on the edge and pulled himself over onto his stomach. His breaths gusted out, hard. He found her ankle and wrapped his hand around it, holding on.

"You're okay, kiddo," Orion said. She was crying, Orion's arms wrapped around her as he held her on his lap.

Ham pushed himself up, not wanting to look down, then trying not to lose it at the distance to the ground. A fist in his chest cut off his breathing.

In the night, sirens blared.

"Here," said Orion, untangling Aggie from his waist. He turned her toward Ham. "I'm going to check on the kids in the car above, see if they're okay. Their car didn't tip as much, but—"

"Go." Ham pulled Aggie to him.

She hung on, still weeping.

He wanted to cry too. "I got you, honey. Don't worry. Daddy's not going to let anything happen to you. You're safe."

He closed his eyes and heard the rest of the last conversation he had with Signe.

"She's safe. I got her."

"Thank God. Please keep her that way, Hamburglar."

Yes. No matter what it cost him, he'd keep his daughter safe.

Below, a fire truck had set up, was disengaging the ladder.

"You did good hanging on."

Aggie sucked in a breath, leaned back, and looked up at him, those big eyes in his, holding him captive. "I was trying to be brave, like Mama always told me to be. She'll be really proud of me, won't she?"

And shoot, he couldn't help but nod.

He wiped her cheek with his thumb and looked out to the lights of the homes that glowed against the darkness. To the horizon and the milky white moon.

To where, somewhere, he just knew Signe was in trouble.

■ ■ ■

Signe didn't want to get dramatic, but the fate of the free world was at stake.

But first, she had to finish her cup of coffee.

Quietly. Deliberately. *Nothing to see here.*

Just a woman sitting in a cafe off the center square of Bad Rappenau, a tiny town southeast of Heidelberg, watching the sun gild the cobblestones and the massive Lutheran church that overlooked the cafe. A nondescript woman in a pair of leggings, boots, a rain jacket, and a hat, her blonde hair tucked up in back. She was wearing sunglasses, but she didn't look any more like a spy than the man sitting across from her, with short dark hair and a blue jacket, black dress pants. He read a German paper.

Or the man who'd parked his bicycle, wearing skinny jeans and a sweater, a scarf knotted around his neck.

Or even the girl at the counter—short black hair, wearing a dress, leggings, and boots.

See, no spy here.

No dangerous information tucked away in her inside pocket, like a grenade should it make it out into the open.

No deep undercover CIA agent holding the world's secrets in her jacket. The NOC list. The list of nonofficial covers of operatives around the world.

She glanced toward the center fountain, the four arched cherubs that shot water out of their mouths. The spray caught the sun, arched it into a rainbow.

The old story about Noah hung in her mind, just for a second. Forgiveness. Fresh starts.

Nursery rhymes and stories that had nothing to do with reality.

The bells on the church rang, scattering a grouping of pigeons, and the scent of fresh apple kuchen from the nearby bakery could make her weep if she hadn't just breakfasted with her old Doctors Without Borders friend, pediatrician Zara Mueller, and her husband, Felix.

Probably she shouldn't have landed on their front step two weeks ago, but she'd run out of options.

Run out of safe houses.

Run out of hope, really.

Because, according to the latest news on CNN, she was also running out of time.

The man with the paper folded it and picked up his coffee. Looked at her and smiled.

She gave him a quick smile back, then focused again on her phone, not looking at anything but her peripheral surroundings. She sat with her back to the wall, in an outside chair, one ear on the conversation inside the cafe, one eye on the fountain.

Roy was late.

No tall, former SEAL who now worked as . . . well, she didn't know his job description, really. Just that he was the one guy she could trust to bring an end to this mess.

Probably there was one other former SEAL she could trust too, but she couldn't involve him.

Roy was supposed to be sitting on the edge of the fountain by the time the last bell tolled, feeding the pigeons. Then, he'd roll up his sleeves so she could identify him by a tattoo of a bonefrog, one of the universal Navy SEAL tats.

She finished her coffee. Glanced at the clock.

Five minutes late.

Yeah, this didn't feel right. She got up and tucked her jacket around her, not sure what to do. But if Roy was late then—

"It's a beautiful day."

The voice, in English, turned her. The dark-haired man who'd sat across from her had also risen.

She stilled, not sure she wanted to speak in English.

He stepped out beside her, close enough to touch her. She closed her hand around a tiny 9mm Luger she'd borrowed from Felix.

Because Felix was on the list. And he had just as much at stake in this meet as she did.

She hoped he was still watching as she ignored the man and stepped into the square, intending to take a walk around the block and maybe through the gardens of the nearby castle as she figured out her next move.

Felix and Zara were probably growing tired of her bunking in their spare room.

"Why didn't you just destroy the list?" Zara's question lingered in Signe's mind as Zara made spätzle and sausage last night, her hair tied back in a handkerchief, so much like the days when they served in the refugee camp together.

Well, actually, Signe was there for other reasons, using the organization to position herself to be in the right place, right time.

Zara was supposed to be her in-country contact, a plan that Signe had talked the pediatrician into.

Signe never planned on staying ten years.

But then again, back then she didn't look too far ahead. Because she'd learned that you simply couldn't trust plans.

The only one you could really count on was yourself.

Well, and maybe Hamilton Jones, but . . . yeah, she'd burned that bridge one too many times.

Love versus her country. Oh, her misplaced ideals had cost her—and Ham—so much. And for what? So she could spend ten years waiting for a warlord to hatch a terrorist attack she hadn't been able to stop anyway.

She should have escaped years ago, but, well, Aggie.

Pavel never let Aggie too far out of his eyesight.

She'd simply gotten lucky, and maybe brave, that night three months ago on his yacht in the Ionian Sea.

"I can't destroy it," she'd said to Zara last night, running her thumb over the edge of her teacup. Felix was out, securing her a fresh German passport. She had her American version, and a Russian Federation version, but it would be easier to travel in the EU with something from the European states. "The NOC list isn't just a Word doc that anyone can open. It comes with layers of encryption, and each copy comes with a master key that is unique to the user authorized to open it. Which means the file contains metadata that can tell us who sold the list out of US hands." And prove her theories about a traitor at the helm of the US government.

"How did you get it away from Tsarnaev?"

Oh, that was a story she didn't want to detail. The short of it, however, was, "I blew up his yacht. Stole a dinghy, dropped my daughter on shore, and ran."

It was just as terrible as it sounded and she looked away, outside, across the red-clay roofed buildings.

Zara had paused then, turning to look at her. "Hamilton's child."

She'd only been barely pregnant when they'd been attacked, but even before that, Zara had been there when Ham reappeared in her life and nearly wrecked Signe's big plans.

Nearly made her abandon her vision, her ideals, and run into his arms.

She'd been strong for her country.

No, she'd been a fool. And clearly was still a fool. Because what if she'd stayed with Aggie and returned home, with Ham?

Well, really, maybe they'd all be dead.

"Did he know about her?" Zara asked.

"Not a clue."

Zara raised an eyebrow.

"I couldn't jeopardize my cover with Tsarnaev. So . . ."

"So you raised your daughter in a terrorist camp."

Signe's mouth tightened, and she looked away. "It wasn't like that." But yes, it felt like it. "When I realized I was pregnant, it was too late." She looked back at Zara. "At least she's safe now."

"With that SEAL."

"He's not a SEAL anymore, but yes. Hamilton has her. Nothing is going to happen to her on his watch, I guarantee it. He's like a Doberman about the people he loves."

About her, really.

Oh, he hadn't deserved the way she treated him.

"Which is a good thing because I've got a target on my head. If I step foot in the US, they'll either label me a terrorist, because of my years with Tsarnaev, or the company will grab me and . . . well, you've heard the rumors, right?"

Zara had gone back to stirring. "About a rogue faction in the CIA who have aligned with Russia and are trying to derail the election?"

Uh, *yeah*?

Zara glanced over her shoulder. "I also heard some rumors that there might be a contract out on you."

Signe stilled. But she should have expected that.

Zara had lost weight after her escape from Chechnya, but then again, being nearly kidnapped by a warlord probably sent her into some kind of PTSD. The fact that she met and married Felix made Signe wonder what kind of counseling Zara had received. Felix had been in the KSK, German special forces, but now sold books at a local used bookstore.

Right.

Now, with the meet a bust, the last thing they needed was trouble invading their lives. She'd have to figure out somewhere else to lie low—

"Signe."

Her name on the man's lips stilled her, and she cringed, painfully aware of her stupidity. She kept walking.

"Roy sent me."

No, no—she didn't stop. Because he'd have to say—

"The sparrows don't fall without someone watching."

She stopped, glanced over her shoulder. The man was a few steps behind, his hands out where she could see them. Okay, so maybe . . .

He gestured into a walkway between the buildings that led out through a park.

Stores had begun to open, a bus stopped nearby and let out passengers. A few wandered through the square.

And from the churchyard, Felix was watching. *Please, follow me . . .*

Except, maybe not. Because people who followed her usually ended up getting hurt. The last thing she wanted was to see one of her oldest friends get burned, or worse.

But maybe, if this wasn't a setup, and she played the game right, they'd all be safe.

She could stop running.

And maybe, someday, go home.

"Don't try to find me."

Her words to Ham still burned her throat.

So she slowed and let the man catch up.

"Where's Roy?"

"Something came up. He sent me."

"Who are you?"

"The name's Martin. Do you have it?"

It was the way he said it. Not the words as much as the tone. Reminded her way too much of Pavel, of the way he'd get when he was annoyed.

And then people got hurt.

She had learned how to handle him. "No. But it's close."

"Didn't trust Roy, huh?" He ended with a chuckle, as if the lives of two hundred people working as nonofficial CIA operatives undercover around the globe was something to be dismissed.

Yeah, it irked her.

"There's a lot at stake," she said calmly, as they came out to the street. Across the street, a cafe hosted breakfasters under red umbrellas. Cars slowed as they drove by on the cobblestone. "The security of our government."

"Which is why we need to get it into safe hands."

Right.

"I'll get it, and meet you back here in an hour."

He grabbed her wrist. "Or, you could take me with you." His fingers bore into her bones. She wanted to twist out of his hold, but here they were, in the middle of the street.

And that's exactly what Pavel would do. Get her in public where she couldn't run and start the threats. Threats that became reality in private.

"Let go of me," she said softly.

"Give me the list," he said, closing the gap between them.

She pressed the nose of the Luger into his gut. "Step back."

He raised an eyebrow, and for the first time, she got a good look at him. A scar across his right eyebrow shadowed dark brown eyes, and pockmarks on his face betrayed an acned youth. Maybe six foot, he bore the brawn of a thug in his shoulders and eyes.

He smiled. "I walk away, and your friend dies."

She drew in a breath.

He pulled his phone from his pocket. Showed her a snapshot.

Felix, blindfolded, wearing the clothes he'd had on when she'd left his flat. Clearly, he'd been taken from the churchyard, and now a gun was held to his head. It looked like . . . yes, he was in his flat, in his kitchen, which meant—

"Don't make us kill him with the wife watching."

Oh—see, this was why she couldn't go home. Because no matter where she went, trouble followed.

People died.

She swallowed hard. "You work for her, don't you?"

Martin cocked his head. "We both work for her."

She shook her head as he put the phone away. "I never wanted this. This was not the plan—"

"I'll count, if that makes it easier. One—"

"This is treason, you know. People who gave their entire lives for their country—"

"Two." His hand went around her gun and drew it out of her grip. Smiled.

A car drove by. Pigeons scattered.

"Three—"

A shot cracked the air and Martin jerked back, away from her.

Signe spun, not looking to see if he was wounded, and took off. Back through the alleyway, into the square, up the hill toward the church, past it, along a footpath to a restaurant. Up the back stairs, three flights.

The apartment door hung open. A whistle shrilled the air.

"Zara!"

Her friend's body lay in the foyer, the blood sticky, drying from the wound across her neck, her eyes glassy.

No—*no*— "Felix!"

She edged past Zara toward the tiny kitchen.

The teakettle sounded from the stove, the steam sweating the cupboards.

The kitchen had been destroyed, the table overturned, chairs broken.

Felix lay on the floor, bruises covering his face, his hands over his gut where blood streamed out between his fingers. The blindfold had been ripped off.

She grabbed a rag and shoved it against the wound. Deep, his intestines spilling out—he'd been gutted. "Felix—I'm here—"

He opened his eyes, seeing her, gasping, and let out a moan. "Go—"

"No, I'm staying—"

"*Run!*" His voice died, breaths coming fast. "Can't . . . they can't . . . find—"

Footsteps up the stairwell made him grab her shirt with his bloody hand. "Out the window—"

She was on her feet, pushing open the tiny window that led out to the clay-tiled roof. The red tiles broke off as she scampered across them.

She ran to the edge. The house dropped away into a thin alleyway, three stories down.

The next roof was six feet away.

She backed up, glanced behind her.

A man was coming out Felix's window.

She turned around and sprinted off the roof. Bit back a scream as her arms windmilled, her legs running—

She landed hard, kicking off tiles, scrambling for purchase.

Found her feet.

The man had cleared the window, was running across the roof.

She jackrabbited across the top, the tiles sliding out beneath her feet. She fell and slid down the slanted roof, tiles flying off the top like dominos.

She stopped just as she careened over the side, her fingers digging into the sharp lip at the edge of the roof.

Kicking, she tried to hook her ankle on the edge of the roof. It slipped and she fell, one grip dislodging.

She pawed at the top, her left hand straining to hold her.

Footsteps ran across the roof, the man having also jumped the gap.

She looked down, her hold disintegrating.

A balcony jutted from below her, maybe ten feet down.

And if she missed it . . . the ground, another forty feet.

Jump, just be brave—

"Gotcha!"

A hand closed around her left wrist.

She looked up at her captor. She'd seen him at the cafe, the bicyclist in the skinny jeans.

Zara's words from last night stabbed at her—*"I also heard some rumors that there might be a contract out on you."*

This was not over.

Because the fate of the free world was at stake.

She lifted her leg and drew out her Ka-Bar from her boot, ran her blade across his knuckles.

He shouted, let her go.

She pushed off the edge.

Fell.

Dropped hard onto the balcony. Pain streaked up her ankle and maybe she'd twisted it.

She had lived through worse—much worse—pain than a little sprained ankle.

Gritting her teeth, she found her feet.

Yanked open the door to the apartment.

Footsteps thundered above as she banged through the flat. Empty except for a cat, which spooked and hissed at her.

She flung herself into the hallway, fled down the stairs.

Then she was out into the street, the pain a dull hum as she ran for her life.

CHAPTER TWO

HAM HAD GIVEN UP any attempt at sleep around three a.m., when visions of Signe running intermingled with Aggie's crying and the screams of onlookers as she dangled from the Ferris wheel basket.

He might never sleep again until he knew his wife was safe.

After two hours of staring at the ceiling, he got up and made coffee in the Marshall family kitchen where he, Aggie, Jenny, and Orion were staying the weekend. A little winery-slash-farm outside of the cities near the town of Lester, Minnesota.

The kitchen was quiet, with a basket of oranges sitting in the middle of a black granite island that seated at least eight. The house was old—a farmhouse that had been added on to over the years and recently renovated. Beamed ceilings arched over a huge range with a double oven, probably used to make the apple and cherry pies the Marshalls sold in their tiny shop. A long farmhouse table with benches and chairs boasted a fresh arrangement of sunflowers in the middle.

All of it reminded Ham of his farm growing up, back when his mother was still alive. Maggie Jones had known how to make a home.

Ham stared out the window as the teakettle heated water, his travel French press filled with dark grounds, his eyes watching as the sky moved from black to blue gray, with hints of red and orange simmering across the horizon.

His mercies are new every morning.

The familiar verse from Lamentations filled his mind, overlaced the nightmares, and soaked into his bones.

He just needed enough wisdom, enough grace for today.

The teakettle started to whistle, and he turned it off before it woke the family sleeping in the many bedrooms upstairs. He filled his press and waited for the coffee to steep.

The town and the nearby communities had suffered a tornado a couple years ago. Ham had driven down with North for a day or two to help with cleanup, had met Garrett Marshall, the owner of the winery, and realized he knew his son Fraser who served with him on Team Three back in the day.

Funny how life worked. Now Fraser worked for Ham, deployed as private security for a humanitarian aid organization in an undisclosed area of the world. And Ham was making coffee in his kitchen, about to sit on the stone back porch to watch the sunrise gild the grapevines that grew in tall rows in the backyard.

Okay, more accurately acres and acres of rolling green. The backyard had a fire pit, a couple wine-barrel tables, a swing, and a patch of pretty landscaping for the occasional private weddings the winery hosted.

The smell of recently cut grasses from nearby fields drifted in through the open windows and stirred up memories as Ham pressed his coffee and poured it into a mug.

Memories of the farm in southern Minnesota. Of chasing Signe's stupid rescue dog, usually with a stolen shoe, sock, or worse, his car keys, through the fields.

Memories of Signe laughing as she tried to ride his only horse, the one who blew up her belly whenever they saddled her so it would fall off.

Memories, too, of those cold days when he'd pull up in his father's pickup on his way to school, holding his hands to the vents as he waited for her to emerge from her grandmother's house.

He took a sip of his coffee, sinking into the sweet memory of her weaving her fingers through his as they sat on the haymow watching the fireworks arch over the Mississippi River. *"Promise me we'll always be together."*

Her words, not his. But he promised.

Of course they would.

Ham shook the memory away and headed outside, the stone chilly on his stocking feet. He found an Adirondack chair and sat down, fatigue embedding his bones.

Tired. Not just from his fruitless night, but tired of waiting. Tired of wondering.

Tired of ignoring his broken heart. And yes, Aggie healed it, mostly. But the ache was deep.

He took a sip of coffee and heard breaths, feet slapping on dry earth.

Garrett Marshall appeared in a pair of shorts, a long-sleeve shirt, and a hat, running down the pathway from the apple grove.

He ran by a classic red barn—their wine barrel storage—and past a new tasting portico they'd built since the tornado, then along the hosta-lined driveway.

But instead of veering toward the front door, he slowed, leaned against one of the posts on the back porch, and stretched his legs.

Then he walked over to Ham.

Garrett always reminded Ham of an older version of Kevin Costner, lean, serious, pensive pale blue eyes, and a rare but sincere smile. He sat down next to Ham. Wiped his arm across his forehead. "We're going to call that five miles, if my wife should ask."

"At least." Ham took a sip of his coffee. "Maybe even seven."

"Let's go with that." Garrett leaned forward, bracing his arms on his knees. "I'm trying to keep my ticker from going out on me, like my brother's did. What's your excuse for getting up so early?"

Ham looked at his coffee.

"Right. Still stuck on a Ferris wheel." Garrett shook his head. "I remember when the tornado blew through here—my son Creed was missing for five days, trapped with his cross-country team. I don't think we slept more than an hour here or there the entire time we were looking for them." He leaned back. "Hate to tell you this, but you don't stop worrying about your children, no matter how old they are. I pray every day for Fraser, out in parts unknown, and Jonas, chasing storms, and Iris in Italy, and Ned, still in SQT with the SEALs, and—"

"Ned is a SEAL? How did I not know this?" Ham said. "Fraser never mentioned it."

"You know how the Navy is—Ned shut down all his social media accounts when he went into BUD/S. SEALs are targets—"

"I know. I guess I've been in my own world."

A hawk screeched out of the sky and scattered a flock of sparrows.

"What's really going on, Ham? You were single last time we met—and now you have a ten-year-old daughter?"

It felt for a second like he'd sat down with his father on the porch, one of those rare occasions when his stepmother wasn't around to shut them down. Ham's chest tightened with the memory.

He liked Garrett. He was a man of faith. Prayer.

"I'm still married to her mother," Ham said. "Her name is Signe, and we got married right after I made it through BUD/S. We grew up together on neighboring farms in a small town just south of Winona."

"What happened?"

Ham took another sip of his coffee. "I don't know. I was deployed right after we were married, and we hadn't seen each other for an entire year—not a great start to marriage, I know. But I thought . . . well, I was pretty idealistic. She'd moved on with her life. Took me five years, but I finally found her. And when I did, she said she thought I got the marriage annulled."

"Is that what you wanted?"

Ham sighed. "I don't know what I wanted. I guess . . . well, maybe what I wanted wasn't fair to her. I mean, I couldn't expect her to sit around and wait for me to come home. She'd always dreamed of a bigger life. Doing something significant. Getting off the farm and seeing the world. And that's exactly what she did."

"What you both did," Garrett said. "Except she did it with your daughter in tow."

He hadn't thought about that. The challenges she must have faced protecting and raising Aggie. "I didn't know I had a daughter until a few months ago. She survived a boat wreck off the coast of Italy."

He was still pushing the fact that Signe had kept Aggie a secret around his heart, trying not to let it land too long in one place, to put down roots and deepen the wounds.

"If I had known about Aggie, I would have gotten out of the military—"

"Really?" Garrett asked. "That's a pretty big sacrifice for someone who's worked so hard to become a SEAL. Maybe that's why your wife didn't tell you. Not that it excuses it, but maybe it might put a little pinprick into that hot ball of anger you have rolling around inside."

"I'm not angry."

"Sure you are. You lost ten years of your daughter's life. Any father would be angry."

Ham finished his coffee. "I'm just . . . well, I wish she would have asked for help." He set the cup on the round stone fire pit. "Fact is, I think Signe is in trouble. Big trouble. And it has me worried. She's still alive. I found a burner phone hidden inside a stuffed unicorn that she'd given Aggie, and I called her. She practically hung up on me, but not before she told me not to look for her."

"Which only makes you want to look for her."

Ham lifted a shoulder. "She grew up pretty rough. Her mother was a drug addict—meth—and Sig lived with her grandparents most of the time. But they were old and weren't keen on raising another daughter, so she sort of ran wild. Got into trouble. And I got her out of it. That's what I do. I look out for people. I help them. I don't sit on my hands and wait. I find them and bring them home."

"Especially if you think they're in danger."

Ham nodded.

"You can't fix this, Ham."

Ham frowned.

"I know you want to—that's the way you're built. You're a good man who does good things for others. But the fact is, despite your desire to help, clearly she's asked you to stay away. And that doesn't just make you worried, it adds to your anger, because now you're helpless."

"Are you sure you're just a vintner?"

"I coach hockey sometimes too."

Ham surrendered to a smile. "No wonder Jenny speaks so highly of you. Said you really helped her when she lived here."

"Jenny was our first foster child. Came to us pretty wrecked—her mother had just been murdered. Lots of counseling. Lots of anger. She dug into school, however, made great grades, and by the time she left for college, she had her head on straight."

"I think Orion is hoping to ask for your blessing to marry her."

Garrett smiled. "I know. Not that I have any say in Jenny's life—she's her own woman. But I'm honored that she still thinks of this place as home."

Garrett got up. "You know, maybe your wife is still trying to protect you."

"I can take care of myself."

"And Aggie?"

Ham drew in a breath.

"Fact is, maybe it's not just your wife but God who wants you to wait. Maybe work a little on compassion. Forgiveness."

Ham picked up his coffee cup, stared at the inside, the fragrance of coffee still emanating from the depths. He hadn't thought about forgiveness—because *of course* he forgave her.

But yes, if he were honest, a dark ball of anger simmered inside him.

Maybe . . .

Well, what he wanted most was a face-to-face with the woman who had broken his heart, stolen the first ten years of his daughter's life from him, and now refused to make it right.

Refused to let him help her.

Refused to come home.

So maybe yes, waiting was exactly the right thing to do. Because he might not like what came out if he were to have that little chat.

Or maybe, in that moment, God's grace would blow in, take over.

That, of course, was the crux of it. Letting God be in charge. Ham blew out a breath. "I need more coffee."

"And I need a shower." Garrett walked over to the door. "Then, wake up your daughter. I have some eggs that need gathering." He winked and headed inside.

Ham followed, poured himself another cup of coffee.

The stairs squeaked and he looked over to see Orion coming

down. He wore a pair of jeans and a T-shirt and was walking barefoot. "You're up early," he said to Ham.

"So are you."

"I heard Garrett talking and thought . . . well, um . . ."

"He's in the shower. But my guess is you'll get a yes."

Orion ran a hand through his brown hair. "Yeah, well, maybe this isn't the right time. It's only been a couple months—"

"Love doesn't have a timetable. If you're ready, then . . ." Ham took down a mug. "Coffee?"

"Black and strong, please."

"By the way, are you up for flying to DC tomorrow? There's a fundraiser White wants the team to attend." He handed Orion the mug.

Orion leaned a hip against the counter. "A fundraiser. Right."

"That's what we're calling it. For now."

Orion took a sip of coffee, and Ham was turning to go back outside when a cry sounded from an upstairs bedroom.

Orion startled, but Ham put down his coffee and was already heading toward the stairs.

The old farmhouse had a plethora of bedrooms, but Aggie was in the one at the top of the stairs, first one on the right, with the twin beds and a faux fireplace. He knocked on the door, then let himself in.

Aggie sat up in bed crying, her blonde hair in knots, the covers clutched to her chest. The sun streamed blood-red fingers into her room, through the eyelet curtains.

"What's going on?" Ham asked and sat down on the bed, pulling Aggie into his arms.

"I dreamed about Mama. I dreamed that . . . that a bad man was after her. That he was trying to hurt her again."

Again. Ham's jaw tensed. "Shh. He's dead, honey. He's not going to hurt her." But oh, he wanted to dig into that statement.

And frankly, couldn't stop himself from adding, quietly, "Did he hurt her a lot?"

She drew in a shaky breath. "She tried to hide it, but . . . yes. Sometimes he came into our room and dragged her out, and I'd hear shouting in the hallway." She leaned back. "He scared me."

Ham's chest had fisted into a hard knot—yes fury, but horror too—but he kept his voice gentle as he pressed his hand to her cheek. "Did he . . . did he hurt . . ." Oh please, no. "You?"

Her eyes widened. "No. He called me his *sladkaya*. His sweetie. He liked to tell me stories about his life in Russia. He never . . . he never hurt me."

Ham had to tighten his jaw against the images of a terrorist talking to, even touching, his daughter.

Thank you, Signe. Whatever she'd done to appease Tsarnaev, it was enough to keep Aggie safe.

Ham could weep with the unexpected, deep prick of compassion.

"Can we call her?" Aggie reached for her unicorn, digging out the phone inside. A small flip burner phone. He kept the phone off to conserve the battery, but Signe had given it to her daughter to keep in touch with her.

Spy craft.

He hated that he suspected it of her, but of course Signe was a spy. There was no other way his brain could compute the choices, the sacrifices she'd made.

Aggie handed him the phone. "Please?"

Wait. But his daughter was staring at him with those big, pretty eyes, so much longing in them, and they just reached in and wrapped around his heart.

He powered on the phone. Felt the bang of his heart as he dialed the only contact in the list.

Listened to it ring. And ring. And ring.

No voicemail. The call simply disconnected.

Ham stared at the phone. Glanced up at Aggie. A tear streaked down her cheek.

"She's not coming back, is she?" Aggie said.

Ham flipped the phone closed. Pulled her against him. And tried to keep the ball of fear—and fury—in his chest from exploding.

■ ■ ■

Today, the whole world would be his.

Orion just needed to figure out the right words.

He sat across from Jenny at Shakey's Pizza, the smell of rosemary, garlic, and basil rising from the open kitchen to her right, a fire crackling in the hearth to her left, country music playing in the background, and the ring box burning a hole in his pocket.

Jenny, I love you. Will you marry me?

Eight words, and they should be easy enough, but they stuck like paste in his throat.

Of course she'd say yes. Right?

He'd been pretty jazzed for the last twenty-four hours, frankly. It started when he reached over Ham's shoulder and snagged Aggie, nearly out of midair. Orion's heart had lodged into his ribs when he saw the little girl dangling from the Ferris wheel, and he climbed up behind Ham without a thought to his knee.

Which worked perfectly, thank you.

Aggie had crawled into his arms and clung to him like he was, well, Jake. *Unca* Jake, Aggie called his teammate—and Orion didn't want to name it jealousy but something inside him did a hooyah when she asked him today to play basketball with her. Had high-fived him after he taught her how to shoot a hook shot.

Ham's daughter was adorable, with her blonde hair and cute smile, and frankly, it had him wondering what his own kids might look like.

Someday.

He might be getting the cart ahead of the horse.

But he'd also been a hero to the kids trapped in the other basket. He'd stayed with them until the firemen extended the ladder to their perch.

Jenny had looked at him differently when he climbed down too. He couldn't put a finger on the change in her, but something . . . well, he hadn't really been on his game since the fall on Denali, and all this PT had made him feel like an invalid.

Not anymore.

So, yeah, he felt the wind under his wings a little, and maybe that's why he'd followed Garrett into the barn this afternoon, after lunch.

He'd cornered Jenny's foster dad in the winery as the man was checking on a batch of fermenting wine.

The place smelled of yeast and oak, big fans keeping the space cool even as the autumn air sneaked inside. Orion wore a flannel shirt and a pair of jeans and probably should have dressed up for this event, but since Garrett wore the same thing, maybe it would earn him points.

Jenny had told him that Garrett and Jenny Marshall—Jenny called them Papa G and Mama J—had given her the home she never thought she'd have when she went into foster care. Somehow in his gut, Orion knew that asking Garrett for his blessing to marry Jenny was the right move.

Garrett only confirmed it when he said, over his shoulder to Orion, "I love her like a daughter, so if you hurt her, you'll answer to me."

That took the wind out of his sails a little. Still, "I won't hurt her."

Garrett had been inspecting a temperature gauge, but he turned and pulled his readers off his nose. "Good. Because Jenny is a special girl. She's one of the bravest women I know. When she first came to us, she'd gone through so much, but she refused to let it beat her. She went out for basketball and made varsity in a year. Came home every day after practice and shot baskets for hours, in the dark, even after it snowed, when her hands were ice cubes. She doesn't do anything halfway."

"I know that."

"Good. Then you know that if she's in, she's all in. But . . ."

It was the *but* that put a fist in Orion's gut. The but and the long pause and then he tried to temper it . . . "I know about her past, Garrett."

"Then you know how her mother died."

"She was killed by her boyfriend."

"Yes. Jenny might look put together, but she hides her wounds well."

He knew that too. Because she'd managed to hide the fact that she worked for the CIA while they were serving together in Afghanistan, managed to hide the fact that she had a nervous breakdown, even managed to pretend she didn't know him when she ran into him later, in Alaska—not wanting to dredge up the past and the guilt she felt at her part in an op-gone-south.

Not her fault. But still, the woman had the capacity to walk wounded like no one he knew. So, he nodded. "I know. But Jenny and I don't have secrets." Not, at least, anymore.

"Good." Garrett had walked over to the next barrel of wine, replacing his glasses to read the gauge. "The thing about making wine is that you have to know when to stop the fermentation process, rack off the wine, and let it sit. And you can't rush the process. But if you can wait . . . well, it's always worth it." He looked back at Orion.

Orion stared at him. "I'll remember that if I ever make wine."

Garrett pursed his lips. "Why do you want to marry our Jenny?"

He was ready for this. "I've loved her for years, really. But when we found each other again, it was like . . . I don't know, maybe an answer to a question I didn't know I had. She makes me better and I think—well, it's time." He followed Garrett as he walked out of the back of the barn, toward the apple orchard.

Aggie and Jenny were picking apples from a tree down the lane. She wore her blonde hair down, and it shone a deep gold under the sun.

"Time for you? Or time for her?"

Orion looked at him, frowned. "Time for us. I'm ready to start our lives. To get married, have children . . ." He looked back at Jenny. "I don't want to be Ham and realize that we could have had more but didn't grab our chance."

"According to Ham, he didn't even know his daughter was alive."

"No, he didn't. And the last time he saw his wife was ten years ago at a refugee camp in Chechnya. I don't know the whole story. But I do know that she was kidnapped by a terrorist and Ham thought she had died. He regrets not going after her anyway."

"And you'll go after Jenny?"

"Always."

"That, son, was the right answer." Garrett turned then and held out his hand. "Here's hoping she says yes."

Here's hoping.

Please.

"We used to come here after our basketball games," Jenny said now, scooping up a square piece of pizza. "Fraser would challenge his brother Jonas to a pizza-eating contest. It never went well for Jonas."

"I haven't met him."

"He's a storm chaser in the summer, but works in Oklahoma during the winter months, researching tornados."

Now? Nope. "Aggie could play basketball. She's got a great hook shot."

"Yes. I saw you trying to teach her." She picked up her glass, took a drink. Set it down. Wiped her fingers. Looked at the fire.

Huh.

"Ham wants us to go to DC tomorrow for some fundraising event."

"Good. Fine."

Now? Maybe—

"That Ferris wheel accident was really . . . wow." She gave him a tight smile. "Scary."

So that was the problem. Maybe it touched off her PTSD. He touched her hand. "Everybody was okay. Aggie was so brave, though, wasn't she?"

She nodded. Turned and wove her fingers through his.

"She called me Uncle Ry today."

It coaxed a grin from her. "Sweet."

Now. Yes. "Jenny, can I . . . uh . . ." And shoot, *Just do it, man!* He stood up, dug into his pocket, and then, without a hint of pain, knelt down on one knee. He still had a hold of her hand. Ran his thumb across the top of it.

Her eyes widened. "Ry—"

"Just listen, Jenny. Since you came back into my life, I've known . . . well, even before then, I knew you were the only girl for me. You're beautiful and brave and kind and I can't imagine spending my life with anyone else."

Yes, see, that came out easily enough. He took a breath. "And I don't want to." He let go of her hand and opened up the ring box. A solitaire. Something pretty yet simple and perfect for the woman he loved. "Babe, will you marry me?"

She'd wrapped her hands around her waist and now stared at him.

And the restaurant had gone quiet, waiting for her answer.

He grinned at her.

"No."

Huh?

He might have frowned because she shook her head, and got up, nearly knocking him over. "No, Ry—"

He scrambled to his feet. "Jenny—"

But she was backing away from him, shaking her head, her expression pained.

No more than the terrible squeezing of his heart.

"No, Orion. I can't—I won't marry you." Then she turned and sprinted for the door.

Taking the world with her.

■ ■ ■

It was a simple room, but safe.

With a lock on the door, a single clean bed, a small table, and windows that overlooked the river Main—a dark snake three stories below. Most of all, the room came with a large, grumpy woman at the front desk who looked a lot like Signe's fourth grade teacher, Mrs. Nicholson.

And no one got by Mrs. Nicholson.

Felix's fresh new documents had done their job—Signe Kincaid was now Sigfreda Katz, and she checked in with euros, just like every other traveler at the hostel Jugendherberge.

Signe had spent the day hiding, watching as the police secured the flat, then doubled back when it got dark and took Felix's VW Passat to Frankfurt. She'd ditched it a mile away and walked to the hostel, the darkness pressing into her, the air breathing a chill into her bones as the wind stirred off the molten black river. Not even a moon to light her way, although maybe that was in her favor. No one to watch her as she limped along the sidewalks.

No one to watch as she purchased a backpack and filled it with essentials—toiletries, a flashlight, a map of Frankfurt, water, a scarf, and socks.

Signe didn't know why, but socks were always on the list. If she wore socks, at least her feet would be warm. Protected.

Socks meant she wasn't completely destitute.

But she was hungry. She'd eaten nothing—too upset by the images of Zara and Felix lodged into her mind—and now, as she set her backpack on the bed and stared out the window, her stomach roared to life.

She shouldn't leave the room. Maybe she shouldn't have even stopped, but really, where was she going to run that the CIA wouldn't find her?

Or, for that matter, the Russian mob?

Oh, things had gotten way too complicated from the day she'd seen the NOC list on Pavel's computer and realized the jig was up.

Frankly, she didn't understand why she wasn't already dead, because Pavel would have killed her if he'd actually studied the list.

She'd had no choice but to leave him for dead aboard his burning yacht and escape with her daughter.

No choice but to send Aggie to her father.

No choice but to run.

But with Roy possibly dead, well . . .

No. She couldn't call Ham. Because she knew him.

Knew he'd come running.

Shoot. It wasn't fair what she'd done to him.

Over. And over. And . . .

She picked up her backpack, grabbed her key card, and headed outside to the cafe still lit up across the street. The outside patio was alive with music and patrons drinking beer and coffee and eating piles of French fries that had her mouth watering. Signe slid into one of the rattan chairs at a table along the riverwalk's edge and read the menu card propped in the middle.

A waitress in black pants and a white oxford approached the table. "*Guten abend,*" she said.

Signe pointed to the fried potatoes, with bacon and onions. "*Die Bratkartoffeln, bitte.*" She ordered water in a bottle, with gas—no need to stand out as an American—and sat back to listen to the skinny kid at the mic plucking at his guitar.

Her ear tuned to the German conversation around her but found nothing of interest. Mostly people smoking or listening to the music, and she let herself breathe.

She'd gotten Roy's name from Felix, had contacted him through email, although she knew how easily those could get hacked, so it didn't surprise her that it had been hijacked.

She'd pinned way too much hope on a stranger.

"Mama, can I have an ice cream?"

The question, asked in German, came from the voice of a little girl that wheedled through the crowd noise. Signe spotted a family in the corner. A little girl, her blonde hair in two ponytails, sat on her knees on a chair, reaching across the table to grab a fry.

Her mother rescued her cup of tea before it went over. "*Achtung, Marie!*"

Be careful. The little girl pulled back her hand, and for a second, Signe wanted to get up, the instinct to step in front of the girl nearly rising to possess her limbs.

Then the woman smiled and picked up the plate of fries, handing it to her.

Signe pressed a hand to her gut.

Aggie was safe. It was good to keep reminding herself. Safe with Ham. Who would never beat her, threaten her, or even emotionally abuse her.

Thank you, Ham.

Oh, she hadn't deserved him.

The singer at the mic finished his song and another person took his place, a woman with full arm tats and a flute. She began to play, something light and airy, and Signe's fries showed up, along with her water.

She couldn't seem to pull her gaze away from the family. The little girl was probably two years younger than Aggie, and sudden laughter when her father kissed her on the neck nearly swept tears into Signe's eyes.

Stop. Spies didn't cry. Now that Aggie was safe, Signe should just walk away.

She only brought trouble into people's lives.

Now Zara and Felix were back in her head, and regardless of how hungry she was, she couldn't possibly eat.

A whimper near her ankle caught her attention. A dog that looked like some kind of terrier mix sat at her feet, eyeing her fries.

"Oh, buddy." She slid him a fry.

He leaped for it, nearly taking off her hand. Then sat again and whimpered.

"Offer him a Cheeto, Ham."

She simply couldn't stop the memory. Nine-year-old Ham, crouched at the end of a drainage pipe, digging into his Cheetos bag. Oh, he was cute even then, with his dark blond hair still summer long, tinted by the sun, and those blue eyes. He wore a T-shirt, cut off at the arms, a pair of jeans, and if she remembered correctly, his mother was still alive. Fading, but still alive.

Water poured out of the culvert after last night's massive autumn storm. Clogged with trees and leaves and debris, it was half full and she would have never seen the dog except for the whimpering.

The sound found her ears as they were biking home from school. She'd stopped and spotted the dog following her.

That's when he ran into the culvert.

She'd beckoned Ham back and found the dog, a mixed-breed hound with big brown eyes, tucked into the debris. No collar.

He shivered, and her heart broke in half.

Maybe because she knew how it felt to be alone, scared and needing rescue.

"I'll climb in," she'd said after the animal grabbed a Cheeto Ham tossed to him.

"Be careful, Sig." Getting on her hands and knees, she held out her hand for the dog to sniff. "C'mere, buddy. It's okay."

The animal growled, backed away. Snapped at her.

"Sig—"

"It's okay, Ham. He just needs time to trust me." She kept her hand out, waiting.

And waiting.

Ham handed her a Cheeto, and she offered it with the other hand.

Slowly the dog eased forward, sniffed the Cheeto, and then began to lick it. She touched his head, began to rub behind his ear. "There you go, pal. You're safe now."

She backed out, and the dog followed her. She fed him another Cheeto, then petted him, finally pulling him into her arms.

"He's hurt, Ham—he's favoring his leg."

Ham looked at it with all the wisdom of his youth. "I don't think it's broken."

"I'm taking him home," Signe said, aware that the dog had slimed her T-shirt and chinos. Her grandmother would kill her.

Maybe she could sneak in after her grandmother fell asleep. Her grandfather wouldn't care, of course.

"Are you sure?" Ham asked. "I don't think—"

"She won't know. I'll keep him in the barn."

Even then, Ham had a way of looking at her, worry in his eyes.

"It'll be fine."

"Okay." Ham helped her situate the dog in the basket on the front of her bike, but the animal wouldn't stay put, so they ended up walking the bikes home. The sun had nearly reached the horizon by the time they settled the animal into the barn. She'd already made up her mind to drag out her ratty Scooby-Doo comforter off her bed to keep the animal warm.

Maybe sleep out here with him.

Ham knew that too. "I don't like you sleeping out here all by yourself."

"I won't be alone. I'll have Caesar."

"Caesar?" He raised an eyebrow.

"I just like it." She rubbed the dog's ears.

Ham put his hand over hers, also rubbing. "He likes you."

It was the first time she could remember wondering if Ham might like her too.

Wishing it.

"I gotta get home." Ham had gotten up. "But I'll be back first thing in the morning, I promise."

It was the only promise he'd ever broken.

Because his mother had died that night.

She'd seen him a week later at the funeral, and shoot if he didn't look at her the same way Caesar had when he was trapped in that tunnel.

She swore that whatever it took, she'd get him out, into the sunlight.

And later amended it to include into her arms.

Her throat tightened now as she slid a couple more fries to the terrier.

"Shoo!" Her waitress came around the table, stomped on the pavement. "Shoo!"

The terrier barked, then turned and ran into the night.

"*Nein!*" She turned to Signe. "*Füttere keinen Hund!*"

Right. Don't feed the dog. She held up her hands. "*Entschuldigung.*"

The woman gave her a look, shook her head.

Yeah, that was familiar too—the look her grandmother had given her when she'd discovered Caesar. Tried to shoo him away.

Caesar kept coming back.

Not unlike Ham.

"*Lucky dog. He picked the right girl to follow home from school.*" Ham's voice, whispering in her ear so many years ago when he'd found her in Chechnya. "*He wasn't the only stray you took in.*"

Oh Ham. If only he knew.

Now she was the stray.

And he was the one calling her into the light.

Signe dug into her jacket to grab her wallet, and her hand closed around her phone.

It was an errant, forbidden impulse that made her draw it from her pocket.

Two missed calls.

Breathe. Only one person had her number. Well, two, but either voice at the end of the line could be lethal. For them.

For her.

For any hope she might harbor to keep everyone safe.

She pulled out some euros and left them on the table.

Then she got up and headed back to the hostel.

But on the way, she stopped in the middle of the bridge and dropped her phone into the water.

CHAPTER THREE

IT WAS THE HELPLESSNESS, the not knowing, that was driving Ham crazy.

That and the hum of frustration right under his skin that buzzed, kept him from sleeping.

He needed answers. Confirmation of his suspicions.

Some way to *fix* this.

Because his nightmares were playing out a scenario in his head that had the woman he loved—yes, he would always love Signe Kincaid—running around Europe with the Chinese or the Russians chasing her, the NOC list in her hand.

So he'd never been so glad to get on a plane. Because Ham couldn't get his conversation with White out of his head, either. Crazy hope had lit inside him that maybe—*please*—White's request had something to do with Signe.

Which would only mean, of course, that Signe was in trouble. That dragged up visions of her body washing up in some murky canal.

She hadn't answered the phone. Twice on Sunday morning, and then five more times during the last twenty-four hours.

Ham wanted to throw something against a wall.

"Would you like a drink, sir?" The flight attendant stopped by his row on the morning flight to DC.

"Coffee, please," he managed, without the growl he felt in his throat.

She filled his cup and set it on the tray. She posed the same question to Orion, who sat next to Ham, but he had his earbuds in so Ham nudged him.

Orion pulled them out. "Coffee."

She filled a cup and he took it, turned back to the window.

So maybe they were all grumpy this morning. All but Jake Silver, who'd shown up wearing his earbuds and a grin.

Apparently, things were going well with Aria. Finally. Ham had invited her on the trip, but the pediatric cardiothoracic doc had surgeries scheduled. Still, Jake seemed a little less at loose ends, a little more focused since Aria had walked into his life and stayed.

But that's what happened when you found the one your soul loved. You felt complete. As if the world had steadied beneath your feet.

Ham drew in a breath, tried to ignore the deep ache inside.

"Maybe your wife is still trying to protect you." Garrett's words stirred in his head.

That wasn't her job. He was supposed to protect *her*.

He glanced over at Orion. "You okay?"

Orion nodded, his jaw tight as he stared out at the clouds.

Yeah, sure he was.

Ham didn't have to do the math—Jenny had turned Orion down. Which made no sense to Ham, but then again, he was batting zero in the understanding-women category lately. They'd returned from dinner out on Sunday afternoon and Jenny had driven back to Minneapolis in her own car, while Orion rode with Ham. Orion said exactly nothing for two excruciating hours.

They arrived separately to the airport this morning too, and

Orion barely spoke to Jenny, although she'd tried to engage him in conversation.

Nope. Orion could be stubborn when he wanted to be, and he'd walked ahead of them, bought a cup of coffee and sat three seats down from Jenny and Scarlett as they waited for the flight. Jake had shown up late, of course, wearing headphones, probably listening to a podcast, and now sat next to the women, watching a movie.

Once they got working, maybe things would work themselves out. Depending on what White said, Ham had planned a few days of urban SAR training with Pete Brooks, who ran point on one of the Red Cross SAR teams. Pete wanted to connect them with a K9 handler to familiarize the team with working with rescue dogs and some new tech they were utilizing.

It only made Ham think of that mangy dog Signe had loved so much.

Aw, shoot, he'd loved Caesar too.

Now Ham's thoughts were back to Signe, and how when she believed in something—like rescuing a drenched dog—she went all in, refusing to give up.

"More coffee?" The flight attendant leaned over him with a tray of coffee cups. He took one. Nudged Orion.

Orion took two and set them on his tray.

"Need me to open a vein for you?" Ham said.

Orion looked at him, his eyes a little cracked with red. "How long is this field trip?"

"Fundraiser's tomorrow night at the Patriot Hotel. Then we're going to do some urban K9 SAR training for a few days."

"Yippee," Orion said. He looked back out the window. But not before his gaze fell on Jenny, sitting with Scarlett.

"Okay, buddy. What's going on between you and Jenny?"

Orion sighed. "She said no."

"I got that part."

"It gets better." Orion's mouth tightened around the edges. "She practically shouted it for the entire town to hear. 'No, I *won't* marry you, Orion.' Then she ran out of the joint like I was some kind of a jerk. I caught up with her at the car, and she was crying so hard she couldn't talk, and when I tried to comfort her, she pushed me away like I really *am* a jerk and . . ." He shook his head and glanced at Jenny again, so much pain in his expression Ham had to look away.

How well Ham knew that expression. "So, she didn't give you a reason?"

"Nope. We went back to the Marshalls', she packed and left for Minneapolis. I tried to call her, but she didn't pick up." He shook his head. "I don't know what to do."

"Maybe there's nothing you can do."

Orion shot him a look. "Yeah. How are you doing with not being able to fix things between you and Signe? Having fun yet?"

Ham said nothing as Orion stared back out the window.

The sky over Reagan airport was overcast and dour, rain spitting down. Ham ordered an UberX and they drove inside the Beltway to their hotel, just off the National Mall.

The Patriot Hotel, circa 1847, was a grand twelve-story building with white columns and had so much history embedded in its gilded walls, Ham felt as if he'd walked back in time. He stood outside the golden-hued reception area with more two-story columns and grand chandeliers and inhaled the sense that the place held a thousand secrets.

"Seriously?" Jake said as he came in, his duffel bag over his shoulder. "This is where the fundraiser is being held? I guess I should have brought a suit."

Ham looked at him, a little wide-eyed, and Jake winked. "Just kidding, boss."

"A lot of history in this place," Ham said. "You probably need to wear a suit to bed."

"I heard there are tunnels from the Patriot to the White House," Orion said, walking toward a red, round conversation sofa that looked straight out of the Gilded Age.

Jenny stood at the entrance, surveying the ornate ceiling.

Scarlett, his new communications tech, walked past her, on her cell phone. Ham had met the former Navy petty officer just three months ago while on an op in Ukraine. She hung up the phone, glanced around the lobby, and Ham's gaze followed her search until it landed on a man sitting in one of the gold brocade Queen Anne chairs. Military in his bearing, he was wide-shouldered, with his dark hair cut short, wearing a pair of jeans and a long-sleeve blue oxford rolled up to the elbows.

Right. Ford Marshall, Scarlett's boyfriend. Ham should have expected to see him here, maybe, but the man was an active-duty SEAL, so who knew where and when he'd show up.

Ford came over to Scarlett, gave her a hug and added a kiss.

With him was a burly black man, also exuding a military aura, with a wide smile aimed directly at Scarlett.

"Hey, Trini." She glanced at Ham. He walked over and shook the man's hand. Also a SEAL, Ham guessed.

"Ford and Trini have a ninety-six, so I invited them. Hope that's okay."

Ham refused to compare Scarlett to Signe. Because had Signe, even once, contacted him while he was on leave, he would have been on the first plane to anywhere.

He should probably get his brain off Signe and the what-ifs. "I have one extra ticket for tomorrow's event—"

"I've got family to see, so I'm out," Trini said.

Ford slid his arm around Scarlett's shoulders. "Thanks, Ham."

Ham headed to the front desk and checked his team in. White

had given them all separate rooms, so Ham handed out keys then headed up to his own, on the eleventh floor.

There, he dropped his bag onto the white bedspread and went to the window.

The view looked out onto the National Mall, the spire of the Washington Monument spearing the blue sky, the trees that blanketed the horizon an array of yellow, fiery orange, and pale green.

Signe, where are you? Please be okay.

Ham pressed his hand against the window, the pane cold against his palm. But it didn't stop Signe from reappearing in his memory, opening the closet door, and sitting down opposite him after his mother's funeral.

"Want a Rice Krispies bar?"

She'd pulled her dress over her knees. She wore tube socks and tennis shoes, so he guessed the dress was her grandmother's doing.

His eyes had adjusted to the darkness, and in the thread of light, he made out her face, her tentative smile.

He hadn't realized how much he'd missed her until this moment. For the first time in a week, it seemed he could breathe.

"How's Caesar?" he asked.

"Grandmother found him and I got a whipping, but she said he could stay in the barn so . . ." She grinned at him. "It was worth it." Her smile vanished. "I'm sorry about your mom."

His eyes welled up. "It's okay. Dad says she's in a better place now. Not suffering anymore."

"Do you really believe that?"

He gave her a slow nod. "Yeah. I think so."

"Your mom was really nice, Ham. She made cookies for my birthday."

Silence.

Then, "Ham, do you think *my* mom's in heaven?"

What did he know? "I guess so."

"Grandmother says she isn't. That she threw her life away on drugs and God turned his back on her." She sighed. "Do you think God does that?"

He shrugged.

She was quiet for a long time. "Grandmother says that I'm a bad person because I don't obey. I ask too many questions. I get in the way. And, because I don't have a dad."

Sometimes Ham really hated her grandmother. He knew it wasn't right to hate—his mother had said that Signe's grandmother was just grieving, and that it made her say things she didn't mean. But when she screamed at Signe and hit her, it sure seemed like she meant them.

"Do you think your mom can tell God that . . . that I'm sorry?"

"Sorry for what?"

"For being bad. I won't throw my life away."

He didn't know what to say. He just knew that he really wanted to climb back into bed with his mother, feel her arms around him. Listen to her sing her hymns.

Remind himself that he wasn't alone.

He drew up his knees, locking his arms around them. Signe said nothing when his weeping became audible. Then, Signe's hand slid through the light from under the door and held out a Rice Krispies bar.

Now, he touched his forehead to the window. *Please, God, don't let her throw her life away. Help me find her.*

Ham stepped away from the window and shook away the memory before he lost his mind.

The team met for dinner at the hotel's Cafe Du Parc. Ham ate seared rockfish and watched as Orion sat picking at his braised short ribs. Jenny and Jake had a conversation about the best way to serve oysters. Scarlett had abandoned them for a date with Ford, and frankly, Ham couldn't get through dinner fast enough.

Especially when Jenny touched Jake's arm and laughed and Orion threw down his napkin, got up, and stalked away.

"You might go easy on the guy," Ham said to her.

She looked like she'd been slapped and he felt like a jerk, and then she ground her jaw, as if trying not to cry, and yeah, he wasn't the guy to fix anything.

"Jenny?"

She fled from the table. Jake raised an eyebrow and Ham just shook his head and handed the waitress his credit card.

It was after ten by the time he returned to his room, but he was still dressed, still staring out at the lights of a darkened DC when his cell phone rang. "I'm here."

"I know," White said. "Go down to the service level. Someone will be waiting."

Ham nearly sprinted to the elevator.

A moment later, the doors opened to the basement floor, and Ham got out. A man stood at the entrance, his back to him, wearing a gray suit coat, his hand stuck into the pockets of his dress pants. He turned.

Ham's heart stopped. "Logan?"

Petty Officer Logan Thorne, one of the SEALs Ham had rescued in Afghanistan. His brown hair was cut short, his green eyes solemn, but he wore a slow, deliberate smile Ham would never forget.

"Chief." Logan held out his hand, but Ham bypassed it and pulled him into an embrace.

"Seriously? What—I don't—" He put him away. "Orion said you were on the lam in Alaska!"

"I was. Long story. I'm back and working for White now on special projects. One of them concerning an out-of-pocket NOC list." He walked to a door at the end of the hallway and keyed in a code.

It opened and he held it open for Ham. "Down three flights."

Ham took the stairs down to another secure entrance. Logan opened it and they went inside to a corridor with dim lighting and the smell of age emanating off the cement.

"I knew there were tunnels down here," Ham said.

"They lead all over the mall area, but this one in particular leads to White's favorite restaurant, the Hamilton."

"I like the name."

He followed Logan down the corridor, up another flight of stairs, and into the back room of a kitchen. Logan walked through the area without blinking and came out into a larger room that reminded Ham of an old speakeasy, with a long, deep walnut bar, chandeliers, and cigar chairs.

Logan led him into a back room and closed the door.

Senator Isaac White sat alone at a table, drinking a cup of coffee. He was impeccably dressed, of course, in a gray suit and blue tie, but Ham easily remembered the day when White wore muddy BDUs and night-vision goggles. The man cleaned up well, his blue eyes warm as he met Ham's grip. "Thanks for meeting me, Ham."

"Anytime, Senator. Or should I say, Mr. President."

"Isaac, please, and it's too soon for that. But thanks for the sentiment." He laughed, though, and offered Ham a seat.

Ham would have preferred to stand, the buzz under his skin nearly lighting him on fire. "So, what is this all about?"

Isaac ran his thumb around the edge of his mug. "Logan, can you give us the room?"

Logan left, the door closing softly behind him, and Isaac leaned forward and reached into his pocket. Pulled out a piece of paper. "This is a copy of an email I was forwarded from a contact I have in Europe. It's a request for contact from one of our operatives in deep cover. The operative calls himself simply Three, and we think he or she has the NOC list. The contact claims that they stole it from the Russians and need to get it into safe hands."

Ham picked up the email. "Who did you get this from?"

Isaac considered him. "The Prince. Also known as Roy."

The name punched Ham, and he drew in his breath. "Royal Benjamin." He glanced at the door. "Does Logan know this?"

"Yes. He is aware that Roy has been working as a blacklist operator for a few years now." Isaac didn't continue, but Ham had a sense that Logan knew it because of his run-in with a rogue CIA group at work inside the company—a story he'd told Orion a year ago when he showed up shot in Alaska, on the run and in trouble.

Ham didn't ask how Logan had hooked up with White, but the senator had told him once that Logan was safe, so . . .

"Then why did you have him step out?"

"Because I wanted you to be free to say no," White said.

"No?"

"Roy sent me a message and told me the meet went south. He was there, scoping out the scene before the meet, but so was someone else—possibly a rogue agent. How he found out about the meet, Roy doesn't know. Just that he intercepted Three, and when Roy tried to chase the operative down, he failed. Which means the NOC list is still at large."

"And where do I fit in?"

"Somehow, Roy was compromised. He said that the operator won't trust him, and that he needs someone Three might agree to meet with on sight."

Ham frowned. "I don't understand."

Isaac sighed. Nodded. "I remember what happened in Chechnya, Ham. That you lost your wife."

Ham took a breath.

"I also know about your daughter, and the idea that your wife didn't die, but in fact embedded with a rebel Chechen group for the last ten years."

His heart had begun to drown out Isaac's words.

"We have reason to believe that . . . well, Three is in fact Signe Kincaid. Your wife."

His wife.

And although he suspected it, even longed for it, the words out of Isaac's mouth flattened Ham. He had nothing, even when Isaac produced a picture on his phone, laying it in front of Ham.

It was blurred, and just a side view, so it was hard to tell, but the woman wore her blonde hair tied up in a bun, a pair of sunglasses, and her profile . . .

Yeah, Ham would know Signe anywhere. He bit back the crazy urge to cry.

"If we can reestablish contact with her, would you be willing to set up a meet and recover the NOC list?"

Oh, he'd do much more than that.

You can't fix this, Ham.

Oh yes, he could.

He would bring her home.

■ ■ ■

Jenny should probably quit the team. Because it didn't take a doctor of psychology or a former CIA profiler to recognize the pain her very presence caused Orion.

Just like the pain his presence caused her. Because the man cleaned up oh, so very well. He wore a black suit, white dress shirt, and navy-blue tie, and had shaven. Frankly, one look at him made Jenny want to turn around and leave the ballroom, despite the glitter of the event with its golden chairs, white tablecloths, and ornate chandeliers dappling magic around the room, enhanced by the classical music playing from the small ensemble at the front.

The Red Cross knew how to throw a gala. She thought she spotted a few celebrities in the audience—Trace Adkins, Sara Evans, and even Eli Manning milling with the crowd.

None of them caught her eye like Orion Starr. He'd walked into the room with Jake, a hard set to his jaw, and when he looked her way, she'd averted her eyes.

She simply didn't know what to say to him.

Oh, what a debacle.

Now, he sat across from her, with Jake, Scarlett, and Ford between them to her left, Ham and his Red Cross friend Pete Brooks with fiancée Jess Tagg on her right. Which meant Jenny had a nearly unobstructed view—save for the orange bird-of-paradise flower arrangement in the middle of the table—of Orion and the way he just wouldn't look at her, either.

It was all her fault.

She could have handled her response to Orion's sweet proposal much, much, *much* better.

She'd simply panicked—a reaction, really, that had been building for the nearly twenty-four hours after she'd watched him rescue Aggie and the two other children at the carnival.

Of course he scrambled up that Ferris wheel after Ham.

Of course he rescued the two other children in the other basket.

And of course he'd relish darling Aggie's affection, the way she called him Uncle Ry.

Watching him teach Aggie how to shoot baskets had nearly turned Jenny into a puddle. He wasn't just devastatingly handsome, with his dark brown hair, those pensive green eyes that could see right into her heart—or most of it—but he had a rescuer's heart.

She'd always known that, birthed in the days she'd watched him deploy and rescue soldiers working in-country in Afghanistan as a pararescue jumper.

Yes, Orion was a hero.

But he was downright dangerous to her heart. Because inevitably—and shoot, she should have known this would happen—he'd want more.

Marriage. Family. *Children.*

It wasn't until she saw him with Aggie that that last truth had clicked in and destroyed everything.

"Are you finished, ma'am?" A waiter gestured to her half-finished chicken cordon bleu, asparagus, and mashed potatoes. She nodded and turned to listen to the speaker just being introduced.

Presidential candidate Isaac White's running mate, Senator Reba Jackson. An impressive woman with blondish-red hair, tall, striking, dressed in a white pantsuit with a blue-and-white handkerchief around her neck. She had taken the podium after the welcomes and talked a little about how the Red Cross had saved lives after the Hurricane Lucy disaster in the Keys. And how, once she and White were elected, they would continue to support the work of the Red Cross, blah, blah, blah . . . Jenny had tuned her out, every cell of her body focused on Orion and his comments to Pete during today's introductory training.

Comments about how Pete had invited him to work for his Red Cross Rescue team.

She liked Pete. He had a charming smile, wore his blond hair long and behind his ears, and exuded a slight Montana aura, maybe due to his western drawl. He sat with his arm propped on the back of his fiancée's chair. Jess could have been a model, with her tall, willowy figure, a peacock-blue dress that could stop a crowd, and her blonde hair left long and golden. But she had real SAR chops, showing up today to work with the K9 team Pete had assembled, led by a woman named Dani Masterson. Pete and Dani showed them some cool new tech they used with the dogs to track their searches, like Kevlar paw protectors and orbital cameras, and that was interesting, but her ears perked up when Pete suggested Orion join his team. Ham and Pete had a good-natured verbal tussle over Orion, and she simply tried to stay calm while her heart tried to leap, screaming, from her chest.

Please. No. She'd joined this team because of Orion. Because she wanted to be in his life.

Because he gave her a fresh start, and because, most of all, she felt whole with him.

Until, of course, being with him made her realize she could never truly be whole. Wow, she so didn't see that coming.

God sure knew how to blindside her. And deservedly so. She should have realized the truth before she dove into a relationship with this amazing man.

She had no business dreaming of the kind of future Orion wanted. He deserved better. And she would not be the cause of his leaving.

Jackson finished her speech and introduced her running mate for president, Senator White.

He started in on his speech, more blah, blah, blah about the Red Cross, although probably super interesting if a gal wasn't fine-tuned to everything Orion was doing.

Leaning back in his chair. Sighing deeply, as if in pain.

She couldn't take it. Wadding up her napkin, she got up, ducked her head as if trying to remain unseen, and left the room.

The room was half-darkened, but as she slipped out, walking past six hundred or more eyes, she drew in a full breath, every bone in her body thin and brittle.

Outside, she leaned against the wall of the hallway, pressed her hands against it.

"Jenny, are you okay?"

The voice surprised her—mostly because Scarlett Hathaway might be the last person Jenny thought would follow her. The communications expert had joined the team just recently, and even then this had been her first training event. Still, Jenny liked her. Petite, with short dark hair and dark brown eyes, she seemed tough, no-nonsense, and just the kind of person they needed to direct verbal traffic during a rescue.

Now, Scarlett wore a simple black-and-silver sequined dress that caught the lights of the room, something spunky and surprising.

Maybe Jenny should have tried harder than her simple black dress, her hair in a braid down her back . . .

It didn't matter. The more Orion noticed her, the more the pain sharpened between them.

She sighed. "I'm not feeling well. I think I need to go back to my room."

"I'll walk you."

"No, that's okay—"

"Listen. White already has my vote. And . . ." Scarlett made a face. "I know I don't know you that well, but is there something going on between you and Orion? Because, I thought you two were dating—"

"We broke up." The words slammed into her. We. Broke. Up.

Had they? Probably. But suddenly her eyes filled and her throat tightened, and shoot, now she really needed to escape to her room.

She pushed away from the wall.

"Jenny?"

"I . . . I just . . ."

"Want to talk about it?" Scarlett had stepped back but kept her voice low. "Because I know a little bit about loving a teammate, and the ways it can go south."

Jenny looked at Scarlett, frowned.

"Ford and I used to be on the same team, sorta. And . . . well, we're still working it out, but we had our dark moments."

"Orion asked me to marry him." Oh, she didn't know why she said that—it just burst out of her.

Scarlett's eyes widened. "And?"

"I said no." She winced, her hand covering her mouth.

"Okay, yes, we're talking." Scarlett grabbed her hand and marched her down the hall to the elevators. "Are you on the eleventh floor too?"

Jenny nodded.

Scarlett practically pushed her into the elevator, and Jenny pressed her fingers under her eyes to stop the stupid flow of tears as they rode up. "I'm fine, really—"

"I know," Scarlett said, looking at the numbers. "The kind of fine that needs a room-service pizza and maybe a pint of chocolate ice cream."

Jenny gave a pitiful laugh-cry that dissolved into weeping.

Scarlett took Jenny's tiny clutch out of her hand, opened it, and pulled out her key. "Which room?"

"1101."

She headed down the hall, opened her room, and dropped her bag on the bed. "Comfy clothes, pronto. I'll call room service."

It felt a little like being back with the military, but Jenny obeyed, changing into a pair of yoga pants and a T-shirt.

By the time she came out of the bathroom, Scarlett had taken off her shoes and was scanning through the television channels. She settled on *Cake Boss*, muted the television, and curled up on the blue Queen Anne chair, pulling her feet up beneath her.

Jenny sat on the bed and grabbed a pillow.

"Should we start at the beginning, or just the moment when you decided to tell the man you love that you won't marry him? And don't tell me you don't love Orion, because not only did I see the way you looked at him tonight when he walked in, but hello, he has hero written all over him. Orion is one of the sweetest, most thoughtful—"

"Generous, giving, and brave men I know. And more. He's a man of faith, he's a rescuer, he would be a great husband—"

"And father?"

"Yes, absolutely. And that's the problem." Jenny took a breath. "I don't want kids."

A beat, and then she looked at Scarlett, who was nodding. "I get it, I guess. Kids complicate things. Orion and you would probably have to choose between the team and your family—"

"No, it's not that. I mean, I . . . I really don't want children." She made a face. "Truth is, I guess I never really admitted it to myself—more of a feeling than an absolute, but . . ." She sighed. "When I saw the way Orion reacted to Aggie, I could see him with a child—a bunch of kids, really, and I knew he would be a great dad. And he *deserves* to have a child."

"And you don't?"

Jenny looked away. "I just don't think I'd be a very good mom."

"What? Why?"

She shook her head. And no, she didn't know Scarlett well enough to dive into all of it, so, "My mom didn't really want to be a mom, and she tried, but it was a big fail. I was more of a mom to her than she was to me."

"Oh, I had one of those moms," Scarlett said. "I was raised by a single mom, and she tried, but she was a disaster." Oddly, her eyes filled. "She died recently, but it's made me wonder about the whole mothering thing too. Although, that probably won't happen for a while, with Ford's lifestyle."

"He's an active-duty SEAL, right?"

"And we also have a slight complication. My little brother is in foster care, and lives with me once in a while. But Ford comes from this big family, and my guess is that someday— "

"There's probably not a someday for me."

Scarlett nodded, took in her words. Then, quietly, "Just because you had a bad mom doesn't mean *you're* going to be a bad mom."

"I think maybe it does. And it's not fair to Orion. He needs to move on and find someone who can give him the family he wants."

"Did you tell him that?"

"I completely freaked out. I didn't see the proposal coming—I don't know why. When he suggested visiting the Marshall family farm—"

"The Marshall family—wait." Scarlett leaned forward. "Ford is a Marshall. His family lives in Montana."

"Garrett and Jenny Marshall were my foster parents. They run a winery in Minnesota."

"Oh. Different Marshalls." Scarlett leaned back. "The Montana Marshalls live on a ranch in midwestern Montana."

"Garrett and Jenny are great people. I went there broken, and living with them healed me in so many ways. Garrett is like my father in a way. But I never dreamed that Orion would ask him if he could marry me. And then, suddenly there he was, down on one knee in the pizza parlor and I just . . . I panicked. I said no and ran out of the restaurant."

"Oh."

"I was crying when he caught up to me at the car, and I just couldn't tell him . . . I knew he'd tell me it was okay, that we didn't have to have children, and frankly, it would just make it worse. So I got into the car and just . . . I just haven't—"

"He doesn't know why you said no? Oh Jenny. You have to talk to him. The guy is in pain."

"I know!" She covered her face with her hands. "I don't know what to say."

"What are you so afraid of?"

"I don't know."

"He loves you, right?"

"Yes. And I love him. I don't want him to give up his dreams for me."

"Even if it means breaking his heart?"

"It's the best thing for him. In fact . . ." She finally looked up. "I think I should probably quit the team."

Scarlett pursed her lips, then nodded. "I get that. But quitting isn't going to make this hurt less, for either of you. You need to talk to him."

"He'll just . . . he'll look at me with those beautiful eyes, and I'll lose my head, and suddenly we'll be at some wedding chapel heading for disaster."

"Or a happy ending."

Jenny looked away. "I think the best thing for me to do is hop on a plane for Minnesota and put us all out of our misery."

Scarlett said nothing.

Jenny got up, went over to her closet, and pulled out her suitcase, putting it on the bed.

"Wait—what, *now*?"

"I'll go to the airport. Sometimes Spirit has these red-eye tickets you can buy at the counter—"

"Jenny, c'mon—" Scarlett had gotten up, but Jenny had already wound her dress into a ball, thrown it into the bottom of the carry-on along with her shoes.

Jenny went over to the drawers, pulled out her workout and training clothes, and gathered them into her arms.

"Don't run, Jenny. Give Orion a chance to fix this. You don't know what he'll do if you don't give him a chance."

She dumped the clothing into the suitcase.

Stared at the mess.

She *was* running. Her classic move, and one she'd perfected on Orion so many years earlier. She was past this. He did deserve an explanation. And maybe, just maybe, they had a chance to fix this.

"Okay. Yes. I'll talk to him in the morning."

"Good girl," Scarlett said. "After ice cream."

Jenny smiled. "And pizza."

A knock sounded at the door. Jenny headed to answer it. Yes, a pizza would help her think more clearly.

Or maybe not, because as she opened the door, her heart simply stopped.

Not room service with a deep-dish pepperoni.

Orion stood in the hallway, his eyes fierce in hers, his hair a little disheveled as if he'd been running frustrated hands through it.

Her mouth opened, but she had nothing.

Apparently, neither did he, because he stared at her, then glanced past her, to the bed, and frowned. Looked back at her.

She didn't think it was possible to hurt him more, but real pain edged his eyes. "Of course you're leaving. Without telling anyone." He shook his head, swallowed. "Maybe you should turn your phone back on."

Right. She'd turned it off before the event. But she didn't have a chance to explain because he continued, almost without a breath. "Before you vanish, Ham is calling a quick emergency meeting. Maybe you could stick around long enough to keep your commitment to him."

Then he turned and headed down the hall.

■ ■ ■

Signe very rarely allowed Ham to step inside her dreams, roam around, pull up the past, and remind her of the what-ifs. But she was tired, having traveled with an eye over her shoulder for the past thirty-six hours. She'd crossed four borders, ridden on so many train cars she'd lost count, and frankly, she just didn't have the strength to keep him away.

So, yes, she let Ham walk into her dreams, behind her closed eyes as she leaned her head on the window of the Paris Métro, the C line looping up along the Seine toward the safe house just across from the Eiffel Tower.

Where she might actually get some sleep and untangle the questions in her brain, like, how had they found her, this rogue group who wanted the NOC list?

But not right now.

Right now she wanted to climb on the back of Ham's Kawasaki 650, her hands around his waist as he drove them up dirt roads, the moon rising above the farmland, the scent of autumn thick in the night air.

He smelled like the fresh shower he'd taken after the game. She'd waited for him until he came out of the locker room—not a groupie, thank you, but his best friend.

And more. Oh, she wanted more. But he hadn't given her even the slightest hint that tucking herself close to him had any effect.

But she could hardly *breathe* around him, especially since he donned football pads three years ago and started playing quarterback.

Now, with the senior homecoming dance just a week away, she was holding her breath for . . .

Except, what if they destroyed this thing they had? This easy, fun camaraderie?

What if she became one of the many girls who traced Ham's name into their notebook, wishing?

So she leaned back and put her hands on his shoulders and let the wind take her hair as he turned them toward their farms.

She noticed, however, that he didn't turn in at her driveway. Or at his. He drove them up the dirt road that ran behind their properties, up the hill, and stopped at a balding rock that overlooked the Mississippi.

"The sky is so clear, I thought . . . well, I have to talk to you."

He reached out and took her hand. A familiar gesture, but it sent a warmth through her that had nothing to do with friendship. They climbed up on the rock and he let her hand go, lay back, his arms behind his head.

Okay. She did the same, the chill of the rock seeping through her volleyball letter jacket and finding her bones. Overhead the spray of stars cast a trail through the dark night sky, winking down at them. In the distance, the river glittered with the lights from shoreline homes. The wind shuffled the dry maple and oak leaves, casting them down.

"My stepmother wants to send me to military school."

Every bone in her body froze. "What?"

"Yeah. She's convinced that I'm a bad influence on Kelsey, so she wants to send me away—"

"Kelsey is seven years old. And you're the best big brother she could ever have."

Ham said nothing, took a breath. "Trisha hates me. I don't know why, but she's convinced my father that I need to leave."

She couldn't breathe, an anvil on her chest. "You remind her that your father loved someone else."

"He married her because of me," Ham said. "Said I needed a mom."

She reached out and wove her fingers through his again. Squeezed. She'd feared someday it would come to this. Ham's father had married the woman, a widow, less than a year after Ham's mother had died. They'd had baby Kelsey almost nine months later, to the day. Signe was old enough to figure out the math on that one.

Trisha had made Ham's life a dark place every day since she'd walked into it. Maybe it was best for him to leave.

Except, it would scoop a chunk out of her soul.

"Can you talk to your dad?" She rolled over, propping her head on her hand. "You only have six months left of school . . . and now you're a big football star." She poked his shoulder.

He grinned at that. "Two touchdowns tonight. I wish my dad had been here to see it."

"Me too." He looked at her and she made a face. "His choices are not your fault."

"Feels like it. Feels like I did something—"

"Ham." She touched his face, moved it to meet her gaze. Let go. "You didn't do anything. She's just . . . I don't know. Like my grandmother."

"Broken?"

"I was going to say mean."

He laughed, then his grin faded. "I don't want to leave you, Sig."

Oh. Her breath caught, his words vising her chest. He too rolled over to one side, facing her. "You're my best friend."

Right. Yes.

But he kept looking at her, those blue eyes holding hers, and she couldn't look away.

He seemed to consider her a moment, then swallowed, and lay back.

She hated the way her heart pounded in her ears, the deep sweep of disappointment.

Friends. Yep. The best kind of friends.

"Sometimes when I look at the stars, I think of my mom, staring down, watching me."

She stared at the stars. "You think she sees you?"

"I don't know. I hope so."

The wind stirred around them. An owl hooted.

"It sure makes you feel small, doesn't it? All those stars. All the worlds," she said quietly.

"God says that he knows all the stars by name. And if he knows the stars, he knows us too."

She liked that about Ham—the fact that even after his mother's death, he didn't hate God. In fact, she sort of needed that from him . . . a faith big enough for both of them. It made her feel like God might care about her too.

"Ham. If you leave, promise not to forget me?"

"What?" He sat up, looked at her. "Forget you? Signe, you're like . . . you're . . ." He stared at her, and she sat up too.

Then his gaze was tracing her face, a vulnerability in it that swept her breath from her chest.

"Signe, I'm in love with you." He touched her face with his big quarterback hand.

Her eyes widened, and she was nodding even as he wound his hand behind her neck. She might have even leaped into his arms as he drew her close and kissed her.

Her first kiss. And oh, it was magic. It lit her entire body on fire, moved her heart off its axis and tilted her world. She didn't want to ask, but she guessed it might be his first kiss too. He kissed her with a tenderness that only made her yearn for more.

In fact, she could never have enough of Hamilton Jones.

She made a soft noise, and he moved closer to her, tugging at her jacket.

Tugging—

Her eyes shot open and she wasn't in Ham's arms, but on a metro—yes, of course—and someone was quietly trying to remove her backpack from her possession.

She looked up at a young man with dark hair, dressed in a hoodie and skinny jeans, who clearly didn't expect her to wake up.

Or to bounce to her feet. "Back off!"

He looked over his shoulder, and that's when she realized the compartment was empty.

Who knew how long she'd slept?

He cocked his head, grinned at her, and she took a breath.

Fine. "Don't do it, pal," she said quietly, in French.

He narrowed his eyes at her.

She glanced at the metro schedule. Forty-seven seconds to station.

"I'm serious," she said just as he took a swing at her.

Really? She moved fast, pivoted, her left arm up to block. His fist whizzed by her.

She grabbed his arm and sent her right fist into the side of his head.

Bam.

He hit the deck.

"Stay down!"

The kid jumped to his feet. She glanced at the clock. Thirty-eight seconds to station.

"Dude, I don't want to hurt you." She spoke in English now, just in case he didn't understand her the first time.

His hood had fallen back and his long hair flung into his face.

Then he said something, a crisp French reply that told her he wasn't so keen on being taken down by a woman.

Well, get used to it. She hadn't spent ten years in a terrorist training camp not learning how to defend herself.

"Last warning."

He launched at her. She pivoted and shot the blade of her foot in his face.

His head snapped back and he howled, holding his nose.

Yeah, that was broken.

She looked around for a camera, saw nothing, but kept her head down as she picked up her pack and headed for the back entrance.

Hoodie was still shouting when they pulled into the station. She got off and didn't look back.

Outside, the night was lit up with the fanfare of Paris. She'd emerged just north of her destination, on the far side of Eiffel Park.

Her memory ticked off a twenty-four-hour internet cafe not far from here, on the way to her rented studio.

Last time she'd been in Paris, she'd stayed in style at the Inter-Continental le Grand, just a few blocks from the Louvre in a suite that could house a small army.

71

Pavel had nearly imprisoned her inside, but she'd managed to get out and see Notre Dame with Aggie. One of the first times she'd nearly run, disappeared.

Returned to Ham.

She'd used the escape to check in with her then handler, Sophia Randall.

Now she found the cafe open.

A few patrons were at cubicles, checking email.

She checked out a computer and sat down.

Paused.

Maybe she should still run. Hide.

Returning to Ham wasn't an option. Especially since she didn't know exactly how her cover had been blown, how Martin had found her. She feared it might be through her cell phone contact.

Yes, it had been foolish—and maybe desperate—to give a phone to her daughter. But she just couldn't . . .

"Promise not to forget me."

She'd clearly been weak.

Yes. Maybe she should just run, take the NOC list with her and disappear.

Except, as long as she had it, Aggie was in danger.

Especially if she was correct about who had leaked it out of CIA hands.

But delivering it into the wrong hands could cost them all their lives.

So she booted up the computer, then logged on to her encrypted email storage.

One email waited. She took a breath, opened it.

From Roy.

It gave a new date, time, and place.

Catania, Italy.

Three days from now.

Twelve hundred.

High noon.

She deleted the email. After the last fiasco, she'd be better pre-pared.

And then, after she passed off the list, she'd vanish.

She logged out and closed the computer.

Headed out into the night for the walk to her one-room safe house.

Overhead, the Eiffel Tower glittered, bright against the night sky.

I'm sorry, Ham. It's time to forget me.

*

CHAPTER FOUR

HAM'S ENTIRE LIFE was about to change, and he sat on the rooftop terrace of their four-story hotel on the shores of the Mediterranean, in a small town in Sicily, reading the morning news on his phone.

Cool as a cucumber in July.

Apparently, Ham's wife had spent the last ten years in the captivity of a terrorist warlord.

Or at least that's the story Ham was going with, and Orion wasn't going to argue. But he had questions.

Probably Ham did too, but he voiced none of them as he, Orion, and Jenny packed and hopped on a flight to Paris, then Rome, and finally landed at Catania-Fontanarossa Airport.

They drove the forty-plus kilometers to a tiny hotel north of the city.

It looked like it had been a former apartment building, with an antique, gated elevator next to a stairway that circled up four stories. The stairs ended at a terrace with rattan tables and chairs, gardenias in pots, and a view of snow-covered Mount Etna in the background. The volcano rose maybe forty kilometers away. A tuft of smoke gusted from the mountain, as if it might be breathing hard in the autumn wind.

It had erupted two years ago in a blazing display of fury on New Year's Eve, but since then had died down to a simmer, still trying to decide its future.

Orion understood the feeling.

"The coffee any good up here?" he asked as he pulled out a chair.

Ham looked up at him, glanced at his cup of dark brown liquid. "It's moka pot coffee, so it'll take the hair off your chest. So I guess, in your terms, yes."

He motioned to a waitress, a dark-skinned woman with blonde braids, and she came over to them. "Can you get a cup of coffee for my friend Orion, here?"

Orion read her name tag. Nori. "No, thank you, Nori. I'm going to find a pastry shop."

"Very good, Mr. Orion." Nori headed over to another table to clear it.

"I found a coffee shop and *pasticceria* near here—I thought I'd take a stroll and score a pastry." In other words, let out some of the tension that wound up his neck and kept him from a decent sleep.

Ham set down his phone. "Afraid Jenny will walk out here and you'll be forced to sit with her?"

"Ouch, and now for sure I'm leaving."

"Ry. Just talk to her."

Orion sat back, stared past him toward the Mediterranean Sea. A number of catamarans and single-hull sailboats were moored in the harbor, the sun bright off their masts. "She was going to leave the hotel without telling me. Us."

Ham picked up his spoon, turned it over. "But she didn't. She got on a plane with us. She's here. That means something."

"Or, it just means she was too embarrassed to leave."

"You don't know if you don't ask."

Orion looked at him.

"Wait—you don't want to know why she said no, do you?" Orion frowned.

"You're afraid that it's something serious. Something you can't fix. Or something about you . . ."

"What? No." Orion put on his sunglasses. "It was just too fast, maybe. That's on me. I was pushing too hard to get a little closure on the rest of our lives. But now I know, right? She doesn't *want* the rest of our lives. Time to move on." He stood up. "You might consider doing the same thing."

Ham just looked at him. Then, slowly, shook his head. "I made a vow. For better or worse—"

"She *left* you. With your child. I'm thinking maybe she broke a few vows on her side."

"I don't know the full story. And even if I never find out . . . well . . ." Ham looked away, toward the sea. "When I was a kid, my mother died. My father married a broken woman who couldn't love his son. She had a bitter tongue and cruel heart and she hated me. So she would lock me in the coal furnace cellar under our house."

He said it so calmly, without ire. Orion couldn't reconcile Ham's words with the former SEAL he'd been. Capable, fierce, in control and decisive. Not the kind to be trapped in a cellar.

"I'd sit there and sing my mother's hymns to myself until Signe showed up. Sometimes she'd bring me food—Cheetos were my favorite—and feed me through the crack in the door. Sometimes she just sat with me, her fingers in the crack, holding my hand. She was my best friend and I loved her. I still do. I don't know why she did what she did, but I'm going to forgive her."

"What?"

Ham took a breath. "She asked me once not to forget her. And I never have. I don't know what she's gone through, but what if I'm the only one who can show her what real love looks like?"

76

Orion just stared at him. "Really?"

"I was pretty strong in my faith back then. And she knew it. That's why she agreed to marry me, I'm sure of it. Because she wanted us to be together, and she knew I would only . . . well, that we had to be married first."

Ham had never really talked about how he'd ended up married. In fact, the revelation that he had a wife had blown Orion over. But the fact he married someone who didn't believe the same way he did . . . yeah, Orion was trying to unsnarl that in his head.

"I might be the only believer Signe knows. And if she just gets anger from me, well, I think there's more at stake than my feelings. I just know that I want to see her. Because regardless of how I feel, I've never stopped loving her. And I guess that's the part that matters. Besides, forgiveness doesn't really belong to me. It's the currency of heaven, and my job is to dispense it here on earth. So, yes, I'm going to forgive her."

Orion stared at him. "Is this one of your thinly veiled pep-talk-slash-sermons? Because I see right through it. You think I should forgive Jenny."

Ham gave a laugh. "Nope. I'll come right out and just say that. But I *was* being serious. How much do you love her? Because the kind of love that God wants us to have for each other—especially our wives—is sacrificial. And sacrifices hurt. Ask Jesus. My guess is that it hurt to hang on a cross."

"And now we're going to turn to hymn 43 and sing 'Amazing Grace.'" But Orion smiled. "Fine. Listen, I hear you. And I do remember asking God to be in charge of our futures, so . . ."

"Go get a pastry and think about it. My guess is that Jenny might like one too."

"You just can't stop fixing things."

"Just doing my part to keep this team together. Please be back by eleven hundred. I know we ran through the op before, and I don't expect any surprises, but I'd like to run through it one more time. Meet me down at the castello."

"I got your back, boss." Orion took the outside stairs down and headed through the narrow alleyway to the harbor.

The rocky shoreline was congested with fishing boats, whalers, double-masted monohulls and a few catamarans at anchor out in the blue. The air smelled of the sea—fishy, humid, the scent of soggy sea grasses mixed with diesel fuel. He passed a group of fishermen unloading baskets of freshly caught mullet fish, their orange skins bright in the sun. He crossed the street at the ruins of the castello covered in sea moss, then cut into the city, away from the harbor.

In the distance, Etna's smoke had begun to darken as it drifted off the snowy surface.

Orion meandered up cobblestone streets, past ancient stone buildings one or two stories tall, many with terraces on the roofs that overflowed with greenery. Some of the windows hosted tiny balconies; a dog barked at him from one as a woman watered her plants in terra-cotta pottery. Buildings painted pink or yellow with ornate doorframes suggested the masonry craftsmanship of a bygone era.

If only he could erase from his brain the sight of that open, half-packed suitcase on Jenny's hotel room bed.

She had been about to do it again—leave him without a word.

He didn't know what hurt more, her full-out sprint after his proposal—because that was a knife in his gut—or seeing the truth on her face in the hotel room.

It was over. Whatever they'd had, whatever hopes he'd still painfully, foolishly harbored died as he spotted her getaway attempt.

To think he'd been debating actually finding her after the speeches were over, maybe asking her to have a cup of coffee with him and listening to her side of the story.

Apparently, she didn't want to tell it.

Okay, sure, she'd tried to pull him aside more than once over the past several days, but maybe he didn't want to know why he wasn't enough for her.

He should have never gotten on a plane with her to Italy. But Ham had asked Orion to watch his back, and had asked Jenny to join them, just in case, well . . . just in case Signe needed a head doctor.

He turned down another street and found himself headed uphill toward a small church, the wooden figure of Mary in an alcove above the door. As he worked his way deeper into the city, the fragrance of a bakery directed his steps. Tiny European cars clogged the streets, parked on sidewalks or near central fountains. A cat chased a group of pigeons, and people rode by on bicycles.

He spotted a bistro with tiny round tables and headed for it, passing a blue truck with fruit in the back.

The delicious smell stopped him at a large window.

Yes. Thank you.

Crisp almond-cookie amaretti and ricotta-filled cannoli, raisin-filled panettone bread and deep-fried zeppole donuts. They even had jelly-filled bomboloni and Italian waffle cookies—pizzelle. But Orion went inside for a bag of cartocci, deep-fried cannoli.

The aroma of coffee made him want to weep.

He stood in the line and let Ham's words drift back to him. *"I'm going to forgive her."*

Orion drew in a breath. A woman walked by him, eating a round taralli, a bagel-like ring cookie. He nearly followed her out.

See, this was what happened when you spent three months training in Italy, at the Sigonella Naval Air Station some forty miles away—duty he'd landed before deploying to Afghanistan so long ago.

"How much do you love her?"

With everything he had inside him. Or he thought so.

A man carried a bag of zeppole out, popping one into his mouth. Orion could nearly taste the sugar.

"Forgiveness . . . is the currency of heaven."

Okay, so maybe he'd buy her a cup of coffee.

After all, she was here, in Italy.

Not running away to Minnesota.

He stepped up to the counter and resurrected his very bad Italian, pointing to the cartocci and holding up two fingers. *"Per favore."* Then, *"Due cappuccino."*

He paid in euros—thanks to Ham for reminding him to pull money from the ATM in the airport—then waited down at the end of the counter.

A couple of women were seated at a table near the door, looking out the window. One of them stood up, her hand grasping the front of her leopard-print shirt. *"Oh mio . . ."* She pressed her other hand to her mouth.

He frowned, stepped over to see what she might be viewing.

Froze.

The dark gray smoke lifting off Etna had turned black.

What the—

The mountain convulsed, breathed in, and then, like a bottle cork blowing off, it erupted. The blast blew off the top of the volcano. Bright red lava spewed into the sky like a geyser.

The concussion rocked down the mountain and Orion had just a second of realization before he yelled, "Down!"

He yanked the woman away from the window and tossed her onto the floor, grabbed a table and pulled it over her and her friend just as the shock hit the cafe. The windows exploded into the building. Glass rained down.

Screams filled the cafe.

"Get down! Stay down! Close your eyes!"

Then he braced himself on all fours as the sky turned dark and the floor began to shake.

■ ■ ■

A good spy came early. Staked out the handoff location, the ruins of the castello. Watched for any suspicious movement, any hint of trouble.

Prepared for surprises.

Like her former husband showing up with his crew of cohorts.

Signe had watched from her room last night, overlooking the castello as Ham and his group of Americans toured the ruins, took pictures, and generally acted as if they might be on vacation.

Not setting up security for a covert drop of information.

Hamilton Jones, what are you doing here?

Oh, the man looked good. Better, even, than the last time she'd seen him, three months ago. He'd been sitting at a cafe in the central square of Catania, and she'd made the mistake of stepping out of the shadow of a booth to get a better look at him.

She'd lost her heart all over again at the sight of him, his sandy blond hair cut short, his wide shoulders, the way he carried himself, as if, although he shouldered the entire world, he could manage it.

Of course he could. Nothing ruffled Ham.

He'd turned her direction, then, and his gaze fixed on her.

And for a second, the questions flashed through her. What if she told him the truth? Told him how she'd been in way over her head? How she'd longed to change her mind and how she dreamed of him for years storming the camp, yanking her out of trouble like he had their entire childhood.

No. Because the other what-if was too terrible.

What if he hated her?

So, she'd bolted. Sprinted through the crowd, down an alley, her heart in her throat.

Then, as if haunting her, a week later, he'd called her on the secret burner phone she'd given Aggie.

It took all her strength to beg him not to come looking for her. Instead, she'd managed, "Don't try to find me."

Of course he hadn't listened to her. She should have suspected it, but the fact of it still burned like a live coal inside her. Because if he wasn't with Aggie, then she might be in danger. And the one thing she needed him to do—*the one thing*—was protect their daughter.

How had he gotten wrapped up in this exchange? What if he was here to apprehend her? Because it couldn't be coincidence that he'd shown up at the designated drop location twenty-four hours before she was supposed to meet Roy.

Ham did like to show up in her life when she least expected it and complicate things.

Signe had sat up most of the night in her tiny room, staring out at the sea, debating her options.

Making decisions.

She would track him down *before* their scheduled drop, just in case he—or more likely, whoever was following him—had something else planned for her. Then, she'd determine just how he ended up in the middle of this mess, maybe hand him the jump drive and . . . walk away.

Really. She'd walk away for the good of all of them.

Run if she had to.

Now, she stood just out of eyesight of Ham, around the corner, near the serving station on the terrace of his hotel, trying to stir up the courage to walk out and . . .

Not lose her heart, do something stupid, and cost them all their lives.

Yeah, no problem.

The sky arched overhead—cloudless and bright, save for the whispering of gray smoke over a smoldering Mount Etna. The Mediterranean Sea was a clear, glorious blue, the sailboats at dock or moored in the bay. The aroma of moka pot coffee seasoned the air from the nearby two-burner hot plates, and a stack of jelly-filled bomboloni tempted her to grab one.

The waitress had just left to fill Ham's cup with coffee, and then Signe had watched him have a conversation with one of his male friends. A good-looking man with brown hair and aviator sunglasses.

Ham's words had drifted her direction and practically stopped her heart. *"I don't know why she did what she did, but I'm going to forgive her."*

"What?" His friend had voiced her exact thought.

Oh Ham. You don't know what you're doing.

The waitress returned, and Signe wrapped her scarf around her face and walked out to the edge of the roof, out of Ham's view. She lost his voice for a minute but stood beside a planted palm tree and heard the last.

"Regardless of how I feel, I've never stopped loving her. And I guess that's the part that matters."

"Ma'am, can I seat you?" The waitress had come up behind her, a beautiful dark-skinned woman with golden braids.

Signe shook her head, not looking at her. Because her eyes burned.

"So, yes, I'm going to forgive her."

Oh, she hated herself for what she was about to do.

The waitress walked away, and Signe blinked, drying her eyes, staring out at the street below. She spotted the man who'd been talking to Ham emerge and head toward the castello.

Now. Before any of his other cohorts showed up.

She took a breath. Turned.

Ham sat in profile to her, wearing a pair of sunglasses, the sun beautiful in his hair, lifting golden threads from the brown. He hadn't shaved, so a hint of dark whiskers raked his face, and he wore a pair of cargo pants, flip-flops, and a button-down shirt.

She walked up, pulled out a chair, and sat down.

He just stared at her, unmoving. His mouth opened slightly. Then he closed it again and nodded. "It *was* you I saw a couple months ago."

She nodded, her jaw tight.

He drew in a breath, then looked away, and only then did she see it.

The swallow, the slightest tremor of his chest.

Unflappable Ham, biting back his emotions.

Yeah, well, maybe SEALs didn't cry either.

He drew in a long breath, and then he was back. "How are you?"

She opened her mouth and didn't even know where to start, so, "Is Aggie okay?"

"Yes. She's with family friends and she's safe. She misses you, though."

She looked away, refused to let his words lodge inside her. Although, "Tell her I love her."

A pause.

"Signe—"

"Why are you here?" She looked straight at him, seeing his eyes through his sunglasses. Good. Her voice hadn't started shaking. "You're not supposed to be here. I'm supposed to be meeting—"

"Roy. I know."

What? "How do you know Roy?"

He shook his head. "It's a long story, and not for now, but—"

"I need to know, Ham. This is . . . there are people's lives at risk—"

"I know you have the list." His voice was low.

She drew in a breath. "Okay."

"And I know that your cover was blown at your last meet."

She frowned, but yes, he might know that, if he'd talked to Roy. Or maybe Martin? "Was Roy compromised?"

"He just said that you wouldn't trust him if you saw him, and you needed a friendly face." He affected a smile.

Friendly. That was a loaded word. But, *I'm going to forgive her.*

The waitress came over. "Coffee?"

She nodded, just needing something to hold on to. The woman poured her a cup of thick espresso. Set a pot of steaming water on the table for her to add to it.

"Croissant?"

"Yes, please."

Signe wrapped her hands around the warm cup. Inhaled the aroma.

"What's going on, Signe? How did you get involved in this? And how is it that I have a ten-year-old daughter I didn't even know about?"

He didn't raise his voice, didn't sound accusatory, but his question was a knife to her heart.

"You remember Pavel Tsarnaev, right?"

"Yes. The Chechen warlord who attacked the refugee camp you were working at. The man who kidnapped you, and the man I thought the US had killed with a missile strike to his bunker. The bunker you were in."

Only at the end did his voice strain, and she had a small hint of what it might have cost him to watch her die. "We were out of the bunker by then. I wasn't hurt."

He let out a breath.

"It was well into the war in Afghanistan, and the CIA knew he had terrorist training camps. They wanted me to find out who was in those camps and what they had planned. I was supposed to act as an aid worker, establish assets, discover his network, work from the outside. But when Pavel attacked the camp, well . . . I changed the plan."

He took off his glasses. His blue eyes could still hold her captive, especially when he asked, quietly, "Bypassing the fact that you were in the CIA and didn't tell me . . . did you know you were pregnant?"

"No." She met his gaze and silently begged him not to ask if knowing would have made a difference. If she would have left, gone home with him, been his wife.

Probably. She hoped so.

But she'd been pretty idealistic back then.

He didn't ask. "How did Pavel Tsarnaev get the NOC list?"

She studied him. "How did you get this assignment?"

"Senator White asked me to meet you. He knew, given our history, that you might trust me." He left that hanging there, a real question behind it.

She wanted to. Of course she did. It was Ham.

"Senator White is running for president, isn't he?"

Ham nodded.

"And his running mate is Senator Reba Jackson?"

"Yes, why?"

Right then she could have told him. Could have revealed what she'd seen, what she'd heard.

But she paused. Mostly because she didn't know how far into this Ham had gotten. Or if the powers that be intended to use him for something nefarious.

But also because, behind Ham, Mount Etna began to shiver.

She glanced at the black smoke billowing off the mountain.

Ham turned. "Oh my—"

And that was as far as he got before the top came off the mountain.

The boom echoed across the blue sky. Ash and smoke poured out.

Ham dove for her as the cloud rolled down into the valley. He tackled her off her chair, barely cushioning her as they landed on the tile. She heard glassware breaking as the force swept tables over. As the world began to shake, he curled his body around her, holding her against him, one arm over her head, his own head pressed down against hers.

She held onto his arms as the building rocked, as the structure tore from its foundation, as the tiles surged and buckled and cracked.

The floor began to open.

Ham saw it first. "Get up!" He jumped to his feet, grabbing her up. "Run!"

Run where? But he had her hand and headed toward the stairwell in the center of the building.

A terrible roaring followed them as the mountain raged fire and smoke. The air turned rotten, poisonous.

Instead of the stairwell, he pushed her into the open elevator. What?

"Get down!" He crouched over her, slamming his hand on the close door button.

She didn't know much about volcanoes—or earthquakes, but maybe they should find a bathroom or get under a door frame or—

The door closed, and for a second, all went silent as the lift began to carry them down. She looked up at him, caught a glimpse of his face.

His eyes met hers, fierce and blue, and she had this crazy, terrible urge to wrap her hands in his shirt and just hold on. Because even in the midst of crazy, here he was, braced over her, solid, safe—

The elevator lurched. She screamed.

Then everything went black and they began to fall.

■ ■ ■

She just needed a peace offering.

A way to show up at Orion's door and get him to listen to her.

Because Jenny hadn't traveled four thousand miles to let Orion walk away.

Okay, yes, three days ago she'd been the one running, but since then . . . well, since then she'd woken up in *Italy*.

Italy, with the overflowing geraniums and begonias in giant terra-cotta pots flanking the door of their four-story hotel. Italy, with its old-world architecture, the Renaissance windows and ornate marble flooring, even in her bathroom. Italy, with the glorious blue Mediterranean Sea out her third-story window, and the stomach-stirring smell of baking bread and rich, dark coffee beckoning her to throw off her cotton covers and stand at the open window.

Sailboats rose and fell in the soft waves of the sea, the sun glinting off their high masts. Dogs walked with their owners, bicyclists rode along the sidewalk. A few fishermen unloaded baskets onto the dock.

"Don't run, Jenny. Give Orion a chance to fix this. You don't know what he'll do if you don't give him a chance."

Scarlett's words had followed Jenny across the ocean, through two airports, and haunted her all day yesterday as Ham and Orion ran through the meet at the castello down the road. She took pictures as they talked through scenarios and tried not to regret the yes she'd said to Ham when he asked if she'd join them on the trip. Apparently, the contact he wanted to meet was an old friend—and might be in trouble. Ham wanted her to be available should she need counseling.

Or maybe Orion had told him that he'd seen her leaving and suggested Ham rope her into his clandestine mission.

She'd let her guilt speak for her. Because she couldn't escape the look on Orion's face, either. *"Of course you're leaving. Without telling anyone."*

So yes, they should talk. But so far, he'd avoided her like she might have Ebola.

Enough. Orion loved coffee. And maybe if she could find a Starbucks or something like it he'd . . .

Well, she didn't allow herself to dream that they might have a happy ending, but he deserved the truth. Regardless of how it hurt her to speak it.

Jenny stood at the window for a long second, breathing in the fragrant air, then threw on a pair of pants, her sandals, and a T-shirt and headed downstairs.

Ham was up early, of course, and standing at the front desk, getting the password for the internet. He glanced at her. "Going out?"

"Just for a morning stroll. I'll be back."

"Don't get lost."

He was in a good mood today. But then again, Ham was always in a good mood.

She walked out the front door, past the lobby where an older man in dress pants swept the front walk. His white hair had the finest trace of black, and his gaze was warm. A name tag on the front of his short-sleeve shirt read Jacopo.

"Ciao," he said.

"Ciao." She paused, then, "Do you speak English?"

He nodded.

"Do you know where I might find a cup of American coffee? And maybe a pastry?"

Jacopo pointed down the cobblestone street, past a row of parked European cars to a white awning. "Caffe Greco. Best coffee in Sicily." He winked at her and she thanked him and headed down the street.

She walked past a gate thick with climbing roses, then down the cobblestone street, past brick and stone buildings, women holding baskets filled with bread, children walking with backpacks.

The shop hosted a couple tables outside, but she went in and the smell swept through her, found her bones.

Get coffee, offer it to Orion, and tell him, well . . . all of it.

She didn't want to have children, ever, because . . . well, because she didn't deserve to have a child.

Which meant she'd have to tell him about Brendan.

She blew out a breath and got in line, trying to decide on any of the pastries in the glass case, trying to sound out their names.

Too soon she got to the counter. "Two coffees. Americano." She hadn't really a clue what those might be, but hopefully they'd be close enough. Her only real time overseas had been in Afghanistan, and the base there had always served the coffee sludge black.

She also pointed to a chocolate croissant and held up two fingers.

Orion, I'm so sorry I ran from you. Can we please talk?

She paid, then grabbed the bag and went to wait at the counter for her coffee. Around her, patrons drank their morning beverages in white cups with foam on top, or just black. She watched a barista froth milk in the massive cappuccino maker along the wall, another ground espresso into a portafilter, then affixed it to the machine to pull the shot.

Laughter and the hum of Italian filled the tiny cafe.

And she was here, without Orion.

She pressed her hand to her stomach, hating the roil against the emptiness. *Orion, I know I really hurt you. I was panicked, and foolish—but I have to tell you something—*

"Ma'am? Your coffee." A man with a little black hat and an apron set two cups on the counter.

She stared at the coffee, steaming in two white cups nestled in white saucers. Oops. "Excuse me—" What did they say in Italian? *"Scusami?"*

The man turned, walked back to her. "Si?"

"Can I get this to go?"

He frowned at her. "Go?" He looked behind him, at one of the baristas, and said something.

She came over. A pretty blonde, she said, "I speak English. How can I help you?"

"Can I get this in to-go cups?"

She turned to the man and they had a moment of conversation. Then she turned back. "You want to go with the coffee?"

"Yes. In a cup?" She made a gesture that she guessed didn't help at all. "A paper cup?"

The woman sighed, turned to the man, explained, then turned back. "I'm sorry. We have no paper."

No paper. Right. No wonder the shop was full.

She picked up the cups and brought them to the end of the counter. Okay, so her peace offering would be minus the coffee. Still, she had the croissant.

She took a sip of the coffee. Nearly coughed but managed to hold it in, swallow, scalding her mouth.

"You okay?"

A college-aged man in shorts, the sides of his head shaven and the rest pulled back into a bun, handed her a cloth napkin. "Italian coffee takes some getting used to."

"I asked for an Americano. It's on the board, but I guess I was expecting American coffee."

He laughed. "It's diluted espresso and it'll take the hair off your chest. Here." He reached into his backpack and handed her a couple packets of what looked like sweetener. "I always travel with a little coffee kit. Sweetener, some creamer."

He wore a bandanna around his neck and a pair of hiking books. "I'm Harley. I'm from Seattle."

"Jenny. Minneapolis."

"Are you here for the volcano?"

She looked at him. "What volcano?"

"Mount Etna. It's been simmering for the past few months, and a bunch of us are going to climb it and look inside the crater. It's supposed to be gnarly."

He gestured to a group of college kids sitting at a nearby table. A couple girls, one dark haired, the other blonde. Two more guys were dressed similar to Harley. She waved and a couple of them waved back.

"Wanna join us?"

She shook her head. "But I do have an extra coffee to donate. I wanted to get it to go. My mistake."

He laughed. "Are you sure?"

"I was going to bring it back for my boy—" And she caught herself. Then didn't know how to finish, so, "A friend. But apparently that won't work. At least I scored a couple chocolate croissants." She held up her bag.

Harley gave her a face. "Those are probably raisin."

Oh. "I was hoping for chocolate."

"Weren't we all. But they're still good. It *is* Italy. Everything here is good. It's just a matter of letting go of your expectations, letting your taste buds take you where they will. You might be surprised." He reached for the coffee. "Thanks."

She nodded again to his group, then exited and wandered down the alleyway, toward the sea.

"Just a matter of letting go of your expectations."

Harley's words followed her as she came out to the harbor, to the boats docked on shore.

"You might be surprised."

She walked down the hill to a long dock that stretched out into the sea, fifty-foot sailboats moored in rows on either side. A few sailors worked on their boats, hauling out ropes or buckets. Others sat in the back, eating breakfast.

She wandered down the dock, the boards moaning under her feet. Seagulls cried in the air overhead. Circling, as if agitated.

Frankly, her expectations, her analysis of problems kept her safe. Kept her from getting in over her head—well, most of the time.

She couldn't help it when a mountain decided to blow up, toss her off the top, and strand her in a crevasse.

Yeah, she hadn't exactly calculated for that.

But she knew Orion well enough to know that she was going to break his heart.

Or maybe . . . well, he'd surprised her with his forgiveness before. It was possible that—

No. Some things didn't get forgiven, ever. And she should have never caught Orion up in a story she couldn't finish.

Didn't deserve to finish.

She didn't know why she hadn't realized it until now . . . or maybe she'd just hoped that God might forgive her anyway.

But Orion deserved the truth. And, he deserved a happy ending.

She'd reached the end of the dock. A kid, maybe twelve, sat on the end, his pole in the water. Skinny, short black hair nearly shaved to his skull, dark skinned and barefoot. His sandals sat near a sack leaning against a pylon.

"Are you catching anything?"

Probably he didn't speak English.

"No. I usually don't catch anything." He had deep brown eyes and now looked up at her and grinned. "But if I go home, I'll have to do chores."

She laughed. "Your English is good."

"I have a good teacher. He's an American."

"What's your name?"

"Gio Beneventi—"

The noise behind them startled his gaze and he glanced past her. She turned.

Everything inside her stilled as she watched the mountain, the one covered with a cap of white, explode.

Black hurtled into the sky, with a gray plume of debris and earth and fire. Lava geysered into the smoke, bright red, spitting down on the mountain.

The earth began to shake. Jenny grabbed for a pylon. Next to her, the boy scrambled to hang on to another dock pinning.

Sailboats at dock slammed into each other as the cloud of smoke began to thunder down the mountain toward the city.

A protoplasmic cloud of ash and sulfur and toxic fumes and—

"We gotta get in the water!" She turned to Gio. "Jump!"

His eyes widened. He shook his head.

She grabbed his hand. "We need to get into the water or that cloud could burn us alive!"

"I don't swim!"

"Well I do! C'mon." She turned and didn't even pause before she launched herself—tugging Gio with her—into the sea.

They landed and went deep, but she kicked up to the surface hard, pulling him with her.

He surfaced, sputtering, clawing for her.

She grabbed his arms. "I got you!" She turned him around and pulled him against her. "We're going to hang on to this pylon!" Kicking them over to the post, she pushed him against it. "Hold on. And when the cloud hits, take a deep breath and go under. Don't come up for as long as you can."

Thunder filled the air, and it thickened with smoke and ash.

She pressed herself to the pylon, her hand on his arm. "I'm here, Gio. I won't leave you."

Then, as the roar filled her ears, she said, "Now!"

She pulled him under as death rolled over the water.

CHAPTER FIVE

HAM'S WORLD HAD ROCKED, given out from under his feet long before the volcano blew. Long before the lift to the building tore from its axis and plunged toward the ground.

And long before he found himself trapped in the stone rubble of the ancient hotel building.

It started when Signe sat down at the table, just like that, and looked at him through her cat-eyed sunglasses. A white flowing scarf hid her head and face, and a linen cargo shirt rolled up at the elbows covered a tank. Her black cargo pants ended above flat tennis shoes.

Just in case she had to make a break for it, maybe.

And, no. She hadn't known she was pregnant.

But yes, she'd been a CIA agent all along, and never told him.

He understood that, maybe, but as she sat there, cupping her coffee, not looking at him, her jaw a hard line, he had to drag up his words to Orion and cling to them.

"I'm going to forgive her."

Please, God help me. Because he wanted to dispense forgiveness. At least in his head.

In his heart, the betrayal, the rejection roiled hot in his core.

It only made it worse that she wouldn't even look at him. She stared at the sea, her blonde hair falling out of her scarf to whisper against her face. He could trace her profile in his sleep—her cute nose, those pretty lips, a light dusting of freckles that had nearly vanished. A pensive expression, always, but when she looked so mysterious and distant he wondered . . . well, maybe he'd been assuming he knew her.

Maybe he had never really known her.

To confirm it, he'd asked, subtly, if she still trusted him.

It almost felt appropriate that, right then, Etna decided to blow. Because he'd felt his own fury building in his chest. *What did I do to you to make you walk—no, run—away?*

But he never got that out because her horrified glance over his shoulder made him turn.

Instinct made him dive toward her. Pull her to himself, protect her.

They landed on the tile of the terrace and he'd curled himself around her as best he could. The building shook, tile cracking, breaking. A line fractured across the rooftop as smoke descended over them.

He hauled her up. "Run!" He grabbed her hand and spied the waitress headed for the stairway near the end of the building.

Then it occurred to him—

Volcano ash was deadly. Sulfuric, toxic. And if he remembered his history lessons of the Mount Saint Helens's eruption, sometimes volcanoes spurted out a pyroclastic cloud of hot gas and rock. Leveling forests and maybe cities and certainly suffocating them—

They needed cover. He headed for the stairwell near the lifts, pulling Signe with him, then pushed her in front of him. "Go—go!"

A glance over his shoulder showed the mountain covered in black, thick smoke that was heading toward them.

The hotel was shaking so hard he nearly fell. They needed a windowless room—maybe a bathroom, or a closet or—

Except, if the ash didn't kill them, the rubble might.

They also needed something to protect them.

He practically pushed Signe into the lift, hoping he hadn't just killed them. "Get down!"

It was an old cage lift with a wooden box, maybe three feet square. But it had metal girders holding it up. Ham closed the wooden doors, then crouched over her, on his knees, his arms braced over her body against the wall.

Closed his eyes.

Oh God, keep us alive!

The lift shuddered, but yes, they might live through this.

Then, the light flickered out, the lift gave a lurch.

Falling!

He wanted to shout. Instead, he reached for Signe, pulled her to himself, and braced them both for the drop.

The lift stopped so fast, they bounced—maybe the emergency brakes kicking in—but he fell back, hitting the wall, Signe on top of him in the darkness.

She was gripping his shirt.

Roaring filled the compartment, the hint of wind, the smell of cement and dirt and sulfur.

"Close your eyes." Maybe the ash wouldn't find them here, but he didn't know. He rolled them over and pushed their heads to the floor of the lift. "Put your hand over your mouth, breathe through your fingers."

The building was still shaking, and he just dug in and started to breathe.

Oh God, don't forget us!

The terrible howl continued, and around them, rocks and pebbles kept falling, pinging against the lift box.

He didn't know how long they crouched there, listening to the building groan and shift, the wind moaning. He smelled smoke, a hint now of gas in the air.

Please let the electricity be off. The last thing they needed were live wires sparking into all that gas.

Finally, the building settled.

"Are you okay?" he asked as he got up.

"I think so." But her voice trembled.

Ham dug his cell phone from his pocket and turned on the flashlight.

Beheld the destruction.

The lift had probably saved their lives, the antique metal casing dented in around the sides, splintering the wood, but still intact.

The electrical panel was dark—probably a good sign—but when he got up and tried the doors, they opened to a cement wall.

They were between floors, but he hadn't a clue how far down. But he could touch the ceiling, and for right now, they weren't moving.

He shined the light down at Signe.

She'd sat up, her scarf off her head, her shirt and hair grimy and covered in gray dust, her green eyes big as she stared at him. "What just happened?"

"Pompeii?"

She gave out a huff—half laugh, half disbelief. "Thanks."

"For what?"

"I would have gone down the stairs."

"Don't thank me yet. We might be trapped in this thing forever."

He probably shouldn't have said that because his words turned her expression stricken.

She got up. "These old elevators have escape hatches on the top. Maybe we can climb out. If the shaft isn't clogged."

He directed his light up, scanned it across the panels. They'd just covered urban rescue scenarios, including elevator rescue, during his training in DC. But his guess was that no K9 was going to find them down here. "I think we probably need to sit tight for a bit and let that ash cloud disperse. It's full of tephra, which are jagged edged particles—"

"I remember our Mount Saint Helens's report, Ham. I think I wrote most of it."

"I did the construction, thank you. We got an A."

"Because of my report."

"Ours was the only volcano that actually erupted."

Just like that, he was back in the seventh grade, working on the volcano on his kitchen table, late at night, listening to Boyz II Men and wondering if it was possible to fall in love forever at the age of thirteen.

He couldn't stop himself. "Signe, did you ever really love me?"

Her eyes were bright in the glow of his phone light. It flashed him to her expression the night he told her he was being shipped off to military school. Sort of desperate and pleading and hoping that he had the right answer for her. Only now it was him wondering what answer she would give him. Had she forgotten him? Or maybe he'd never been to her what she'd been to him.

"Ham," she said softly, almost a whisper. "Of course I loved you. I loved you with everything inside of me, every cell of my body."

He stilled, not sure what to do with her words. Or the past tense of them. But he didn't want to ask the follow-up question—*Do you love me now?*

Instead, "What happened to you? All I remember is that we got married, we spent an amazing weekend together, and then I came back from my first deployment and you were gone. I know we talked about that, but then five years later I find you and again we spend the most amazing weekend together and then you're gone. This time, I think you're dead, but ten years later I find out you're *not* dead and I have a child. What *happened*? Why didn't you come back to me?"

She sighed then, and the defeat on her face shook him to the core. He'd never known Signe to be defeated. She was light and life and curiosity and a force to be reckoned with. But sitting there in the lift with ash covering her body, she turned into a ghost in front of him.

And right then . . . no, he didn't know her at all.

"It's a long story," she said quietly.

He sank down, his back to the wall. "We're not going anywhere. I'm listening."

■ ■ ■

Jenny.

Orion had one thought as the world stopped shaking, as water sprayed from a broken line in the coffee shop, as people around him cried or screamed.

Get. To. Jenny.

He'd dived under a table with two women, both middle-aged, dark hair. Now, as he leaned up, he saw one bled from her arm, a jagged piece of glass embedded in the flesh of her bicep. The other woman curled into a ball, her knees up, her head down. When she looked up, blood dripped down her forehead from an open cut.

"Don't move." He scrambled out from under the table. Around the cafe, others had also taken refuge under tables or behind the counter. A few simply lay on the floor, hands over their heads. A couple young bucks were getting up and he pointed at the water spraying through the cafe. "Turn that off!"

Maybe they spoke English, or maybe they simply caught his meaning, because one of them scrambled over the counter.

The other turned to a young woman who was holding her bloody leg and crying.

Orion hit his feet and grabbed a couple cloth napkins that had spilled onto the floor. He came back to the women and pressed one to the woman's head. "Hold this here."

She nodded, her eyes wide, and he turned to the other woman, the one in the leopard shirt. The glass still protruded from her arm, and he couldn't tell if it had nicked an artery.

He should probably wait until she could get to an ER before he removed it, but given the tragedy, even in this little coffee shop, that could be hours.

He held her arm, met her eyes. "Can I see it?"

She was a pretty woman, big brown eyes, olive skin, maybe midforties. "Si."

He pulled back the skin around the wound and she whimpered. But it didn't look that deep.

What he really needed was a way to stop blood flow, just in case.

She wore a scarf in her hair. He motioned to it and she nodded. Taking it off her, he put it around her arm, then grabbed a nearby butter knife and fashioned a tourniquet around her upper arm, above the wound.

"I'm going to take this out, okay?"

The other woman reached out and took her hand.

"I'm Orion. What's your name?"

"Federica."

"Okay, here we go. On three."

He counted, and pulled on two. She cried out, and blood surged, but he pressed the cloth over the wound and tightened the tourniquet. The flow stopped. "Hold this on here until help arrives." He tied off the tourniquet.

Federica grabbed his shirt. "Where are you going?"

"To find my girlfriend." The words came out easy, as if nothing had changed between them.

Maybe, right now, nothing had.

So she didn't want to marry him—right now, all that mattered was that she was alive and safe.

Orion pulled his cell phone from his pocket. No signal. Outside, sirens blared in the distance, a car alarm honking somewhere in the fog. Most of the windows in the coffee shop had shattered. Smoke darkened the streets.

Smoke filled with ash and volcanic debris. It might even be toxic. "Cover your mouths!" he said, the realization sinking in. He grabbed more napkins off the floor and tied one around his mouth, handed them out to the patrons now mending their wounds, trying their cell phones.

The water had stopped spurting, but the floor was slick and muddy with ash, coffee stirred into the mix. A barista had been scalded and one of the young bucks was pouring water over her hand and arm.

Orion stepped out into the street, trying to get his bearings. He couldn't see the sky, the world gritty and dark. Ash layered the cars, the blue fruit truck parked in the street. Flowerpots lay smashed on the sidewalks, having toppled from balconies, and a couple buildings were cracked, terra-cotta roof tiles in broken piles along the road. The cobblestones had buckled, and the tables outside the cafe were flung over, glass from storefront windows scattered all the way down the street.

He had no idea which way to go. He pulled out his phone, pulled up his GPS, but it gave him nothing.

"Orion. Where are you going?"

Federica called to him from where she sat on the floor, through the space of the open glass.

"To my hotel. It's on the harbor."

Federica pointed to her right. "That way. Four or five blocks."

He took off in a jog down the street. The air smelled of burned rubber, sulfuric and toxic. Water gushed from cracks in buildings onto the street, and overhead electric cables sparked.

His eyes burned and he stopped, leaned over, grabbing his knees. He closed his eyes for a moment, trying to let them tear and cleanse out the rubble.

Please, Jenny, be okay.

He passed a couple buildings that were cracked, one leaning to its side, and one with its entire frontside crumbled onto the street. "Hello? Anyone here?" He stood at the edge of the rubble, not even sure where to start looking. He probably should have paid better attention during the urban SAR training they'd done in DC, but frankly he'd been too focused on, well, being angry.

Pouting, his father might have called it.

"Orion, can we talk?"

Jenny had come up to him at the airport, right before their flight to Amsterdam, and he'd barely looked up from his phone—he'd been listening to a podcast—and shook his head.

Shook. His. Stupid. Head.

No talking, just pouting, and now he felt sick.

Please, Jenny, be alive.

Overhead, the air was still clogged with a gassy current of ash and debris, the sidewalks littered with the carcasses of tree limbs, sand, rocks, stone, and dirt.

Covering his eyes, Orion stumbled over the debris of the house, back toward the harbor. He nearly tripped over a bicycle, toppled over on the ground, half buried in dust.

Bracing his hand on the buildings, he worked his way down the street.

He spotted a fire blazing from a building a block or so away. He picked up his speed, his heart thundering, but when he arrived, people were standing away from the burning house, a woman holding a baby in her arms, both of them grimy, enclosed in the embrace of an equally dirty man. They were quietly crying. The house had fallen in, the roof gone, the place ablaze.

A group of local men were spraying water onto a nearby home, trying to save it.

Orion's eyes watered, his sight turning blurry.

He turned back toward the harbor—or what he hoped might be the harbor. If he found it, he could follow the shoreline all the way to the hotel.

He passed the church with the Madonna above the door and spotted a crack all the way up the outside wall. The bell tower had broken off at the top, a great splinter along the yellow stucco.

He turned and headed down the street, a straight shot down the hill to the harbor. An eerie quiet pervaded the air, something prickling his skin despite the chaos, the fire and smoke and reek of sulfur. As if something else were poised to attack, maybe another fiery blast, maybe an aftershock.

Maybe . . . and as he came out to the sea, the air clearing slightly, he saw it.

The sea was beginning to recede from shore, the water scraping over rocks as the harbor emptied. Sailboats were beached at their dockings, fishing boats dug into the sand, and farther out, at the mooring balls, a few sailors scrambled to put their dinghies down and motor to shore.

Tsunami. The earthquake from the volcano had ruptured the seabed somewhere and—

Orion broke out into a run. He was probably only a kilometer from the hotel, but he could make it.

He *would* make it.

Jenny's room was on the third floor, so maybe she was safe, but if the hotel had collapsed, and she was trapped inside, she'd drown.

He ran down the middle of the road, past the castello, now in even more ruin, past a dry harbor of beached rowboats and whalers, past one of many long docks, the boats like horses tied up to a hitching post.

"Help!"

The voice rose over the expanse of water and the distant thunder and tripped Orion up. He nearly flattened on the road, but slowed enough to spot a man running toward shore through the shallow waters.

He'd abandoned his dinghy, held two kids, one in each arm as he fought the pull of the seabed.

Thirty feet out, his catamaran was being grounded by the vanishing water.

Orion glanced down the street and spotted the hotel. It looked mostly intact, but he couldn't tell.

"Help!"

Aw, he couldn't stop himself from turning, running off the road, onto the boardwalk, then down to shore. The man was still fifty yards away. "My wife is still on the boat with our daughter!"

Oh, perfect. And then, as if to add to the horror, a deep rumble tremored the air.

The roar of the sea, lifting, rushing toward them.

For a second, Orion was standing on the shore on a frigid day in January, watching his father trying to save his mother and little brother out of a raging, frozen river.

Yeah, he wasn't going to stand by and watch another family be decimated.

Orion took off toward the man, yanking his feet out of the muck, the going too slow. He reached him, an American, given the Minnesota Vikings hat he wore over his long blond hair.

The man shoved his two sons—Orion guessed them to be about nine and seven years old—into Orion's arms. "I gotta get back—"

"You don't have time, man!"

Vikings looked at him, his gaze fierce. "My wife is back there, with our daughter. Keep my sons safe!"

Then he turned and fought his way through the muck toward the boat.

Shoot.

Orion spun toward shore and worked his way back, fighting to hold on to the boys, not looking behind him as the water raced toward him.

He reached the sand and put them down, gripped their hands, and sprinted up the beach, practically dragging them. He aimed for a set of brick stairs leading to higher ground.

He glanced out to sea.

The surge had reached the catamaran and lifted it, the foamy, violent front wave dislodging it from the seabed and pushing it along like a toy.

Orion reached the top of the stairs and for a second was caught by the sight of the entire seabed rising, the leading edge of the water overrunning the boats, grabbing them, pushing them to shore like litter.

Seagulls scattered, crying overhead.

The helplessness of it caught Orion around the chest, squeezed.

Sort of like when he'd seen Jenny standing in the parking lot.

He wanted to help. Wanted to be the one who carried her to shore, kept her safe.

Lord, keep us alive so we can find each other.

The sea hit the cement barrier of the castello with a terrible boom, the water careening toward land at a terrific speed.

He took off again, the boys clinging to him, crying.

And with everything Orion had inside him, he prayed for mercy.

■ ■ ■

For the first time in what seemed like ten years Signe felt safe. Which was entirely crazy because she *wasn't* safe.

She was trapped in an elevator hovering somewhere between the first and fourth floors, the electricity off, sitting in the darkness with only a flashlight for light, pinned under the scrutiny of a man whose heart she'd broken.

If she were honest, this was more of an interrogation than a conversation between old friends, because Ham wasn't exactly here on personal business. For all she knew, he worked for the CIA and was here to determine whether she was a patriot . . . or a terrorist.

And why not? She'd vanished from his life and, to the naked eye, joined a jihadist organization. Not to mention hid his daughter from him.

So, yes, he had every right to eye her with what looked like suspicion.

She'd stick to the facts. And really, that was all she could give him because if she let him take a good look at what was going on inside her head, or worse, her heart, well, yes, that would be a catastrophe of epic proportions.

As soon as this conversation was over—and they'd escaped their tomb—she would disappear. Because she still hadn't figured out who he might be connected to, and who might have followed him, and frankly who might be waiting for them outside the elevator.

But right now, right this moment, she was safe. So she could give him the truth—or most of it.

"You need to let me get all the way to the end before you start shouting."

His mouth opened. Then closed. And he nodded.

She ran her hands together. "Sort of reminds me of the times your stepmother would lock you in the cellar of your farmhouse. For one of your perceived infractions—probably you'd forgotten

108

to clean the kitchen or take out the garbage or even simply not given her the right answer when she demanded it."

She didn't know why she led with that.

"She just liked to exert her power," Ham said quietly. "Remind me that I wasn't hers."

For a moment, she wondered if he'd questioned whether Aggie was his. But maybe it wouldn't matter to a man like Ham. He made everyone feel like they were under his wings.

"I never knew how you survived her abuse."

"You," he said quietly, then drew in a breath as if he hadn't meant for that to escape. He looked away. "I'd be sitting in the darkness, singing a song to myself—"

"That's right. You were always singing."

"My mom's hymns. I don't know why, but it helped. And then, suddenly I'd hear your voice." He met her eyes. "You kept me sane."

You too. Because sometimes when . . . well, when she felt so afraid or alone she thought she might break in half, he was there. At least in her memories.

Oh, pull yourself together, Signe! She found a desperate smile. "I wanted to take a bolt cutter to the padlock."

One side of his mouth ticked up, such a familiar half smile, her heart lurched.

"I reported your stepmother to my grandmother once, but that went nowhere."

"It wouldn't have mattered. She was on the PTA board, and no one would have believed you. And, she loved Kelsey. It was just me who made her angry."

"You were a good kid, Ham."

Something flickered in his eyes. "This is about you."

Right. "I don't know where to start."

"Start at the beginning."

"The beginning. You mean when I was thirteen, the day that my grandfather died and I realized that I was alone?"

He drew in a breath.

And no, she hadn't been alone. She'd had her grandmother, and Ham. But right then, she'd begun making plans to do something with her life. Be significant, leave her mark.

Yes, she should start there because then maybe he'd understand. "I was the perfect prey for the CIA."

His mouth tightened around the edges. "When did they recruit you?"

"It was after we got married. You'd left and I was . . . well, I was afraid. I didn't know if I'd ever see you again. I knew your training was so dangerous and then you would be deployed, and I just couldn't be the one waiting for you to die."

"I know," he said softly. "You told me all that. That's why you joined the Peace Corps, right?"

"I wasn't in the Peace Corps." She drew in her breath, suddenly aware of her tower of lies. "I was deep into my first assignment by the time you found me in Chechnya."

He drew up his legs and rested his hands over his knees. "I see."

"Do you, Ham? Because you were out in the world doing amazing things. Jumping out of airplanes, learning how to scuba dive, preparing to go to war. But I'd watched airplanes slam into the World Trade Center too, and I wanted to do something, but I didn't know how . . . and then suddenly I had a chance."

"I don't get it. You got so angry with me in Chechnya. Told me that you couldn't be married to a SEAL. That you couldn't watch me die. And then you go and do exactly the same thing."

She sighed. "I didn't want you to know what I was doing," she said quietly. "I thought you'd try to stop me."

"You're right. I would have tried."

"And then what, Ham? You would have dragged me across the

world, to Virginia, or Pensacola, and then parked me on base so I could wait for you to come back? Like a little housewife—"

"Like *my* wife!" It was the first time he raised his voice to her. Maybe she deserved it.

He drew in a breath, schooled his voice. "What was so wrong with that?"

"Nothing, except . . . I didn't want that. I wanted what you had. To do something important with my life. To know that I didn't waste it."

Her last sentence hung out there, reverberating into her soul. Maybe his too. "Like your mom did."

She looked away from him. "Yeah, I guess so."

"So then you just left. No goodbyes—just . . . gone." Again no accusation in his tone, but enough of truth in it for her to wince.

"I couldn't say goodbye to you, Hamburglar. I knew you'd find me, though. And I dreaded the day you'd show up and talk me out of what I was doing."

"Do you really think I could have done that?"

She gave a huff, half laughter, half incredulity. "Yes. Wasn't that *exactly* what you tried to do when you found me in Chechnya? What our romantic getaway to Ukraine was all about?"

He looked away. "No. Maybe. I don't know." Then he met her eyes again. "You were doing something dangerous and I was afraid, and okay, yes, maybe I did try to talk you out of it. And I would have tried harder if I knew you were *pregnant*."

His words landed like a knife in her chest.

She gritted her jaw against the ache. "I'm sorry I took your daughter from you. It wasn't my intent. When Pavel Tsarnaev raided the camp, one of his men was shot. He took my friend Zara, and I didn't know what to do so I went with her. She doctored the man at a house, and then I talked Tsarnaev into leaving her there in exchange for taking me."

Ham's eyes widened.

"I told him that I could look after the soldier—"

"You've got to be kidding me!"

"Ham, you promised to hear the whole thing—"

"I take it back. Are you completely crazy?"

His response knocked her back.

"Tsarnaev was a terrorist. A jihadist and a militant Islamic. You know what they do to women in those camps—"

She folded her arms, glared at him, then looked away.

Maybe her actions calmed him down because he blew out a breath, ran his hands over his face. "Okay. Sorry. I just . . ." He stared at her then. "I found Zara. She said Tsarnaev had taken you, and I nearly lost my mind, okay? And now you're saying you went with him willingly? Why?" His question hung in the air of the tiny compartment. "Why would you do that—"

"Because it was my job!" She cut her voice low. "I was tasked to infiltrate and find out what Tsarnaev knew—"

"Not by joining his terrorist camp!"

She held up her hand. "Listen. We knew Tsarnaev was planning something. And, like I told you, I was tasked to find out what. When he took me to his camp, I realized it was a much bigger event than we thought. It wasn't just camp—it was practically a city. Three thousand soldiers, all training for jihad. And that was just one of his many camps. They were also using the place as a so-called retraining ground for captured American soldiers. At first I thought I could just smuggle out the location and save the POWs. I did, and some of them got away and were rescued. But then I realized there was a bigger plan. Tsarnaev was planning a *number* of terrorist attacks. It was only ten years out from 9/11 and I thought I could stop something bad from happening."

He was listening now, his gaze hard on hers. Probably because he'd been the tip of the sword back then, still trying to hunt down the players in al-Qaeda.

"The first of Tsarnaev's attacks happened in 2010, only not in America like I thought, but in Russia. In a Moscow subway. Tsarnaev sent two of his women as suicide bombers. I was shocked because I warned the CIA and thought they would stop it. But they didn't. And that's the first time I thought that maybe there was something wrong inside the company. Then less than a year later, one of his suicide bombers blew up Domodedovo Airport. Again, the CIA did *nothing*. A couple more attacks happened—the public transit system in 2013 and a hijack of an airplane in 2015, and finally the explosion in the St. Petersburg metro in April of 2017. All of them connected to Pavel Tsarnaev, and every single time I got word to the company, nothing happened. It was all in Russia, so maybe they didn't want to get involved, but I started to wonder if the information wasn't getting to the right people, or maybe the people I was reporting to were the wrong people."

She had his attention, and his silence, now. "And that's when I started plotting a way to get out."

For a while, Ham had been sitting there, looking down and away from her. Now, he met her eyes. "And where was Aggie all this time?"

"She was with me. She was safe."

It seemed like there was a question in his eyes, but she couldn't bear to answer it.

Instead, "Tsarnaev knew I was valuable. Maybe he thought that someday he could ransom me, or maybe even exchange me for his captured people. So, I pretended I was a double agent and gave him information. The kind of information that hurt no one, but enough so that he could believe me."

Ham was looking at her as if sorting through her words, trying to believe her.

"All this time I was learning Arabic, as well as German and French, and trying to understand his mindset. And Pavel liked Aggie. Something about her blonde hair intrigued him."

He drew back. "Did he ever—"

"No. He never hurt her. I made sure of that."

Ham's jaw tightened.

"You need to know that if I ever felt Aggie wasn't safe, I would have taken her and run."

Please, believe me.

His sigh was audible. "So, then what happened? Why did you run?"

"About three years ago we had a visitor from America."

"This person visited the terrorist camp?"

She nodded. "And about six months later I got access to Tsarnaev's computer and I found a file."

"The NOC list," Ham said.

"Yes. And that's when I started to unravel the plan."

"What plan?"

She stared at him. Debated. Because while she trusted Ham, she couldn't be sure who'd really sent him. So, she kept it cryptic. "The kind of plan that took down governments and rearranged world powers."

He just stared at her.

"I think Tsarnaev bought the list in exchange for services rendered."

"What kind of services?"

The smell of smoke had dissipated a little. "Maybe we should try to get out—"

"What kind of services, Sig?"

"The kind that involve political assassinations, okay?"

"Like a senator?"

"Or a Russian general." Aw, maybe she'd told him too much.

But it could be a test, right? "You heard about the attempted assassination of General Boris Stanislov, right?"

"Yes. Four months ago I was involved in an operation to rescue a woman who was named in his assassination attempt."

Of course he was. She'd wondered how the woman—a CIA operative, according to the rumors—had walked away from the KGB.

Unless she was working with the Russians. But if Ham was involved . . .

"Do you think Tsarnaev had anything to do with the bombing attempt of White's campaign event in Alaska?" he asked.

"I don't know anything about that," she said. "But I did know that with the NOC list in Tsarnaev's hands he could do anything with it. Hold on to it for leverage against the United States or sell it to the highest bidder—whatever served his purposes." She paused. "And there were names on it that I didn't want him to see."

Ham's voice was quiet. "Like yours."

"And others. And I knew that if it got out into the world at large, people would die."

"So why not just destroy it?"

"Every NOC list comes encrypted and can only be unlocked by the personal key of the handful of people in the world who have access to it. So if it was sold, it also came with the decryption key. Unfortunately, I couldn't get my hands on a decryption key, but the right people could decrypt it and match it with the code and . . ."

"Find the source. And discover the traitor in our government."

"Exactly," she said.

"If you had destroyed it, you and Aggie could have disappeared, and stayed safe."

"And Tsarnaev's plan would have still been enacted, and the traitors in the US government never brought to justice."

Ham studied her. "Sig. Did you kill Pavel Tsarnaev?"

She made a face. "Technically he was alive when I left him. But I did leave him sleeping in his cabin and blew up his boat."

He met her eyes and she met his.

"So that's a yes."

"I am not proud of—"

"I always said you were crazy brave. You still are."

No crying. "No, Ham, I'm just . . . I'm just trying to keep ahead of my bad decisions. And just trying to make the next right one. I think you and Aggie are still in danger. I'm sure that whoever found me in Germany is still tracking me." She paused. But she had to know. "Has she been in any danger since she came to you?"

It was the way he looked away, flinched.

"Oh no." A fist squeezed her chest. "What happened?"

"Two months ago, while we were at the Mall of America, a Russian—we think he was part of the Bratva—tried to grab her. We got her back, but he died before we were able to question him."

She pressed on her stomach, trying not to hurl. "I feared something like that would happen. I tried to cover her tracks. I left a note on her for the US Navy to call you. I knew you were out of the Navy, and I thought she'd be safer with you. How did the Russians find her?"

"Maybe it was me," Ham said quietly. "I came to Italy looking for you. Maybe whoever was searching for you saw me . . . followed me home."

"And snatched Aggie."

"Yes. It was that night, too, that I called you on your burner phone."

The phone she'd hid inside Aggie's ratty unicorn. "Really?"

"Yes. Maybe they caught that signal. I don't know, but . . . it could be how they tracked you down too."

She drew in a breath. "Do you still have it?"

116

He nodded. "I tried to call you about a week ago. You didn't answer."

She wanted to lie and tell him that she hadn't gotten the call. That she'd thrown the phone away before—

Aw, she'd never been any good at lying to Ham.

"I was running and I missed your call. Truth. But then, I didn't want you to find me. So I dumped it."

A beat, then, "Why, Signe?"

And she was just tired, and maybe a little frustrated, but, "Because of this! Because of this moment where I look at you and I realize that I've hurt you. And I hate it. I hate the fact that I did this to you, but I didn't know what else to do, and I seem to never make the right choice. And I knew if I heard your voice I would . . ." No. She put a hand over her mouth.

"You would what?" he said softly.

"Nothing. It doesn't matter—"

"It does matter! It matters very much. I didn't trek halfway across the road just to get this list from you. I came to bring you home, Sig. Home where you belong. With me and your daughter. Our family."

Family. But she couldn't allow herself to land there. Instead, she mustered up the woman who'd lived surrounded by hate for the last ten years, the one without hope. "Are you serious? You seriously think that we can be a family after *everything*—" She took a breath. "No, I can't . . ."

He looked like he wanted to swear. Instead, he ran his hand across his head, took a breath. "Please explain this to me."

And there he was. Quintessential Ham—calm, tucking all his emotions back inside.

Yes, well, his soft voice calmed her too. "Until I know that Aggie is safe, that this rogue CIA group or the Russians or whoever wants the list won't come after her, I have to stay away."

"That makes no sense," Ham said. "Why wouldn't they just use Aggie as leverage to force you to come in?"

"They can't use her if they think I'm dead."

He recoiled. "Sig . . . what are you talking about?"

"I'm talking about vanishing. Faking my death—whatever it takes to make sure that Aggie is safe." She met Ham's eyes. "I'm *not* going home with you."

His eyes sparked, and she rushed ahead before he could argue. "But can I give you this information with your solemn promise you will give it to the right people?"

His mouth tightened. "I'll give it to Isaac White."

"Can you trust him?"

He nodded. "But I'm not letting you go, Sig."

"If you want our daughter to live, you will."

He shook his head. "No. You're not doing this again." He held up his hands, then curled them into fists. "I love you, Sig. And I should have never let you walk out of my life. I'm not letting you go."

Oh Ham. "You have to!" Her voice came out just as hot. "Because I haven't endured everything I've gone through for the last ten years to fail at this. To let Pavel Tsarnaev take more, take *everything* from me. I refuse to let him win."

Ham drew in a breath, and his voice tightened to a thread of horror. "Signe, just what did he take from you?" And something in his expression looked so wrecked, she had to look away.

Besides, she couldn't breathe with the rush of answers.

No. She had to put the past behind her if she hoped to survive.

Still, a terrible silence echoed through the elevator, so long and deafening she knew Ham could hear her heart pounding against her ribs.

"Ham—"

A roar filled the silence. It thundered through the darkness, flooding over her, through her, overtaking her cells.

The lift began to shake. "Ham?"

Water seeped into the bottom, saturating the floor.

"Get up!" Ham scrambled to his feet, shining his light on the edges. "Oh no."

"What?" She too stood up.

"Sometimes after volcanoes and earthquakes there are tidal waves."

"Are you talking a *tsunami*?"

He handed her the phone. "We've got to get out of here or we're going to drown." He stood up and searched the top of the box, found a latch. He tried to open it, scattering pebbles and dirt into the compartment. "It's stuck." He turned to her. "We have to get up there. If I lift you, can you push the panel free?"

She nodded. He held out his clasped hands.

She stepped into them, her hands on his massive shoulders, and as if she weighed nothing, he picked her up. Setting her shoulder to the panel, she pushed on it. It moved and she wedged it open and pulled herself up.

"What do you see?"

He'd been right, the lift *had* protected them. Rubble had fallen around the outside of the box, but for the most part the shaft was open all the way to the top. Four rusty metal poles ran the length of the shaft, one on either side of the doors, and along the back. A wan light bled through the metal grates on the floor above. "I think we fell two floors down."

The building had started to shake. She leaned down and put her hand out. "Can you reach my hand?"

"Get back," he said. "And hang on to the cable in case the lift decides to break free."

"What?"

But she did as she was told as Ham jumped, grabbing the edges of the opening. Then, like the super human that he was, he pulled himself up, barely wedging his shoulders through.

He grabbed the cable, testing it. "We need to climb this." He unbuttoned his shirt and pulled it off, revealing the fact that he still had his SEAL physique, then ripped off the arms of his shirt.

He put his shirt back on. "Hold out your hands."

She was too shocked to do anything but obey. He wrapped the fabric around her hands. "Can you do this?"

She met his gaze. "Yes. Of course."

Just for a moment, she got a smile. A glimpse of the old Ham, the one who competed with her in gym class. The Ham who had taught her how to ride a horse, the one who'd been her best friend and told her he'd never forget her.

Clearly, he'd kept that promise.

Of course he kept that promise.

She looked away and grabbed the pole.

"Climb as fast as you can, Signe. Because I'm afraid this building is going to go down."

She wrapped her hands around the cable and started to inch up. But she didn't know what was more dangerous—the tsunami or the unforgettable pull Ham had on her heart.

CHAPTER SIX

SIGNE WAS SCARED. Ham got that.

He'd just have to prove to her that he could protect her. *Them.* Because she *was* going home with him.

Aggie needed her mother. And, regardless of the betrayal that ground through him, Signe was his wife.

They'd figure that out after they made it to the top of the elevator shaft, after they escaped this disintegrating hotel, after she handed over the NOC list, and, frankly, after he got her home and got to the bottom of . . . well, *"I haven't endured everything I've gone through for the last ten years to fail at this. To let Pavel Tsarnaev take more, take* everything *from me."*

Sheesh, now he had way too many dark scenarios in his head and it only added to the panic as he ascended the rope behind Signe.

Who was struggling.

"You okay?"

"Golden. Call me Catwoman." But she'd started to slip a little, even with the cloth around her hands.

"Just a couple more feet, you're almost there."

She had her legs wrapped around the cable, her hands inching her up, but in truth, the cable was oily and rough and even he was fighting, his hands starting to bleed from the fibers in the cable.

The building was still shaking, battered by what he assumed was debris-filled water. The bricks of the elevator shaft broke free as they climbed, falling to shatter on the box below.

The entire structure could go down.

The lift was dark, with no more than a graying smudge at the top where a vent had dislodged. The air reeked of sulfur and ash.

The two-story drop fell to darkness.

"What if I pushed you—"

"Keep your hands to yourself, there, Batman." She moved another few feet. "I can almost reach the ledge." She leaned out, trying to touch the edge of the next floor. Missed.

She grabbed the line, and it shook. Metal fibers bit into his hands.

"Signe—"

"I got this! I just need a second."

They didn't have a second. "Next to the ledge is the metal girder. Just transfer your weight there, dig your feet into the edge of the bricks. Then, climb up to the ledge holding on to the girder."

She leaned out, and her fingertips just grazed the metal.

"I'm going to climb up underneath you and brace you. Give you something solid to push off." He moved up underneath her and her feet met his shoulders.

"You're going to fall—"

"We'll both fall if we don't get off this—now brace your feet on me and grab that ledge!" He was using his senior chief voice, but he didn't care.

"On three," he said. "Grab the girder and pull yourself up."

She let out a noise—half frustration, half pain—and launched.

The girder shuddered as she grabbed it, but she clung to it like a koala.

His grip was slipping, but he had to get her off that metal before he joined her or it could detach from the wall and send them both southward.

"Can you reach the door?"

She made another sound of effort and scrambled up the pole. Atta girl.

A weird sense of pride swept through him, an old, errant feeling that he'd thought was dormant.

His girl.

Yes, they had to get out of here and fix . . . everything.

She put her foot on the ledge and grunted her way higher until she could stand on it. Then she braced herself on the metal pole with one hand and reached out for the metal grate covering the doors with the other.

The grate was designed to zigzag back.

Please let it not be wedged. Please let him not have made a lethal mistake.

It shuddered with her efforts.

"Keep pulling." He tightened his legs because his hands were slipping.

She got her foot into the space and widened it, maybe two feet. "It's stuck."

Below them, he heard the water banging into the lift.

"Okay, maybe I can reach it. Hang tight."

The skin on his hands might be peeling back, but he worked his legs, grit his teeth, and shimmied up the pole.

The only easy day was yesterday. The SEAL motto hung in his head as he focused on the edge. He was nearly even with it now. But if he put his foot out, his hand would slip—

"Grab my hand. I'll pull you over."

"I'll yank you right off—"

"Grab my hand, Ham!"

He blew out a breath, then entangled his hand with hers. It was a crazy wide step, but if he could get his other hand around the grate, he could wedge it open. Then he could kick the doors in.

"Don't miss, Batman." She gave him a look, then smiled.

Oh, his old instincts were igniting. *Game on, honey.*

He put out his foot, ready to catch the ledge.

On her mark, he let her force tug him over, and he sprang for the door.

His hand closed around the metal bar, his foot landed on the lip—

The lip gave way.

She shouted as he fell, but he had one hand on the grate.

The other hand in hers.

Which saved her life because just as he suspected, his weight tore her from her perch and she fell into the chasm. Her scream echoed into the chamber—

"Hold on!"

She dangled from his grip. "Ham!"

"I'm not going to drop you. Just hang on!"

Please.

He still had ahold of the door, and now scrabbled his feet into the bricks, trying to find a foothold.

"Swing me to the pipe!"

His feet caught, a three-point hold. "Can you grab it?"

She nodded, a fierceness in her eyes. He swung back, then forward with everything he had in him.

Her hand closed on the girder and she clung to the metal pipe, letting him go.

He grabbed the door and scrambled up to the opening. Wrenched open the gate. Kicked open the wooden doors.

Then he crouched inside the door and reached out for her.

She went into his arms as if she'd always belonged there, as if she knew he'd catch her.

As if they were once again a team.

He used one arm to pull her against himself, the other to hold on to the door. Then, he simply fell back to safety, holding her tight, breathing hard.

She had her arms around his waist, also breathing hard.

"You okay?" he said.

She lifted herself, met his eyes, something unreadable in them. Then she blinked hard and pushed herself off him. "Let's go."

She was right. No time to explore what-ifs and once-upon-a-times.

They were back on the terrace, and he followed her across the roof. A terrible gash in the tile ran the length of the building, and the shaking had toppled planters of begonias and even a couple tall palm trees. Dirt and glass and plates and food debris, broken tile, plants and overturned furniture littered their path, and everything was covered in a film of ash.

She made it to the edge of the building. "Oh no . . ."

He joined her, and the sight took his breath.

The sea had risen, maybe twenty feet, sweeping over the water breaks and taking with it everything in its path. Fishing boats, cars, wooden structures, and probably even people, although Ham couldn't see anyone, all swirled in a cauldron of black water. The wave moved through the city, breaking windows, tearing down buildings. Already, the house two doors down had dislodged from its moorings.

The water reached to nearly the second floor of the hotel, flooding in the windows.

"If we'd stayed in the lift, we'd be under water by now," Signe said.

"Don't think about it." He took her hand, and miraculously, she gripped his back. "We need to get off this roof before this house goes down."

So much for the "old and quaint" hotel listing. Next time he was going for new, sturdy, and very boring with lots of exits and far, far from volcanoes and other natural disasters.

He glanced back toward the volcano, but it was still shrouded in a gassy cloud, the city haunted with eerie smoke. A few fires flickered, but he couldn't get a good fix on them.

"How?" Signe said, referring to his suggestion. "We're surrounded by water."

Good question. But they were situated in the lower side of the city. Just a block to the south, the city rose on a hill . . .

"We need to get to those buildings," he said and pointed to the higher ground. "And nearly every building is connected."

"Except ours." She had let go of his hand and walked over to the side of the building. "There's a ten-foot gap here."

"But our building is taller."

"No, Ham—"

"Signe. You're one of the best long-jumpers—"

"You're out of your mind!"

"There's no other way off this building! And—"

His words cut off as the building gave a terrific shudder.

"We gotta go."

She gave him a fierce, angry look, her jaw tight. "Okay, let's line up a couple tables and get a running start."

Atta girl, Catwoman.

They dragged over four tables and lined them up perpendicular to the railing, like a runway. Signe got on one and tested it. "This is a stupid idea."

"You can do this. It's only ten feet—"

"And four stories down!"

"Remember that time we found that rope swing out over the river?"

Horror filled her expression. "I've never been so scared in my life! That was forty feet high!"

"But you did it. You just decided—and you did it."

"If I remember correctly, there was some name-calling involved."

A terrible whining sound wove through the air, probably the foundation separating from its moorings.

"Don't be a chicken."

"I hate you." But she backed up, wiped her hands on her pants. "Oh, geez—"

"Just—"

She took off running. When she launched, she screamed, her arms windmilling as she fell.

Please!

She cleared the wall and landed on the terrace, on her feet, scrambling until she stopped herself against a table.

"Your turn!"

He climbed the tables. They were more rickety than he'd thought as he put his foot on the first one.

"Hurry!" Signe had gone to the wall. "The building has a massive crack up the side!"

Yeah, yeah, no problem. She weighed about a buck twenty while wet and he was over two hundred, and getting his buffalo body over that gap—

"Just jump, Ham! Don't be—"

He took off, four big steps across the tables—

Just as he launched, the last table tipped. He managed to get a foot on the edge but didn't get the oomph he needed.

He tumbled like a brick through the air, dropping hard and fast.

His fingers brushed the edge of the building.

Then he was plunging into the alleyway below.

■ ■ ■

Signe just knew that Ham was going to get killed trying to save her. She screamed as his hands scraped the edge.

She tried to reach out for him, but she was too late, and she caught herself before she nearly went over too.

Below her was a cauldron of lethal water, rebar, wood, and broken metal, ready to impale him.

Batman caught the railing of the next balcony down.

His roar tore through her bones, but he hung there, moaning, refusing to let gravity have him.

It took her a second to get it through her head that Ham hadn't landed as a splat on the dirty rapids of water below. "Hang on!"

She ran across the broken terrace to the doors to the stairwell, avoided the lift, thank you very much, and ran down to the next floor.

Apartments, and it took her a second to figure out which one might be right. She banged on the door but got no response.

She backed up and slammed her foot into the door, at the lock.

It broke and the door eased open.

She was through it, weaving around broken glass and toppled furniture all the way to the French doors.

Ham dangled from the balcony, his face a knot of pain.

She grabbed his belt, and he got his feet up on the balcony and then he tumbled over the railing and into her arms.

She just wanted to hold on. Never let go.

Never. Never. Never.

"We have to go." He rolled away from her, but as he did, he winced and brought his arm in close to his body. Let out a moan.

"Is it dislocated?" She reached out for him.

He caught her arm before she could touch him. "It's okay."

"It's not okay. You're in pain."

"I'm fine. It's probably just sprained." But as he got up, he let out a grunt.

"It's more than sprained." She could be just as stubborn as he could, thank you. She ran into the apartment, found a towel, and returned. He was right behind her.

"What's that for?"

"A sling—"

He grabbed the towel from her. "I'm fine."

"You're so stubborn! Why can't you admit you're hurt?"

He stared at her. "What good would it do? So, I'm hurt. The danger doesn't stop because I got an owie."

"Let me fix it!"

"Really, now you want to fix it? Now you care?"

She stared at him. "What are we talking about here?"

He drew in a breath. "Sorry. I . . . listen. Let's just get out of here."

She didn't move. "Ham. I've always cared. I never stopped thinking about you. I *never* stopped loving you."

Her words seemed to stymie him because he just stared at her.

"C'mon. We gotta go," she said. "But let me sling your stupid arm."

He handed her the towel. She ran it up under his wrist, then around his neck, to knot it. He had to lean over a little, and the familiarity in his scent wove through her, a swift and brutal memory of being in his arms, his breath on her neck.

"You okay?"

She stepped away from him and his devastating presence. "Yeah. Yes. Fine."

"Your hands are a little dinged up there." He'd caught one of her wrists.

"For cryin' in the sink, it's a scrape. Yours are like raw meat." She tore away, walked out of the apartment, then back up the stairs.

The next building was attached and a little lower. She easily lowered herself down.

Through a break in the clouds, she spotted lava spitting into the air, bleeding down the slopes of Etna. Below them, the confused, blackened sea swirled with wreckage. Water rushed over a catamaran wedged between buildings.

The next building was separated by a three-foot gap, and she easily leaped it. Ham landed almost immediately next to her. Back stairs led down into a gated garden filled with water.

A sea kayak floated in the middle, the paddle wedged into the webbing on top.

Almost as if waiting for them.

Ham pointed to it.

"Good idea, Huck."

He grinned, and the light from it found her soul. "That was your terrible idea, if I remember correctly."

"Blame it on our sixth-grade teacher. She's the one who made us read *Huckleberry Finn*." She grabbed a broom, climbed down the stairs, and hooked one end onto the kayak.

"But you were the one who said we could take a raft down the Mississippi."

She dragged the edge of the kayak toward her. "Not so much a raft as a dinghy."

"Milton Anderson's dinghy, to be specific."

She pulled the kayak close. "You get in first. I'll sit in front."

Ham grabbed the kayak and eased into it. Propped his legs on the side.

For the first time she noticed that his leg was bleeding. "Ham?"

"Just a flesh wound. I've had worse." He gave her a slow grin.

"Stop," she said, but the old quote from one of his favorite Monty Python movies loosened her own smile. She climbed in, crouching in the well in front of him. Grabbed the paddle. "I guess I'll have to do all the work here."

"Just don't dump us." Ham pushed off.

"That wasn't my fault."

"You were driving."

They reached the gate and she maneuvered over to the latch.

"I got this." He worked the latch, then wrestled with the gate. It eased open, and she helped pull them through.

The waters in the alley still churned, but the debris wasn't as thick.

"The road rises to the south," Ham said, pointing.

"I know. I've been here a couple days." She started to move them into the current. Ham tried to push aside debris.

"Really?"

"I saw you arrive. Saw your team scope out the castello. I just wanted to make sure you weren't being followed."

They paddled past more gated entrances, downed palm trees, cars slammed into stone walls, and the occasional completely submerged house. Fires crackled on the hillside above them, smoke blackening the air.

"Were we?"

"I don't think so. But I was careful last time too. Maybe you're right, maybe they traced me through the burner phone when I answered your call. But then they would have had to track me through Italy, then Croatia, and Bulgaria—"

"Wow."

"I finally made it to Germany. I stayed with Zara." She glanced over her shoulder at him. "They killed her and her husband Felix."

"Who's they?"

"A guy named Martin—or so he said. And possibly others. Russian, American, I don't know. One of them nearly caught me, but I got away. I opened his knuckles with my knife."

She turned back around.

"I'm normally pretty good at taking care of myself. At least when I'm not caught in the apocalypse."

"I'm sure you are."

"The good news about the world ending is that maybe whoever is trying to kill me is currently under a building."

"You really think they'll find you here?"

"I don't know." A terrible cracking and the whine of metal rending made her turn around. Glance past him. "If I knew who—oh wow."

He turned too.

Their hotel moved completely off its moorings, cracked, then dissolved in a cloud, falling into the black sea.

Ham said nothing. Turned back and met her eyes. "So much for that croissant." He gave her a wry smile. "Sorry. Bad taste, I know. Jake's stress humor is clearly rubbing off on me."

She looked at him. For Pete's sake. But oh, she missed him. The thought just erupted from her heart, filled her entire body with heat. She probably never knew a time when she didn't love Hamilton Jones.

This had gotten so messy.

She kept paddling, heading toward the hill where the water shallowed. The air had cleared, just a little, and she made out a wall, stairs rising above the water that led to higher ground.

The air smelled rotten, and another tremor shook the earth as they pulled up to the stairs. Or maybe it was just her body, trembling, feeling Ham's body behind her, his legs around her. She was very, very aware of the effect being around him had on her soul.

She had to get out of here.

The water pooled to the third step, but beyond that, it was clear. Ham held the boat as she climbed out. He followed her.

"Now where?" She looked out across the devastation, buildings toppled over in the water, a gray landscape of water, ash, and smoke. Ham's body was covered in ash too, which was still lilting from the sky.

"We find shelter. Then we figure out if my team is still alive. They both left the hotel. Hopefully they didn't return."

His team. Right. The people who actually knew him.

Who would return home with him—if they were still alive.

She started up the hill.

"Where are you going?" Ham asked.

"There's a pizza joint up this way."

"You're hungry?"

"Starved, but that's not the point. My guess is they'd have internet, if there is any. And maybe bottled water."

The cobblestones had hiccupped from the earth, cracks in buildings scattered debris, cars sat parked, dented, dusty. Trees were whitened, ghostly arms reaching to the skies.

"Sig."

She glanced over her shoulder. Ham was keeping up, holding his arm. "You know I forgive you, right?"

Aw, shoot, don't go there. "I think it's right up here." She pointed to a blue building with a gated area, the tables on the sidewalk toppled over.

"I never forgot you."

Her jaw tightened. She came to the gate and opened it. The place was empty.

She walked up the steps and went inside.

She'd eaten here two nights ago, had a pizza with fresh tomatoes, basil, arugula, and burrata cheese.

Funny that she'd remember that, and the fact that she'd watched every person who came into the place. Clearly, she was too conditioned because even now, she scoured the place for trouble. Noted the exits.

"This place smells amazing," she said.

No response from the man behind her.

She turned. Ham was standing at the doorway, his gaze on her. Fine.

"Ham, the fact is, you don't even know what you're forgiving me for. You have no idea—"

"It doesn't matter, Sig." He came into the room. "I don't need to know. And you never have to tell me."

"There isn't enough forgiveness—"

"Nope. You're wrong there too." He walked over to a standing cooler and opened it. Grabbed a water and handed it to her. "Forgiveness has no limit. There's an endless supply."

She took the water. Oh Ham. "I don't understand how you can say that after . . . well, what your stepmother did to you. Or what I did to you."

He made to open his water bottle but struggled with his hand in a sling, so she opened hers and handed it to him, took his.

"Thanks." He took a drink. "I guess the fact is, if I walk around with anger in my heart, it just darkens my own soul. Forgiveness is hard, but really, it costs me nothing because it doesn't come from me."

Oh. Right. "So, you never lost your faith."

"It's the one thing that never let me down."

She drew in a breath, but yes, she deserved that.

He met her gaze. "Including me, Sig. I'm not perfect. I've done a lot of things that I'm ashamed of. But God seems to keep forgiving me, even when I let myself down."

She took the cap off her water, took a drink. It filled her parched throat, her cells, and she closed her eyes.

When she opened them, Ham stood in front of her. He touched her face.

The world began to shake again.

"Seriously?" Ham grabbed her hand and pulled her over to a table. He pushed her down under it, then climbed in beside her.

Then, without asking, he pulled her against him, his good arm around her.

Shoot, she'd let him. Because right now, with the world crashing down around them, tomorrow didn't matter.

Her sins didn't matter.

Just the fact that right here, at this moment . . . she was home.

"I hope someone comes by to take our order," Ham said. "Because I'm really hankering for a deep-dish pepperoni and mushroom."

■ ■ ■

Jenny couldn't move.

She just stood on the rooftop of Caffe Greco, her hands pressed to her mouth, unable to breathe at the sight of her hotel disappearing into the sea.

No. No, no—

"Jenny, just breathe."

Harley touched her arm.

Jenny turned away from him, ran to a garbage can, and lost the bile left in her stomach.

Then she sank down into a ball, put her hands over her head. *Wake up. Wake* up!

She closed her eyes, tracking through the past hour—

The taste of the Mediterranean still stung her lips, her clothing soggy from her dive into the sea. She'd clung to the pylon, her arm around Gio as they ducked under the water, holding their breaths until her lungs wanted to burst.

She surfaced, gulped a breath, and went down again. Gio's arms were around her by then, and when she felt him panic, she hit the surface again.

This time, she bobbed, searching the horizon.

The cloud of volcanic debris blanketed the air, hanging over the sea, and she could barely make out the shore. "Pull your shirt up over your mouth," she told him as she did the same, tucking it over her nose.

135

That's when the sea betrayed her.

At first, as the water fell away from shore, she thought it might be a normal wave. But when the sea swept past the dinghies tied at the dock, when it fell to reveal rocks and boulders and the debris of the shoreline, she knew they were in trouble.

"Run, Gio!"

Jenny grabbed Gio's shirt as they stumbled up the shoreline, past huge sailboats now dug into the seabed, past fishing trawlers and nets and buoys. She lost her flip-flops and Gio tripped and fell, cutting his knee on a rock.

"Get up!" She didn't mean to scare him, but she could already hear the deep, dark thunder of a tsunami.

She didn't realize they had tsunamis in the Mediterranean, but of course they did. Turkey had been hit with one a few years ago, right?

They hit the shoreline and kept running.

"My grandfather!" Gio pulled away from her, heading toward the pier.

"Gio!"

The shout came from an elderly fisherman in canvas pants and sandals. Ash covered his hat and vest, and he ran down the shore and scooped Gio into his arms, shaking, weeping.

"Nonnino!" Gio struggled free and said something in Italian.

His grandfather turned, took one look at the sea, and took his hand.

"This way!" Jenny said, not sure why, and took off up the road, toward the coffee shop.

Toward the hotel.

Back to Orion.

She couldn't remember where it was except to retrace her steps, but as she ran, her hand over her mouth, she thought of turning around, going back along the harbor.

The hotel overlooked the sea.

Gio and his nonnino ran past her, and she glanced back. A wall of gray sea roared toward shore, foaming, hungry, gobbling everything in its path. It hit the sailboats at anchor beyond the docks like they might be toys, scooping them up, swamping them. Spray filled the air and she could already taste the death.

She sprinted up the hill, passing Gio and his grandfather, flinging herself into the coffee shop.

People were hurt, bleeding, crying. She spotted the Americans. Harley was wrapping a cloth around the hand of one of the girls.

"Tsunami!" Jenny shouted and Harley looked at her.

She turned to a barista. "Stairs—where are your stairs?"

He pointed to a door in the back, and Jenny pushed Gio and his grandfather toward it. "Go, go!"

Already the thunder had turned deafening and water crashed into the open, broken windows of the cafe.

She sprinted up the stairs, followed by the screaming patrons fighting to get up as water flooded the ground floor. Jenny looked down as she hit the second floor and spotted the water rising on the lower level stairs. Harley was at the bottom, pulling people in.

So much like Orion.

Two apartments were on the second floor, and she banged on the doors as she ran by. "Get out!"

She ran up to the third floor. Someone had already opened the door to the terrace and she ran out, past spilled planters and toppled furniture, all covered in ash.

She cupped her hands over her eyes and watched the sea erupt in fury, tearing at apartments, taking down trees.

Their building shivered, but it was protected by the buildings around it, the higher altitude.

People were crying—the two American women holding hands, staring at the sea, then the mountain.

Harley came up beside her, breathing hard. "We got everyone out. Thank you."

She nodded but didn't really see him. Because behind him, along the shore, she watched an apartment building as it surrendered, collapsed into the sea in a foamy splash.

Oh.

No.

An *entire* building.

"Are you okay?"

"My boyfriend is in a seaside hotel on the second floor." She searched the horizon. "The one with the green umbrellas."

"There's no way to get there."

"I need to try." And then, as she watched, the umbrellas on the roof began to shake and . . .

The hotel fell into the sea.

No . . . wait—*what*?

Her legs nearly buckled.

"Jenny, just breathe."

She fled to the trash can . . .

Now, Harley crouched in front of her. "Hey. Can I get you anything?"

She shook her head, emptied. Numb.

"Maybe he got out," Harley said. His expression betrayed worry.

Gio came over to her. "My nonnino wants to thank you."

Right. Okay. Because what else was she going to do?

She got up and Gio led her over to the old man, now seated on a chair, breathing hard.

She crouched in front of him. *Focus. Move forward.* "Hi. Are you okay?"

Gio translated.

The man pressed his chest but nodded. *"Grazie."* He clamped his hand on Gio's shoulder. A tear spilled down his face, and he wiped it away.

"You're welcome," she said, and glanced at Gio. "What's your grandfather's name?"

"Marcello."

"Marcello, you have a brave grandson."

Gio translated and Marcello smiled.

Then, to her horror, he groaned and doubled over, holding his chest.

Oh no. "Gio, ask him where it hurts."

The boy translated. Marcello made a face.

"He says it's just his blood pressure."

Maybe angina. Maybe not. "Let's get him down on the ground. Loosen his clothing."

Harley had come over. "What's going on?"

"He might be having a heart attack. Gio, ask him if he has any medicine he takes."

Harley translated instead. "Yes, but it's at his house."

"Do we have any aspirin?"

"I do!" said one of the women. "But it's in my pack . . ."

Jenny got up. "Stay with him," she said to Harley. "Loosen his clothes and if he stops breathing—"

"Where do you think you're going?" Harley hit his feet and followed her.

She ignored him. "What does your pack look like?" she said to the woman.

"It's orange. It's got my name—Angie Hunter—on a tag. And—oh, a green ribbon—"

"You're not going down there," Harley said.

"Marcello needs his aspirin."

"Hey—no!" Harley stood in front of her. "You are *not* going down there—"

139

"I absolutely *am* going down there. I'm getting Angie's orange backpack and I'm only telling you once to step back, pal. I know I don't look like it, but I served in Afghanistan alongside special forces, and trust me when I say I'm giving you just one warning."

Harley's eyes widened. "Okay. Um." He glanced at his friends, back to her. "If this is some kind of psychotic break—"

"I'm a psychologist, for Pete's sake, and right now, I need to do *something*. Okay?" And she might be scaring herself, but she couldn't . . . oh. She pressed her hands to her gut, fighting the words in her head.

Why didn't I just say yes to Orion? Tell him she loved him, and that if he wanted a family, then . . . well, she'd just figure it out. They could adopt. Or maybe . . . maybe the doctors were wrong.

Whatever. Wow, she'd been stupid, and the rush of it nearly made her cry out.

Instead, she drew in a breath and met Harley's green eyes.

Orion had green eyes.

Stop. "Listen, I'm a climber and a swimmer and I'll be fine. Hopefully the pack is still there. I'll go look, and if not, then I'll be right back—"

"I'm coming with you."

Yes, okay. Because maybe, like her, he needed something to do also. "C'mon."

The stairwell was only filled to the bottom four steps, the water dark and gritty, debris swirling in a mass. She stood at the edge of the water and peered into the shop.

Wood, Styrofoam, plaster, foam, rubber, clothing, even plastic dishes filled the room. However, near the corner, a pile of clothing, purses, and yes . . . an orange backpack.

"I'm going in."

"I'm right behind you."

She gasped as she plunged into the chilly water. It came up past her waist, and she clung to the bar as she worked her way over to the corner. The current hit the wall, then rushed away, rocketing water throughout the tiny cafe. Harley pushed a piece of wood away from her.

The pack was caught in a debris pile, near the back, past a cauldron of water.

"Be careful," Harley said as she neared it.

"I got—"

The current grabbed her.

Swept her feet out from under her. She went under, the water collapsing over her head.

Something whacked her, she opened her mouth, managed to swallow water, scraped her foot on the bottom but fell before she could right herself.

No. Not like this—

Hands hauled her up. Pushed her against the bar.

She clung to it, coughing.

"You okay?" Harley said.

She was a stupid fool. Headstrong, thoughtless, cruel . . . and she began to weep as she coughed.

Harley stood there, his hand on her back.

She bowed her head into her hands. "He asked me to marry him, and I said no." Her breath washboarded in. "I said no!"

Harley said nothing, just nodded.

She looked at him. And maybe it was because he was a stranger. And so terribly reminded her of Orion. And because her regret, more than the water, was drowning her. "Because I had an abortion when I was nineteen and there were complications." She looked at him. "The doctor said that I probably can't have kids. But Orion *loves* kids. And I didn't even think about that when we first met—we were overseas in Afghanistan, and having a family was the furthest thing from my mind. I mean, who thinks of having kids while you're in a war zone, right?"

Harley nodded, lifted a shoulder.

"And then we found each other again and I . . ." She closed her eyes. "I was so selfish. I was so . . . stupid. I was . . ." Her breaths caught again.

Somewhere in there, Harley's arms went around her and he held her in the swirling mass of filthy, lethal water.

She didn't know when she came back to herself but, finally, "I'm sorry, I'm so—"

"Stop. Just stop. It's okay."

She looked up at him. He wore concern in his eyes.

"I'm sorry I'm so unraveled."

"Tsunamis do that to people." He gave her a small smile. Then he reached around her and snagged the orange pack, providentially dislodged from the pile of debris. "Let's go."

She followed him back up the stairs, out of the darkness.

Marcello was sitting up, breathing better, but Harley dug through Angie's backpack anyway and found the aspirin. Marcello chewed a couple.

Jenny went over to the railing and stared at the space where the hotel had been. And right then, Scarlett's question found her, the one she'd asked in DC.

The one that really mattered.

"What are you so afraid of?"

This. She was afraid of this.

The moment when God took away her happy ending.

Because she didn't deserve one.

I'm so sorry, Ry. Jenny sank down on the floor of the terrace, brought her knees up, curled her hands around them, and wept.

CHAPTER SEVEN

HE WAS REALLY HURT.

Ham leaned against the wall of the dark pizza place, listening to Signe's breathing, watching as the world outside turned dark with the smoke off the mountain, trying not to move.

He'd broken his wrist, he was sure of it. Every time he moved it, a flash of pain spiked up his arm and consumed his entire body. So, that was fun.

He hadn't noticed the gash on his leg until he stopped running. Now, it burned, and his blood was probably swimming with bacteria.

He needed a hospital. Or at least a splint and a shot of penicillin.

Never mind the fact that in the back of his mind, he kept seeing their hotel vanish into the sea.

Please let Orion and Jenny not have returned to the hotel. He'd tried his cell phone a couple times, but the towers were down and that only fueled the frustration buzzing through his body.

He needed to be on his feet *doing* something.

But sitting here with Signe was . . . well, maybe an answered prayer.

143

Please, God, keep her from running from me. Please help her to trust me.

In fact, he'd spent the last hour simply praying as the building shook around them. *Please protect us. Protect Orion and Jenny. Protect Aggie and restore us as a family.*

So maybe, right now, not moving was the exact right action. In fact, he'd willingly stay here forever, enduring the pain if it meant keeping Signe safe.

He ran his hand over the funny scar on her upper arm, the one she'd gotten while building the tree house near the river when they were thirteen. A nail he'd half pounded in the tree stuck out and she'd snagged it, hopping down to the ground.

A thick, bumpy scar that had probably long since blended into her skin. But he knew it was there.

Her words kept reverberating through him. *"Because I haven't endured everything I've gone through for the last ten years to fail at this. To let Pavel Tsarnaev take more, take everything from me."*

His imagination was having a field day.

Oh yes, he really hurt.

Another tremor reverberated through the stone floor of the restaurant.

"That's the third aftershock." Signe leaned away from him.

He barely restrained himself from tugging her back.

She got up. "I'm going to see if I can find us something to eat."

"Sig . . ."

She walked over to the kitchen area and opened a refrigerator. "There's leftover pizza in here."

"I'm dying here. I know it's only going to kill me, but . . . what did Tsarnaev take from you?"

She had come over to the long bar that separated the kitchen from the cafe, holding something wrapped in parchment. The shadows hid her face, but her tone was clear. "Ham . . . I—"

"Did he hurt you?"

She was quiet. And he knew—he just *knew*.

"Did he rape you?"

Paper crinkled as she opened the parchment. "It's a margherita pizza."

"Signe!"

"What do you think, Ham? It was a terrorist camp." She didn't raise her voice, just kept it small and even, as if she were giving a sit-rep.

Though he'd suspected it, the words punched him, right into the center of his chest.

He struggled to breathe. *Lord, give me the right response*—

"It just happened once. Right after I arrived. Once Tsarnaev realized I was pregnant, he didn't touch me again."

He didn't know what to say to that.

She came over carrying the pizza in the parchment and set it down in front of him, sat down cross-legged.

He couldn't possibly eat.

"We never talked about it, but he might have thought Aggie was his."

Right. Then, wait— "Aggie protected you from him, didn't she? As long as he thought she was his, then you weren't in danger."

She picked up a piece of pizza.

"Signe . . . what aren't you telling me?"

She took a bite, set the pizza down. "Nothing you need to know."

Except . . . "Signe, if he thought you were the mother of his child, then . . . did he marry you?"

"As his wife I had access to so much. His private quarters, he took me on business trips, he—"

"You *married* him?"

Oh, he didn't mean to let the horror leak in, but—

"Are you familiar at all with Sharia law? If I didn't, he would have accused me of adultery—"

"He *raped* you."

She flinched, and he felt like he'd hit her.

"Oh Signe, I'm sorry." He scrubbed his hands down his face. "The thought of you married to that . . ." He didn't say the rest, but inside, he was screaming.

"I didn't have a choice, Ham. In order to be exonerated I had to produce four male witnesses to the crime. Right. Not a chance. So, it was either marry him, or I was going to be flogged. Maybe even executed."

He might be ill right here on the floor.

"I realize my stupid choices." She picked up her pizza, then put it back down. "But once I got there, I had to go all in. Which meant . . . I had to be Pavel's wife."

Pavel. "You're *my* wife."

Silence.

He looked away from her, out to the street where the day was darkening.

Oh, he should have gone after her into that bunker. Never stopped looking for her. He gritted his jaw, his eyes burning. But everything inside him was ripping asunder.

You're my wife.

Clearly not anymore.

"Ham, I know you were hoping that maybe we could put things back together. Be a family. But . . ."

"What else did he take from you?" He didn't know why, but for some reason, he knew that wasn't all. "*To let Pavel Tsarnaev take more, take everything from me.*"

"I think we need to get out of here—"

"What, Signe!"

She stared at him, her jaw hard. "He took my son, okay?"

What?

She got up and paced away from him, standing at the cracked picture window.

Ham had nothing, the words stripped right out of him. She had a *son*.

She ran her hands down her face, then pressed them to the window, and the old Ham, the one who always, *always* came to her aid, wanted to go to her. To hold her.

But he also wanted to hit something, to rage with the roil of heat inside him. She had a child with a *terrorist*?

"He was born a year after Aggie. His name is Ruslan." She turned around to face him, folded her arms, her face hard. "When he was six, Pavel sent him to live with relatives in eastern Russia. Said he was safer there. I haven't seen him in three years."

Ham just stared at her, not sure what was worse—not knowing you had a child and missing ten years of her life or . . .

Or knowing your child was growing up without you.

"I get pictures of him every year. Sometimes a phone call, but I have no idea where he is."

He pushed to his feet, biting back a groan.

"Sit down!" She came over to him. "Your leg is still bleeding."

He looked down to see a puddle where his leg had been resting.

She pulled a red checkered tablecloth from the floor and bit it, tearing a long swath from it. "Let me wrap that."

And wow, they were alike with the need to keep moving, fix something, do *anything* to push back the hurt.

He stayed quiet as she doctored him, aware that he knew so very little of her life now.

So very . . . wait.

He stilled. If Pavel had her son, did he also have control over her?

The kind of control that would make a woman sacrifice her life . . . or betray her country?

He studied Signe. She'd long since lost her head scarf, her face sooty and dirty. She wore stress in lines around her eyes, and her lips had thinned.

But she was still the most beautiful woman he'd ever seen.

He had no doubt that Pavel Tsarnaev had fallen in love with her. But love didn't trump ideology.

What if Tsarnaev wasn't dead, as she said. And what if the information she wanted to give Ham also contained a virus or something that could compromise the security of the US? Ham didn't want to think that way, but he'd been a special operator for over a decade. He was trained to look for danger.

"You need stitches."

"Signe, who was the person who came to the camp? The one who you said was from the US government?"

She looked up at him. Her jaw tightened.

"You don't trust me."

"I *do* trust you, Ham. I just don't trust the people you might work for."

"Why?"

She paused. "I believe there is a rogue CIA faction that was working with Tsarnaev. And that faction is trying to kill me."

"That's not going to happen."

"Why? Are you Superman? You can stop speeding bullets, see through walls, be everywhere at once?"

"No. I'm your husband! I'm going to protect you!" He didn't mean for that to emerge quite so hot, but he had a very thin hold on his emotions and—

"You can't protect someone who doesn't want to be protected!"

He stared at her.

"I'm a big girl, Ham. I know I asked you not to forget me, but really, that's the best thing for you to do—forget me. Because as soon as we get out of here, I'm gone—"

"You're going to leave Aggie." It was more of an incredulous statement than a question. "You're going to walk right out of her life, like your mother did you."

Signe drew in a breath, and for a second he thought she might slap him. "This is *nothing* like my mother. I am doing this *for* Aggie. For you. Believe me. If I could, I would go home with you." Her voice broke. "Ham. You're the love of my life. Don't you think I want to be with you?"

He just blinked at her.

"You don't, do you? Do you believe *anything* I'm telling you?"

He nearly reached out to her, her words resounding over and over inside him. "I love you too, Signe. I would give my life for you. And I want to trust you. Help me trust you. Tell me who came to your camp."

She studied him. "I can't, Ham. People—you, Aggie, . . . me. It could cost lives."

"Sig. Let me protect you. Protect Aggie. Give us a chance." He made to take her hand.

She pulled away and seemed like she might be trying not to cry.

"You don't have to be afraid, Shorty." And he wondered if maybe he said it as much for himself as her. "You don't have to be brave or strong or anything . . ." *Just be my wife.* But he didn't say that because he didn't want to scare her. His voice quieted. "You're not alone anymore."

Her expression softened. "I really did miss you, Hamburglar." She put her hand on his face, leaned in and kissed him.

And he just didn't know what to make of it. It lit a fire inside him, something he didn't quite have control of, but he didn't move.

Maybe he was dreaming.

Maybe this was a kind of test. Especially since her kiss was sweet, absent the passion that had always accompanied their romance.

He didn't have the strength to stop himself from kissing her back.

And maybe he needed to remind her what they had before it was too late.

So he ran his hand behind her neck and pulled her closer, putting a little of that fire into his touch.

She tasted of pizza, and the sense of it hearkened him way back to the beginning. The first time they'd kissed, right after a football game on a hill overlooking the Mississippi River.

The first time he realized that he would always and forever belong to her.

Signe. He was winding his fingers into her hair when she leaned away, ran a thumb over his lips. "You remember our first kiss?"

"Of course I do. I never forgot you, Sig. And now that I found you, I am bringing you home."

She closed her eyes, and his heart nearly exploded when she nodded.

Mission accomplished.

■ ■ ■

Miracles did happen and people did survive the impossible.

At least, that's what Orion wanted to believe as he motored up the murky waters in the dark-as-night streets searching for survivors.

He'd seen it with his own eyes—while serving as a pararescue jumper in Afghanistan, and today.

Watching from the third-floor balcony of an apartment building overlooking the sea.

He'd practically tossed the two boys he'd carried over the gate cordoning off the yard—mostly because he had nowhere else to go. Then he scaled the wall himself, ran up an outside stairway, and just as the water thundered onto shore, he kicked in a door and took cover in the apartment.

He found a terrified mother and her three-year-old daughter hiding in the bathroom. Shoving the boys in with her, he went to watch from the balcony.

The sea bubbled and roared as it swept past them, rising to the second floor, and he nearly went after the woman to bring them to the roof. But the waters spread out, into the city, and instead he fixed his gaze on the catamaran, tumbling like Styrofoam through the tumult. It hit the stone stairway, bounced off, turned, then was carried up over it and into the garden of a nearby house.

Most of the one- and two-story houses along the seaboard were under water or destroyed, boats piled up in gated areas. The sea was a lethal soup of destruction, the air smelled like ash, and all Orion could think was . . .

Jenny. Please be alive.

His heart lurched when he spotted the man emerge on the catamaran deck, probably from where he'd taken cover inside, and begin to search for an escape. He wore a life jacket, a silly headlamp, and Orion remembered his words about a wife and a daughter.

One pontoon was wedged into the balcony of the house, shattering the window. The waves tossed it but couldn't dislodge it. Orion traced an escape route for him—if the man was to climb along the pontoon, he could maybe grab the upper rail of the balcony above and pull himself to safety.

Perhaps he had the same idea because he started to inch out on the pontoon.

He slipped. The man's cry echoed into the air as he tumbled off the pontoon. His hand closed around one of the lines, but the water gobbled him and yanked him away from the boat.

"Help!" He bobbed in the water, trying to haul himself in.

Orion's heart nearly stopped when a woman wearing a life

jacket stepped out onto the deck. A little girl, maybe age five, gripped the back of her jacket.

The woman pushed her daughter onto the hard-topped Bimini. The little girl screamed as the woman left her there, trying to make her way down the boat toward her husband.

She was going to fall, and then that child would be stuck, and scared, and alone, and . . .

Orion went into the bathroom to check on the family. He found the woman sitting on the floor, singing to the kids. "Stay here. I'll be back for you." He hoped she understood English.

He'd spotted a dinghy stuck in the garden and sprinted back out to the balcony. The water roiled, the currents lethal, but he eased down, managing to get a leg over the edge of the craft. It was bouncing against the wall, between the balconies, but it looked seaworthy—the motor up, as if it had been brought to shore.

Oh God, don't let them die.

Orion tumbled into the boat, grabbed the front seat.

A life jacket was still shoved underneath. He pulled it on.

Ham would be proud of him.

Ham. Shoot. He'd tried his cell phone a couple times, but no signal. *Please, God, let Ham be alive too.*

Orion glanced at the catamaran. The woman had gotten ahold of her husband's line, was trying to tow him in.

Inches from going in herself. Her daughter was screaming, the waves pounding the cat against the building.

Orion put the motor down, aware of the litter swirling in the water. *Please start.* He ripped the cord, and the motor coughed to life, gas stirring in the already toxic air.

"Hang on!" Of course, the people couldn't hear him, but it just helped him stay focused.

Helped him not give in to the desire to turn the dinghy toward the hotel.

He opened the throttle and tore over the wall, kicking up grimy spray as he gunned toward them.

The noise alerted the woman and she looked up. Shouted, waving. Orion searched the water.

There. Yellow life preserver. He was fighting to stay up.

Orion measured the current, then cut the motor just as he came up beside the man.

"Grab my hand!"

The man stretched up his hand. Orion grabbed it and fell back, using his weight to pull the man over the edge.

He rolled into the dinghy, breathing hard.

Orion grabbed the throttle, gunning it toward the cat.

The woman had run up the pontoons to rescue her daughter. By the time he reached the port side, the man was on his feet, reaching for the railing. His wife passed their daughter over to him and he set her in the middle of the boat, safe.

The current slammed the boat against the pontoons, then away.

"Get closer!" the man yelled.

Orion fought to direct them back to the boat. The man held open his arms. "Jump, honey!"

The woman stared at him, a look of horror on her face.

The cat jerked in the waves and she fell. Her husband caught her and pulled her to himself, nearly weeping.

"Get down!" Orion said, and backed up the dinghy, away from the thrashing cat.

He fought the current, the debris, and his own emotions as he returned them all to the apartment.

"I gotta go find my girlfriend," he said to the man as they climbed out. "I'll be back."

Orion turned the boat out into the water.

He guesstimated he was less than a mile from the hotel, but as he drove along the shore, he couldn't seem to find it in the row of buildings. He remembered it as a tall blue four-story building with balconies on the front. He motored all the way down to where the harbor curved, all the while fighting the swirl of the confused water.

When he motored back, he searched again for anything that seemed familiar. Just debris, broken fishing vessels, wrecked sailboats, homes half-destroyed, others completely off their foundation and disintegrating into the sea.

The hotel was old—so old it had an ancient elevator and questionable plumbing.

So old, maybe, the foundation had worn away. The realization came to him like poison in his veins as he trekked the route a third time, along the seawall, and back.

The hotel was gone.

Just vanished, gobbled by the sea.

No.

He just stared at the way the waters engulfed the shoreline, all the way up the hill, and he knew.

Jenny was gone.

Orion was numb by the time he returned to the apartment. He tied up the dinghy and found his way inside.

The family sat with the woman and her daughter in the main room of their home. The man rose when Orion came through the door, walked over, and without a word, embraced him.

Orion just stood there.

"Thank you," the man said. "I thought we were dead."

Orion's chest tightened. He couldn't speak.

"My name's Keith. This is Renee, my wife. And that's Jack and Finn and this is Katie." He picked up his daughter and kissed her cheek.

Orion tousled Jack's head. He guessed the kid might be nine. Too young to watch his family die.

"Did you find your girlfriend?" Keith said. He had long hair, now slicked back and dirty. They were all filthy, covered in ash and grime and stinking of the sea and sulfur.

"No. I don't know where she is. Our hotel . . . it's . . ." He looked away, out the window, toward the sea. "It's gone."

Silence.

He closed his eyes.

Keith's hand touched his shoulder. "I'm sorry, man."

Breathe. Just . . .

He opened his eyes. "Yeah, well. We probably need to get you guys to safety. I don't know how long this building is going to stay up with all that debris smashing into it."

Keith nodded and that's when the women of the house—Irene and her daughter, Noemi—suggested the church on the hill.

"We will go to St. Mary's and pray," Irene said.

It didn't sound like a terrible idea. Especially when she added, "They have a medical center and a school. It is where we go at times like these."

And maybe where Ham and Jenny might go, if they'd survived.

By the time they arrived two hours later, the place was packed, people sitting on pews, more in the school gymnasium and on the floor of the hallways, and even more in the tiny medical clinic that was designed for the students more than the general public.

Orion walked past people with broken bones, lacerations, contusions—too many wearing despair.

He should probably add himself to the line.

The bell had fallen into the center of the church, but a small group of men were working on hauling it into the courtyard. An assembly of women worked in the kitchen, trying to figure out how to feed people.

He found Keith with his family in the cafeteria.

"Is she here?" Keith asked.

"No."

Keith glanced at his family—Finn and Jack sat at the table eating a bowl of cold oatmeal. Renee held Katie on her lap, a blanket over her shoulders.

"Let's go," Keith said. He picked up his headlamp.

Orion frowned at him.

"Let's go look for her. Get the dinghy and we'll go down to the harbor. I heard a couple people say they heard shouting from rooftops and balconies—"

"The hotel is gone!"

"But maybe she got out. Or maybe"—Keith clamped a hand on his shoulder—"a crazy man showed up in a dinghy to save her life."

Orion wanted to smile, but his chest hurt and really, he just wanted to shout, maybe throw his fist into something.

"Take a breath, son. Just take a breath."

For some reason, Orion obeyed him, pressing his hand to his chest. "I just don't know what to do." He sank down onto a nearby bench. "I just found her again after losing her for three years and . . . I can't lose her now."

He closed his eyes.

Hands touched him. He looked up and Keith's hand was on one of his shoulders, Renee's on the other.

"I don't know if you believe in God, Orion, but you are never helpless when you are in God's hands. God does not give us a spirit of fear but of power and love and self-control. Which means we do not despair. We do not let the enemy take control of our hope. Hope is the weapon of the Lord, and right now, we are going to wield it, in Jesus's name."

Orion just stared at him. The man was channeling Ham.

"Now get up, we're going to find your woman." Keith glanced at his wife. "I'll be back, I promise."

Orion had the strangest urge to weep. Or maybe high-five some-one.

They'd left the dinghy on the sidewalk, where the water stopped two blocks before the church, and now found it in the darkness. Keith flicked on his headlamp.

They got in and Orion pushed off, the waters dark and thick with wreckage. He waited until they were free, then pulled the motor.

It growled to life.

He drove them down to the harbor and discovered he wasn't the only one looking for survivors. The Italian coast guard and local Catania police lit up the shoreline with searchlights, and he passed a couple rescue boats helping people to safety from their apartments.

"Where was your hotel?"

Orion pointed to a darkness between a couple apartment build-ings.

They pulled up to the front of one of the buildings and tied up the dinghy, and Orion shouted up into the darkness. "Hey, anyone there?"

No one shouted back.

"Jenny!"

"Maybe they're on the roof," Keith said.

Orion looked at him.

"Sometimes we just need a different perspective."

It took everything Orion had to climb onto the balcony. Keith followed him, guiding their way with the headlamp.

So maybe it wasn't silly.

The doorjamb was busted, as if someone had broken in, but the flat was vacant. They took the stairs up and emerged on the roof.

Orion walked to the edge. "I think the hotel was right here." He pointed to the water, and Keith looked down, shining his light on the ruins.

Indeed. Rubble filled the space, a mound of tile, stone, wood, and probably dead bodies.

As if he could hear her voice, a cry lifted in his heart. *Orion!*

He closed his eyes. Heard it again, an echo deep inside. *"Help!"*

"You hear that?" Keith said, and Orion turned.

"Really?"

"Shouting." Keith turned his light across the water, to the next building, then around to the other side.

Nothing.

Orion took a breath, tried to listen.

Nothing but the splash of water, the dark pang of despair.

"Let's go," Orion said, and returned to the stairwell.

He was halfway down the stairwell when he heard it again. "Orion! Help!"

He turned back, his heart in his throat as he ran back up the stairs.

Keith was already at the back edge of the building, waving.

Please, please— Orion sprinted over to the edge.

For a second, he didn't recognize the people standing on the roof on the house behind the apartment. The water had lipped over the edge of the three-story building, but it was on higher ground, and they stood on a small enclosed stairwell.

The woman was dark skinned, her hair in braids. She stood with an elderly gentleman, and Orion thought he recognized him as the concierge.

Nori?

"Mr. Orion! Mr. Orion!" Nori waved at him.

"You know her?" Keith asked.

"She was a waitress at our hotel." Orion waved back, not sure what to do with the emotions that bubbled inside him. "Hang on! We'll come around and get you!"

He and Keith scrambled down to the dinghy, untied it, and motored it around the block, Keith's light dragging along the fencing until they found the house. Orion brought the boat up to the edge of the building, and Keith helped the concierge and Nori into the dinghy.

Nori curled her arms around herself. She wore her black skirt and a grimy blouse, her tennis shoes. Keith put a life jacket on her, and she shivered. Only then did Orion realize the temperature had dropped.

The older man sat next to her.

Probably they should bring them back to the church, get them warm.

Orion sat down at the motor. "Nori, did you see a blonde American woman in the hotel this morning?"

"I did," interjected the older man. "She spoke to me when she left the hotel. Asked me where a coffee shop was."

Coffee.

Orion couldn't breathe.

"Can you tell me where it is?"

He pointed toward the end of the street. "I can take you there."

Keith was grinning at him under his shiny, silly light. "Do you believe in miracles?"

■ ■ ■

They needed help, right now.

Marcello was in trouble, his chest still tight, and with everything inside her Jenny wished she had her roommate Aria's training as a heart surgeon.

But even then, what was Jenny going to do here on a roof, in the darkness, the temperature dropping, the stink of death rising around them as the water lapped the buildings?

At least the air had cleared, slightly. She couldn't make out stars, but in the distance, the terrible glow of Mordor testified to the angry mountain.

She sat next to Gio, who sat next to Marcello.

Harley and his group had made a sort of circle of comfort not far away, sharing the meager rations from Angie's orange backpack. A Snickers bar. A pack of gum. A packet of airplane peanuts.

"Why did you come to Italy?" Gio asked.

The answer didn't seem to matter anymore. "To meet a friend. Actually, no, for our friend to meet a friend. Sort of."

In the face of all the tragedy, she had barely thought of Ham, or his contact, but now, staring out at the place the hotel had been, she let herself give in to the ache inside.

Ham was a good man. He'd believed in her, given her a job, although she guessed that job offer had more to do with getting Orion out of Alaska and down to Minnesota.

A move she'd been entirely in favor of.

Wow, she was selfish. She hadn't even thought about Orion's feelings, the way he'd uprooted his entire life for her. Because he loved her.

Wanted to marry her.

She pressed her hand to her mouth.

"I hope my mama is okay," Gio said. He pointed into the darkness, away from the city, to the southwest of the mountain. "She lives out there, near the military base."

The military base. Right. Fifty miles away was a small city filled with American servicemen. Maybe that's who had arrived in the harbor an hour ago, with boats and searchlights. She and the others had wasted their voices shouting for help, but they were a good three blocks from the harbor, so probably no one would find them.

They had to find help themselves.

Jenny looked at Gio. "I'm going to get your grandfather to a hospital."

She walked over to Harley. "We need to get off this roof. It's getting cold out, and Marcello is not doing well."

Harley hadn't said a word about her breakdown and now he looked past her, to Marcello. "How? The water hasn't receded, and it's dark out. Angie does have a flashlight, but the batteries got wet."

"The water is probably not terribly deep—maybe we walk him out."

"It's like a cesspool down there. And where are we going to take him? We have no idea where the hospital is."

"Maybe someone here knows."

She turned. "Gio, where's the nearest hospital?"

"We go to the base, or to Catania," he said.

The base. But that was forty, maybe fifty miles away. "What we need is to get the attention of one of those boats," she said and pointed out to sea.

And maybe it was there before—she hadn't seen it, but she might have missed it—but a light flickered on the building near where her hotel had been. She ran to the side of the roof. Too far to see, but maybe they could hear her. "Help!" She waved her arms.

Which was silly, because it was too dark out to see. Still, the light panned as if searching for her voice. And the crazy, desperate woman in her added, "Orion!"

No. She couldn't let her hope stir, find footing.

The light stopped, turned toward them. "Help!" She jumped up and down, and now Angie joined her. "Over here!"

The light moved down, then away.

"No! Come back!"

It disappeared off the roof.

A rock fell through Jenny's chest. Okay. What had she learned climbing Denali last summer? That God showed up, even when things felt impossible.

"I'm going to get help," Jenny said.

"Oh no, not this again." Harley shook his head. "Really?"

"Yes. There are a ton of boats out there. I just need to find something to float on, find a paddle and get out to one of those lights."

"Jenny—"

"I can't sit here one more second!" She schooled her voice. "Listen, Harley, if you want, you can come with me—"

"Oh, thanks."

"But if not—"

"I'm going. Sheesh." He followed her to the stairwell, but she stopped at the top.

"Yikes, that's dark. Once we're down in the coffee shop—"

"We were there. We remember what it looks like, right?" Harley said. "A bar to our left, the door in the center—"

"And lots of broken glass."

"What about this?" Angie ran up to them, holding her phone. "There's not a lot of juice left, but maybe enough to get you out of the building."

The light shone from the tiny spot on her phone.

Jenny took it. "Are you sure? What if you need it to call home, or—"

"This is more important. When I need to call, I'll find something. Go get help."

Jenny shined it down the stairwell. The light scattered the darkness.

"Let's go," she said and started down, Harley behind her. "Where are you guys from, anyway?"

"All over. We go to a Bible college in Amsterdam, but we're taking the fall semester off to tour Europe and share the gospel."

"And climb volcanoes."

"We're rethinking that day trip," Harley said.

"So, Mr. Bible, where is God in all this mess?" Jenny rounded the second floor and shined her light onto the water.

"Right here. In this stairwell."

She glanced at him. "I mean—"

"I know what you meant. Can't he stop the volcanoes, the earthquakes, the tsunamis? Yes. But this is also the natural order of the world. Tragedies happen. People get hurt. People hurt other people. But it's in suffering—as well as joy—that we find our faith. In times of trouble, we either draw near, or we run."

She reached the bottom, shining light across the darkness. No boats. "And if we run?"

"Then God chases after us. That's the thing about God. We might give up on him, but he never gives up on us."

Harley pointed to a door floating in the water near the entrance.

"You remember the *Titanic*, right?" she said.

"Jack could have totally gotten on that door," he said and plunged into the water.

She held the light on him, and he rolled onto the door. It wobbled but held him. "C'mon."

Jenny hid a gasp as she stepped out into the cold water and waded over to him. On the way, she picked up a couple floating serving trays. She put the phone in her mouth as he helped her onto the door.

She crawled to the front and handed him one of the serving trays.

He dug in on his side and nearly swamped them.

She pulled the phone from her mouth. "Stop! We need to be coordinated!"

He waited. "Ready?"

She flicked off the phone, and the night settled around them, the smells of the dank water ripe and rancid.

"You hold the light. I'll paddle," Harley said.

She flicked it back on. "Just don't swamp us."

He leaned over the side and began to move them through the water. They bumped past cars and wood and wreckage of boats. The current played with them, moving the door around in circles.

"We're not going anywhere," she said. "I'm getting out and swimming."

"Have you lost your mind? The water is full of disease and wreckage and—"

She just stared at him, and maybe it was something on her face because he stopped paddling. "What if that was your boyfriend on the roof?"

She shook her head.

"What if he's still alive?"

"Stop."

"You don't know for sure, Jenny. And risking your life to prove something to—who?—isn't going to make you feel better."

"It might! Maybe I help rescue Marcello and somehow I live with myself instead of regretting not banging down Orion's door and telling him I loved him. That yes, I would marry him! That I was a fool to believe that . . . that . . ."

"That he couldn't forgive you."

She swallowed.

"He, as in Orion? Or he, as in God?" Harley said.

Her breath caught.

"He can, and he does, you know. In fact, he grieves for you and your pain. He can do that—forgive you and hurt for you."

"What if he's punishing me?"

"Well, thank you very much, then, because I didn't do anything to deserve being in a tsunami-slash-volcano eruption."

She stared at him.

"God isn't punishing any of us, Jenny. But he does want you to trust him when he says he loves you. That he has a good plan for you. That there is therefore no condemnation for you, if you've been forgiven." He put down his serving platter, his face half in shadow. "Have you asked for forgiveness?"

"Too many times to count."

"Once is enough. Leave it behind. He has."

She drew in a long breath.

"God doesn't write tragedies. He's all about the happy ending. We just have to stick with him through the story, right?"

A motor sounded in the darkness. Harley heard it too.

She shined her light down the street and realized the current had taken them way past the coffee shop, to a flattened area.

Tugging them out to sea.

"We have to paddle back!" She tucked the phone in her shirt and picked up a serving platter. Harley turned around, and the door nearly went over.

"Harley!"

"Sorry!"

They paddled together. A spotlight shone at the end of the street, near the coffee shop entrance, and she didn't have to say anything to Harley to have him speed up.

"We're leaking here, Jenny." Harley pointed to a spot under him. "I think my knee went through."

"Keep paddling."

The spotlight grew larger, and then, just like that, it winked out. What?

"No—no—they have to stay. They have to get Marcello!"

"Jenny!"

But they were only thirty yards away, and with her eyes adjusted to the darkness she could make out a dinghy, with people.

"I'm going in—"

"No, you're not!" Then, just like that, Harley was in the water. He grabbed the edge of the door and started to drag it along. She paddled with him, the door sinking fast.

Oh, this was stupid. They were so close she could see two people sitting in the dinghy, and one wore a life jacket.

"Hey!" She waved.

The door tipped.

In a second she was under the water, the chill closing in over her. But she kicked, and her feet touched something solid, and in a second she surfaced.

Harley grabbed her. "You okay?"

She nodded. "Swim!"

The dinghy was tied to the entrance, too big to get through the door, and as she came up to it, she recognized the concierge.

"Jacopo!"

He reached out for her. And something inside her gave a hard tug. Hope.

"God chases after us."

She let go of Jacopo and swam through the coffee shop, hit the stairs, and slogged her way out of the water.

Then, sprinted.

Please, *please*—

He was standing in the middle of the roof, his back to her, with a bigger man who turned at her shout and blinded her with his headlamp.

She threw her hand up to shield her eyes.

But she heard his voice. Orion's sweet, thunderous voice that could find its way under her skin to turn her entire body from frigid to hot.

"Jenny!"

The light moved away just in time for her to see Orion, his clothes sodden, his handsome face grimy, his eyes gritty and red, sprint toward her.

Then she was in his arms. Caught up, her breath lost as he held her. As he wept.

She wrapped her arms around his amazing shoulders, her legs around his hips, her entire body clinging to him, unable to let go, unable, really, to restart her heart.

166

"Oh, oh—" She pressed her face into his shoulder and sobbed.

So, yes, they were a mess. Orion finally set her down, took her face in his hands, and glued her with those beautiful green eyes. "I thought you were dead. I couldn't even find the hotel—"

"I thought *you* were in the hotel—I went out for coffee. I wanted to get you one, and I was going to tell you I'm sorry—"

"No. I'm sorry. I was such a jerk to you. I love you and I don't have to marry you—we can just . . . whatever you want."

Oh, Ry. "I want *you*. Yes, I will marry you—we just have to talk and then, maybe you ask me again—"

"Yes. Whenever, always." Then he kissed her. He was reining it in for their audience, but she could still taste his desperation, the all-out passion that was Orion. He dug his hands into her hair, pressed his forehead to hers. "Yes, I believe in miracles."

She frowned, but he grinned, nodding.

"And that ends tonight's edition of *Survivor*," Harley said, breathing hard, sopping wet. "Jenny and Orion are voted off the island."

Jenny looked over at him. Harley winked at her. "Happy endings."

She closed her eyes and listened to Orion's beating heart.

Oh, she hoped so.

She finally pushed away from him. "We have to get Marcello to a hospital. And then . . . have you heard from Ham?"

Orion shook his head. "Last time I saw him . . . he was on the roof."

No.

"But so was Nori, and she made it off, so . . ."

"Nori?"

Orion took her hand. "The waitress at the terrace cafe. She's in the dinghy."

"With Jacopo."

Harley and the others had started to gather around Marcello, maybe to lift him.

"What's wrong with him?" Orion said, letting go of her hand.

"I think he's having a mild heart attack." She walked over to Gio. "This is Gio, his grandson."

"Hey, kid," Orion said, and tousled his hair.

Oh, he'd make such a great father. She'd have to figure out how to drop her bombshell into his life.

No condemnation.

"Oh my!" Angie's voice made Orion look up, and in his eyes, Jenny could see the reflection.

Flames fractured the darkness from a building down the street. Just one more in the many that flanked the horizon, but this one was close enough to hear it roar.

Then, as they watched, a terrible boom shook the air and a fireball burst from inside the inferno, rolling out into the sky. Gasps, and a couple people ducked.

"Wowza," Gio said. "I think that was Angelis Pizza Parlor."

"I hope it was empty," Orion said. "C'mon, let's get Marcello into the boat. We'll send help for the rest of you."

Then he turned to Jenny. "But not you, sweetheart. You're coming with me."

CHAPTER EIGHT

OH, WHAT WAS SHE DOING?

Because she was clearly in over her head.

Signe sat shoulder to shoulder with Ham, his leg against hers, his body warm as they finished off the cold pizza.

She could still taste him on her lips, the familiarity, the spark, the way he made her feel at once out of control and safe.

So much for her ability to walk away.

"Now that I found you, I am bringing you home."

She'd nodded. As if she'd *agreed* with him. As if she wasn't going to break his beautiful heart and flee.

Oh, she shouldn't have kissed him. But they were here, and it might be the last time they were together. She'd simply surrendered to the terrible impulse to let herself be in his arms.

Even if it couldn't last.

He reached out and nudged her hand, and she let him weave his fingers with hers.

Oh Ham. Heat poured up her arm and through her entire body.

"Why did you leave the SEALs?" she asked quietly. "I know you started a chain of athletic clubs around the nation."

"You do?" He glanced down at her. "Of course you do. Best research partner ever."

She laughed. "Only because you were busy playing football."

"I was busy because I hated doing homework." He pressed a kiss to her forehead. "But we were a good team. Hamburglar and Shorty."

The old nicknames found their way to her heart. "Yeah, until your evil stepmother shipped you off to military school."

"Just for my last semester. I came home in time to take you to prom." He waggled his eyebrows. "Now, that was some fun."

Oh, how was she going to walk away from this man?

"Tell me why you're so scared, Sig," Ham said quietly.

"You didn't answer my question. Why did you leave the SEALs?"

Ham drew in a breath. "An op-gone-south. Teammates were taken. I broke a few rules going after them."

Her breath hitched. And then he said it—

"I wasn't going to sit around and let the enemy take the people I cared about. Not again."

Right. Because watching her disappear was enough.

"Were you court-martialed?"

"No. The Navy let me go with an honorable discharge. But it wasn't optional."

"Oh Ham, you worked so hard—"

"It's okay, Sig." He squeezed her hand. "If I were still on the Teams, I couldn't take care of Aggie."

He always did that—found the positive spin. "You were a great operator. I am sure you're missed."

"I convinced a few of my former teammates to join me—I started a small private security and SAR outfit. That's what Orion and Jenny do—they are part of Jones, Inc."

"You don't miss being an operator?"

"We can't live in the what-ifs, Sig. We have to live in the now. The fact that we have a second chance." He met her eyes, held them. "Right?"

And again, she found herself nodding.

He had the skills of an interrogator to make her say what he wanted to hear.

What she wanted to say.

"Your turn. What has you so rattled that you can't tell me who you saw, Sig?"

Oh. And this was where she listened to her brains, and not her heart. Where her training kicked in.

Because Ham was a patriot, right down to every cell in his body, and if he knew what she knew, he'd have to risk being a traitor to the country he loved.

The country he swore to protect.

No. She was about to shake her head, when—

"Do you smell that?" Ham took his hand away, started to get to his feet. "Smoke—"

Boom! The explosion rocked the air, shook the building.

Ham tackled her, pushing her to the ground, covering her body with his.

She didn't scream but grabbed his shirt and hid her face in his shoulder.

Like a long-buried reflex.

He smelled of dust and old water and sweat, and she just wanted to curl into his strength and never leave.

The building shook, but no fireball rolled over them. He jumped up. "We gotta get out of here!" He reached for her and pulled her up. But when he took a step, he nearly collapsed.

"Ham!"

"I'm okay." But he'd grimaced, holding his leg. "Just a little rush of blood flow. C'mon."

Tough guy that he was, he practically ran from the building, hardly a limp.

The sky had turned eerily orange, and not from the distant

volcano—impossible to see from the smoke clouding the sky—but from the inferno of a nearby restaurant.

Flames shot from the windows of the building next to it.

"The gas line has been damaged. It's only a matter of time before this entire block explodes." Fire reflected in his face, his eyes. Already the street burned with smoke. She coughed.

"The pipes run under the road," Ham said. "We need to get back to the water."

"What—but—"

"C'mon!" He tugged her down the street, back toward their kayak beached at the end of the street.

He found it in the night despite the dark sky and lack of stars, and she supposed she shouldn't be surprised. "Get in!"

She sat down in front of him, like before, and he climbed in the back, pushing them off.

They had just cleared the pavement, floating free, when the voice lifted in the distance.

"Aiuto!" Help. Again. *"Aiuto!"*

"Where are you?" Ham shouted back.

He didn't say it in Italian, so she translated. *"Dove sei?"*

Screams, then, *"Qui! Qui!"*

"There, Ham." Signe pointed to a building, half submerged in the water, and the dark outline of someone waving their hands.

She turned on her phone's flashlight as Ham paddled them toward the woman.

The woman wore a grimy leopard-print shirt, a dirty rag wrapped around her arm, her hair gray with soot. She knelt on the first-floor landing of an apartment complex, nearly hysterical as she reached out and took the hand of someone below.

"Oh no," Signe said quietly.

"I see it," Ham said. She recognized his SEAL voice—cool, detached, the one that got business done. He used the same

172

one in Ukraine, when she told him she would be returning to Chechnya.

"Is that a kid?" Her heart froze at the face pressed to the open window. Only a kid's arm could weave through the metal security bars. They were old, decorative, and lethal for trapping someone inside the building.

The woman ran to them. "Grazie—grazie—" She erupted into Italian, but Signe got the gist.

"Her daughter is caught in the house, and the water level is rising," Signe said. She shined her flashlight onto the window.

The bars protruded at the bottom of the window maybe a foot, mostly to allow the window to open. It was hinged at the top.

"That's not the only problem," Ham said. "Look." He pointed to flames burning against the first-story windows.

Burn or drown. No wonder the mother was screaming. Ham pulled up to the landing, but Signe was already out of the kayak and over to the window. She landed in the well in front of the window, the water chest deep, grabbed the bars, and put her foot against the wall.

They didn't budge.

Ham joined her. "Again!"

They strained together, but nothing budged.

Inside, the little girl, maybe twelve years old, was banging on the half-opened window.

"Hang on," Ham said to her. "We're going to get you out!"

Signe wanted to believe him. But the fire had broken an upper window and the water seemed to be rising.

Ham ran up the steps. Put his hand to the door. Yanked it away. "We can't go in that way."

"This stone is old. Maybe we can break it free," Signe said.

He sat down on the landing. "Stand back." The bars shuddered

173

with his kick. He gave another devastating kick, and the bars shook. But they moved.

"Again, Ham!"

He kicked again, and the bar began to wiggle, slightly.

"If I had a grinder—" he said. The heat of the home began to radiate out into the street. The girl began to cough.

"How about a lever?" Signe said and pointed to a street sign up the road, still out of the water.

A car had plowed into it—maybe a casualty of the earthquake—and bent the pole over the end, severing it.

He ran, no hint of injury, toward the sign. Picked up the pole and carried it back. It looked heavy, especially as he moved it into the space at the bottom of the window between the grate and the stone wall of the house.

He leveraged his leg against the house and began to pull on the bars with his good arm, working them free.

The stonework crumbled around the edges where the bolts fixed to the stone.

"You need help." Signe pushed next to him. "On two."

They heaved together, and probably she didn't add much to his strength, but the bars began to shift.

"Kick it at the base as I pull," Ham said, even as the girl disappeared from the window.

Ham heaved. "God—please!"

Signe braced her back on the edge of the landing, took a breath, submerged herself, and put her feet against the base of the bars.

Then, she kicked. And kicked. Surfaced to the mother screaming, grabbed a breath, went back down.

Kicked. The bars shuddered. She surfaced, gasping.

"Almost," Ham said, his eyes wide. "You okay?"

She ignored him and went under again, heard Ham's voice in her head. *God—please!*

Kicked again, and again, and again.

Her breath slipped to a tiny wisp.

Kicked again.

And just like that, the grate broke free at the bottom.

She surfaced, gulping air.

Ham broke the metal free from the bottom of the window like he might be Hercules, raising the bars as far as he could. It was enough for her to squeeze in. Then, he put the metal bar through the glass, swept it around the frame.

Signe took a breath and dove up through the opening.

No way Ham could have fit. As it were, the metal tugged at her as she pulled herself through.

The little girl had crawled onto a table, curled into a ball, her hands over her mouth. But her eyes were open as Signe surfaced. Signe coughed, the air smoky.

"Take a breath," she said.

The girl nodded, and Signe grabbed a gulp of bitter air and pulled the girl under.

She pushed her out of the window, and into Ham's waiting hands.

Pushed herself out the window.

The metal bars grabbed her.

Ham surfaced, climbing out of the water.

Signe tugged on the bars, wrestling to work herself free. The metal locked onto the hem of her pants, trapping her.

She was running out of air. And Ham had left the water.

Ham!

She thrashed, fighting, then reached for her waistband to wiggle free.

Her brain had turned foggy, to dots and blotches, and even as she unzipped her pants, began to dim.

Hurry!

Don't breathe. Don't—but her body wanted it.

Oh, she was going to die right here, in a dirty basement apartment—

Hands closed around her arms, reached down her leg, and suddenly, she was free.

Her head broke the surface and the air turned to fire as she gulped it into her lungs, coughing.

Ham held her above the water, his hands gripping her arms as she writhed out the smoke from her lungs, tried to come back to herself.

"Are you okay?"

She nodded, still coughing. Spittle had formed at the edges of her mouth. Oh, that was pretty.

No, what was pretty was the mother holding her daughter, shaking with her weeping.

Signe wanted to weep, to shake.

To hold her daughter and never let her go.

She looked at Ham, who was searching her face, and saw the same sentiment in his eyes. She swallowed, her throat burning.

Ham helped her out of the courtyard and onto the steps. He ran his hands over her arms, then turned to the woman. "Are you okay?"

Maybe she knew some English because she nodded, still holding her daughter.

"What's your name?" Signe said to the woman.

"Federica, and this is Rosa." She looked at Ham, then back to Signe. "Are you Americans?"

Oh. Um . . .

"Yes," Ham said.

"I met one today. In the coffee shop," she said.

"Where?"

Federica shook her head to Signe's question, but added, "He might have gone to the school."

"Where is it?" Ham asked.

Federica got up. Took Rosa's hand. "I will show you."

Signe's stupid legs almost refused to move, but she pushed to her feet.

"Babe. You're a little . . . undone, there."

She looked at her pants.

Ham raised an eyebrow.

"I was trying to free myself."

"Good idea. Glad we didn't have to go that route."

Her pants were ripped at the bottom, but she refixed her zipper and buttoned them.

Then Ham took her hand, his firm and solid in hers.

Hamburglar and Shorty.

The murky smell of old water, sewer, smoke, gas, and even the rancid odor of fish followed them through the cobblestone streets.

"Now that I found you, I am bringing you home."

Her eyes burned, and for the first time in hours, she thought of the jump drive, still secured in the zippered pocket of her cargo pants, along with her various passports, thankfully, all in plastic, waterproof cases.

"Help me trust you. Tell me who you saw."

They came to a courtyard that edged what looked like a church, the roof imploded. Federica opened a gate and let them into the yard.

Soggy, sooty, and ash-gray survivors sat in groups in the yard, some of them under blankets, a number of them holding sleeping children. A giant bell sat in the middle of the yard.

A church, attached to a school. People slept in the hallways, but the smell of coffee lured Signe down the hallway.

They came into a lunchroom, with tables and chairs and people eating. Bread, bowls of noodles and sauce, and every person looking as if they'd been through war.

Maybe they had.

And survived.

And come together to find each other. To regroup.

To eat with families.

"Ham!"

The voice turned her, even as Ham jerked.

"Orion!"

The man had brown hair and with him was a blonde woman who broke into a run as she dodged tables. Ham caught her up. "Jenny!"

Huh. Signe refused the spurt of jealousy. Because he wasn't hers anymore.

Or maybe he was. Because he hadn't annulled their marriage.

Except, she'd married someone else, so there was that.

Ham set her down. He met Orion's hand, then pulled him in for a quick slap.

Orion scrubbed a hand down his face.

Ham swallowed, looked away.

Men, for Pete's sake. But she got it.

Spies didn't cry either.

"You okay?" Ham said then.

"Yeah," Orion said. "I found Jenny on a roof. Where were you?"

Ham looked at Signe and smiled. "We went out for pizza."

"We can't live in the what-ifs, Sig. We have to live in the now. The fact that we have a second chance."

She smiled back. "And a little late-night swim."

He put his arm around her, pulled her against him. "Ry, Jenny. This is Signe. My wife."

Yes, yes she was. Right now, she was his wife. So she held out her hand to his team. "Nice to meet you."

■ ■ ■

Orion just had to stay focused on the current problem. On examining Ham's wrist, on splinting it so that whatever damage he'd done to it didn't become worse.

Then, on checking on the patients lined up in the hallway, most of them already attended to over the past four hours. Lacerations, butterflied with the meager supplies in the health center of the school, hematomas, and a few broken bones that he'd splinted to the best of his ability.

Jenny was helping too, as were a few local doctors and nurses, but one look at the survivors told him that they needed help.

Yet all he could think about were Jenny's words. *"Yes, I will marry you—we just have to talk."*

"Go easy there, bro," Ham said, his voice thin as Orion turned his wrist to gauge movement. Ham sat on the grimy floor and looked fresh off a mission. Scrapes marred his face and chin, filth embedded his hair, and he smelled of smoke and body odor.

Maybe Orion looked the same.

Darkness enfolded the corridor, and the rank smell of old water, stone, dust, and the hint of gas still layered the air. The electricity and phone lines had died with the earthquake, and the occasional crying or moaning filtered down the hallways, bouncing against the hard surfaces.

Daylight couldn't come soon enough.

Daylight, and The Talk.

"Sorry," Orion said. He held his cell phone light over the wound. "Without an X-ray I can't be sure, but it definitely seems broken." He reached for a piece of cardboard he'd found in one of the classrooms. Folded over, it would keep Ham's wrist protected until he got to help. He bent it into a U-shape and tucked it against Ham's arm.

"How'd this happen?"

"I was jumping between buildings," Ham said without a hitch. "Missed the edge, fell, caught a balcony."

"Of course you did." Orion shook his head. "Were you still on that roof when the volcano blew?"

"Yep. Took cover in an elevator—"

Orion lifted his gaze, raised an eyebrow.

Ham held up his hand. "I know. But I kept thinking about all those toxic fumes and that outweighed the fear of getting crushed. Besides, it was an old elevator, the sturdy kind."

"So you hid out in an elevator."

"Until the tsunami hit. Then we climbed out—"

"And you pulled a Superman."

"Hardly. Broken wrist, remember?"

Orion had cushioned Ham's arm with a piece of cloth. Now he wrapped it with packing tape, pulling it snug against his arm. "Did you get the information from Signe?"

Ham was watching his ministrations. "Not yet. But I will."

Orion broke the tape off. "I have to admit, I was worried we'd lost you."

Ham was nodding as if he got it. "How'd you find Jenny?"

"A miracle. I went back to the hotel—which isn't there anymore—"

"I know. We watched it go down. I was praying you and Jenny weren't inside. Or anyone else."

"Yeah," Orion said. "I found our waitress, Nori, and the concierge on a nearby roof, and they'd seen Jenny. Like I said, miracle."

"And?" Ham said.

Orion frowned.

"Did you two talk? Are you okay?"

Orion was looking at the laceration on Ham's leg.

"Ry?"

"We're . . . I don't know." Orion ripped open Ham's pants leg. "You need stitches."

"You don't know if you two are okay?"

The wound ran down Ham's calf, maybe six inches, and knuckle deep. Orion recognized the subcutaneous layer. "I need to close this up, at least temporarily."

"Dude."

He leaned back. "Okay, yes, we . . . I think we're okay. She said she'd marry me—"

Ham raised an eyebrow.

"But that we needed to talk first."

"So, you talk."

"We will. As soon as things calm down, but . . ."

Ham frowned.

"I can't get it out of my head that it's something bad. Something I can't fix."

Ham fell silent across from him.

Orion reached for the first aid kit. "What?"

"Nothing. I'm just wondering what it was that made her so scared to talk to you."

Orion considered him, and the way that Ham glanced down the hall toward Signe, who was also helping people. Orion could barely make her out in the glow of a cell phone light beam as she examined a wound on a little girl.

Clearly her years surviving in a terrorist camp had taught her survival skills, as well as first aid.

"Do you think I somehow frightened her?" Orion found the first aid kit and pulled out some white medical tape and iodine. The thought ran a fist into his chest.

"I don't know. But she had a pretty visceral reaction to your proposal."

"I gotta clean the wound," Orion said. "This is going to hurt."

"Right," Ham said. "Sorry I said anything."

Orion grinned. "It's not personal."

Ham laughed. But he stopped when Orion poured iodine onto a cotton swab and then bathed the wound.

He blew out a breath in a long stream.

"I'll give you a lollipop when I'm finished."

"Just hurry up."

Orion broke off the tape to close the wound.

"Let me help," Ham said and grabbed the tape.

Orion held the edges of the wound closed. Ham made a sound deep in his chest, but his hands were steady enough to put the tape over the wound.

"It felt like the same gut response as in Afghanistan, after she found out you were hurt," Ham said. "She blamed herself and ended up having a nervous breakdown."

Orion held the next section closed. "She was upset, not suffering from a psychotic break."

"Right. Maybe it's something *she* did that put her on the run. Is there anything she did that would make her believe you wouldn't want her?"

"Like what?"

Ham shrugged. "I don't know. Maybe, like, she's married to someone else?"

Orion's eyes widened. "No, dude. I don't think . . . she's not . . . are we still talking about Jenny?"

Ham's mouth tightened.

"You okay, boss?"

"Yep. Let's get this over with."

Ho-kay.

"Nothing she's done would keep me from loving her," Orion said. "Or wanting to marry her."

"Does she know that?" Ham said quietly, now looking up at him.

"I thought so. But . . . maybe she doesn't. It feels like she doesn't trust me." He held together the edges of the wound for the next strip of tape. "Go."

Ham grunted but placed the tape over it. "What if it's not about trust, but shame?"

"You're saying it's something so terrible that she's afraid to tell me? That she would run from me rather than talk to me?"

Ham ripped off more tape. "Some wounds run so deep, you think they're healed until . . ." He glanced again down the hall. "Until something reopens them. And you discover that they're not healed at all." He put the last strip on the wound.

So, they *were* talking about Ham and Signe. Orion gave a slow nod.

"Maybe it's just too fast, you know? You only found each other a few months ago. Maybe she needs more time."

Orion frowned. "What do you mean?"

"In lieu of finding Roy, you decide to get married?"

Orion reached for the gauze. "I can admit that finding Roy is a burr inside me, but no. Maybe. I don't know."

Ham leaned back as Orion wrapped the gauze around the wound. "I just know how you hate loose ends."

"I hate regret. I hate failure. And I hate being angry all the time. But that's over. It's time to move on, right? I learned that on Denali." He looked up at Ham.

But Ham was watching Signe. She was walking down the hallway, into the darkness, on a mission to find more wounded.

"What if Roy doesn't want to be found," Ham said softly. "What if he isn't the same person we knew?"

Orion ripped the gauze at the end, then tied it around Ham's leg. "Do you think Signe has been brainwashed?"

Ham looked at him.

"You said she was in a terrorist camp for the past ten years—"

"No."

Orion held up a hand in defense and Ham closed his eyes. Reopened his eyes. "Okay, fine. Signe is still hiding something. She's convinced there's a traitor in the CIA, and she knows who, but she's not saying."

"Seriously?"

"Yes. White said the same thing."

"Do you think this traitor is behind the assassination attempt in Alaska?"

"Maybe. And maybe also the one in Seattle a month ago. On Senator Jackson."

"I saw that on the news. A shooter, at the pier?"

"Yeah. I don't think they caught him."

"So, someone, maybe even inside our government, is trying to derail the election? That's a Vince Flynn novel."

"And Signe knows about it."

Orion closed up the kit. "And you're not sure if you trust her."

Ham's mouth made a tight line.

Bingo, but Ham wouldn't admit it.

"Who do you think it is?"

"I don't know. And although my heart wants to believe that Signe is going home with us, my gut says . . ."

"That she's going to run."

Orion's gaze tracked to Jenny. She sat against the wall now, her knees drawn up, her arms propped on them, her eyes closed.

"I know Signe. She's smart. Always thinking, always looking at everything from all the angles. She agreed to come home with me, but it feels . . . I don't know. Maybe she's telling the truth, but I can't pry it out of my head that there's something else going on."

"You need to get that list from her. That's the mission."

"I know."

"Before she runs."

"I *know*."

Orion considered him. "It's Afghanistan all over again. We were betrayed by someone we knew, someone we trusted, and guys we cared about didn't come home. I know you love her, Ham, but what if she's—"

"She's not a terrorist, Ry." But Ham's voice was soft, almost a declaration to himself.

Orion said nothing.

Ham shook his head. "Would you do it? Choose your country over Jenny?"

Orion looked away.

"Listen. She's afraid, and I need to figure out why. Then maybe I don't have to choose."

"Yeah," Orion said quietly. "Maybe. Try to get some rest. No one is going anywhere tonight."

And, to confirm his words, Signe came back toward them. Exhaustion lined her grimy face, her clothing soiled and torn. "We need to get medical help to these people," she said as she sat down next to Ham. "Some of them are significantly wounded."

"I know," Orion said, and noticed how Ham wove his fingers through Signe's. "I was thinking about the Sigonella Naval Air Station. There's a clinic and a hospital there. But I'm not sure how we get there."

"I have an idea," Signe said and looked at Ham, something soft in her eyes. "And I think you're going to like it."

Maybe Signe didn't notice the hunger on Ham's face, the desperate hope that he could trust this woman he loved, but it made Orion's gut tighten and he had to look away. "I'm going to get some winks. Let's regroup in a couple hours."

He walked over to Jenny.

Sat down next to her.

"I'm exhausted," she said and put her head on his shoulder.

He put his arm around her.

"You okay?" she asked.

At the moment? If he ignored the hole inside him, the buzz under his skin, the frustration of knowing that something still lingered between them. Maybe now—

"Jenny?"

But her deep breaths said she was already asleep.

"Nothing she's done would keep me from loving her. Or wanting to marry her."

Please, God, let his words be true.

■ ■ ■

Of course Signe was going back to Minnesota with him. She'd practically said as much.

Ham was simply letting the past taint his future.

Because, in his mind, he was standing in front of her tiny apartment in Berkeley, flowers in hand, his life slowly shredding as Signe's roommate told him she'd left.

Him.

And he was hearing her voice in the elevator . . . *"I'm just trying to keep ahead of my bad decisions. And just trying to make the next right one."*

Please, let the next right one be to return home, with him.

Because he also couldn't forget, *"You're the love of my life. Don't you think I want to be with you?"*

That sat in his chest like a hot ember, spreading through him.

The *love* of her life.

If only she hadn't left him already—twice.

His conversation with Orion hadn't helped either, one he kept turning over in his head.

"Do you think Signe has been brainwashed? You said she was in a terrorist camp for the past ten years—"

Shoot, it too closely mirrored his own thoughts, and . . . *"Would you do it? Choose your country over Jenny?"*

He couldn't go there.

Please, God, don't make him choose.

Better to just keep holding on to Signe, to try to sleep despite the throb in his arm, his leg.

His heart.

So really, so much for sleeping. He lay down beside Signe and apparently finally dozed off, because when he woke, Signe was up and nudging him. "I found some coffee."

Sunlight drizzled in through the windows. The hallways had filled up—people moving in from the courtyard, or perhaps just finding the school as a place of refuge. Families, dirty and injured, huddled under blankets, their faces betraying the stripping of their lives.

A woman nursed her infant under a jacket, her husband standing over her, his arms crossed, as if a sentry. An elderly man lay with what looked like his school-aged grandson next to him.

"Can you sit up?" Signe crouched next to him.

She had washed her face, put her hair back in a messy bun, and now she held the coffee out to him. "The stoves are working, so the gas hasn't been shut off."

"We need to get out of here and get some medical help to these people," Ham said as he sat up, trying to bite back a groan. He took the coffee.

"I told you I had an idea."

"I'm all ears." The coffee fed his bones, strong and bracing.

"Is the ability to hot-wire a scooter still in your bag of tricks?"

He glanced at her. "You remember that?"

"Mmmhmm. Did you ever find the keys to your bike?"

"Nope." He took another sip. Yes, they just might survive this.

Jenny came down the hallway, carrying a glass of water. She

stopped next to the elderly man and helped him take a drink. He grabbed her hand and said something to her. The boy translated, and Jenny nodded.

"Jenny," Ham said quietly, but his voice echoed down the hallway.

She came over to him. "You okay?"

"Yeah." He nodded to the kid. "Who is that?"

"His name's Gio. I rescued him off the pier. I promised his grandfather we'd take him to his mother. Apparently, she lives near the base."

"Where's Orion?"

"A group of survivors came in. He's out in the yard checking on them."

"Did he get any sleep?"

"I don't know. When I woke up, he was gone."

Always a PJ. "Okay," Ham said. "Tell him we need to get going."

"Where are we going?"

"To the base. We'll drop Gio on the way. And then . . . we're going home."

Jenny flashed a look at Signe, then back to Ham. "Roger."

Signe had said nothing.

He looked at her. "Right?"

"Of course."

Of course.

Huh.

Signe got up and held out her hand. "Ready, tough guy?"

He let her help him off the floor. "Signe, give me the jump drive."

She stilled. Swallowed.

He expected a fight. Not for her to lean down and unzip a pocket in her pants leg. She pulled out a jump drive and put it in his palm.

Smiled. "Let's go home."

He had no idea why he felt punched in the stomach as he followed her out of the building.

Signe had hidden a couple Vespas under a piece of plywood in an alleyway.

"When did you find these?" He knelt beside the bike.

"Last night, when you and Orion were catching up."

He didn't want to ask her why she'd been on the street.

If she'd been thinking about leaving him.

Because she hadn't, had she? She was still here. Going home with him.

"Of course."

See, he could stop panicking.

He made to move the scooter away from the wall but winced, so she helped wheel it free.

Orion arrived with Jenny and Gio. "Vespas? Cool."

"You'll have to hot-wire it. Take off the front panel, find the steering lock, and break it off. Then cut the starter wires. You'll need to turn on the kill switch, but then you can kick-start it," Ham said.

"As long as the battery isn't dead," Orion said, but he was already maneuvering his Vespa away from its hiding place. "Just like a snowmobile."

Ham pulled off the front panel, but Signe reached in and broke off the steering lock. Then she produced a folding knife from her pocket—really?—and cut all the wires attached to the starter.

"I suppose you want to drive too."

She grinned at him. "Always."

Orion's scooter revved as he kick-started it, and he got on, Jenny behind him. Gio sat in front of him. "Okay, kid, get us out of here."

Signe jumped on the starter once, twice. The third time their scooter started. "Hop on, number three."

Three. His jersey number.

His conversation with Isaac White in the restaurant returned to him. The mysterious contact, known only by a number.

His.

She was grinning at him.

He threw his leg over the back and wrapped his good arm around her waist. "Try not to kill us."

"Payback." She eased them away from the church and up the road.

The cobblestones had broken, the path jagged as they drove away from the shoreline, between buildings. Smoke still blurred the sky, but the morning sun simmered an eerie blood red through the clouds, and in the distance, just barely, he could make out the volcano, still exhaling flame and smoke, streams of lava cutting down its side.

"Wait until Aggie hears about this," Ham said into Signe's ear. "We should call her when we get to base. She's really missed you."

She might have tensed, but maybe it was her navigating around a cluster of cars stopped on the street. "Yeah, good idea."

Good idea.

Orion's navigator led them out to an abandoned highway, with cars in the ditches or on the side of the road. They wove in and out of the stopped traffic as they traveled southwest.

"What are you going to do with it?" Signe asked the question over her shoulder.

"With what?" He liked the feel of her close to him, her body stronger, although leaner than it had been a decade ago.

It also stirred up memories that probably he shouldn't revisit. Not quite yet.

But yes, someday.

"The NOC list."

"I'm giving it to Isaac White." Funny, she'd asked him that before.

She continued driving. Said nothing more about it as they hit the highway.

This part of the city hadn't suffered as much damage, although he spied collapsed stone walls, houses with broken roofs, torn pavement and debris clogging the streets. Signe kept pace with Orion, who slowed often to avoid cracks in the road.

They were skirting the city of Catania. He could barely make it out in the distance but knew from the map that it sat about forty miles from the base.

"How are we on gas?"

"We'll make it."

The wind seemed to have blown the smoke north, and over the next two hours, he made out fields of olive trees and vineyards to the west, probably cultivated in old lava fields.

In front of them, Gio pointed to a small suburban area, and Orion turned off the highway, east toward a tiny community with red-roofed homes, small apartment buildings, and gated gardens. Signe followed, and they drove through the relatively undamaged streets until they came to a two-story white building.

A dog barked at them through the railing on the second floor. Orion stopped and Gio got off and shouted at the dog. He whined. A woman came out onto the porch. "Gio!"

Ham didn't catch the rest.

Gio opened the gate and ran into the yard. Jenny got off the bike and followed him.

"I guess we're going in," Ham said as Signe stopped.

Orion parked the bike but left it running as he went in.

Signe did the same. Ham took her hand as they walked inside, he wasn't sure why. Maybe just because . . .

Well, because they were almost home. And seeing a family reunited stirred the image of Aggie's smile when Signe walked off the airplane.

He squeezed her hand and smiled down at her as Gio introduced them to his mother. "I speak English," she said. "My name is Luna."

She appeared to be in her midthirties, pretty, with dark olive skin, dark hair that hung down her back, and dark eyes that swept over the team with such gratitude Ham nearly agreed to let her make them tea.

"We gotta go," he said.

Signe had let go of his hand and asked to use the bathroom. Luna motioned to a room down the hall.

"You're headed to the base?"

"Yes," Ham said, not sure what else to tell her.

"I used to live there," Orion said, filling in a gap.

"I'm dating a corpsman," she said as she went to the kitchen. "Please sit."

Ham glanced at Orion and shook his head, but Orion frowned. And Jenny sat.

"I can call him and tell him that you're here. He can get you in the front gate," Luna said. She returned with a couple sandwiches in plastic wrap. "These were for our dinner, but Gio didn't return last night." She handed one to Ham, whose stomach suddenly roared to life. He took a look—salami, ham, tomato, lettuce, and mozzarella cheese. He might weep.

"I'll make you one," Luna said to Jenny.

Orion looked at his sandwich, then at Ham, waggled his eyebrows.

Fine. Ham sank down onto a straight-back chair, about to open his sandwich when . . .

Wait.

"Where's Signe?" Orion said, voicing Ham's thought.

Jenny went down the hall. "The bathroom is empty," she said, coming out. "And the window is open."

Orion went to the balcony. "Ham!"
No, oh—
He limped over to the window.
Orion's bike lay on its side, the engine off.
Signe's bike was gone.

CHAPTER NINE

PERFECT. Not only had Signe lost her mind, she couldn't even escape this stupid town. Round and round she went, driving through narrow side roads, past graffitied buildings, vacant lots, and the occasional palm tree, looking for the highway.

If only she'd paid just a little attention to the route she'd taken following Orion instead of the way Ham had his arm hooked around her waist. The feel of his legs against hers.

The sense that she could have this—all of it—if she played it right.

Or not. Because her brains, instead of her heart, kept reminding her that the second after she gave Ham the real drive, she had nothing. No leverage to prove she was telling the truth.

Convince the CIA Good Guys that she wasn't a terrorist wheedling her way back into her country.

Hello, black site holding facility.

And while her heart said she could trust the one man who hadn't given up on her, her head said that the CIA Bad Guys still wanted their hands on the drive. On her.

Worse, Aggie was caught in the middle.

Nope.

She needed to get away. Regroup.

Figure out how to get Aggie back and to safety.

She might have panicked a little bit when Ham's words bounced down the hallway toward her last night at the school. She'd been minding her own business, taking care of survivors, and out of the darkness heard . . .

"You need to get that list from her. That's the mission."

"I know."

"Before she runs."

"I know."

His words were a searing red poker to the heart.

Ham might have at least tried a smidgen to hide the fact that he knew she'd betray him.

Okay, maybe she deserved that. Because here she was, doing exactly that.

Although, admittedly, not well.

She bit back a word as she turned down yet another narrow, nameless street. Past ochre-colored stucco two-story homes with pink bougainvillea spilling off the balconies. Past gated gardens, their walls blanketed with ivy. Past boys kicking a soccer ball in a vacant lot and a fenced olive grove.

The place felt so untouched by the chaos forty miles to the north, it almost felt surreal.

As if she were trapped in suburbia.

And worse, her heart kept shouting at her. *Go back.*

Nope.

Because the second she gave the drive to Ham, he'd pass it off to Isaac White. She'd even asked him—twice.

And then . . . well, everything she'd sacrificed for the past decade would be for nothing.

Stupid Ham. He'd almost talked her into a happy ending. Made her believe, for a split second, they might go home and live as a family.

The highway rose ahead when she turned onto another street. Hooyah.

She gunned the engine, turned—

The road dead ended at a parking garage, a stone wall between her and the highway.

Yeah, that felt right.

She turned the Vespa around.

This was the plotline of her life. Flee, run into a dead end, get trapped . . .

Hide.

Hide and forget and—

She sped down the way she came, but just as she turned the corner, the Vespa sputtered, jerked her forward.

She gunned it, and it sputtered again.

Oh no . . . *no* . . .

And of course, it died, right there next to a couple of old, rusted Fiats.

Her brain might have also reminded her not to test fate when she was up against Ham. She knew what side she landed on.

Maybe she should start looking over her shoulder for a hurricane. Hail. An epic blizzard.

Or maybe Martin and his thugs, having survived the apocalypse, could suddenly show up to give her a lift.

Signe got off the Vespa and refrained from kicking it. Clearly she shouldn't have been so flippant about having enough gas.

Now what? She scrubbed her hands down her grimy face. *Think, Sig!*

She thought she remembered seeing a gas station down one of the side streets, maybe.

Or she could boost one of these beaters . . .

She peered into the grimy window of a Volkswagen. Too late—wires hung from under the steering column.

Stay calm. Think.

Except, all she could hear were Ham's words—*"We can't live in the what-ifs, Sig. We have to live in the now. The fact that we have a second chance."*

Sorry. She didn't live in the same "it'll all work out" world Ham inhabited. In her world, people didn't shake off their sins, didn't get do-overs. Didn't return home to build successful, multimillion-dollar businesses.

They fought. Hated. Died.

And if they didn't, they lived with the dark scars.

The rumble of a car's engine made her look up. A tiny red Fiat covered in dust, the fender dented. She climbed to her feet and raised her hand. Maybe the driver could point her to a gas station and . . . *oh goody.*

She had nowhere to run as the car stopped and Ham stepped out of the driver's side.

He shut the door. Looked at the Vespa.

"I ran out of gas."

His mouth made a tight line as he nodded, as if it might be expected.

Then he pulled out the jump drive, held it on his palm. "Did you swipe this from the school?"

"I found it in one of the teacher classrooms."

He looked away from her, and it looked as if his eyes glistened. "How did you find me?"

"Really? That's the big question here?"

She lifted a shoulder.

"Fine." He advanced toward her and she stiffened, backed up. His eyes widened. "Seriously. You think I would hurt you?"

His tone burned through her, but, "I don't know. Would you?"

"Check your leg pocket."

What? She slid her hand down to her other zippered leg pocket.

His cell phone. The one she used last night for a flashlight. She hadn't returned it.

"I called my communications officer and she was able to ping my GPS."

She opened the pocket and felt like an idiot as she handed him back the phone.

He took it, rubbing his thumb over the case. "So, were you playing me the entire time, or just for the past twelve hours?"

She folded her arms. "I tried the truth. You didn't listen."

"Try me again. I'm all ears. You can even use the big words if you want."

"It's so easy for you, isn't it? Everything is black and white. You show up and I'm supposed to fall into your arms like you're my savior—"

"Husband."

"*Ex*-husband."

His eyes narrowed.

"I don't need you."

He took a breath.

"I don't. I survived on my own for ten years, with my daughter—"

"*Our* daughter."

"You're not hearing me. If I give this information to the wrong people, I have nothing to prove I'm not lying."

He folded his arms.

"Nothing to protect Aggie. Or you."

"I don't—"

"Nothing to prove that I haven't wasted my entire life!"

Shoot. That wasn't supposed to come out. But Ham had this way of loosening the dark secrets from her soul. Even now, he just stared at her, unmoving, and she ached to pour out everything.

The years of abuse, of fear, of longing, of regrets.

The fact that she longed to go home almost as much as she feared it.

How could this man possibly want her after all she'd done?

Sometimes she hated how calm he could be when her entire life was splitting at the seams. "Say something!"

"What do you want me to say? Yes, you wasted your life?"

He could have slapped her with less effect.

"You're a jerk."

"And you stole ten years of my daughter's life from me and gave it to a terrorist." His jaw tightened. "Sorry. I told myself I wouldn't say that."

But she had backed away, her hand up. "I knew it. You were all, 'I'll forgive her' and 'We're together now,' but I was right, Ham. There's not a hope we can put this back together. Because deep down, you hate me."

He swallowed, shook his head, but she held up her hand.

"Yes, you do. That's why you came to Italy, isn't it? So you could face me and tell me that I hurt you. That I was wrong. What do you want to hear, Ham, that I regret my life?"

"Okay, yes. How about this—how about that you regret leaving me. You regret taking my daughter. You regret breaking every single promise you made to me."

His tone had turned lethal.

She knew he had it in him.

"Nice. See, that's the real truth between us, Ham." She shook her head, started to walk past him. "We haven't a hope of fixing this."

He put his hand on her arm. "Sig—"

She yanked out of his grasp. "Don't touch me."

He held up his hands. "Fine. Give me the jump drive and I'll leave you alone."

"No."

"Signe! I promise nothing bad is going to happen to you, or Aggie, or—"

"You're so obtuse! You don't get it—"

"Help me get it!" And now, finally, Ham was shouting. His eyes shone, his jaw tight, his chest rising and falling.

"Fine. You're in bed with a traitor."

He recoiled. "I—what?"

"Isaac White."

He stared at her, as if trying to wrap his mind around her words. "What?"

"Isaac White, and more specifically, his running mate, Senator Jackson, are traitors."

"You're—"

"Crazy. Yeah, or a terrorist, according to your friend Orion, but I know what I know."

"Okay, I'll bite. What do you know?" He folded his arms, stepped back.

"Jackson is the one who came to Tsarnaev's camp. She's the traitor."

A beat. Ham blew out a breath. "And you're sure it was her?"

"Yeah, I'm sure. And, brace yourself—that's how Tsarnaev got the NOC list."

Ham sat down on the stone wall. "You think a US senator gave away national secrets?"

"Sold them."

He ran a hand over his forehead.

"I'm telling the truth—"

"I believe you."

The words ripped her breath from her chest. "What?"

"I believe you."

Stupid, forbidden tears burned her eyes. No, *no*— "You do?"

"Of course I do. Sig— I know you, or I did. You might hide the truth. Even run from the truth. Even betray me without looking back. But you're not lying."

"You knew I wasn't coming back with you?"

He lifted a shoulder. "I wanted to believe that, but yes." He met her eyes.

And it nearly felled her, the look of hurt in his gaze.

"Sit down. Tell me what you think is going on." He didn't reach out to her, though. Just folded his arms, his face grim.

She sat down next to him. "I did some research—"

"Of course you did."

"Jackson was on the Senate Armed Services Committee, so she probably had oversight of anti-terrorism activities. It probably wouldn't have been impossible for her to get a copy of the list."

"But why give it to Tsarnaev?" Ham asked.

"I don't know. Like I said—maybe to secure his services."

"Like the destabilization of Russia? But why?"

She ran her palms on her pants. "I think some of her humanitarian aid organizations are cover for arms dealing."

He just looked at her. "Senator Jackson is a weapons trafficker?"

"I know it sounds crazy! It's just a theory. Or, maybe she's after the presidency. Or maybe . . ."

"White is in on it."

She nodded.

"Oh Sig. That's—"

"Treason. And now you know why I can't go home. Because if White is in on it, then if he becomes president, my accusation is treasonous."

"White can be trusted, Sig. I served with the man. I know him. He's a patriot."

"I want to agree with you. But even if he's not mixed up in this, Jackson is. And she knows me and what I've done."

He looked at her.

"She's the one who gave me the mission to track Tsarnaev."

"What?"

"She's the reason I embedded with him. And when Jackson arrived at the camp . . . I thought it was to see me. But she didn't even talk to me. And Pavel didn't let me out of my room and . . . I started to wonder if maybe she'd been using me all this time to get in with him. She'd given him a CIA operative and earned his trust."

"You think Tsarnaev knew you were an operative?"

"I don't know. Maybe that's why he didn't kill me when he got the list. My name was on it, and I feared he'd see it—but maybe he already knew."

"You think maybe he was using you too? Giving you false information?"

"Or maybe the right information to the wrong people—I don't know. I just know that Jackson is up to something, and White chose her for his running mate."

Ham took a breath. "Research."

"I'm a chronic insomniac."

He uncrossed his arms, and for a moment, she thought he might take her hand.

Stupidly wished it, really, her heart peeking out to take over her brains.

Nope.

He got up, turned to look at her. "Okay, listen. I can't make you trust me, but I promise you, we're going to figure this out."

"Ham. Think. The CIA is going to meet me at the airport and that's it. I'm chained to a wall eating soft foods in a black site until the end of my days."

"I'd find you." He said it without a smile, his tone cold.

Oh. Okay. And there went her heart again, leaping up to say *Listen, you idiot.*

He held out his hand. "Signe, give me the jump drive."

"I'll give it to you when we land in America."

He studied her. "Okay."

"Really? Just like that?"

"If we're going to be married, then we need to start trusting each other. I'll go first."

"We're not married, Ham."

"Stop overthinking things, Sig. I don't have a hidden agenda. Whenever you just can't see a way out, you panic. Then you run and hide and I have to climb up into the tree fort and talk you down. Or keep you from packing up the dog and taking off down the Mississippi in a stolen dinghy."

"You knew I was running away?"

"Best friend."

And she couldn't contradict him.

"Why do you keep showing up?" she asked softly.

"That's how I'm built."

Yes, he was.

"Fine. What now?"

"We go to the base, talk to the commanding officer, and get a lift home."

Oh boy.

"And then we see our daughter."

The man was a sniper with his words. And there she was, nearly crying again. Sheesh.

"Aw, Shorty. I told you that you weren't alone anymore."

That's what she was afraid of.

Then Ham reached out and pulled her to himself, wrapping his arms around her.

She closed her eyes, wanting to resist.

But shoot, the man had powers beyond hers. She sank into him.

His cell phone vibrated in his pocket and she stepped away as he answered it. "Ham here."

His intake of breath stopped her heart in her chest. Especially when his eyes met hers, widening.

But his voice was steely cool. "We'll be right there."

He hung up.

"What is it?"

She'd seen him snap into warrior mode before—but now he wore something akin to fury on his face.

"Orion's in trouble. Apparently, your friends from Germany are waiting for you. And they're going to kill Orion, Jenny, and our Italian friends if we don't bring them the list."

See? The cosmos hated her. "What are we going to do?"

His phone vibrated again. He looked at it and smiled. Looked back at her. "Do you trust me, Sig?"

She cocked her head.

"It's now or never. Give me the list."

She drew in a breath. Then she reached into her pocket and handed over her life into his palm. "Don't get me killed."

■ ■ ■

Jenny saw the look on Orion's face and knew . . . they were going to die.

They would die and Orion would never know the reason why she told him no. Told him no and broke his heart. Told him no and nearly lost him to a tsunami because they weren't together.

And now she was going to lose him to the thugs who'd broken into Gio's mother's apartment.

Mostly because Orion didn't go down easily.

Two big men simply broke down Luna's door—the metal one probably left open after Ham tore out of here. And in that moment, Orion had changed from the rescuer she knew to the warrior he'd trained to be.

And to think, for a whole minute she thought everything was going to be okay. At least for them. For Ham . . . oh, poor Ham.

He'd paced the small house as he got ahold of Scarlett, who in turn contacted a hacker friend, and together they pinpointed Ham's GPS.

Jenny had never seen him quite so undone, and Ham didn't unravel easily.

Luna gave him her car keys, then set on a kettle to boil.

Apparently, they were having tea.

Orion got back on the phone with Scarlett then, and Jenny heard him talking about their friend Jake, and arranging a ride home, and then she was listening to Gio tell his mother about the earthquake, tsunami, and his big adventures. She made out a few of the Italian words, including *nonno*—grandfather.

They needed to get to the base and send help to the school.

Right about then, the men came through the door.

They were tall and nondescript and when they shouted at her and Orion, she thought it might be in Russian, but it could be Ukrainian, or even Polish. Maybe Chechen?

She got the gist of their words, however.

Hands up.

She obeyed.

Not Orion, of course.

He dropped his phone just as one of them rushed him. The man put a fist in Orion's gut, bent him over, and slammed him into the wall.

Jenny screamed as the second man advanced on her. She took a step between her and Luna and Gio. "Stay back!"

The third man through the door looked American. A scar traced his forehead, looking relatively fresh, and he wore a suit. As if he might be the one in charge.

Orion rebounded, rolled, and sent his fist into his attacker's ear.

He howled, and Orion got behind him and cranked his arm around his neck.

The man tried to headbutt him, but Orion held on. Smaller but wiry, he hooked his legs around the Russian's waist, wearing him down.

Until Russian thug number two jumped in. He pulled Orion off, then hit him so hard Orion spun and hit the bookshelf, fell against a table, broke a lamp.

Then the man aimed a kick at Orion's knee, and he hit the floor.

The thug stood over him, grabbed his shirt, pulled back his fist.

"No!" Jenny took off and launched herself onto the Russian holding Orion. He elbowed her in the gut and she fell off, but rolled and picked up the broken lamp. Swung it at the first thug, now finding his breath.

Luna screamed.

"Stop! Or I kill the kid!"

Jenny froze.

Gio had run at the closest man with a kitchen knife. Now, the man had Gio around the neck, a gun to his head. He'd dropped the knife.

Orion had found his feet, picked up a shard of the lamp, and gone after the Russian. Blood dripped down Orion's face, his lip broken, his nose bleeding.

For a second, no one breathed. They just stood there looking at each other, and then Orion dropped the lamp shard and put his hands up. "Don't hurt him."

Gio was kicking at the man, so the American pushed his head against the wall and shoved his gun against his spine. "I said stop."

"Don't move, Gio," Orion said.

Maybe it was the calm in his voice, but Gio stilled, just a whimper emerging from him now.

Luna stood frozen, her hands glued over her mouth.

Orion shot a look at Jenny. "It'll be okay," he mouthed. Or at least that's what she thought he said. Maybe it was just her heart hoping the words.

"Get down on your knees, both of you," the American said.

Orion obeyed, and that's when she noticed his wince. She caught his tiny groan as he went down.

She got down beside him, her heart pulsing in her throat. He was really hurt.

"Who are you?" Orion said.

"Where's the woman?" the man said.

Orion looked at Jenny, back at the American, and raised an eyebrow. "What woman?"

"The one you came to find. The woman married to Hamilton Jones."

"Oh, *that* woman," cheeky Orion said. "Hate to tell you, but she's gone. Ditched us. Buh-bye."

He was making the man angry. What was his game?

The man said something to the Russians, and one stepped up and picked up Orion's cell phone.

"Call him," the American said. The Russian held out the phone to Orion.

"Call who?" Orion asked nicely.

"Your boss. Jones."

"He's not going to answer."

"If he doesn't, she's dead." And he turned the gun to Jenny.

Orion took a breath, and all the fun and games vanished from his face. He looked at her, and she saw his words in his eyes—everything he'd said on the roof last night, when he'd found her. *"I love you and I don't have to marry you—we can just . . . whatever you want."*

"*I want you.*" She'd said it then, and she meant it now as she stared back at him.

"I'll do it," Orion said quietly.

"Make it snappy," the American said.

Orion dialed. Waited. It must have gone to voicemail because, "Ham. It's me, Orion. So, some friends are here looking for Signe. Do you suppose you could come back around when you get done with whatever you're doing? Perfect."

He hung up. "We're all set."

The man spoke again to the Russian and he ripped the phone from Orion's hand.

The American checked the phone. Looked up at Orion.

Then he took the gun off Jenny and advanced to Orion, pressed the gun to his forehead.

"Who did you call?"

"My boss."

The American hit him across the face.

Jenny closed her eyes.

When she opened them, the man was scrolling down Orion's speed dial contacts. He pressed a number and handed the phone to Jenny. "Let's try again. And no funny stuff because I promise, I'll shoot him right here, right now—"

"Fine!" She grabbed the phone. The man had put it on speaker, and Ham's voice came on the line. "Ham here."

She kept her voice even. "The guys that are after Signe are here. They want the list. Can you come back?"

He didn't even hesitate, his voice cool. Quintessential Ham.

"We'll be right there." He hung up.

The man swiped the phone from Jenny's grip. "On the floor, both of you, face down."

She lay flat, and a foot came down between her shoulder blades. Hands pulled her arms back.

Her wrists were taped, and she turned her head and saw that the other thug was doing the same to Orion. His face was to hers.

Orion's breathing was even, as if he was thinking, but all she could think about was the fact that he'd never know. She'd never told him why she'd broken his heart.

Last night simply hadn't been the right time. Not with rescuing people from the coffee shop, taking care of Marcello, finding the school, and then of course Ham arrived and there was the joy of knowing that he hadn't perished. None of it felt like the right time to talk to Orion, to say the words that might derail their future.

She wanted a quiet moment. A moment when he could ask her questions and she could tell him the whole story. And then tell him that he could walk away if he needed to. But at least he would know that she loved him.

Now. She had to tell him before . . . well, before Ham arrived and who knew what happened. "Orion."

The men had stepped away to tie up Luna and Gio.

"Orion."

He was looking right at her so she didn't actually need his attention. She just had to figure out how to say the rest. She cut her voice low. "I need to tell you something."

He just looked at her, clearly listening.

Okay. Deep breath. "I know I should have told you, but . . . okay, so when I was nineteen years old I met a guy who—never mind. The short of it is that I had an abortion. And when I did . . ." She swallowed. He hadn't even blinked. "I'm not sure I can have kids. And I just didn't want you to marry me without knowing that because you love kids and—"

"Shut up over there!"

Jenny closed her mouth.

Orion was just staring at her. Didn't frown. Didn't add a look of concern or disgust or even anger. Just stared.

Then, quietly, "When I tell you, I need you to roll away and get small, okay?"

Huh?

"Just wait for my signal."

Um . . . "Okay."

"I said shut up!" The American came over and kicked Orion, right in the face.

Jenny screamed. "Stop!"

He ignored her. One of the Russians grabbed Orion's collar and moved him away from her, shoved him against the sofa.

Orion sat there, his back against the sofa, his knees up, his warrior face on.

And did not look at her.

Not even once for the next twenty minutes as they waited in silence.

That's when she decided to actually use her head—stop worrying about herself and start figuring out how she could get them out of this mess.

She had no idea what was going on with Orion, but he seemed to be disconnected from the world. Clearly he'd taken a severe hit to the head with that kick.

Oh, God, make me brave. "My name is Jenny," she said quietly. "What's yours?"

She wasn't talking to the Russians, of course, but the American, and he looked at her and smiled.

"Martin," he said, surprising her, really.

"You're an American," she said, not a question.

"I am."

"So, I don't understand. We're Americans too. What's going on?"

He picked up a chair and sat down, leaned his arms against the back of the chair.

"Well, here's the problem, Jenny. You're working with a rogue CIA agent who has sensitive information, and we've been tracking her across Europe trying to secure it. She keeps eluding us. We tracked her to this house and realized that the only way we were going to get close to her is to ask her to come to us."

"Us too!" Jenny said. "We're clearly on your side. Just let us go."

Martin shook his head. "Sorry. We don't know who to trust. We'll get the information, take you back to the US, and you can sort it out with the CIA."

Jenny glanced at Orion. He still hadn't moved.

She looked back at Martin. "There's been some misunderstanding. We were sent here by the CIA to retrieve the very information that you're talking about. So, like I said, we're on the same side."

Martin got up and looked to be walking away.

Jenny closed her eyes. *Think negotiation techniques. Empathize with him. Make him believe you're on his side.* She opened her eyes. "I'm not actually in the CIA but I can imagine it's really hard to be able to trust people."

Martin turned around. Folded his arms and rested his hip against the kitchen table. "You think so?"

"I used to be a profiler in Afghanistan. My job was to vet our sources. But sometimes that's not easy, is it? I got it wrong once and it cost lives."

Martin raised an eyebrow.

"It's hard to have so many lives at stake. You can't afford to get things wrong."

Martin studied her.

"What if you're wrong about this informant?"

"Oh, I don't think so," Martin said. "She killed her husband and another man on a boat in the Mediterranean. And she left two of my men dead in Germany. She's lived the last ten years in a terrorist training camp. I don't think we can trust her."

She hadn't known all that about Signe. Just knew that Ham trusted her. Loved her.

Maybe he didn't know.

"What are you going to do with us after she comes back and after you get the list?"

Martin stood up and went to the window, looked out. "I told you we're going to bring you back to the US."

He was lying. Classic technique—don't look at the person while delivering the lie, and they can't see your telltale eye shift.

Stay steady, Jen.

"So you're going to kill me and Orion. I get that. What about that boy right there?" She looked at Gio. "He's done nothing. You're just going to kill them and walk away?"

Martin glanced at Gio, who was tied up with his mother, and lifted his shoulder.

Deep breath. "What if you let them go right now. Put them in the back bedroom? They don't speak English. They don't know what's going on."

Martin shook his head.

C'mon, Jenny. You can do better than this. She was a licensed psychologist. Knew how to counsel, even interrogate people.

Orion still wasn't moving.

"You know it's going to cause a ruckus when you shoot us. Orion is not going to go down easily, you've already seen that."

And maybe she shouldn't have said that because that's when Orion came out of his catatonic state for a moment. She couldn't decipher the look he gave her.

Then he looked away again, head down. At least his nose seemed to have stopped gushing.

"Listen, you come at us and we're all going to start screaming. You can't kill us all at the same time. People will hear you. But if you let Luna and Gio go, Orion and I will sit here quietly. We won't make a problem when Ham returns, and we'll tell him to give you the information. Then, we'll let you do whatever you want to us."

Martin looked at her.

"Put them in the back room," she said. "By the time they get to help, you'll be gone. And you won't have had an international incident to clean up. Just us Americans. Isn't that what you want?"

Martin glanced at Gio. Back to her. Then he said something to the Russians.

Jenny let out her breath as they walked over, grabbed Luna and Gio, and shoved them into the bathroom.

The door locked.

And maybe she and Orion would never get out of here. But at least she'd told him the truth.

Now she just had to tell him that she loved him. So, she looked at him and said, "Orion Starr, I love you. I was afraid that you wouldn't love me because I can't give you children. But I give you my heart. You are my hero, now and forever."

For the second time Orion lifted his head and broke his catatonic state. He looked at her, smiled, and shouted, "Now!"

Huh?

The glass broke in the big window behind her, and she huddled into a ball as a soldier came through it. Two pops and the Russians went down. The door burst open and another soldier came in.

She got small.

But just in case she didn't, Orion, his hands free, launched himself over her, his body encasing hers. "Stay down!"

So not catatonic, apparently. Cunning, freeing himself.

And planning some sort of stealth attack.

Martin had flipped over a table, and she saw him darting through the flat, toward the back.

One of the soldiers went after him.

The other spoke into an earpiece. "He went out the back."

Right about then, Ham appeared in the door. "Hey!" He headed inside. "Did you get them?"

Orion rolled off her. "I need a towel. My nose is broken."

The first soldier crouched beside her, ran his Ka-Bar under her taped hands, freeing her.

She rolled over. Looked at him, her eyes wide.

"You okay, Jenny?"

"Jake?"

Jake Silver grinned at her under his helmet. He wore head-to-toe protective gear, but his blue eyes glimmered. "That's the last time I stay home and babysit."

■ ■ ■

Hope was not a strategy.

But so far, it was working, and Ham wasn't ready to abandon it quite yet.

He sat on an examination table in the medical clinic of the Sigonella Naval Air Station, his leg draped, a male physician's assistant about to sew his leg back up.

Gio and his mother had been taken to a hospital not on base, but Lt. Shelly Hollybrook from the naval base had cleared Ham, North, Jake, Orion, and the rest of the team to be treated at the medical clinic.

Ham now sported a less-than-convenient plaster cast on his hairline-fractured wrist—something he'd call overkill.

Hooyah, his team had shown up, just like he'd trained them when he set up their private group-messaging system.

Although reading his mind hadn't been an upgrade he thought he'd chosen.

"How'd this happen, exactly?" Jenny sat on a chair, an ice pack to her bruised rib where Igor One had sent his elbow into her side. "One second I'm on the ground, Orion is staring at the floor like his brain is scrambled, the next he's on top of me and a handful of Rambos—"

"Ex–special operators," Jake said from where he held up a wall with his shoulder. "We still got it." He bumped fists with North Gunderson, who seemed in a surly mood after losing Martin in the tiny alleyways of Librino, Gio's suburb.

That sat in Ham's craw too.

This wasn't over.

Signe's words about White hadn't helped. He needed to buy himself some time and do a little investigating.

"Blame Orion," North said. "He's the one who called in the text. We have a voice-to-text system that sends the message, along with a GPS location, to everyone's phone."

"So that's the call he made," Jenny said. "But—"

"We were in-country," Jake said. "As soon as we heard about the volcano, and Scarlett couldn't reach Ham on his cell, we got on a plane for Italy. We got to Palermo and had to drive the rest of the way. We figured even if you were okay, there might be others who needed our help."

"And you brought *weapons*?" Signe said. She was standing away from them, her arms folded, staring out the window at the activities on base, as if she expected Navy MAs to kick in the door and take her down to the floor, haul her away.

Over his dead body. But the thought sat in the back of his brain, along with her words—*"I'm chained to a wall eating soft foods in a black site until the end of my days."*

She hadn't been kidding.

He hadn't either when he told her he'd find her.

Please, let it not come to that.

But his chest still burned with the hard punch of realizing she had betrayed him.

And the fact that deep in his gut, she might be a little right. He *had* come to Italy to confront her.

And maybe a part of him did hate her for choosing the mission over him.

He shook the thought away. "We always bring tactical weapons."

"On a commercial flight?"

"Who said we went commercial?" North said. He leaned up from the wall. "I'm going to call Selah, tell her we're okay." He patted Jake on the shoulder as if that might atone for the fact that North was dating Jake's kid sister.

"You own a plane?" Signe said, looking at Ham.

"No. But we have a contract with a private charter company when we need it."

"Chief, this is going to hurt," said the petty officer. Ham looked at him. Young guy, blond hair worn high and tight. Blue eyes, and manners. Wore the name Samuels on his badge.

"Do it," Ham said and looked away as Samuels administered a needle of novocaine.

"I need to debride the wound a little—there's a bit of an infection."

"Blame the water. And by the way, did you guys get the location of the school?" He directed his attention to Jake.

"Orion is taking care of it right now," Jake said. He looked at Jenny. "He tells me you were amazing. Talked the guy into letting the family go."

"I didn't know what else to do," she said. "There might have been some panic. And Orion was playing stupid."

"Listening. Waiting for us to get into place," Jake said. "He gave the signal for us to come in."

"Oh. That's what that was." She gave a laugh that didn't sound anything like humor.

"You okay, Jen?" Ham said.

"How about if I get you something to eat," Jake said.

"I'm good, I'm just . . . okay, a coffee sounds good." She followed Jake from the room.

Then it was just Ham and Signe and Samuels, quietly sewing up his wound.

Maybe the PA had something for the bitter ache inside.

"Signe. You still with me here?"

She turned, her lips tight. Lifted a shoulder. "Where else am I going to go."

"Nice, Sig."

She didn't answer him. Turned away.

Four hours later, she still hadn't looked at him as they boarded the chartered jet. She sat down in the padded leather chair, running her hands over the armrests.

He took the seat next to her, not sure why, but maybe just because he couldn't leave it alone.

He wasn't the bad guy here.

"Signe, you okay?"

"Yeah, sure. Super."

"Nothing is going to happen to you, I promise."

"I hope you're right," she said. "How did you get the plane here?"

"The wind shifted, and my pilot was able to get in. But we need to leave now if we want to get out before it shifts again."

"Do these fancy seats go back?"

He indicated an electronic pull on her armrest.

She put the seat down, grabbed her pillow, and curled up, her back to him.

"The only easy day was yesterday," Jake said as he sat down across the aisle from him.

Ham looked at him. "Yesterday was off the hook. Today's not much better."

"It's a little better. I scored you a grape soda from the nurse's stand." Jake reached into his backpack and pulled it out. "Get some shut-eye. Tomorrow is a new day."

"When we land, it'll still be today."

"That bad, huh?" Jake nodded toward Signe and her less than friendly posture.

Ham looked at her. "I got a plan."

"Of course you do." Jake pulled out his pillow as the plane began to cycle up.

At least the private plane had more leg room, but Ham couldn't wait to put his seat back. Orion sat ahead of him, beside Jenny, a pillow under his head, his nose taped, his knee under ice.

North and the rest of the team had taken the back seats, stretched out.

The captain came on and prepped them for takeoff. Ham stared out the window as they left the runway, the plane rising above the Catania-Fontanarossa airport.

In the distance, Etna still spit lava, a great cloud of black ash hovering above, raining down its slopes. Streams of red lava dug trenches into the hillside, scarring the terrain as it seeped death into the villages below.

It would take a lifetime for them to recover, if at all.

Signe stirred, punched her pillow, and fell back to sleep as they flew into the clouds and left the destruction behind.

CHAPTER TEN

MARTIN WAS STILL HUNTING HER, and no amount of pretending was going to make that truth easier.

Signe stared out the window as the pilot came over the loudspeaker and announced their descent. She'd slept a total of 13.3 minutes since leaving Italy, rolling what-ifs through her brain.

All of them ended with her on the run, sometimes with Aggie, sometimes without, using her passport to cross into Canada, and from there . . . vanish.

Next to her, Ham put up his seat. "You ready?"

He'd slept on the flight, his lean, strong body relaxing as they headed into the sunset. His even breaths stirred to the surface the night they'd spent together at the school. The way she'd let herself relax next to him, relish the warmth of his presence.

She'd always felt safe next to Ham.

It was the world that scared her. The world she needed to figure out, order, control. The world that made her want to grab one of her aliases and run.

She just had to decide if she should take Aggie with her. Probably not.

Being on the run was no life for her child. For anyone, really.

"Sure," she said now to his question. Signe looked out the

window. They had cleared the clouds, and all of the Minneapolis/ St. Paul area stretched out across the horizon. Neighborhoods nestled in a jeweled array of red maples, yellow poplar, and orange oak trees, the lakes deep indigo and the twilight shining off a silver-domed stadium.

"Is that new?" She pointed at the stadium.

Ham looked out her window. "US Bank Stadium. Where the Minnesota Vikings play."

"Do you still have that crazy hat?"

He shook his head but offered a slight smile. "But I have season tickets."

Of course he did.

In fact, his entire life had risen its head and shaken her. Not to mention the differences between the man she'd known and this man.

This man who had a private jet on retainer.

But, it also meant he had resources—the kind that just might unravel the conspiracy she knew was brewing.

She just needed some time to research.

Time, and a computer, and security clearance, and maybe a really good hacker.

And Aggie.

She needed her arms around Aggie, the smell of her daughter's hair, the sound of her laughter.

"You okay, Sig?" He put his hand on the armrest, as if to take hers, but she slipped her hands into her lap, folding them.

This wasn't going to work and no amount of hope or wishing was going to make this disaster turn into a fairy-tale ending. She couldn't just morph and become the wife, mother, and whatever that Ham envisioned. She didn't even know what that looked like. Him, trotting off to manage his megalosphere of gyms while she attended ballet lessons? Maybe soccer games?

All of it could be moot anyway, because the moment she got off the plane, a cadre of CIA suits might be waiting to cart her away.

The airport came into view.

At least Aggie wouldn't have to see her mother get arrested.

"We'll have to go through customs, and passport control, but then Aggie will be waiting with Jake's parents."

Oh, for cryin' in the sink. "Aggie knows I'm coming?"

"No. I wanted it to be a surprise."

Surprise! Your mother, who dumped you off on the beach with only a ratty stuffed animal and a burner phone, aka, *abandoned you*, is back. Okay, Signe had called the emergency services with an anonymous tip, but . . . she pressed her hand to her stomach.

She'd thought she would have more time to figure out her words.

"Are you worried about passport control?" He was watching her gesture.

"No." She'd perfected acting years ago, when her life and Aggie's depended on her performance. But, there was the other thing . . . "By the way, my passport says Stephi Jones."

He looked at her. "You used my last name?"

"It's an old passport. I didn't . . . well, at the time, it was all I had."

"Jones is a good name."

She looked at him. "Yes, it is."

"It's still yours if you want it." His mouth tightened around the edges, and his word, *husband*, echoed in her brain.

Oh Ham.

This was going to be very, very ugly. In fact, it might be better if she simply took Aggie and vanished.

Nice, Sig. Because clearly she hadn't hurt him enough.

"Aggie will be so glad to see you. She lost a tooth a couple weeks ago. Did you know that kids lose teeth until they're twelve?"

"Really?"

"Yeah. And . . . oh, I should probably tell you. Last week we had a little scare with the Ferris wheel."

"What? Was it the Russians—"

"No, just a freak accident. She's fine. But you might hear about it."

"Aggie has always been a little independent. Likes to wander. Once, we lived in an area that had been an old minefield. That was—"

"I don't want to know." Ham drew in a breath. "Not now, okay? Just let's be together."

He said it with quietness, such a dark, pained earnestness, she nodded.

Tonight, they could be a family.

She'd figure out how to escape Martin and find a new life tomorrow.

The plane touched down, wetness on the tarmac, and as they descended the stairs, the wind scattered leaves into puddles, the air brisk.

"At least it isn't snowing," Jake said as he descended. He went to the baggage area to claim their gear. Orion and North did the same, but when Ham reached for a bag, Signe picked it up for him.

"For once, you don't have to be the tough guy."

He narrowed his eyes but said nothing as they walked into the passport control area.

She stood in line behind Ham, and maybe he purposely got in front of her, to suggest they were traveling together, because when she stepped up, the officer gave her passport a quick glance, then stamped it and marked her through.

Orion and the guys were left in customs to inspect the bags, and Jenny stayed back to help, so just Signe and Ham headed to the receiving area.

Signe slowed. "I just . . ." She pressed her hand to her chest. "I guess I just thought I'd never see her again. I had to shut off my feelings, compartmentalize. Stay focused on the job."

"Breathe, Shorty. It's going to be fine."

"Right." She followed him past the screen.

Aggie wore braids, a pair of jeans, and a jacket, and stood with a young woman, maybe seventeen, in black leggings, flip-flops, and a baggy blue sweatshirt with the word Skippers on the front. She looked a little like Jake with her blonde hair.

"Daddy!" Aggie took off running, clearly seeing Ham first.

Then she spotted Signe. Aggie's mouth opened and she burst into tears, launching herself at Signe.

"See," Ham said, pressing his big hand on Aggie's back. Aggie had her legs and arms wrapped around Signe, who crushed her daughter to herself.

Aggie. She smelled different, but the feel of her skin, the form of her body, the way she sobbed—Signe sank to the floor and just rocked them both.

Don't cry. But her body had turned into a fist, trying to contain the rush of emotions.

Freedom. It just . . . it felt too wide. Too much, too fast, and Signe started to hyperventilate.

"Okay, you're okay." Ham knelt beside them, pulling Aggie away. "Let's give your mom some room, there, kiddo."

She closed her eyes.

"In, out. In. Just like we used to do."

She listened to his words, his breathing, with hers.

"You're okay," he said again.

Her breathing slowed down. When she opened her eyes, the team was standing around her, not a few of them wearing worry in their expressions.

"It's a thing," Ham said, looking over at Orion, who had crouched beside him. "She used to hyperventilate when she got overemotional."

"Thanks. That's exactly what I want everyone to know about me. Maybe my bra size too?"

Ham widened his eyes. "I uh . . . don't know—"

"Loosen up, Hamburglar."

There she was, the girl she could depend on. In control. A little cynical.

Signe reached again for Aggie, pulling her tight. "You okay, sweetie?"

Aggie nodded. "I have my own room."

Probably only Signe knew what that meant—both the privacy and safety in being able to lock her door. "I can't wait to see it."

Jake introduced his sister Ellie, then caught a ride with her. Orion and Jenny had taken separate cars, and Ham led them to his Jeep in long-term parking.

He got in at the wheel.

As Aggie buckled in the back, Signe slid in the passenger seat.

Ham started the car, then moved the transmission into reverse, put his right hand on the wheel—

His left arm was in a cast.

"Oh, for Pete's sake. I'll shift."

"I can do it."

"Just drive."

He pulled out, pushed in the clutch, and she put it into first. He hit the gas, clutched again, and she switched to second.

"You just had to get a stick shift," she said.

"Never had a problem until now," he growled.

He paid for parking, then they took off onto the highway, working in tandem. Overhead, the sky was dark, stars falling into the bright lights of the downtown skyline.

"Where do you live?"

"On Lake Minnetonka."

"Right on the lake?"

"Yeah. I bought an old seventies rambler and gutted it. Did most of the work myself—beamed ceiling, dark wood floors, floor-to-ceiling glass windows that look out onto the lake. Three bedrooms."

Three. "It sounds nice."

"Yeah. It's quiet." He looked behind them. "Aggie's sleeping."

"It's late."

"I was thinking. Tomorrow I need to meet with my team, and then maybe we head up north. I have a cabin off the grid there, and it'll be a good place for us to lay low."

"Ham." She looked at him, the unshaven profile of the man she'd always loved. Hard-jawed. Capable.

The perfect man, really.

If she were the perfect woman. "I think it's best if I don't stay."

He glanced over at her, frowned.

"Car!"

He looked back. A car had swerved in front of them. He slammed on his brakes, hit the clutch.

She shifted on reflex.

He straightened the Jeep out into the next lane.

They drove for a second without speaking.

"What about Aggie?"

"I can take care of her—"

"Have you lost your mind?" He blew out a breath, schooled his words to just above a whisper so as not to wake Aggie.

"That guy—Martin—is still out there. And you want to take Aggie and run?" His mouth tightened. "No. Over my dead body."

"She's not—"

"My daughter?" He looked at her. "Of course she is. I see myself in her as much as I see you. Not for a second do I believe she's a terrorist's daughter."

Her eyes glazed. "She doesn't know you."

"She does now. Wasn't that the point, Signe? For me to protect her?"

"You did great. But I'm her mother."

"And I'm her father. And your husband, and you're not leaving."

She stared at him, her eyes hard. "Oh, I see. I go from a terrorist to a dictator."

He closed his mouth. "You know I don't mean it like that. It's just . . . you're tired, Sig. And you're scared. And, c'mon. Let me take care of you, just a little. Let things get back to normal."

She looked out the window. "What is normal for us, Ham? What does that even look like?"

He turned quiet. "Our exit is next." He touched the brakes and she shifted down, then again as he looped up to Highway 7.

They drove west, the night arching over them.

"Just stay for a week, while we unravel what's on the drive," Ham said. "Then . . . you can go where you want. I won't stand in your way."

She looked back at Aggie. She wasn't carrying her ratty unicorn but a huge stuffed moose, her head on its massive body. "You get that for her?"

He signaled, turned off, and she shifted. "Won it at a fair. Sharp-shooting."

They slowed on winding roads that curved through old neighborhoods toward the lake. It glistened between the yards.

Then, finally, they pulled up to a long drive that wove to the house hidden in the trees.

She'd expected a mansion, maybe, not this unassuming modern ranch, despite his description. Ham got out and came around to get Aggie, but Signe already had awakened her, pulling her woozy body next to hers. "Where's her room?"

Ham keyed in a code and let them in.

For a moment, the grandeur of the house stilled her. The lake shone through the massive windows and giant Edison lights hung from wires attached to the beams. He flicked on the entry light, and it splashed luminance onto the stone flooring.

"Down the hall, second door on the right. The guest room is right beside it."

She slid off her shoes and walked on the carpet down the hall. She passed a small room with a way-too-inviting fluffy queen bed.

A butterfly night-light glowed from the next room, the queen bed overwhelmed with purple pillows. The word *Dream* was stenciled on the wall above. A disco ball light fixture reflected the light from the front entry, and a white wicker chair hung from the ceiling, a book and stuffed rabbit tucked inside.

The room of a beloved daughter. It made her want to weep.

Signe eased Aggie down on the bed. She wrapped her arms up around Signe's neck. "Don't go, Mama."

Signe kissed her cheek. "I'll be here when you wake up."

She pulled the covers over her.

"Really? Promise?" Ham was standing near the door.

In the wan light, he looked rough. Tired, broken, worn, fierce, handsome, and perfect.

Wow, she'd missed him.

If only she wasn't such damaged goods.

If only she didn't bring danger right to his front door.

If only, inside her, didn't beat the heart of a woman whose mission wasn't over.

"A moving target is harder to hit, Ham," she said as she walked over to him. "But tonight, I'm going to snuggle with my daughter."

He looked at Aggie, back to her, and for a second what looked like relief washed over him. "I'm locking the door and setting the security system."

"And sitting outside the door," she said quietly.

He met her eyes. "Probably."

She put her hand on his chest. "You're a good man, Hamburglar."

"Husband," he said quietly.

She let it go and climbed into her daughter's cozy purple bed.

Aggie rolled over and pressed her hand on Signe's cheek. "Mama?"

Signe wove her fingers through hers. "I'm here, baby."

"Are we safe now?"

The door had clicked behind Ham, but she saw his shadow stretching under the door. He was standing just outside, clearly intending to camp outside the door.

Signe tucked her body against her daughter, felt the thump of her heart, the warm curve of her body.

Sank into it, her throat thick. "Yes, honey. We're safe."

For now, tonight, they were safe.

■ ■ ■

"When morning gilds the skies . . ." The hymn hung in Ham's mind as he sat out on one of his Adirondack chairs at his cold fire pit, watching the sun rise. The horizon had turned from pewter to molten gold, not unlike the brilliant red lava he'd seen spouting from Etna. Only this lava flattened over the horizon and spilled into the lake, across the waves, tipping them in copper. A brisk wind scattered the leaves that scraped across the stone fire pit, and in the distance, a flock of Canadian geese landed in the tiny inlet nearby, their honking breaking through the silence of the dawn.

Ham wore his thick flannel jacket, a wool hat, and had his hands shoved hard into his pockets, and still he shivered. Maybe not as much from the air as the chill from Signe since that moment in Italy when he realized she'd betrayed him.

The moment, the realization, still swept his breath from his chest, still made him want to let out a growl from the deep ache he felt all the way to his core.

He still hadn't found his footing.

Especially since she kept knocking him over. *"I think it's best if I don't stay."*

What?

How—why—*what* had he done to make her keep running from him?

He leaned forward in his chair, his head in his hands. "Lord, I don't know what to do. I don't know."

The wind stirred, lifting the fragrance of autumn—crispy, drying leaves, a hint of smoke in the air, the deepening loam.

Everything dying in the face of winter.

"I don't know how to reach her. How to tell her that she's safe. How to bring her home . . . how to be her husband."

He waited, but nothing of wisdom filled his soul. Just the sun upon the platinum waters, turning it from dark to light.

He couldn't deny the hard clench of relief in his chest when he spotted Signe in the kitchen with Aggie when he finally went in. He'd left her a pair of sweatpants and a T-shirt in the hallway and she was wearing them, frying up a couple eggs.

Aggie sat at the counter, her legs wrapped around the high-top chair, licking peanut butter off a piece of toast. "Mama is making eggs!"

Ham shed his jacket and closed his sliding glass door. "I see that. There's some bacon in the fridge too."

"We don't eat pork," Signe said. She wore her hair down, finger combed.

"Oh, uh . . ." He looked at Aggie, whose eyes had widened. Oops. "Why?"

Signe looked at him, frowned. Back to the eggs. "I guess . . . oh, um . . ."

Because Tsarnaev had been Muslim.

He hadn't even thought about how her faith had been affected by her tenure in Tsarnaev's camp.

Or if any of it still existed.

Signe slid a couple fried eggs from the pan onto a plate. Brought them over to the counter. "Over hard, the way you like?"

"Thanks." He slid onto a stool beside Aggie. She'd changed into a pair of flannel pajamas, fuzzy pink slippers.

Signe handed him a fork. Met his eyes.

Her gaze held sadness, and he tried not to panic.

She returned to the stove and sliced a wedge of butter into the pan.

"I have to meet with Scarlett this morning. She has a hacker friend who might be able to decrypt the list. We'll get her to work on it, and then I'd like to head up north, to my cabin."

Signe drew in a breath. "Ham—"

"For Aggie. It's gorgeous and . . ." And maybe they could figure out how to start over. "You're tired, Sig. You need a break. It's safe. No one is going to find you there, I promise."

Signe looked at Aggie, who was nodding.

Smoke rose from the pan. "Oh, the butter!" She took it off the heat, then broke a couple more eggs into the pan. "Okay."

He watched her fry eggs, then, "You'll be here when I get back?"

She looked at him. Then gave a slow nod.

The gesture sat in his gut, a sort of ember of dread and fear until he returned home, the jump drive left safely in Scarlett's hands.

He also hadn't returned Isaac White's phone call.

They just needed time.

Time to unravel Signe's story.

Time to be a family.

Time to figure out how he could fix this.

Signe had packed Aggie a bag and was scanning through television channels on his flat-screen as they waited. "You have over five hundred cable channels."

"I know. I watch about three. Ready?"

Aggie was armed with all her stuffed animals—the moose, her ratty unicorn, the oversized dolphin, and her furry rabbit. She'd changed into a purple sweater and leggings, her hair braided.

Signe hadn't changed, and when she walked over to him, he handed her a bag. "Scarlett sent these over."

She looked inside and frowned. "Why would she give me clothing?"

"Because you don't have any?"

She drew in a breath, then fished through the bag and pulled out a pair of fuzzy socks. "Right. I'll go change."

By the time Signe returned, he'd gathered Aggie's bag, his own overnight bag, which he'd packed last night, just in case he had to take off quickly, and some snacks for the five-hour drive.

She wore a pair of jeans and a baggy sweater, and with her hair up in a messy bun she looked every inch a suburban soccer mom. "You want me to drive?"

"No. We're taking the truck," he said and glanced out to his Silverado in the driveway.

"How many vehicles do you own?"

He picked up Aggie's bag and his own, and managed the door by himself. "Three, counting the Corvette."

She picked up the bag of snacks and followed him out. "How rich are you?"

He loaded the gear into the bed of the truck, took her bag from her, and pulled the top over the bed. "I can afford what I need for me and the team." He opened the back door for Aggie to climb in. "And for you and Aggie. Here, honey, you're in charge of the chips. Don't eat them all at once." He handed Aggie the bag of goodies as she settled her farm around her. "Oh, and I brought your book." He pulled the book they'd been reading from his back pocket. "I thought you'd like to finish it on the way up."

He wondered if Signe noticed the cover.

"You're reading her *The Farthest Away Mountain*?"

So, yes.

Signe walked around and climbed into the cab. "Where did you find it?"

"Used bookstore." He joined her in the driver's seat.

She smiled at him and it nearly lit his chest on fire. "I can't believe you remembered."

"You wouldn't stop talking about that book, and how you wanted to go on your own adventures."

Yes, she did.

He set the security system, then glanced in the rearview mirror. Aggie was already inside the book. "Did you teach her to read? She speaks excellent English, and her teacher says she's the top in her math class."

"Yes. Tsarnaev allowed us wives to raise our daughters."

"Wives? Plural?" He pulled out onto the highway. The sky overhead had turned a wispy, light blue.

"He had several. But most of them were political alliances with neighboring tribes."

He really didn't want to know.

"He wasn't as cruel as you might think. He cared for his wives, and—"

"No, Signe." He cut his voice low, but really, he didn't care if Aggie heard him. "Evil disguised as kindness is just manipulation. And manipulation is emotional abuse when it's used to control people." He looked at her. "You did a brave, honorable thing. But let's not pretend you weren't also physically, mentally, and emotionally abused in the process. Tsarnaev is a terrorist, and terrorists are only interested in themselves and their agenda."

She stared at him, her eyes hard, then turned away.

Nice, Ham.

Lord, give me wisdom.

As they headed north, the trees deepened their bejeweled colors—gold, red, and deep purple, the slightest hint of frost on the cattails and pussy willows that lined the marshes along the highway.

"Where is your cabin?" Signe asked.

"It's near the town of Deep Haven, overlooking Lake Superior."

They stopped for coffee at Tobies, a donut shop halfway to Duluth. Ham turned on the radio, and for a while they listened to the news. Signe's hands went a little white when updates of White and Jackson's campaign came over the radio.

He resisted the urge to touch her. "Scarlett will get to the bottom of this."

"Who is her hacker? Is she with the CIA?"

"No. Apparently, her boyfriend's brother is engaged to a superhacker. Scarlett is flying out to see them this weekend, so she'll give her the drive then."

"It feels strange for it to be over, you know?"

"I do. When I separated from the military, I didn't know what to do with myself. I came home and bought the house and started remodeling it—"

"You did that yourself?"

"Mostly. I gutted it, did the rewiring, the plumbing, the structural work. I had some help—North left the same time I did, and he came back to Minneapolis with me. I spent very little while I was serving, so my bank account was flush when I returned. I used it to set up my first GoSports shop in Minneapolis. We started with a weight room, a boxing area, and a climbing wall. We're open 24/7, and when we realized we were maxed out, we opened another location in the western suburbs. That membership maxed out within a few months, so we opened another shop in Arden Hills, and from there, started a franchise."

"Wow."

"Yeah. I got lucky—I had a contact with the Minnesota Vikings, so we had one of their wide receivers sign on as our spokesman. Even ran a Super Bowl ad our second year that exploded our franchise sales. Now, we're national, with our first international club opening in a few weeks in Vancouver."

"So, very rich, then."

He laughed. "No. I'm always putting back into the company. I even teach, sometimes. We specialize in alternative sports— everything from climbing to triathlon swimming, with individualized plans to help people realize an active lifestyle. You won't find any Jazzercize classes, but we do have a Pilates teacher, a hot yoga room, and a spin class. Our most popular classes are the ice-climbing and kite-surfing classes."

He topped the hill over Duluth, and immediately the air changed, chilled, Lake Superior unfurling in deep blue in the valley below.

"Is that a bridge?" Aggie said, leaning forward and pointing to the arched aerial bridge that spanned the channel between Minnesota and Wisconsin.

"Yes. Want to stop and see it?"

She nodded, and Ham exited at Canal Park.

Aggie tossed chips to the seagulls as they walked the barrier along the channel, all the way to the lighthouse. Signe shivered, and Ham took off his jacket and wrapped it around her.

She didn't shrug it away and he counted it as a win.

An oceangoing cargo ship came in, and Ham held Aggie's hand as they stood under the bridge, watching it go up.

"Cool," Aggie said.

Ham bought her an ice-cream cone, then they got back into the truck and headed up the shore.

Signe dug into the bag for a couple sandwiches. "Cheese and baloney. It was all I could find in your fridge, but if I remember correctly, they were your favorite."

"You used to bring them to school, just in case my stepmother refused to make me lunch."

"And Twinkies."

He took the sandwich that she'd unwrapped. "I would have gone hungry without you."

"Hardly. I wasn't the only girl in school who had a crush on you."

"You were the only one who knew how terrible my stepmother was."

She took a bite of her sandwich. "Is she still alive?"

He swallowed, put his sandwich down, and took a drink of water. She took his thermos and capped it as he shook his head. "She and my father were murdered in Central Park about fifteen years ago."

"What?"

"Yeah. They'd taken Kelsey to *The Lion King* on Broadway and then decided to take a walk through the park. They were jumped by a gang of three guys. They killed my father and my stepmother and left Kelsey for dead."

"Oh my."

"Yeah. Thankfully, she was found, but she was badly hurt. I was deployed, but the Navy got ahold of me and I left as soon as I could. It still took me ten days to get to her. She was asleep when I arrived and I just sat there, looking at her, trying not to blame myself for not being there."

"Of course."

"I realize how crazy that sounds, but—"

"But that's how you're built."

He shrugged.

"How old was she?"

"Fourteen."

"Oh, wow. I remember you playing with her. Taking your horse out into the fields. Remember her? The horse used to blow up her stomach so the saddle would fall off after you cinched it."

"Yeah. I was the only one who knew how to saddle her."

"What happened to Kelsey?"

"She went to live with family on her mother's side. A cousin who lived in Wisconsin, not far from the farm. The hardest thing I ever did was leave her there. It was . . . I felt . . ." He drew in a breath, surprised by the sudden burn in his eyes. "I felt like I was abandoning her."

He glanced at Aggie in the rearview mirror, but she was still reading, her ice-cream cone gone.

Signe had her gaze on him when he looked back at the road. When she looked away, her jaw was tight.

"Kelsey's okay now," he said, trying to figure out what he'd said wrong. "She's actually the lead singer in a country band called the Yankee Belles. And I think she's engaged."

"So, then, you talk every day."

He frowned.

"You *think* she's engaged?"

"I . . . I walked out of her life about fifteen years ago and we haven't really stayed in touch. I got an update from a mutual friend a few months ago."

"Why haven't you stayed in touch?"

They'd gotten behind a slow-moving car. Off the passenger side, the waves were tossing themselves into the rocky shoreline. The sun had passed the apex of the horizon, was falling to the backside of the day, the sky bruising with the hour.

"I don't know."

"It's because you're ashamed."

236

He frowned. "What?"

"You hated leaving, and you decided you were a bad person for doing so—even though you had a country to protect—and now you can't face her."

He stared at her. Closed his mouth and looked back at the road. "I was an active-duty SEAL."

"Yep."

"And I was in the middle of a deployment."

"Mmmhmm."

"And my team needed me."

"This was what—about a year after I left you?"

He drew in a breath.

"The team was all you had. But you still think you're a bad guy for leaving her."

"I was all *she* had."

"You never were good at forgiving yourself."

He floored the truck and passed the car.

"You were always nice to your stepmother."

"I had no choice. My father married her. And if I—"

"If you said anything, she beat you. Or locked you in the cellar. Or didn't feed you—"

"Okay, that's enough, Signe." He settled the car back into cruise. "A lot of people have rough childhoods."

"You deserved a better stepmother. And frankly, a better father. He should have stood up for you. But just because they didn't doesn't make you a bad person, Ham. You're one of the most heroic, kind—"

"Yeah? Then why are you thinking of leaving me?"

She drew in a breath.

Aw. *See, Lord?* He schooled his emotions, tamped them back down to a hard ball.

"Signe. You deserved a mother who didn't choose drugs over

you. Who made you feel important and worthy of sticking around. But we can't live wishing for what we don't have." He looked at her. "We have to live with what we've been given."

She met his eyes. "And what's that?"

"I think you know," he said quietly.

"Hey, are we almost there?" Aggie leaned forward.

Ham looked back to the road. "Yep. Just a few more miles."

Signe looked away. "It's really pretty up here."

And how. Somehow, the moment he entered the picturesque town of Deep Haven, he left behind his problems, the weight of his thoughts, and slipped into another mindset.

The tiny town wrapped around a small harbor—restaurants, gift shops, pubs, and hotels edging the pebbled beach. Sailboats still waiting for haul-out sat at anchor or were moored at the docks by the fish house, and a trail of gray smoke twined from the smokehouse in town.

Deep blue water raked the shoreline, and seagulls hunted for snacks among the rocks. A white lighthouse sat at the end of the breakwater, the cold froth of the lake splashing against it. A hill rose behind the town, bejeweled with the golds, reds, and oranges of maple, oak, and poplar intermixed with deep green balsam and fir trees. Overhead, the sky was turning mottled purple, dappled with a deep blush along the far horizon.

A place time and worries forgot.

Ham pulled into the gas station, filled up the truck, then went in to pay while Aggie used the restroom. A man stood at the counter, talking to the cashier.

"Pastor Dan?" Ham held out his hand to the pastor of the Deep Haven Community Church. Brown hair, medium build, the pastor had once served on the volunteer fire-fighting team. In fact, his wife had been the fire chief, if Ham remembered the lore correctly. He'd attended the church a few times during his escape weekends.

"Hamilton Jones, whattaya know?" Dan gripped his hand. He wore a pair of cargo pants and a flannel shirt, sported a baseball hat. A couple frozen pizzas sat on the counter, waiting for checkout. "Date night," Dan said, nodding to the pizzas.

"Not a bad idea." Ham headed to the frozen section to grab dinner.

Dan was waiting for him when he returned. "You going to be around for a while?"

"I don't know. A week or two."

"Maybe we can get in some fishing. Think you can handle a rod and reel in that cast?"

"That's not the problem. I got skunked the last time we went out. I'm not sure the fish like me."

"Yeah, well, they're there. You just have to keep trying. Find the right bait, the right hiding place. Coax them out." He picked up his pizzas. "It's like being a Minnesota Vikings fan. No matter how many times they choke in the fourth quarter, we still keep trying, right?"

Ham laughed, and Aggie came walking up. She took Ham's hand.

"Who is this?" Dan asked, smiling down at Aggie.

"This is my daughter," Ham said.

"I'm sorry we've never met before." He shook her hand.

Ham nodded. "Honey, go on out to the truck. I'll be right out." Dan watched her go. Raised an eyebrow.

"Her mom and I were separated for a long time," Ham said. "But we're back together . . . sort of, and . . ." He ran a hand around the back of his neck. Now was not the time, but . . .

"Ham, I've discovered in nearly eighteen years of marriage that the key to a good marriage is sacrifice. Setting aside what you want for the good of someone else. It's a daily surrender. And really, it's not about us, right? It's about being Jesus every day to the people we love. Grace. Hope. Kindness. Forgiveness and truth."

"Right."

"Call me if you want to go fishing." Dan pushed outside.

Coax them out. Keep trying. Sacrifice. Surrender.

Be Jesus every day.

Okay, Lord. He bought the pizzas and got back into the truck.

"Who were you talking to?" Signe asked.

"Just a fishing buddy," Ham said. "Ready? The cabin is just a few miles up the road."

"Yes." She leaned her head back and closed her eyes. "I think this place is magical."

That's what he was hoping for.

CHAPTER ELEVEN

O H, **SPECIAL OPERATOR HAM** knew *exactly* what he was
doing when he packed his family into his truck and drove
to the end of the earth to a gorgeous two-story home deep in the
woods of northern Minnesota.

What he called a *cabin* she termed a six-bedroom vacation
home with a home theater, gourmet kitchen, great room, an expansive deck that overlooked the lake, and the whisper of safety
and calm in the thick fir trees that surrounded the property.

When he'd said "off the grid," she'd expected an outhouse.
Gas lighting. A hand pump for water. A rickety futon in the family room.

He gave her the master bedroom, with the Jacuzzi tub and the
view overlooking the lake.

She noticed he dumped his things in the bedroom downstairs,
next to Aggie's. Interesting. And, he hadn't said under his breath
or otherwise—not even once—the word *husband*.

She tried not to let it get under her skin, irk her as he made
pizza, then played a game of Sorry! with Aggie, who giggled every
time he sent her piece back to home with an exaggerated "Sorry!"

The man was the perfect father. Sweet, engaging, and when he swung Aggie into his arms to whisk her off to her bed, singing "You Are My Sunshine," Signe physically hurt, her body a knot of confusion.

How could she leave this man?

No, how could she take Aggie from her father? They still weren't safe, with Martin on the loose, but Aggie was safe with Ham, Signe knew it to her soul.

Signe made hot cocoa and went out to the deck, taking a blanket with her as she sat on the swing, staring at the stars. The wind carried a nip and scurried broken leaves across the deck, but the blanket trapped the heat.

Ham slid the door closed. "Sorry that took so long. Aggie wanted me to read the rest of her book with her."

"Did Dakin find her prince?"

"Again, yes." Ham grinned, then knelt and turned on the burner to the fire table. Flames burst to life, flickering up through the clear rocks.

"Wow. You thought of everything."

"You have room under that blanket for me?"

Oh. Uh.

His smile fell. "Sorry. I just—"

"Yes." She scooted over on the swing and held up one side of the blanket.

"You sure, Sig? I don't want you to feel uncomfortable."

Husband. She nearly said it but bit it back.

Still. "I'm getting chilly. Yes or no?"

"Yes." He sat down and pulled the blanket over his lap, then stretched his arm out behind her. She didn't lean into him, but she could if she wanted to.

Maybe she wanted to.

She stared at the flames, her hands around the mug. "Hard to believe that three days ago, we were escaping a volcano."

"More like four, but yes." His voice was soft, and he rocked the swing slightly.

"I hope Gio and his mom are okay."

"I asked Lieutenant Hollybrook to check on them."

Of course he had.

"Look!" He pointed to the sky. "A shooting star."

The stars spilled into the wash of the Milky Way, so vivid she could reach out and touch them. "I don't see it."

"I guess it's just my wish, then."

"What did you wish for?"

"I can't tell you that."

"Remember that night on the rock when—"

"When I said that God names the stars?"

She looked at him.

"I was thinking the same thing, is all. That in my wildest dreams, I never thought . . ." He drew in a breath. "I never thought I'd see you again. But sometimes, before Chechnya, I'd be in country, on watch, or on a night mission and the sky would be particularly clear and I'd think about you."

He met her eyes.

Yes, she remembered that night, that sky. Because that was the night he'd kissed her for the first time.

He swallowed, looked away.

So maybe he was thinking about that kiss too.

"I didn't always live in the camp," Signe said. "Tsarnaev had an estate outside Tbilisi, in the republic of Georgia, and we went there sometimes when he was doing international business."

He'd tensed next to her, but she kept talking. "My room had a balcony off the second floor, and at night, I'd sit out there and look at the stars and . . ." She set her cocoa on the fire table. "Ham, you were never far from my thoughts."

He said nothing, his breaths rising and falling.

"Do you think Scarlett will be able to crack the code?"

"I hope so."

"Do you think we'll find Martin?"

"Yes," he said. "We will." He said it in his former warrior's voice. The voice that she'd heard in her head every time she thought about contacting him.

The one that said he would do anything for her. Even die.

That, she could not live with.

She gave in to the urge to lean her head against his shoulder. He smelled good—maybe the soap from his morning shower, but also the scent of Ham—strong, sure, right, big, safe. Her eyes were trained on the sky when she spotted a star unlatch, arc, sweep through the night in a blaze of quick light. "There!" She sat up, pointing. "Did you see it?"

He was looking at her, a heat in his eyes. "Nope."

Oh. His gaze found her core, lit it on fire. No, no . . .

"That's your wish this time," he said, his tone burrowing under her skin.

Her wish. Oh, she couldn't bear to voice it. Her eyes burned. *No!*

"Signe?"

"I wish I'd never walked away from you."

"You're not supposed to *say* your wish."

"Yeah, well . . ." She swallowed. "There it is."

"I wished the same thing."

She looked at him. "Perfect. Now neither of us will get our wish."

"Or maybe we can." He curled his hand behind her neck. "I love you, Signe. And I know you've got scars, but God brought you back to me, and I don't want to let you go."

Ham. She pressed her hand to his chest, right over his heart. "I mess everything up. I shouldn't have married you like I did—"

"But you did. We did—and now we have Aggie, and everything is different."

She couldn't look at him. "It's not. I'm still on the run. I'm still trouble—"

"And I'm still here, running to your rescue."

"And nearly getting yourself killed. Ham . . . I'm not worth it."

"What? Yes, you are." He turned her face to meet his. "You are worth it to me."

Shoot.

Then he lowered his mouth to hers, and she hadn't a bone in her body that wanted to resist, so she lifted her chin and met his kiss.

Soft, gentle, the kind of kiss he'd given her so long ago, on the rock overlooking the river. The kind of kiss that hinted at a deep fear that he'd somehow scare her away.

Not tonight.

If she left, it wouldn't be because she was scared of Ham.

His heart thundered under her hand, and she sank into him, deepening her kiss. It took only a moment, but he responded with enough *hooyah* that she recognized the younger version of him. His whiskers scraped her face and he tasted of the night, of safety and hope and all the things she'd remembered and wanted.

All the things she'd married and lost.

And now, found. *Ham*.

He deserved to have his wife back.

She curled her hands into his shirt, about to suggest more when he broke away, his breathing a little hard. "Sig, I'm not sure what's going on here, but—"

"Husband," she said quietly.

His mouth opened slightly. "Really? Are you sure? I mean, I want to be all in, but only if you—uh . . ." His gaze held hers. "I love you. But maybe we should wait until we've gotten to know each other again."

"I know you, Ham. And you know me and—"

"You married someone else."

She stilled. But maybe she deserved that. "The ceremony with Tsarnaev wasn't official—not really. I'm still . . ."

He raised an eyebrow.

Yours. She couldn't say the word.

No. She could never belong to a man again. Tsarnaev had made that term ugly and suffocating. "I'm still married, legally, only to you."

He considered her. "I can't give myself to you again, can't hold you in my arms and survive you walking out of my life. Last time . . ." He blew out a breath. "It wasn't pretty. I wasn't myself for a long, long time."

The power of his confession, the deep opening of his heart shook through her. She'd thought he'd forgotten about her. Moved on.

Found someone else to love.

Clearly not. Maybe he loved her too much, and that scared her to her bones. Because he just might pull her into his vortex and then . . .

She wouldn't survive leaving him, either.

It simply . . . she couldn't . . . Except, maybe she could. Just like she had with Pavel, she could put on a role. Give Ham what he wanted without sacrificing her heart.

She leaned in and kissed him again, put more ardor into it, ran her hand over his chest.

He caught her wrist, then leaned away from her, frowning. "Did you hear me?"

"Yeah, I heard you. But I'm here, now, and I know you want to be with me, right?"

His expression darkened. "Wait. Signe, do you think . . . are you doing this because you think I expect this?"

She stilled.

"No. Not like this. Not like . . . Signe, there's so much between us and—"

"Fine. No problem." She leaned away, smiled. "It's all good." Aw, and for a girl who knew how to push her feelings into a corner and ignore them, her chest was hurting, her eyes smarting.

She was a stupid, out-of-the-box mess.

"Signe—let's talk about this—"

A scream echoed down the hallway, out past the slightly open sliding door.

"Aggie!" Signe found her feet.

He was already at the door, sliding it open.

Signe was the first one through. She ran down the hall. Aggie was thrashing in her bed, screaming, her stuffed animals on the floor. Signe flicked on the light. "Aggie!" She sat down on her bed and grabbed her arms. "Aggie, wake up. Wake. Up."

Aggie's eyes opened and she stared first at Signe, then Ham, then back. "Mama!" She broke into tears.

Signe gathered her into her arms, pulling her tight, rocking her. "It was just a dream, honey. Just a bad dream."

"No, it wasn't. It wasn't!" Aggie pushed away from her. "I *saw* him!"

The sheer terror in her tone raised the hairs on Signe's neck. "Who?"

"Daa!"

Signe froze. "What? When?"

"Saw who?" Ham said from behind them.

"Oh, honey. No, Daa is not . . . he's never going to scare you again."

"Who. Is. Daa?"

Signe held up her hand to Ham and the tremor of fury in his voice.

"I saw him from the Ferris wheel!"

Signe stilled, turned to look at Ham. "What is she talking about?"

Ham wore a stricken expression. "What are you saying, Aggie? Who is Daa?"

"It's Tsarnaev. He made her call him—"

"Father." Ham's mouth made a tight, lethal line.

Signe nodded.

Ham crouched next to the bed. "When you say you saw him at the Ferris wheel—"

"That night. When I went to get cotton candy. There was a man there—he talked to you."

Ham was frowning.

"What is she talking about?" Signe said.

He shook his head. "I don't know."

"The man, Daddy! The man you were with."

"I don't remember—*oh*."

Signe raised her eyebrows. "What?"

Ham took Aggie's hand. "No, honey. That was just a stranger. He had kids riding on the Ferris wheel. He looked Middle Eastern, but we have a lot of immigrants here, sweetheart. They're not terrorists."

Her eyes were wide. "Are you sure?"

"*I'm* sure," Signe said. "Daa is . . . he is gone. And he's not coming back."

Aggie reached for her unicorn and Signe handed it to her. "Lie down, sweetie. Mama will be right here."

She got up. Ham rose too.

"Ham—"

"I get it," he said quietly, holding up his hand. "I'm going to make a call anyway."

"I thought we were off the grid."

He made a wry face. "I have a sat phone in my office."

Of course he did.

"See you in the morning," she said, and pressed her hand to his cheek. "I promise." And for some reason, the words took hold of her bones.

Shoot, because she had a bad feeling that she meant it.

■ ■ ■

Signe had left him.

No, she'd *lied*, then left him.

Ham stood barefoot on the front step of his cabin, staring at the empty dirt driveway where his truck sat just last night. *What?*

"Signe!" His shout, more agony than question, laced the air, the sky overcast and dour. *"Signe!"*

Wow, he was a fool. Because he'd actually believed her last night.

Believed because of the way she'd kissed him, at least the first time, and by the tenor of her voice, that they had a real chance at happily ever after. "Husband," she'd said.

Yeah, right.

Ham stepped back inside and shut the door, pressing his hand against it, trying to keep from unraveling.

He'd stayed up late talking to the coroner in Italy he'd met a few months ago, asking him to confirm DNA on the corpse that had been washed ashore. The one identified as Pavel Tsarnaev.

Aggie's dream had loosed a worry in his bones he couldn't shake.

Then, the fatigue of the past few days had caught up to him and, after checking on Signe and Aggie tucked together in the queen bed, he'd fallen hard into his own bed.

He woke to the honking of Canadian geese and the patter of rain on the window. And a deafening silence throughout the house.

When he checked Aggie's room, her stuffed animals were gone. All of them, including the moose, and even her bag was missing.

Signe's clothing bag was untouched, but then again, he didn't expect her to take anything with her. Nothing that he could use to identify her, probably.

That's when he went out to the empty driveway and called himself every kind of fool.

Now, he pulled on a T-shirt, a flannel shirt, and a pair of jeans, shoved his feet into boots, and headed toward the door.

She was probably headed for the Canadian border, less than an hour away.

Hopefully, she didn't have that large of a lead on him.

He opened the garage door and headed to his dirt bikes, still grimy after last year's outing with Jake. Pain shot up his wrist as he pulled one of the bikes off its kickstand, but it wasn't untenable.

Not like the pain in his chest.

He grabbed his helmet, shoved it on. Then wheeled the bike out of the garage, threw his leg over the seat, and kick-started it.

Mud spit up as he spun the bike around and headed to the road.

Please, Lord, let me catch her.

And even with the prayer, a terrible fury burned through him. How *could* she?

His wrist burned as he motored to the highway. He turned and rode on the shoulder, north.

The drizzle had died to simply a mist in the crisp air, the lake angry, edged with spittle as it crashed upon the rocky shore. The rain had turned the shoulder spongy, and he wrestled with the bike as he motored over ruts and weeds and mud, the burn in his wrist spiking through him.

A mile up the road, he'd worked himself into a full boil.

Really, Signe? After everything? Last night he'd even reached inside himself, bared his heart to her. *"I can't give myself to you again, can't hold you in my arms and survive you walking out of my life."*

What a pansy. He'd even alluded to how he'd been taken apart after he thought she'd died.

Not again. He'd survived by wadding those feelings into a hard ball. By not letting them escape into the open and wreak wounds and scars all over his life. He'd survived loss and rejection over and over again. His mother, his malicious stepmother, his family. His team in Afghanistan. His career with the SEALs.

He could survive this.

The bike hit a rut, a culvert running under the road. The wheel jerked, turning toward his weak wrist.

He didn't have the strength to right it.

The bike turned over and Ham went flying. He had the presence of mind to duck and roll, and he landed, bruised and sore, in a soft puddle of marshland.

As mud seeped into his clothing, Ham stared at the gray sky and just tried to breathe.

And because he was alone, because he was lying in a ditch on the side of the road, because somehow, he hadn't actually escaped the dark, cold cellar, he let out a shout.

More of a scream, but it rent the sky, fracturing the morning.

A swell of sparrows lifted from nearby, startled.

Yeah, well . . .

Not far away, a car crunched dirt as it pulled to the side.

Perfect. Now he'd have company in his misery.

The door shut and Ham rolled over, groaning, trying to push to his feet.

"How hurt are you?" Pastor Dan Matthews was jogging toward him, wearing a suit, dress shoes, and a jacket. "Ham?"

Ham had made it to his knees and now realized he'd probably banged his shoulder pretty good. "Yeah." He sat back on his haunches and unsnapped his helmet strap, worked off the helmet, and let it fall into the grass.

"Your front wheel looks bent," Dan said as he crouched next to Ham.

"I hit the culvert. Couldn't correct." He held up his casted wrist.

Dan frowned. "What's going on?"

Ham closed his eyes. Shook his head.

"I'm on my way to services in Portage, but I have a few minutes to give you a lift home."

Ham looked at the man. In his midforties, Dan had a quiet, no-nonsense preaching style. Usually got right to the bones of the problem.

So, "My wife left me. Again."

Dan didn't even blink. Just a quiet pursing of his lips. "I'm sorry."

"It's not really a surprise." Ham grabbed his helmet and forced himself to his feet. "I'm just angry that I didn't see it coming. Again. That I talked myself into believing that this time would be different." He walked over to the bike. The front tire was bent, the fender broken.

So much for stopping Signe at the border.

Dan helped him haul up the bike.

"Don't get your suit dirty," Ham said.

"The suit isn't sacred, Ham. But your soul is." Dan pushed the bike with him from the ditch.

"My soul isn't in any danger."

"Isn't it?" Dan wheeled the bike with him to his F-150. "You might be calm on the outside, but I see a storm raging inside. Let's talk about *again*. My wife left me *again*."

Ham held the bike while Dan pulled down the gate. "I don't even know where to start."

"At the beginning?"

Ham gave a harrumph. Moved to lift the bike into place.

"I got this, Ham," Dan said and lifted the front of the bike onto the bed.

Right. Ham stepped back and let Dan lift the back tire onto the bed, although he grabbed the tire with his good hand. Hid a wince as he lifted.

Yeah, maybe he'd done some real damage to his shoulder. Felt okay, though, to hurt on the outside—to match the agony inside.

"We got married on a whim, about fifteen years ago. It was a rash decision, based on impulse."

"You loved her." Dan got the bike into the back, then climbed up to the bed.

"We were childhood friends, and it grew from there. I'm not sure when I started loving her."

"And you never stopped."

Unfortunately. "Even when she left me to . . . work overseas."

Dan set the bike on its side.

"I found her years later, and we . . . well, that's when Aggie was conceived."

Dan smacked the dirt off his hands. Looked at him, no judgment in his eyes. "And?"

"The short of it was that she left me again. She had her reasons, but I spent the last ten years thinking she was dead. And I didn't have a clue about Aggie."

"Wow."

"I only found out the truth recently and I went to . . . get her. I thought we had a chance. I mean, she's been through a lot, but we're still married—although—" He stepped back as Dan jumped off the bed. Ham noticed his dress shoes were caked with mud.

"Although?"

"She married someone else in the meantime. Someone bad."

Dan raised an eyebrow.

"He's dead, so . . . but . . . I don't know. She has scars, that's for sure, but last night . . ." He looked away.

"Last night?"

"Whatever. She said she would be here this morning, and she's not and I think she's headed to the border. With Aggie."

"Huh."

"I'm just tired of the lies."

"And angry."

"Of course."

"And hurt, and you have every right to be." Dan pulled out a handkerchief, handed it to Ham. "You're bleeding." He indicated a place on Ham's chin.

Ham pressed his fingers to the wound and found a nick where his chin strap had been. "It's nothing." But he pressed the handkerchief to it.

Dan closed the tailgate. "In Luke 22, Jesus tells Simon Peter that Satan asked to sift him as wheat. And Jesus says that he is praying for him, that he would not fail. It sounds like you're being sifted, Ham. The enemy wants to win this one. Don't let him."

Ham shook his head. "I don't know how to win this."

"I know. Right now, the hurt, the offense feels overwhelming."

Ham's jaw tightened, but he could hardly breathe.

"Try this. When you look at your wife, I want you to picture Jesus standing over her. He's saying, *Ham, every piece of anger and fury you hurtle at her, you are hitting me. Because I've already paid for her sins. And even if she doesn't accept that forgiveness, you know it's true.*"

"That's not fair."

"But it's true, right?"

"Are you going to give me a ride home?"

"Get in."

Ham climbed in the passenger side. Dan got in behind the wheel. "You'll have to point me in the right direction."

"Up the road a mile or so. First right."

Dan pulled onto the road. "Ham, nothing is impossible with God."

"It feels impossible."

"I hear that. But believe it or not, God has a plan."

"I wish I knew it." His shoulder was really starting to ache.

"Do you? Because maybe it's going to get worse before it gets better. And if we knew the big picture, I'll bet we'd say, no thanks."

Maybe.

"The answer isn't in knowing the plan, but trusting God, daily, to give you direction. To help you sacrifice your own desires, and to love."

"What if that isn't enough?"

"It *is* enough. Because what you're not seeing is that it's not just about your marriage or your wife. It's about you. It's about getting to the heart of your relationship with Jesus. You're a good man, Ham. But God doesn't want just a good man. He wants a man who is his. This is why Jesus allowed Satan to sift Simon Peter. Because when Peter denied Christ, he came to the end of himself and truly became a new man. God's man. And that's who you need to be to get through this." Dan turned on his blinker. "This one?"

Ham nodded.

Dan slowed the truck. "Ham, when you were a SEAL, you walked around with a target on your back. You were always aware that you could be attacked. So, you were on the defensive— sometimes even on the offensive, right?"

"And?"

"You're still at war, buddy. If you're a Christian, then you have a big target on your heart. Satan is a very real enemy who wants to take you out. He wants to destroy your testimony and take out the power of God in your life. Undermine your faith. And he does it by making you doubt God's love. By distracting you from the person God says you are and the future he has for you. The enemy wants you to rush ahead and try to fix your problems on your own, and then say, 'See, God doesn't care.'

"But God calls you to be a warrior. To train, to wait for his command. And that's why you have to lean hard into him. Fill your mind with prayer, with Scripture, with truth. Let God be to you all he says he is—strength, peace, grace, love, . . . joy."

He turned onto the dirt road to Ham's place.

"Second left," Ham said.

"You need to hunker down into what you know, Ham. God is good. God is love. And God's timing is always perfect."

He slowed as he pulled into Ham's driveway.

Ham stilled.

The Silverado sat in the driveway.

Signe was pulling Aggie's duffel bag from the back end. It was stuffed with her animals. She handed the bag to Aggie, then grabbed a bag of groceries.

Dan stopped the truck. Looked over at Ham.

"Grace and forgiveness don't belong to you, Ham. They're the weapons of heaven given to you by your Savior to destroy the darkness in their lives. To give them hope. To glimpse their real Savior, Jesus."

Signe turned, frowned, then lifted a hand in greeting right before she grabbed another bag from the back.

Ham couldn't breathe.

"No power of Satan can pluck you from the hand of God. Stand in his power, Ham, and you will have everything you need. The time for mourning is over." He looked at Signe heading now into the house. "The time for joy is at hand. And get that shoulder looked at, okay?"

Ham nodded. "Thanks."

"Let's get your bike unloaded."

Signe had returned from the house by the time Dan had the bike in the driveway. "What happened?" She looked at Ham. "I thought you were still sleeping. I went to town for groceries. And Aggie had to bring the whole farm with her. No more carnivals, okay?"

He just stood there, unable to move.

She took a step toward him. "Are you okay? You're bleeding."

Ham caught her wrist softly just before she touched him. "I'm fine."

She frowned. Ham released his hold.

"Warrior," Dan said quietly.

Right.

"Call me if you need a fishing trip." Dan pulled out of the driveway.

Signe stared at Ham. She was wearing a flannel shirt and leggings, her boots, her hair held back in two pigtails. Innocent. Pretty.

He left the bike there and headed for the house.

"Ham?" Signe followed him. "What's going on?"

He ground his jaw. Shook his head.

"Did you take the bike out?"

He rounded on her, his breathing fast, hard. "Yes. Okay? *Yes.* I went looking for you!"

"Why? I just went to the store—"

"I didn't know that." He knew he should be schooling his voice, but it all simply spilled out, uncensored. "I thought you left me. *Again.*" He held up his hands. "I know you're standing here right now, but I can't live like this, Sig. I can't—" He blew out a breath. Shook his head. "I can't wonder every time you leave the house if you're coming back to me. I can't wonder if someday I'm going to come home and find you gone." His throat tightened. "I can't—"

"End up in the cellar again, wondering what you did to be rejected."

He stared at her. Then, quietly, nodded.

She wrapped her arms around her waist. "And I can't bear the idea that I'll do something that will cause your death."

The wind stirred around them, leaves skittering across the dirt.

"I'm not Caesar."

"It was my fault. He should have been secured."

"It was a car accident."

Her eyes blazed. "I'd been drinking."

"I don't believe you."

"You weren't there! You left and I was alone—"

"Because I was at military school! I didn't *choose* that."

"I know, but . . ." She shook her head. "After you left, I made some bad decisions, Ham. And I was too ashamed to tell you about them." She looked away. "And then it happened all over again, in Chechnya. Only this time it was you who was going to get killed."

"What?"

Her eyes were hard. "I saw you in Chechnya that day, when you came after me."

He just blinked at her.

"Tsarnaev and I were out of the bunker, and you and your men were hunkered down, but Tsarnaev had a sniper on you. And I begged him to let you live."

"You did *what*?" He shook his head. "Signe—"

"I told him I'd go with him peacefully if he'd let you live."

He turned away from her. "No. No, this can't be my fault—"

"What? No, Ham—it's *my* fault for going with him, but . . . don't you see? I've always brought trouble into the lives of people I love, and I can't—"

"No." Ham rounded on her, his breaths coming in hard. "You've always brought comfort into the lives of people you love. Aggie. And your grandmother, who was grieving the loss of her daughter so hard she couldn't see the gift she had in you. And me. You were comfort to me, Sig. Just like I was safety to you."

Her jaw tightened.

"Are you going to leave me?" He said it quietly, met her eyes, tried to keep his voice from shaking.

She took a breath. "I don't know what this looks like for us. What normal is."

"We can make our own normal."

She stepped up to him. "Ham, I do know what I've been given. And my daughter deserves a safe life with her father."

"And you?"

She bit her lip. "Promise you won't die because of me?"

He frowned, shook his head.

"Because you're looking a lot banged up here, Batman." She touched his chin.

"I think I might have broken my shoulder," he said, his gaze holding hers.

She swallowed, forced a smile. But it went right to his heart, lighting it afire.

"I guess I'd better stick around, then. Someone needs to take you to the hospital and feed you baloney sandwiches."

He closed his eyes, fighting the burn in them. *Lord, I don't know—*

She touched his face, bringing his gaze to hers. "This war isn't over. But like you said, we're together now, right?" Then she rose up on her toes and kissed him. Nothing ardent or deeply passionate, but something solid and true and . . .

When he opened his eyes, she was still there, smiling at him.

They were together now. And he intended to keep them that way.

The door opened. Aggie stood holding her dolphin, her hair

in long braids. She held a donut in wrapped paper, wore sugar around her mouth. "Want a donut?"

"We stopped at a little shop called World's Best Donuts. I had to see if they were telling the truth," Signe said.

"Research," he said quietly.

"Daddy, where were you?" Aggie said. "I looked for you and you were gone."

"I'm sorry, honey," he said, looking at Signe, then his daughter. "But I promise, I'm not going anywhere."

CHAPTER TWELVE

THIS IS ABOUT the most extreme case of avoidance I've ever seen, and I'm not even a psychologist!"

The voice came from below Jenny, at the bottom of the climbing wall where her best friend, Aria, was belaying her. A harness hugged Aria's lower body, webbing attached to a clip on the floor. She stared up at Jenny, her voice having echoed throughout the entire massive climbing center at the Edina GoSports facility.

Good thing it was after nine and Aria needed a little de-stressing after a long surgery. She'd been easy prey for Jenny's restless energy.

She just had to shake off her frustration, and nothing helped her work a problem like a 5.12 route. Even if it did only drop to a spongy floor some sixty feet below.

The entire center resembled a gigantic cave, with vertical and overhang walls for both climbing and rappelling. Beyond the glass windows were two stories of exercise equipment, from treadmills and ellipticals to rowing machines and cycles. In the next room, a second-story track rounded a massive Olympic-sized pool, deep enough for scuba lessons on the far end.

The Minnetonka location had a cold room for ice climbing, but tonight, she needed the heat to match her mood.

"Do you want to talk about it?"

"No!" Jenny said as she reached for a jug just above her left fingers. This particular route included an overhang, one that she had yet to nail. She'd spent the past two weeks trying to figure it out. Figuring out her hand holds, her movements, her weight distribution, trying to figure out why Orion had just stared at her when she'd bared her heart to him.

"I had an abortion."

Those words had emerged from her mouth, right? Because she had a very vivid memory of the acid pooling in her gut a moment before she admitted it.

That and declaring her love for him, just in case they died.

Both times he'd ignored her.

Or just . . . didn't care?

"Just so we're clear, I'm not going to go climb Everest with you just because you're in denial," Aria said.

Jenny caught her fingertips on the jug and worked her grip in, then moved her foot to an indentation and twisted to press up. "I'm not in denial. I'm just moving forward." She shoved her right hand in a crack near the overhang.

"You haven't talked to Orion since you got back from Italy two weeks ago. This is hardly moving forward."

Jenny clipped her line into a carabiner hooked into the wall. "He has a cell phone. He can call me." She found another handhold and pressed out, smearing up the wall before her left foot found a lip.

"Jenny. Call him. It'll be easier than trying to climb this stupid wall every night."

Jenny traded hands in the crack, then twisted her hips in and reached for another jug. Her right foot found the top of an undercling, and she pinched it with her left. "Listen. I bared my soul to him and the guy just looked at me—"

"You were being attacked!"

Jenny wiped her forehead with her arm. "I know. But I used all my emotional energy saying it the first time. I'm not saying it again." Her arms shook, sweat dripping between her shoulder blades. She reached up for a slope with her left hand and cupped her hand over it. Her hand was slick, though, slipping fast.

"Why not?"

Jenny looked down at her. "Really?"

Aria's mouth closed. "It's just . . ."

"If you tell me to give him a chance, I'm going to—"

"What? I have your life in my hands," Aria said, grinning.

Jenny stuck out her tongue at her.

"I just think you were both under a lot of stress and—be careful!"

"I got this!"

"You're almost there!"

She moved her left foot onto the top of an undercling and pivoted to the outside edge, moving her center of gravity in.

Oh, her entire body had started to shake.

"You can do it!" Aria shouted.

Yes. She needed a win today, something to make her stop thinking about whether Orion wasn't calling her because, well, because she'd been right all along.

He wanted a wife who didn't come with her kind of scars.

Her kind of sins.

A wife who could give him a family.

She shoved her right finger into a pocket to steady herself, then moved her right foot out to a slope and used the dynamic energy to grab a jug with her left hand and walk up the wall, pressing hard for the overhanging ledge above.

Really, she didn't blame him. He wasn't the first guy who'd walked away from her. And he probably wouldn't be the last.

No, he would most definitely be the last.

Her right hand closed over the skinny ledge and she wrapped her thumb around her fingers for extra support.

There, see, she—

Her foot slipped.

She careened off the rock, swinging in midair.

Aria caught her. "I saw that coming."

Jenny looked down at her. "I almost had it."

"Yeah, you did," Aria said as she lowered Jenny to the mat. "You okay?"

"Are you?"

Aria wore her dark hair back, no makeup, her brown eyes bright despite a full day at work. Jenny blamed Jake for her best friend's constant happiness. "Yeah. But I promised to meet Jake tonight, so I don't have time for another go."

"Really?"

"He taught a scuba diving class tonight. I haven't seen him all week." She worked off her harness. "I really think you should talk to Orion."

Jenny grabbed a towel, wiping her face. "That's the last thing I'm going to do."

"Jenny—"

"Listen, I get it. I took the chance that he'd walk away from me when I told him, and now I just have to . . ." She blew out a breath, refused to let the ache pool in her chest. "I just have to live with it. I'll be fine."

She made to move past her, but Aria caught her arm. "But he won't."

Jenny stilled. "What?"

"He's not okay, Jenny. According to Jake, he really hurt his knee in the assault, and he's been working out for two weeks trying to get himself put back together."

Jenny stared at her.

"Could it be that maybe there's something going on inside his head that isn't about your conversation and might just be about the fact that he didn't protect you?"

Jenny could barely form the words. "You think Orion is staying away from me because he thinks he should have *protected* me?"

"Heart doctor," Aria said quietly.

"Huh," Jenny said. She picked up her water bottle and headed toward the door.

Scarlett stood at the glass on the other side. She wore a pair of yoga pants, a workout jacket, and running shoes. Her hair was wet.

Jenny opened the door. "I didn't know you worked out here."

"Yeah. I just started," Scarlett said. "North got me fixed up with a membership. I came to swim. But I saw you two climbing. Good job. I'm not much of a climber, but that looked hard."

"It is," Aria said. "You headed home?"

"Actually, no. I need to talk to Ham, but I don't know how to get ahold of him. I've called a couple times, but his phone goes to voicemail."

"He's up north, at his cabin," said Jenny. "I think it's off the grid."

"Jake says he has a sat phone," Aria said. "He can probably get you the number. Why?"

Scarlett made a face.

"We know about the NOC list, Scarlett," Jenny said. "And that you were working on decrypting it."

"That's the thing. I gave it to a hacker friend of mine who worked on it."

"And?"

"I think Ham's in danger."

Jenny looked at Aria. Back to Scarlett. "What do you mean?"

"That woman who had the list—"

"Signe? His wife?"

"Yeah. His wife." Scarlett shook her head. "She's lying. And not just about Jackson. Signe Jones is a terrorist, and Ham is in serious trouble."

■ ■ ■

"Come at me again." Orion's voice emerged on a hard breath. Sweat dripped down his face, his back. He took a step back, shook the acid out of his arms, facing North, breathing hard.

"Seriously, Ry. You got this—"

"Again!" Orion's voice nearly thundered through the MMA arena of the downtown GoSports location. While a pair of boxers worked on one of the center rings, North and Orion grappled on one of the massive mats. Night poured through the tall windows that surrounded the building. The entire place contained a Gold's Gym vibe, with a loud weight-lifting room, a sauna, and plenty of hanging bags.

Orion preferred a real human being coming at him. Someone he could grapple with, someone he could fight.

Someone he could pretend was an angry Russian thug.

North wore protective gear—a padded head wrap, shin guards, body protection. Orion too wore gear, especially since his nose still hurt. He'd wrapped his knee and padded his hands, but mostly he wanted to be free to move.

He had to figure out how they'd taken him down so fast, and how to never, ever let it happen again.

He couldn't get Jenny's scream out of his head.

"Ready?" North asked.

"Just—"

North rushed him, and Orion sidestepped him, pivoted, and slammed his fist into his ear as the man went by. Shot his knee into his leg, then swept it.

North hit the mat. Stared up at Ry. "I think you got this."

Orion danced back. "Again."

North got up. Unclipped his head wrap and dropped it on the mat. "Nope. I'm tappin' out. You're a lean, mean, fightin' machine, and I need a burger."

Orion picked up his water bottle and squirted water into his mouth. His knee hurt tonight. But he needed a little hurt in his life to remind him of his stupidity. He'd been off his guard, a little lovesick, thinking way too much about Jenny and her arms around him as he'd driven them through the city on that Vespa. Thinking about their future and whatever it was that still stood between them.

Then, *Bam!* He'd been flattened and—

"Shake it off, Starr. You're okay. Everybody lived." North tossed a towel at him.

Orion looked at him. North had a quiet, almost lethally cool manner about him. He never got rattled. Not even in Afghanistan with his buddies dying around him.

If it hadn't been for North, Orion might not have made it home, so he respected the guy. But it was still a little unfair that North didn't walk around with any demons.

North peeled off the rest of his gear. "Is this about Jenny?"

Orion was unwrapping his hands. "It's about me being off my game. Letting a couple Russians jump me. I know better. I trained better."

"You're not a one-man army," North said.

"What you mean is that I'm not a SEAL."

North grinned. "Yep."

Orion threw one of his gloves at him, and North ducked, but he grabbed his water bottle and headed toward the locker room.

Jerk. Especially since the PJs went through Hell Week and spec ops training too.

But Orion was trained to save people under fire. Not to start the battle. Still, he should be able to take down a couple untrained street fighters from Moscow. Sheesh.

Orion followed North into the locker room. North had already stripped down to a towel and was heading to the sauna. Orion joined him.

They sat in the heat for a while. Then, as the steam rose, "Jenny had to negotiate. She traded our lives for the kid's and his mom's freedom. But she was ready to *die*—"

"That's not on you."

Orion leaned back on the cedar bench, let the sweat drip down his face. "Who else am I supposed to blame?"

"Royal climbed back inside your head, didn't he?"

Orion lifted a shoulder.

"I knew it. Your knee went out on you, and it only brought back the fiasco with Royal and Logan on the mountain."

Orion drew in a breath of hot air. "We should have never left them behind."

"We couldn't get to them, man. Don't you think I still have nightmares about leaving them?"

Orion looked at him, met North's dark eyes. Huh. So maybe North did have a few chinks in his cool Viking armor. Still, "You went in after them. I sat in a German hospital and tried to walk again."

North hung a towel over his head. "You gotta make peace with it, Ry."

"Royal's still not home, is he?"

North leaned forward, his arms on his knees, head down. "I guess not."

A beat. Then, because North wasn't looking at him, "I thought I made peace with it. Or at least learned to live with it. I even convinced myself that by proposing, I was moving on." Orion scrubbed his hands down his slick face. "But the truth is, I'm not at peace. Not until I find him."

"And then?"

"I don't know. I keep hearing her scream, you know? And I'm just sitting there, trussed up like a pig, unable to move, listening for you guys to save us. It sits in my gut every night. I haven't been able to face Jenny."

"You think she blames you?"

"I would."

North nodded, pulled off the towel, and leaned back.

"She was talking with Martin—I can't wait until we find him—and I told her to wait for my signal and all the while I was thinking, *What if one of the Russians comes after her?* My stupid knee was twisted, and I was working my hands loose, but I knew I couldn't stop them. And it made me crazy. If you guys hadn't showed up—"

"But we did."

Orion shook his head. "I nearly lost her, now, twice, because I couldn't take care of myself. And there's no guarantee that my knee isn't going to crap out on me again." He got up. "I'm an invalid. I wouldn't want me either."

North made a noise of disagreement, but Orion ignored him and pushed out of the sauna, headed toward the showers. Yes, he probably owed Jenny an explanation. But the last thing he wanted was her pity. He made himself a little sick thinking about the conversation. She'd tell him she loved him, that it was okay, that they made it and that was the important thing. And maybe it was.

He still couldn't look at himself in the mirror. Or dial her number.

He finished the shower, wrapped his knee, and dressed. "I'm headed home. Thanks, North."

"Anytime, bro," North said as he packed his gear.

Orion walked out into the cool night. Overhead, the stars hung bright in the cloudless sky. The wind lifted the collar of his jacket.

Let it go.

Not hardly. Because North was right. Royal had climbed into his brain like a specter, and Jenny's screams only kept it alive.

If he wanted freedom, he needed to find Royal. Then maybe he and Jenny had a chance.

If she could forgive him for not protecting her.

Orion got in his Renegade, threw his workout bag on the passenger seat, and headed to the three-bedroom house he shared with Jake. The guy had purchased it only a couple months ago, on his sister's recommendation, but it sat in a quaint St. Louis Park community, right across from a park, and Orion figured Jake had Aria on the brain when he'd put in his offer.

Jake pretty much always had Aria on his brain.

Orion lived in the basement bedroom, with Jake in the finished attic bedroom. So far, neither of them had killed the other.

But Orion had been thinking about houses too, before the trip to Italy.

Now he was just thinking about ice for his knee and maybe a bowl of cereal.

He pulled up beside Jake's Subaru in the alley garage. So, back from his date with Aria.

The back light was on over the deck and Orion came in the back entrance. Set his bag on the floor.

Heard voices and froze.

Oh no.

He closed the door just as Jake came around the corner. "Hey. Took you long enough. We gotta talk to you."

We? His gut tightened as he walked into the front room.

Jenny sat on Jake's sofa, next to Scarlett, peering into a computer open on the coffee table.

When she looked up, she wore the same stripped, panicked look he was probably giving out. "Hi."

"Hi." His throat tightened. *I'm sorry I didn't call*—the words lodged in his throat.

Thankfully, Scarlett spoke up. "We need to contact Ham."

Oh. Orion looked at Jake, who was standing near the fireplace, his arms folded. Aria came out of the kitchen, holding a glass of water.

"Hey, Ry."

He nodded, then turned to Scarlett. "He's still up north, at his cabin. But he has a sat phone. We can call him if we have to. But he's trying to reconnect with his family—"

"We think he's in danger," Jenny said.

Orion frowned. "Why?"

Scarlett scooted back and turned the computer around to face him. "This is the NOC list."

She could have punched him with less effect, until—

"And Signe is not on it."

"Are you sure?" Orion sat on a nearby chair and pulled the computer toward him. "Did you check aliases? She came into the country as Stephi Jones."

Scarlett nodded. "Ford's sister, Ruby Jane, is a CIA analyst. She was able to get a list of all Signe's known aliases. We ran it through the database. And yeah, we got a hit, but not on this list."

Quiet. Orion looked up at her. Then Jenny, Jake, and back. "What?"

"She's on the disavowed list," Jake said quietly. "The CIA issued a burn notice on her over a year ago."

"Basically, it means to disregard all intelligence gathered by her," Scarlett said. "Because she's untrustworthy."

"Then how did she get through passport control?"

Scarlett raised a shoulder. "Maybe they saw Ham's name, and hers matched, so it didn't raise any flags."

"Which means she used Ham to get into the country," Jake said, his expression grim.

"And what about the story about Jackson?" Orion asked.

"There's no decryption signature package in the coding, so that was a lie, according to my hacker source," Scarlett said. "Ruby Jane said that they were sending someone to take her into custody."

"Ham is going to lose it," Orion said quietly. "We need to warn him."

"And what if she runs?" Aria asked. "Who knows what her plan is, and if she takes off, we'll never know."

"You really think she's a terrorist?" Jake said. "Ham seems to trust her."

"Ham wants very desperately for his family to be put back together," Jenny said quietly. "That can cause you to make bad decisions. Overlook truths."

Orion looked at her, but she wouldn't meet his eyes.

"She did run, in Italy," Orion said. "What if Martin was telling the truth?"

Jenny shook her head. "I don't believe it. There was something about him that just . . . it didn't feel right." Now she met Orion's gaze. "Didn't you sense that?"

He had nothing except a siren of panic resounding in his head. "Jenny, the truth is, I wasn't really paying attention to him. I was just thinking about how we were going to survive."

She just looked at him. "Really?"

"It's all a big haze to me. I do remember you offering to let him kill us, though."

And that shut down the room. Jenny's mouth tightened. Then, "Truth is, in the back of my mind, I thought . . ." She lifted a shoulder. "I guess I thought you'd save us. You were acting so weird, though, I couldn't be sure . . ."

He stared at her. Swallowed. And he *knew* it. He'd failed her.

"It could be that this Martin guy thought you were in league with her," Scarlett said.

That broke the spell. Jenny turned to Scarlett. "What are you going to do with the list?"

"Ruby Jane works for Isaac White, on a special task force, and she's already handed it over. He's sending someone here, right now, to meet us."

"And they want us to lead them to her," Jake said. He folded his arms. "I don't like it."

Orion looked at Jenny. "What do you think we should do?"

"I'm not sure we have a choice. If Signe has been using Ham to get into the country, then she's betrayed all of us, especially him."

Orion nodded. "We need to get there first. At least Jake and I do. And we'll keep her there until you guys show up."

"I'll give you directions, Scarlett, but try to delay them," Jake said. "We need to give Ham time to figure this out."

"Let's hold on to the hope that she hasn't played us all," Jenny said.

Orion got up, but Jenny had also found her feet. "Ry?"

He looked at her. Jake and Aria went into the other room. Scarlett was typing.

"Yeah?" Wow, she was pretty. Always, but not having seen her for two weeks took a slice out of him. Sometimes he couldn't breathe around her. Now, she wore a pair of loose jeans and a white fleece jacket, her blonde hair back, her blue eyes shiny.

I'm sorry. The words filled his chest. *I'm sorry I didn't protect you—*

"Stay safe. She could be dangerous." She swallowed, and it

seemed her eyes glazed. Probably thinking of the way he'd been practically helpless on the floor.

"I love you. You are my hero, now and forever." The words whispered in the back of his head, like a memory, but he shook them away. Wishful thinking.

He nodded and gave her a bland smile. "Don't worry, Jenny, I got this. Just, please, stay out of the way, okay?" He managed not to wince as he walked down the stairs to retrieve his gear.

By the time he emerged, packed and ready to go, she was gone.

■ ■ ■

For the first time in two weeks—maybe longer—Signe woke up without the nightmares. Without Tsarnaev and Jackson chasing her through shadowed, cobbled streets or down narrow alleyways. Without the quickening of her heartbeat as she opened her eyes, trying to get a footing on her surroundings.

Today she woke up safe. With the glorious sunshine whispering through the gauzy curtains and across the carpet of Ham's master bedroom suite. With the geese honking as they flew overhead and the smell of bacon—

What?

That's when she noticed Ham's absence in the bed beside her. They hadn't quite made their way back to intimacy, Ham holding fast to his idea that they needed to know each other better. But he'd burst into her room one night after she'd screamed in her sleep, and she'd convinced him to stay.

She'd fallen asleep with his arms around her, and she hadn't slept so soundly in years.

So yes, she'd give him time. She was just happy hearing the sound of his breathing every night.

And the timbre of his voice, singing hymns in the morning, as he made breakfast.

Now, she could hear his voice downstairs, even if she couldn't make out the words, and Signe guessed he was talking with Aggie, probably telling her one of his many childhood stories, censored and embellished for her ears.

Your mom had this dog named Caesar . . .

She lay there, watching the overhead fan spin. So, this was what happily-ever-after felt like. No pounding headache, no hyperventilation, no sense of dread in her gut. Just glorious golden skies and the man she loved—and oh, how she loved Hamilton Jones—making her breakfast.

Bacon. Yes. She'd started eating it again this week, and maybe that's what had broken her free. The realization that Tsarnaev no longer had a hold on her.

She wasn't leaving. She'd made that decision on the doorstep, seeing Ham's broken expression, hearing his heart.

She believed him when he said he'd keep her safe. When he said that they could create their own version of normal.

They'd spent the past two weeks doing just that—hiking, playing games with Aggie, making meals together. Ham had even taken them fishing, and Aggie had spotted a real moose in the reeds. They'd watched movies in his basement theater, drank hot cocoa by the fire, roasted marshmallows on the beach, and listened to the waves crash upon the shoreline.

Somehow, the trauma of the past decade had started to recede, wash away with the tide, leaving behind only the skeleton of her regrets. But even those were beginning to crumble.

This was her future. Her new life.

The one she'd been too afraid, really, to believe in.

The smell finally beckoned her out of bed, and she threw on a pair of yoga pants and a sweatshirt, pulling her hair up in a messy bun.

She was exiting the bedroom, on her way down the stairs, when

Ham's voice rose, something lethal and dark in it. "Over my dead body."

Then the stairs moaned under her foot and the conversational hum in the kitchen stopped.

She peeked over the railing, expecting—or hoping, maybe—to see Aggie swirling her pancakes through syrup.

Her breath caught.

Orion and Jake sat at the kitchen table, drinking coffee. A plate of bacon sat in the center of the table, and both had messy egg plates, already finished with their breakfast.

They looked up at her, something of a stricken look on their faces.

Then they looked at Ham.

He was leaning against the peninsula countertop, his arms folded over his chest, wearing such a wretched expression it looked like someone had died.

Maybe—and in the back of her brain, something was clicking, but it didn't form before she asked, "Did you find him?" She came down the stairs. "Did you find Martin?"

Except, it occurred to her just as she hit the landing, that Ham would be packing, anxious to interrogate the man—so, no. Something *else* . . . "What's going on?"

He looked back at Orion. "I don't believe it."

"Ham," Jake said, something of warning in his tone, but it didn't stop Ham from turning to her.

"You're not on the NOC list."

She cocked her head. "What?"

"They decrypted the NOC list. You aren't on it."

"Oh." Huh. She slid onto the bench across from Jake and Orion. Reached for a piece of bacon. "I guess that's why Tsarnaev didn't kill me."

Jake just blinked at her. Orion's mouth opened, closed.

"And you guys came all the way up here to tell us that?" She grabbed a napkin. Looked at Ham, frowned. "Is your sat phone not working?"

"It's working. It's just . . . there's more, Sig."

It was the way he didn't move, the way he was looking at her, no *through* her, that made her set down her napkin, smooth it on the table. "What?"

"You're on the disavowed list," Jake said quietly.

The words sifted through her. Silence.

"Scarlett has connections with a CIA insider—"

"I told you that you can't trust the CIA!" She didn't mean to raise her voice, but this—this moment—was exactly why she should have run.

Probably without Aggie.

"She's working separately, on a special task force for Isaac White," Jake said.

Signe's mouth opened, closed. "Ah, I see. And you came up here to tell Ham not to trust me. That I was lying."

They said nothing. Jake looked away.

Orion, however, stared at her, his jaw hard.

Wait. No. "You came here to *protect* Ham. I would never—"

"Calm down, Sig. They came here to warn me, so *we* could think up a plan."

She got up. "Did the CIA send people? Are they on their way?"

Ham nodded. "But it doesn't matter. I'm not going to let them take you."

"Seriously. Ham. What are you going to do? Form a perimeter and have a standoff?"

His mouth tightened.

Oh boy. And this was worse. A standoff with her daughter and her husband—yes, *husband*—caught in the crossfire. "Why don't I just go? The border is only an hour away—"

"No!" Ham came across the room, and she startled at his burst of emotion. "You're not leaving."

She recoiled, and because his tone had sheared off her protective layer—actually, hardly any of it remained, anyway—tears raked her eyes.

Get. Ahold. Of. Yourself.

She was tougher than this. *Compartmentalize. Think.*

"You're right." She held up her hands, backed away from him. "If I run, then they'll take you and Aggie in and . . . I can't have her terrorized that way."

Ham caught her arm. "Stop. It's going to be okay—"

"In what world?" She shook out of his grip. "I knew this would happen. Jackson did this—she disavowed me. She's behind this whole thing! Did you not see her name in the decryption key?"

"There was no key," Orion said quietly.

"No . . . no . . . that's not . . . I *know* there's a key."

"How?" Jake asked.

She looked at Jake. Back to Ham. "Because when I got the list, the first thing I did was contact my former handler, someone I trusted. Sophia Randall. I told her about the list, and Jackson, and my fear that there was a rogue group inside the CIA. She told me to hang on to the drive because all NOC lists come with a key."

"Not this one," Jake said.

She swallowed. "What if this one was a decoy?"

Silence.

"Why would Jackson give Tsarnaev a decoy?" Orion said.

"Maybe he knew it was false," Jake said. "What if it's not about the list, but about you. Maybe they were counting on you coming to America with it."

"Maybe you have something they want," Ham said quietly.

She looked at Ham. "What? How would . . . I'm nobody."

Ham's mouth tightened. "Not to me."

"What if this is about you, Ham?" Orion said. "White *did* send you to get her."

Ham stared at him for a beat. Then, "No. Isaac sent me because he was there when I lost her to Tsarnaev." Ham held Signe's gaze. "He knew what it would mean to me to find her."

Her chest tightened. "If it was fake, then this was all a setup. I was played."

Ham took a step toward her, but she turned away from him, her hands around her waist.

And that's when she spied Aggie standing at the end of the hallway. "Mama, are you okay?"

Signe held open her arms. Aggie walked into them and she stayed there, holding her, as a car drove up outside.

Ham put a hand on her shoulder. "I'm not going to let them take you."

She kissed Aggie's cheek. "I don't have anything to hide."

Orion had stood up as well. "Ham, we got your back."

"This isn't a standoff, Ry. We're just going to talk."

Outside, car doors closed. Signe turned to Aggie. "Sweetheart, why don't you go make a fort for your animals in your room?"

Aggie's eyes widened, but she nodded and headed down the hallway.

Signe turned as a knock came at the door. Took a breath.

Ham opened the door. Jenny Calhoun stood there with two other women she didn't know. But it was one of two men in suits that made her still.

"York?"

She didn't recognize the one with sandy brown hair, green eyes. The other, however, had blond hair, cut short and tight, and she would know that scar anywhere—the one that ran from his ear halfway along his neck. York Newgate. US intelligence officer and one of her former contacts.

Rumor was that he'd been on the disavowed list. So apparently this was a meetup of sorts, of former operatives left out in the cold.

He too paused, hesitated. Looked over his shoulder at a dark-haired woman, then back to Signe. "Stella?"

Oops. She made a face. "Signe. Jones, but yes."

"You're behind all this?" He walked into the house, followed by the other man. "You brought in the NOC list?"

"Yeah. What are you doing here?"

"How do you know each other?" Ham said, but before she could answer, he looked at the dark-haired woman behind York. "Ruby Jane Marshall?"

"Hey, Ham," she said. She wore a pair of black dress pants and a blouse, her dark hair up. "This is York, by the way."

Ham shook his hand. "So you're the one."

Signe had the distinct impression she was missing something. Ham turned to her. "Remember that woman who was framed for shooting General Stanislov? This is her."

"The one who mysteriously escaped Russia with the FSB on her tail?" Signe shook her hand. Then looked at York. "Now it makes sense. You were a part of that, weren't you?"

"It's a long story," York said. "Ruby Jane is a former CIA analyst who got caught up in something. But we're here about you. What's going on?"

"No—first, how do you two know each other?" This from the other man, with brown hair.

About that time, Orion said from behind her, "Logan Thorne? What are you doing here?"

Logan looked at him. "Orion. Last time I saw you, you were fighting fires in Alaska." He shook his hand.

"Last time I saw you, I helped sew up your gunshot wound. How'd you get back to the Lower 48?"

"Took a chance on love." Logan smiled. "Now I work for Senator White. I'm the head of an off-the-books group looking into this mess with the CIA and any connection to Jackson."

"See!" Signe said. She turned to Logan. "You need to talk to Sophia Randall."

The intake of breath from Ruby Jane made Signe turn. She wore a stricken expression. "Sophia Randall?"

Signe nodded, but it was the added expression of horror on York's face that formed a knot in her gut. "What?"

"She was my boss," Ruby Jane said. "She was murdered about two months ago."

Signe reached out for the table. "What?"

"We think it was by a rogue officer named Martin, but we're not sure," York said.

"We met him!" Jenny said. "In Italy. Chasing Signe."

Signe hadn't seen her walk in. Or the other woman, with short dark hair.

"Wait. So Martin killed Sophia, then tried to kill you?" Logan asked.

"I have history with him too," York said. "Once upon a time we worked for the same organization. But our roads diverged when he nearly killed me." He pointed to the scar at his neck. "He works for Jackson."

"See?" Signe said. She turned to Ham. "I'm not lying."

"Of course you're not," Ham said quietly. "It's possible Jackson stripped off the decryption key to hide her involvement with the sale of the NOC list."

"That makes sense," Ruby Jane said now, nodding. "But how do you know Sophia?"

"She was my former handler, a contact in the agency I thought I could trust. When I got the list, I called her and told her everything."

"When was this?"

"About four months ago."

Ruby Jane looked at York. "That's about the time she went missing. Now we know what started her search."

Signe drew in a breath. "Did I . . . did I get her killed?"

"No," York said. "She got herself killed. She dug too deep. Just like Tasha."

Signe stared at him, feeling punched. "I'm so sorry, York. I didn't know."

"Yeah."

"Who is Tasha?" Ham asked.

Signe turned to him. "I met York about three years ago at a resort on the Black Sea. I was there with Tsarnaev. York came with his girlfriend, Tasha, who was a reporter for an underground newspaper. I think she was trying to get dirt on Tsarnaev. Meanwhile, I handed off information to York about an upcoming terrorist attack."

"Yes. Unfortunately, I also handed it off—to the wrong people. The attack happened on Russian soil," York said.

"What happened to Tasha?" Signe asked.

"She reported a rumor about a Russian general sleeping with an American senator. Apparently, Tsarnaev was bragging about how he'd set them up."

That shut down the room.

"Tasha was killed by an assassin for hire, a few months later," York said quietly. "We're not sure who was behind it, but we suspect Martin."

"Which leads us back to Jackson," said Ruby Jane.

"Why are we not freaking out that Jackson is running for vice president?" Jake said, having stood up to join the group. "The election is in three days!"

"I know," Logan said quietly. "And so does Isaac White. But it's too late to pull her from the ticket, and if we did, we couldn't regain the ground lost. Isaac will get elected, then work from the inside to confirm our allegations. Then he can decide what to do."

"We can't have a traitor in the White House," Jenny said.

A beat, then Signe turned to York. "Are you here to take me in?"

York looked at Logan. "He's in charge."

Um, not by the expression on Ham's face, but she said nothing.

Logan was shaking his head. "No one but a small circle knows you're here. Until we get to the bottom of this, we'd like it to stay that way. But I do need to hear everything. And, I need you to stick around, okay?"

Ham took her hand.

"Yes," she said, squeezing Ham's hand. "I'm not going any-where. And I promise . . ." She looked at York, then Orion, Jenny, and Jake. "I'm going to find out exactly what is going on."

CHAPTER THIRTEEN

THIS COULD BE THEIR NEW NORMAL.

A normal Ham never thought he'd ever have, really.

The intoxicating fragrance of the turkey roasting in the oven, stuffed with homemade thyme dressing. Potatoes peeled and soaking in water on the stove, ready to boil. His normally empty table set for thirteen, and the sounds of laughter outside as Jake, Orion, Aria, and Jenny played a game of pickup football.

His broken shoulder was still on the mend or he'd be out there playing too.

Signe was in his office, dressed in an oversized Berkeley sweatshirt, jeans, and a pair of wool socks, researching.

In the three weeks since the election, since White swept the electoral college, she'd become obsessed with uncovering Jackson's grand plan.

If there was one.

The door to his backyard slid open and Jake came in, sweating. "I know I already ate dinner with my family, but that smells amazing, Ham." He closed the door. Leaf debris littered his thermal shirt. "I've worked off meal one, and I'm ready for meal two."

"Don't track mud through my house," Ham said.

"Okay, Betty," Jake said, and toed off his shoes. "I'm just here to grab Signe and Aggie and see if they want to play."

"Betty?" Ham said.

"Crocker." Jake pointed to the dish towel Ham had tucked around his waist. "I certainly hope there's pie in my future." He came into the kitchen and opened the oven.

"You're letting out the heat."

"Who knew the Senior Chief could cook?"

"That's what happens when you're a bachelor into your late thirties." Ham untied the makeshift apron. "Aggie is in her room. I'll get Signe."

"Wait." Jake closed the oven. "Actually, Orion and I were talking. Boss, we're still trying to wrap our brains around Signe's story. You have to admit, the entire thing sounds far-fetched. A senator selling state secrets to a Chechen warlord? Why?"

"I don't know, but it's not just Signe's word anymore. York, Logan, and Ruby Jane corroborated it. That's why Signe's been working so hard—so she can prove it."

Jake looked at the potatoes.

"What?"

"It's just . . . she was in that camp for a very long time. Are you sure—"

"I'm sure." Ham met Jake's expression. "I know Signe. I know when she's lying. She's not."

"Okay. I trust you, Ham. So I'll trust her too. It's just . . . isn't it a little strange that you and she got invitations to the inaugural ball?"

"Why? White is a friend. Of course he'd invite me to the inauguration."

"And an inaugural ball? Signe is supposed to be on a CIA burn list."

"The invitation was written to me and my wife. Mr. and Mrs. Hamilton Jones."

"It just has the little hairs on my neck rising."

He didn't want to admit it, but he'd had the same reaction. Not because of Signe, but because for the first time, he'd realized . . .

He wasn't in this alone.

He had a family at stake in this game.

And sure, Aggie had entered his life a few months before, but it hadn't sunk into his bones that, just like that, he finally had the home he'd always longed for.

As if God knew the dreams unspoken in his heart.

The goodness of his sovereign God took his breath away.

"That's what I have you guys for," Ham said and clamped a hand on Jake's shoulder. "I called the office of the president-elect and nabbed invites for you and Aria, Jenny and Orion, North and Selah, and even Scarlett and Ford. I was going to give them to you tonight, but, *surprise*."

"Super. Now I suppose I need to rent a tux."

"Buy, buddy. You never know when you'll need one."

Aggie came out of her room in a pair of leggings and an over-sized shirt with a turkey decal. "Hey, Uncle Jake."

"Wanna play some football with us?" Jake said and crouched to get a hug.

"Yeah!" She ran into his arms and let him lift her over his shoulder, fireman style. "What's football?" she said, laughing as Jake slipped his shoes back on.

"I'll get Signe," Ham said.

He dropped the makeshift apron on his counter and headed across the great room to his office.

Signe sat with one leg up on his office chair, scrolling through what looked like bank records, the sweatshirt off, wearing a tank top.

"What's this?"

His words startled her, and she turned, her eyes wide.

He froze at the fear in them. "Sig?"

She took a breath. Blew out. "Sorry. Reflex."

He didn't want to ask about what, because anytime she talked about her life with Tsarnaev, it turned him inside out, made him prowl the house at night, wanting to get his hands around the man's dead neck.

Worse were the occasional nightmares she or Aggie had. When they woke from a sound sleep, screaming.

Yeah, he wanted to go back in time and follow Tsarnaev into that bunker. Even if the man had a sniper shot aimed at his head. He'd give his life if Signe didn't have to suffer those ten years.

The coroner hadn't been able to confirm DNA from Pavel, but reconstructed facial recognition had the man cold on a slab in the Catania morgue, and now in the ground, so . . . everyone could stand down to DEFCON 4. At least that's what he told himself, standing on his cold hardwood floor, staring at the dark lake at 2:00 a.m.

No one was going to hurt her again if he could help it.

He leaned over her shoulder. "Whose records are these?"

"Pavel's."

He hated it when she called him by his first name, but bit that back. "How'd you get into his accounts? And . . . why?"

"I'm trying to find payments from Jackson. This is one of his Cayman accounts, but so far, nothing." She scrubbed her hands down her face. "Although I've been looking at numbers for so long my brain is shutting down."

"The guys want you to play football. Aggie is out there, and they need even teams."

She looked up at him. She wore no makeup today—her blonde hair up. He leaned down and kissed her, and for a moment, he debated forgetting the game and taking advantage of the babysitting . . .

No. He and Signe hadn't stepped into all the intimacies of marriage yet, although she'd moved right into his room when they returned from the cabin, and he didn't want to rush it.

He wanted this restart to be perfect.

Still, he pressed a kiss to her neck, and because she'd taken off her sweatshirt, he kissed her shoulder too.

Only then did he notice the scar, right behind her shoulder, in the fleshy area, a bumpy, distorted patch of skin. He ran his thumb over it. "Where did you get this?"

She pressed her hand over it. "Oh. That was . . ." She made a face. "That was a tattoo."

"Really?"

"Yeah. It was a symbol of Tsarnaev's organization. Everyone had to get one."

Ham froze. "What?"

She met his eyes, then grabbed her sweatshirt and pulled it over her head, hiding it. "It was a way to prove my loyalty. But after I left him, I had a friend burn it away with an iron."

"Burn it."

"I didn't know how else to get rid of it." She stood up. "Football?"

He had nothing as she walked away.

Tsarnaev had *tattooed* her. Ham pressed his hand to his gut, not sure if he was going to hurl, fighting the urge to put his fist into the wall.

She already had her Cons on—the ones Jenny had given her—and headed out the back door.

Breathe. Just . . . today was a new day.

Ham slipped on his tennis shoes and joined her. He still wore his cast, but maybe he could referee.

The sun hung halfway down the sky, the trees in his backyard a glorious bronze and burnt gold, autumn waxing into winter, the leaves a blanket beneath his feet. Jake and Jenny played Aria and Orion, who had nabbed Aggie for his side.

Signe joined Jake's team.

Ham went over to the fire pit and grabbed an Adirondack chair, dragging it across the yard. "Goal line one."

Jake was already dragging another the opposite direction. "Goal line two."

"Toss me the ball," Ham said to Orion. He caught it with one hand. "Okay, this is easy. Two-hand touch. I call it down. I'll hike for each team. Don't hit me."

Orion rubbed his hands together. "We flipped. We get the ball first." He called his team in, and they huddled up. He was explaining the rules to Aggie. "Just run out and I'll throw one of you the football." They clapped and headed up to the line.

Ham lined up at center. Looked over his shoulder at Orion.

"Ready? Hike!"

Ham handed him the ball, and Aria and Aggie ran out for passes. Orion threw it over Aria's head.

Jake ran to get it.

"Really?" Ham asked.

"I was a lineman," Orion said.

"Ham was our starting quarterback for two years," Signe said, a little twinkle in her eyes as she went into Jake's huddle.

Sometimes, Ham could still hear her cheering for him. Still see her waiting for him outside the locker room after the game.

Still feel her arms around him as he drove them home on his bike.

Normal. He'd take it however she wanted it.

Orion lined up again, and this time when Ham hiked it, he kept the ball and went through the center, just past Ham.

Jake met him and tackled him a few feet past the line.

"Hey, I thought this was two-hand touch."

"I touched you all the way to the dirt," Jake said, hopping up, grinning.

"I'm going to touch you a fat lip, buddy," Orion said, but grinned as he tossed Ham the ball.

Apparently, his knee was back in working order. But Ham hadn't missed the strange coldness between Jenny and Orion since he'd returned from the cabin.

Something still hadn't shaken out between them. Jenny wouldn't quite look at Orion, wasn't her usual exuberant self.

Not like last time, when she'd tried to pretend all was well. She wasn't selling any sort of hocus-pocus this time. The poor woman was nursing serious injury.

It was Orion who was dancing around the truth—he could see it in Orion's driven mode, the way he drilled down to take on the world, avoiding hard whatever pain throbbed between them.

Which meant the man meant to win this innocent, friendly game of Thanksgiving football.

They went to the line again, and this time, Aria caught the hike. She dropped back as Jenny rushed her. Threw a lopsided pass to Orion. He caught the ball and stiff-armed Jake, who tried to tag him. Jake went sprawling and Orion shot across the yard, on his way to a touchdown.

Except for Signe. She came at Orion with a look on her face that made Ham chuckle.

Until it didn't. Because as she headed for Orion, he stuck out his arm to block her.

She grabbed it, moved it away from her, turned behind him, and swept his leg so fast, Ham wished for an instant replay.

Orion sprawled into the grass, rolling, the ball bouncing away. Signe snapped it up. "Fumble!"

Then she took off for the other goal line, unopposed.

She danced into the end zone.

No one moved, save for Orion, who rolled to his hands and knees, shaking the sense back into his head.

"Are you okay, Ry?" Jake said, running over.

He pushed Jake's hand away. "This is supposed to be *touch* football! Sheesh—what is with your team? You're a bunch of maniacs!"

He was muddy, his jeans stained, and he didn't appear to be kidding.

In the end zone, Signe stopped jumping up and down.

"Okay, flag on the play," Ham said, but he walked toward Signe.

She looked at him. "What?"

"Where'd you learn to do that?"

"Do what?"

"Sig, did you *train* in Tsarnaev's camp?"

Her eyes hardened. "No. I trained with the CIA. But yes, I sharpened a few skills in Chechnya. A person has to stay alive." She shoved the ball at him. "Game time is over."

She headed toward the house.

Jenny came up to him. "You okay?"

Ham stared after her. "I think so. I just . . ."

"What?"

He gave the ball to Jenny. "I need to check on the turkey."

The smell of roasting bird could knock him over, but not as much as the sight of Signe, standing in front of the lit fire, just staring at the flames.

Her face was stoic, but tears glistened on her cheeks.

"Sig?"

She drew in a breath, as if coming back to herself. Wiped her cheeks and turned to him. "There's a lot about me that you don't know."

He came over to her. "I know what I need to." He put his hands on her shoulders. "I know that I love you. That we're figuring this out. And that it's time for joy, not mourning. What's past is past."

"It's like I'm drowning, and every once in a while, I come up for air. And it's sweet and fresh and then something drags me back under. And everything is hazy and dark and I haven't a clue how I'm going to survive."

He frowned. "I don't—"

"Regret. It's suffocating me."

"You gotta forgive yourself, Sig."

"How?"

"For one, you have to trust that God had a plan for all of it, so there can't be any regrets with him."

"Really, you don't have regrets?"

"Of course I do. But the minute I start living in that regret is the moment I doubt God's plan. God takes our twisted paths and makes something beautiful out of them, and no power of darkness or a terrorist's evil agenda can stop that. God wins. In the end, God wins."

She turned, stared up at him. "I want to believe that."

"Believe it. Because when you do, everything changes. You're no longer caught up in the pain of today or the fears about tomorrow. You just have to do what God asks of you today—and you can trust him for the rest."

She touched his chest. "It's always been so easy for you."

"Easy? Hardly. I'd do everything—*everything* in my power—to be kind to my stepmother, and she would twist my words to my father, tell him I'd been disrespectful, or even violent to her. He was trapped between the two of us. He didn't know what to do, so he'd let her lock me in the cellar. And I'd sit there and try to figure out what I did to get her to hate me. And for my own father to betray me."

"I know, I remember."

"Then you also remember me singing. Because that's all I had—my mother's hymns reminding me that everything would be okay. That I wasn't alone. In fact, it was in those moments in that dark, smelly cellar that I knew God was with me. It gave me what I needed, later, when I went to war." He cupped her face. "That's what it means to say the joy of the Lord is my strength. Because when we have nothing, when we *are* nothing, then that's when we see that God is already there, holding us up. Fighting the battle for us. He is enough, and more. He can heal our broken hearts, save us, give us peace. Eternity."

She turned back to the fire. "I remember right after my grandfather died, I was devastated. He was the only one who . . . ."

"Who loved you?"

She lifted a shoulder. "Maybe. I remember coming home after our volcano project—we won the blue ribbon—"

"Yeah we did."

"I brought home that stupid volcano and he put it in his office, along with our silly blue ribbon." She wrapped her arms around herself. "About a week after he died, my grandmother cleaned his office and threw out the volcano. I asked her why she threw it out, and she said it was garbage."

Ham slid his hands over her shoulders again. "You aren't garbage, Signe. Not to me. Not to Aggie. And not to God. You are his beautiful, perfect, amazing daughter and he loves you. Period. No qualifications necessary. Or even allowed."

She said nothing, just stared at the fire.

For a moment, he had this terrible sense that no matter what he did, what he said, she couldn't hear it. He would have turned her, met her eyes, put a little more *oomph* into his words, but the sliding glass door opened.

"You can smell that turkey into North Dakota," Orion said. "Please, sir, may we have some food?"

Signe glanced at him. "Sorry, Orion. That tackle was a little extreme."

"I can handle a takedown, Signe. But I choose you for my team next time."

"If you want to win, you will," Signe said.

Ham laughed and headed into the kitchen. "Call the team, Ry. It's time to feast."

See, everything was normal. Perfect, in fact. Signe wasn't a terrorist, Pavel Tsarnaev wasn't alive, Vice President–elect Jackson wasn't a traitor, and he hadn't burned the turkey.

They were all going to live happily ever after.

Then why did he feel like he was in the cellar, in need of a good hymn?

■ ■ ■

He was still alive.

Signe knew it.

Pavel Tsarnaev was alive and coming for her.

Signe stared at the ceiling of the bedroom, Ham asleep beside her, and tried to tell herself it was just her stupid fears talking. Her worst nightmares rising to destroy her suddenly, surprisingly perfect life.

Or, nearly perfect, if Ham's team would stop eyeing her with suspicion. She knew that Orion and Jake still weren't convinced that she wasn't lying about something. Sure, they said they believed her—after her story was corroborated. But she couldn't dismiss a niggle of suspicion, by the way they sometimes looked at her, the quiet tones of corner conversations, that they thought she was still lying.

Probably, because she was.

She should tell Ham, but maybe she was overreacting. After all, perhaps one of his men had stolen Tsarnaev's banking information and started draining his account. And that accounted for his massive withdrawals, his current activity.

Really.

Besides, if Ham thought Tsarnaev was alive, he'd be on a plane, hunting down the terrorist.

And die doing it.

Ham lay on his back, and she watched him, traced the curve of his face, his lashes closed on his cheeks. The five o'clock shadow thickening on his chin.

Oh, he was a handsome man. And his solid good looks only deepened with age.

She so didn't want to leave him.

But if Pavel was alive, he'd hunt her down . . .

Ham stirred next to her, and she froze, not wanting to wake him. After all, last night he'd prowled the house for the better part of two hours, unable to sleep.

Maybe he'd been putting together the dollhouse he'd purchased for Aggie and set it up under the tree, as if Santa had arrived.

He rolled over to face her, his eyes open.

"Hi," she said.

"Merry Christmas." He put his hand to her cheek. Ran his thumb along her jaw. Tiny eddies of warmth spilled through her entire body. "I never thought I'd wake up with you on a Christmas morning," he said quietly.

Oh Ham. He could make her weep.

Then he leaned in and kissed her. Sweetly, gently, but with a hint of heat under his touch. She surrendered to his kiss, her arms moving around his shoulders.

"Aggie is still sleeping," he said, moving away, his eyes darkening.

Oh.

Oh.

She nodded, her chest tightening.

Silly. She didn't have to be afraid. This was Ham. Her *husband*, Ham.

The man who'd crossed an ocean to find her. Who'd never stopped loving her.

Oh, shoot. He'd gotten too far inside her heart because when he came back to her, kissing her, her entire body erupted in heat and panic and—

No.

No!

His arms curled around her, but suddenly, she wasn't in Ham's warm bed, but in a tent, Pavel's earthy smell pressing her down, his roughened hands on her body and—

"No!"

Ham moved off her so fast her body might have been electrified. He stared at her, his eyes wide, something stricken on his face. "Did I hurt you?"

She shook her head. Then nodded, pressing her hands over her eyes.

"Signe?"

"I thought . . ." Her breaths trembled out. "I thought I was ready. That I could . . ."

He was silent for so long, she opened her eyes.

Tears glistened on his cheeks, his jaw flexing so hard she thought he might break molars. "This is about Tsarnaev, isn't it?"

He did know her. Too well.

She sat up, drew up her knees, locking her arms around them. Nodded.

"I could kill him all over again."

"I thought . . . I mean, I want to, and I thought I was ready, but then, suddenly . . ." Tears burned down her cheeks. Oh! She'd turned into a sappy, uncontrollable mess around Ham.

But maybe she wasn't a spy anymore. Not here. Not now.

"I could compartmentalize when I was with him. Tell myself it was part of my job. That it meant nothing."

"But it did mean something," Ham said. "It meant you were being violated."

She looked away.

"It's too high," Ham said quietly.

"What is?"

"The price you paid for your country."

She met his eyes. "I'm not dead. And I'm not wounded."

His gaze softened. "Yes, Shorty, you are."

She caught her bottom lip between her teeth. "You just love me too much, Ham. It's overwhelming and breathtaking and it scares me." She looked away. "I can't compartmentalize you."

"Good."

"Not good. Because what if I lose you? I'd lose *myself* too."

"You're not going to lose me."

She paused. "I have to tell you something."

"Merry Christmas!" Aggie burst into the room, dragging her rabbit by one ear. "Santa was here!" She wore a flannel nightgown and now jumped on the bed between them.

So. There went that moment. Ham sat up and caught her in his arms. "Really? Did he leave anything for you?"

"A dollhouse! And a purse. And books!"

"Oh my. He must really like you," Ham said, looking over at Signe, winking.

The man had gone completely overboard in his gift-buying for Aggie.

It made her wonder what he would do for a son.

Stop. That part of her life was over.

"You go back to the presents, Aggie. Mama and I will be down soon." Ham set her on the floor and she ran out the door.

"You told her about Santa? Ham. She's too old to believe—"

"You're never too old—hey—"

She was getting up, but he touched her arm. "What?"

"Santa left something for you too." He reached over to his nightstand, opened the drawer with one hand, and pulled out a white box. "Merry Christmas."

Her eyes widened and she sat back down on the bed. He handed her the box.

She opened it, and out fell a black velvet case. "Ham . . ."

"Just open it."

No, no—but she opened the box, and sitting in the plush velvet was a wide, white gold ring, with a massive diamond in the center, flanked by two smaller diamonds. "Ham—"

"The diamond was my mom's. But I had it reset. And two more added on the sides."

"Ham—"

"I should have gotten you a better one than that stupid cubic zirconia one in the Vegas gift shop—"

"Ham."

He met her eyes, so much of his heart in them, she couldn't breathe.

"I can't. I can't accept this."

"What?"

Ham got up, and for a second, she thought he was walking out of her life.

Instead, he shut the door. Turned to her. "What are you talking about?"

She closed her eyes. *Calm down. Breathe.* She opened her eyes. "Ham. Pavel Tsarnaev is still alive."

He stared at her. Then, "Okay, so that was not what I thought you were going to say." He paused. "How do you know?"

"I was tracking his checking account, and there's been with-drawals."

"That doesn't mean it was him," he said. "His identity could have been stolen." He ran a hand across his mouth. "Okay, so I confess, I called the coroner in Italy after Aggie's dream."

"You did?"

"It was sort of freaking me out too. But he said that the facial reconstruction on the face matched Tsarnaev's, so . . ."

"No, Ham. His brother was on board too, so it could've been him."

Ham leaned forward and took her hand. "Tsarnaev's dead, Signe. And you're home. And it's Christmas morning." He took the ring out of the box. "Marry me again. I've waited ten years—no, fifteen—to have you back in my life. I know you have scars and fears, but if you let me, I'd like to stick around and help heal them."

She pressed her hand to her mouth.

"Shorty, I love you."

"You scare me to death."

"Again, not really what I thought you were going to say, but if you wear my ring, I'll promise to try not to."

"What am I going to do with you?"

"I have a few ideas. But they can wait until you're ready." He winked, and she pushed him off the bed, onto the floor. He was climbing to his feet, laughing when she put the ring on her finger.

But six hours later, after the wrapping paper, after Aggie's over-load of gifts, Ham's words still hung in Signe's brain. *"He's dead."*

Oh, she hoped so.

But if he wasn't, she was going to find him.

And this time, she'd finish what she started.

■ ■ ■

Don't look at the ring.

Just . . . aw, Jenny's stupid gaze was riveted on Signe's galactic-sized diamond ring as Signe played with her sweet potatoes and ham.

Like she had lost her appetite. Or maybe she simply couldn't lift her hand to her mouth—

Stop.

"Jenny." Aria's voice, her foot kicking into her shin, tore her focus back to the conversation.

To Ham, who was talking through the details of the inaugural ball they'd been invited to.

Except, all the eyes were on her and she put her fork down. "What?"

"Orion asked if you could pass the salt," Aria said, sotto voce.

Oh. She grabbed the salt and sent it down the table to Orion.

"No problem," Orion said, not looking at her.

Oh, she was so done with this. So done with hoping that he'd call. So done with replaying the rooftop scene in Italy in her head, believing that somehow they might get beyond her past.

She needed to move on.

Put Orion out of her heart.

Outside, snow fell against the windows, and the lake had iced over. He'd made a fire in the pit for Aggie tonight and they'd roasted marshmallows.

She should have gone to the Marshalls' for Christmas like she did every year, but no, she had to accept Ham's invitation to spend Christmas with him.

Because her stupid heart had hoped that Orion might be here. Move. On.

"So, is this thing a tuxedo event?" Orion was asking.

"Really? Yes. And the girls should wear gowns," Ham said.

Aria met her gaze from across the table. Frankly, Jenny expected Aria to be the one sporting a ring this Christmas.

"I probably need to get home," Jenny said. "The weather is getting dicey."

She wasn't running. Not. At. All.

Signe got up with her. "I need to check on Aggie." She'd gone to bed earlier with a tummy ache, which Ham attributed to too much chocolate Santa.

"Thank you for dinner, Ham," Jenny said and brought her plate into the kitchen.

"You're a psychologist, right?" Signe had followed her in. "Can I talk to you?" Signe wore a sexy black dress and looked every inch the kind of international spy Jenny saw in the movies. She'd often wondered about Signe's life, and especially her skills, after seeing her take down Orion at Thanksgiving.

Yeah, that made her smile.

Bad Jenny.

"Is Aggie having trouble?"

"No. Actually . . ." Signe glanced over her shoulder toward Ham.

Oh. A *girl* talk. "Come into my office," Jenny said and headed down the hall. She stepped into Ham's guest bathroom and Signe followed her in.

Jenny shut the door. Locked it. "Would you like a seat?" She pointed to the toilet.

Signe smiled. "This will do." She sat on the edge of the tub and took off her heels, rubbed her feet.

"I was wondering if and when we'd have a real chat," Jenny said. "Ham brought me to Italy because he thought—"

"I'd be traumatized?"

"He didn't know," Jenny said. "He feared the worst, maybe."

"I had no idea what I was getting myself into when I joined the agency," Signe said. "That was probably for the best."

Jenny sat down on the commode. "I had the same thought when I worked for them."

Signe raised her eyebrows.

"I was a profiler, in Afghanistan."

"Right. Did you have trouble . . . I don't know how to say it . . . settling in, after you returned?"

"That's an understatement. I actually had a nervous breakdown after sending a bunch of SEALs into an ambush. Ham was one of them. And Orion was the PJ sent in to rescue the wounded. He ended up getting his knee blown out. So, I settled right into a psychiatric hospital." Maybe that was too much information, but she wasn't ashamed of it. Not anymore. "Everyone goes through stress coming home. No one realizes it—they think you should be glad to be home, but—"

"No, that's not it." Signe wasn't looking at her, her voice quiet.

Jenny knew when to stop talking.

Silence, while Signe breathed. Then, "I was raped while I was overseas."

Oh.

"I mean, of course I was—I was in a terrorist camp. But then . . ." She looked at Jenny. "In order to keep my cover—and really, to protect Aggie—I married him."

"You married your rapist." And just in the nick of time, Jenny changed her tone, so it came out as a statement. "I see."

"I told myself it was part of the job and I got very good at . . . well, not letting my heart engage in the marriage."

Jenny nodded.

"I think I simply tried to forget about the human part of marriage—love, family—and just told myself that I was doing something for the good of my country."

"Something that took pieces out of your soul, little by little."

"For ten years." She looked up at Jenny. "I stopped feeling. And then I couldn't get hurt, see?"

Jenny understood better than she wanted to admit.

"And then along came Ham."

"Ham. Yes. He's a force."

Signe met her eyes. "You have no idea. The man is like a fire hose with his love and forgiveness, and frankly, it's like I'm drowning. I want to open my heart to him, but . . . it's not pretty in there. I mean, there are a lot of scars and wounds and I just don't know if I have it in me to . . . to . . ."

"To receive grace?"

Signe stilled. "I wrecked everything. We had something, and I ran from it. I did this to us. And now I'm . . ."

"Dirty." Jenny could hardly say the word herself.

Signe nodded. "I'm trying to unlock my heart, but I think I've lost the key. And I don't know how to let him in. I don't know how to love him like a wife."

Jenny looked at her. "Signe. Are you thinking of leaving Ham?"

Signe was spinning the ring on her finger. "I'm afraid that Tsarnaev is alive. And if he is, he will come after me. I can't let Aggie get caught in the crossfire. Or Ham."

"Signe, this isn't about Aggie or Ham."

She looked up at Jenny.

"This is about you. And being ashamed. And letting that shame tell you who you are." She leaned forward. "Signe. Let's flip the tables. Let's say that I did something shameful. What would you say to me?"

"I guess it would depend on what it was."

"Would it? Because guilt is about something you've done. But shame is about who you are. At your core. And that's the real problem. This isn't about your actions. It's about who you believe you are. And who you believe you are is not because of what happened out in the field. What happened in the field happened because of who you believe you are."

She leaned forward. "At some point in your life, someone told you that you weren't worth protecting. Weren't really worth loving. And you believed them. And because of that, you went out and tried to prove that you were. Which, in your case, meant joining the CIA and becoming a superspy."

"I'm hardly a superspy," Signe said.

"I saw your mad skills." She pointed at Signe's heart. "You need to fix what you believe in there before you'll figure out how to deal with what is in here." She pointed to Signe's head.

"How do I do that?"

"You start listening to the truth. Ham, your friends, and, if you want, God. Because clearly he brought you back to the starting place. Maybe that's because he wants you to take another look at what he has for you." She made a face. "Not trying to tell you what to do, but I'm thinking that maybe it doesn't involve running away."

Signe smiled.

Jenny met it. "I think maybe I need to listen to my own advice. I've been running away for too long from what I think Orion believes about me. I'm going to just go ask him."

"Really? Okay. Well good then. I'm glad we could have this little chat."

"Thanks, doc," Jenny said.

Signe laughed and Jenny opened the door. Came out to the great room and noticed everyone had gotten up from the table. She heard voices in the kitchen and headed there. Yes, she'd simply pull Orion aside and confront him. And maybe it was over between them. But at least they could both move on.

Or not. Because as she came into the kitchen, she found Aria and Jake in a clench. "Oh, sorry!"

Aria looked over Jake's shoulder, then pushed him away. "We're doing dishes."

"I can see that."

"Where's Ham?" This from Signe, behind her.

"He went to check on Aggie," Jake answered.

"Where's Orion?" Jenny asked.

"He left right after you did. I thought it was to catch you." Jake shook his head. "That idiot. He just needs to get it over with."

Jenny's breath caught as Jake's words settled in. "No, no he doesn't. You can tell him that it's already over."

Jake frowned.

"I have to get home before the blizzard hits."

"Be careful, Jen," Aria said. "It's getting slippery out."

It was way past cold and into freezing as she left the house. Tiny granules of ice pinged on her window, layering it, and she sat in the car for a moment, letting it heat up, blowing on her hands, her conversation with Signe pinging back to her. *"Guilt is about something you've done. But shame is about who you are."*

Just like that, Harley was in her head.

"Have you asked for forgiveness?"

"Too many times to count."

"Once is enough. Leave it behind. He has."

Her breath gusted out in a cloud, and she turned on the defrost. The ice on her windshield began to melt.

So all that was left, then, was the shame.

She turned the car around and pulled out of Ham's long driveway, onto the unplowed street. She could make out tire tracks, just barely, in front of her, and followed them out to another street. Flurries scattered in front of her headlights and they barely cut through the darkness. She edged out, heading down the hill toward the next road.

"It's in suffering—as well as joy—that we find our faith. In times of trouble, we either draw near, or we run."

Lights came at her from the other direction, blinding her. Aware that she was taking up the entire road, she slammed on her brakes.

Her car swerved, spun.

She careened into the ditch on her side of the road.

Snow puffed up, covered her car. Thankfully, her airbag didn't deploy, but she sat there, stunned, immobilized by the seat belt.

Unhurt but clearly derailed.

Stuck.

Nice, Jenny.

She put the car into reverse. Her tires spun, revving hard, kicking up snow.

Perfect. Now she could stay in the ditch and freeze. She closed her eyes.

"And if we run?"

"Then God chases after us. That's the thing about God. We might give up on him, but he never gives up on us."

Yeah, well, she certainly hoped he was in the neighborhood, because she wasn't getting out of the ditch without help.

The other car had slowed as it passed her, and she was unbuckling to check out how bad she was stuck before she called Ham for help when a knock came at her window.

She slid the window down.

She could nearly hear God laugh in the wind as Orion leaned in, snow in his hair, glistening on his eyelashes, looking fresh out of Alaska. "Need some help?"

"God doesn't write tragedies. He's all about the happy ending. We just have to stick with him through the story, right?"

"Get in, hero. We need to talk."

306

Orion paused, swallowed, then quietly, he opened her door. "Let's get in my car, where it's warm."

He held out his hand, and Jenny put hers into it, let Orion help her to his Renegade.

The heat blared full blast.

"We should go back to Ham's house and get a tow rope," Orion said. He still wouldn't look at her.

And that was just *enough*. "No. We're going to sit right here and . . . and . . . just give it to me straight, Ry. I get it if kids are a deal breaker for you, but at the very least, you could have a conversation with me—"

His green eyes widened. "What are you *talking* about?"

"I'm talking about you giving me the silent treatment for nearly two months!"

"I'm not . . . you're giving *me* the silent treatment! You told me that you'd marry me after we talked. But we never talked. You never said a word—"

"Have you lost your mind? Do you not remember anything from Italy? I told you I loved you. I told you about the abortion. I told you that I couldn't have kids. And you just—"

"You had an abortion?"

It was the way he said it that made her stop. Made her throat fill. A hint of horror, of disbelief—

She looked away, out the window in the darkness. Nodded.

His hand lay on top of hers. "Jenny. I'm so sorry. I didn't . . . You told me this in Italy?"

"Yes, during the attack."

"During the—babe, I was completely freaking out because I'd been practically disabled right in front of you, and you were negotiating with a man who was going to kill us, and I . . . I didn't hear *any* of that."

She looked over at him. "None of it?"

He shook his head. "Why on earth would you pick then to tell me?"

She stiffened. "Because I was scared! You were lying there, hurt, and I thought we were going to die—"

"Because I couldn't protect you."

She stilled. "What?"

He looked away from her. "I should have protected you." His voice tightened. "For the past two months all I could think about was how I nearly let you get killed while I lay there like a stuffed ham. I was sick . . ." He exhaled, then looked at her. His eyes glistened. "Babe. You had an abortion?"

She took in a breath.

"How old were you?"

"Nineteen."

"You must have been terrified."

Oh.

His eyes were wet. "And so sad. I'm so sorry."

She just looked at him, her own eyes filling. "I *was* sad. And scared. I didn't know what to do. And I . . ." She shook her head. "I've always just tried to move forward. But suddenly, you were proposing and the past reached out and caught me."

"Maybe because you weren't supposed to move forward without me," he said softly. "We're in this together, Jen. I love you." Then he reached out and pulled her to himself, his coat crunching in the cold as his arms went around her. "I'm so, so sorry."

She had nothing. And then she had everything, his arms holding her, the beat of his heart against hers. "I thought you were disgusted and angry with me."

He leaned away. "I'm angry at the guy who put you in that position."

"Brendan was young and scared too. He gave me money and walked out of my life."

Orion's lips pinched tight.

"The thing is, something went wrong. I bled a lot, and they told me that getting pregnant again might be dangerous. I . . . I'm not sure I can have kids."

Orion said nothing.

"Ry?"

"And?"

"Don't you want kids? You love kids—"

"Of course I want kids, Jen." His eyes gleamed, almost fierce. "But I want you more. You are my future. And remember, we told God he could be in charge, right? We'll leave it in his hands."

She closed her eyes. Nodded.

He nudged her chin up and kissed her. His lips were cold, his chin unshaven, but she grabbed his jacket and clung to him, kissing him back.

This was how it was supposed to be. Together, safe, warm, while the world stormed around them.

Orion. She leaned away. "You really were embarrassed you couldn't overpower two massive Russian thugs?"

He nodded.

"Oh, for cryin' in the sink—"

"I just can't let anything like that happen again, Jen. First Roy, then you—I can't feel that helpless again. I can't watch someone hurt you, ever again."

"It's not a bad thing to be helpless when you're on a team. And, I'm not *completely* helpless. I did train for self-defense in the CIA. I just . . . I panicked in Italy. I saw you go down and—"

"And that's what I'm talking about. You have to trust me, babe."

"And you have to trust *me*. That's what marriage is about, right? A team. You and me? When you're weak, I'm strong. You said it—we're in this together."

His gaze searched hers. "Are you still willing to marry me?"

"You need to ask? Of course—"

His mouth closed on hers. Again. And okay, the man was anything but helpless. He kissed her like he had on the rooftop in Italy, as if he'd found something he'd been searching for. Thought he'd lost forever.

Or maybe she was the one doing that because she held on, digging her hands into his coat lapels.

Never letting him go again.

In fact, she could stay stuck here with him until they found them next spring.

Merry Christmas.

CHAPTER FOURTEEN

HAM SHOULD SIMPLY STOP WORRYING. Because everyone was safe, and it was the dawn of a new season.

Mourning over. Joy ahead.

Overhead, the bright blue DC skies agreed, hardly a cloud for today's inauguration on the Mall. Chilly, to be sure, with the temperatures hovering in the midthirties. He and Signe and the rest of the team had arrived early enough to grab spaces near the front. Signe had slid her hand into his, into the pocket of his wool dress coat, holding tight as first Jackson was sworn in as VP, then White as president.

The Mormon Tabernacle choir sang "Amazing Grace," the US Marine Band played the national anthem, country music star Benjamin King sang "America the Beautiful," and the entire event swept a patriotism through Ham he'd thought he'd forgotten.

The home of the brave and the land of the free. He felt it in his bones.

He'd also stopped feeling his fingers long about hour four and now tried to work heat back into them as he sat at a coffee shop near their hotel just a few blocks off the Mall. The parade had long ago streamed by, and now a crowd pressed into the warmth of the shop.

311

Steam spiraled up from the cups on the table as Jake and Aria, Orion and Jenny—finally holding hands again—and even Scarlett and Ford, who had flown in for the event, chatted about the ceremony. North had opted to stay home, with Selah about to leave on another overseas trip. Ham felt for him.

Signe seemed singularly upbeat, something about her demeanor loosening over the past few weeks, since Christmas.

Since he'd given her the ring. No, since he'd confirmed for her that Tsarnaev was dead.

No longer able to terrorize her.

Yes, sometimes he still woke and had to prowl the house, praying, fighting the darkness that wanted to consume him at the cost of her patriotism.

Not today. Today the good guys won.

Signe's fuzzy white mittens sat on the table, so he found her bare hand and wove his fingers through hers. Felt the ring, cool on her finger.

"Last time we were here we did search-and-rescue training with Dani Masterson and a couple of her dogs," Scarlett was saying. "They had this cool device they put in the dog's eye—a contact that functioned like a camera. So they could see everything the dogs saw."

"Really?" Signe said as Ham took a sip of his macchiato. "How?"

"Through a cell phone connection, I think. They couldn't hear anything, of course, but it did have a GPS, so they could track it as well. Dani said they used it for urban SAR, as well as for some military applications."

"We used a dog on our team," Jake was saying. "He saved our hides more than once by alerting to a bomb or some other kind of danger."

"I used to have a dog," Signe said. "Named Caesar. Ham and I found him together." She looked at him. "We should get another dog."

His heart nearly flipped inside him, but he managed to nod.

A dog.

Which meant a future.

See, he could stop worrying. He should start believing in the happy ending he was living.

"We should get back to the hotel and change," Jenny said. She looked at Orion. "I bought a dress."

Orion's eyebrows went up, and he smiled. "I can't wait."

Ham didn't know what had happened to repair the gaping canyon between them, but something had been put right.

He'd booked rooms at the Patriot Hotel again, the location of the private Patriot Ball, a tribute to search-and-rescue personnel, the Red Cross, and other organizations. After they returned from the coffee shop, and after he'd emerged from his shower, Signe locked herself in the bathroom for a good hour.

Now, he could hear her singing.

Singing.

She had her phone on, but still, her words drowned it out as she sang about them being just kids when they fell in love.

An Ed Sheeran song. Ham hummed along, the words exactly right. He'd found a woman, a love bigger than he ever dreamed. He stood at the window, dressed in his tux, staring down at the snow-covered streets, the whitened spires of the elm trees that stood sentry over the Mall, the frozen ice of the reflection pond.

Only three months since he'd gone after the woman he'd never forgotten.

The door opened behind him and he turned.

"Wow."

Signe emerged from the bathroom, coiffed and so beautiful his heart nearly punched through his chest. The strapless black ball

313

gown had a sweetheart neckline, a pleated satin skirt with a slit up the side, mid-thigh. She wore a simple silver necklace, her blonde hair down, curled, and falling over her shoulders, and open-toed black stilettos.

He clenched his fists at his side, fighting the urge to touch her, trace his fingers down her arms, muss her golden hair.

"Just a little black dress? That's how you described it," he said, almost with a growl. "You're so beautiful, I can hardly breathe."

She laughed, those perfect lips curving into a smile. "You don't look too terrible yourself there, hero."

"I feel like a bum next to you."

She walked over to him. Oh, and she smelled good. "I love you, Hamilton Jones."

He heard a cracking, deep inside, all his rules, his self-designated control breaking away. Now wasn't the time to— "Signe, we'd better go."

Instead, she put her hands on his lapels. Lifted her face to his. "I was thinking that tonight, after the ball . . ." She raised an eyebrow.

His eyes widened. "Really?"

She nodded. "It's something Jenny said—that God brought us back to the beginning, maybe so that I could take another look at what he has for me. Us. I know what I have. And I'm not scared anymore that I'm going to lose it."

He nodded, his hands cupping her face. When he kissed her, sweetly, careful of her lipstick, he ignored the part of his brain that worked overtime to scare him, and again told himself to stop worrying.

They descended in the elevator and met the others in the lobby. Orion and Jake both wore tuxes. Jenny wore a dark navy dress with a boatneck collar and a frilled slit just above her knee, silver heels.

Aria wore a silver V-necked sequined dress, her dark hair up. Jake couldn't take his eyes off her.

Ford Marshall had flown into town for the event and wore his dress whites, and Scarlett joined him in a white satin gown with a twisted neckline and cascading ruffles. Her above-the-ankle hemline showed off a pair of gold shoes.

"Apparently, we are *way* off duty tonight," Orion said.

Maybe. If Ham could get rid of the burr in his gut.

"Relax, boss," Jake said, clamping a hand on his shoulder as he pulled out his tickets.

"I'm relaxed."

"Right. I could play a song off the muscles in your neck. Breathe. The place is surrounded by Secret Service. No one who doesn't belong is getting in here."

Maybe. They found the hall, stood in line, and went through two checkpoints before entering the grand ballroom—showing their tickets, their IDs, checking their coats, walking through a scanner, and even being wanded.

He'd never felt so naked, especially when he realized he'd left his cell phone in his coat. But Signe took his arm and they walked into the massive two-story room. A balcony surrounded the room, golden chandeliers sparkled with grandeur, and soaring marble columns cordoned off the center area dance floor. Gold brocade curtains hung at the windows, regal and stately.

Flags lined the stage, and lights that shone on the marble columns illuminated yet more flags hanging from the ceiling around the room.

A giant round thrust extended from the stage, with the presidential seal embedded in the carpet.

A band behind glass near the stage played "I Will Always Love You" by Dolly Parton, and it only made Ham want to pull Signe onto the dance floor.

Lush bouquets of red, white, and blue roses were centered on each table. Guests in tuxes, dresses, and a few uniforms mingled around the room, drinking champagne and other cocktails. Waiters in white gloves strolled with appetizer platters.

It reminded Ham very much of the smaller event in Alaska where a waiter had held Jenny hostage and tried to blow up White with a suicide bomb.

Oh, for Pete's sake, Jake was right. *Breathe*. The place was swimming with security.

He noticed that Orion had a tight grip on Jenny's hand, though.

The music switched to Bruce Springsteen's "Born in the USA," and Ham wove them through the crowd to an empty table. "I'll get us some food," he said to Signe.

"And some champagne!" She winked and he couldn't help but give her a kiss on the cheek.

He worked his way toward a table of food, spotting a cake among the offerings.

"Ham! Is that you?"

He turned and stilled as he spotted—his sister, Kelsey. "What are you doing here?"

His little sister, now all grown up, wore a blue dress, cowboy boots, and . . . wait . . . a wedding ring?

She threw her arms around him and he hugged her back. Stepped away. Silver earrings dangled from her ears, her brown hair pulled back, long down the back.

"You look great!" He glanced at her hand. Yep. "Are you married?"

"Oh." She pressed her hand to her mouth. "I'm sorry. Yes. Knox Marshall and I eloped a couple months ago."

He tried not to feel the spear in his heart. But there it was, the constant reminder that she really didn't want him in her life. And really, who could blame her—he'd been MIA in her life too. So, no, it didn't make sense, but it still hurt.

He forced a smile. "Congratulations."

"We didn't tell anyone, Ham. It was impromptu. Between gigs. Which we have tonight. We're playing a song for my bandmate's mother when she comes on stage."

Ham just blinked at her.

"Reba Jackson. The new VP?"

Oh. "Wow. I didn't . . . really?"

"Her daughter, Glo, plays in our band. We're doing a quick number right before she comes on—something Glo wrote for the inauguration. We're going with her to all the events tonight, singing it." She lifted a shoulder like it might not be a big deal. "We're just here for a few minutes, then we're headed to the Liberty Ball. I think we're doing ten balls in total tonight."

"That's fantastic, Kelsey," Ham said. He had the sudden urge to tell her about Signe, a weird sort of *See, I put my life back together, also* comment, but he let it pass.

"When will you be in Minnesota next?"

"I don't know . . ."

"I've never met Knox face-to-face, although I met Tate and Ford and Wyatt and Ruby Jane a while back, so—"

"You did?"

"Yes. Uh . . ." He wasn't sure what she knew. "Ruby Jane was in Russia . . ."

"Right," she said, nodding. "Well, we're glad that's over. Tate's been going crazy trying to protect Glo from people who want to take a shot at her mother."

Ham frowned. "I thought you caught the guy in Seattle."

"There was another attempt at Glo and Tate's wedding, although we figured out that the man behind it wasn't after her—anyway, for a while people were saying Jackson was behind the attacks—crazy, right? But she was cleared by Tate, so . . ."

Huh. "I'm glad to hear that." Except, Signe had been so sure.

Then again, he'd been convinced to his bones that he'd watched Signe die, so there was that.

"I'd love to see you, Kelsey, if you get a chance."

"Text me. I'll be in DC for a few days."

He made to move past her, but she grabbed his hand. "Ham?"

He turned back.

"Thank you for what you did."

He just looked at her.

"When you came to New York, after I was mugged. For staying. For reminding me that I wasn't alone. You were a good brother. We can start over, okay?"

Yes. He didn't know why those words tightened his throat. Or why, when she lifted up to give him a kiss on the cheek, he couldn't speak. But he just nodded, smiled.

And then she was gone.

Huh.

Cake. Yes. And champagne.

He scored both and returned to the table.

Signe was gone. He set down his spoils and looked around. Spotted Orion and Jenny on the dance floor.

Ford was talking with someone who looked like him—wait. Tate Marshall. Yes, he recognized the former spec ops soldier. Probably here with the band.

But no Signe. Maybe she went to the restroom.

"Ham."

The voice turned him and he found Logan Thorne standing behind him. "Hey, Logan."

Logan wasn't smiling. "Where's your wife?"

It was the tone, more than the question, that had the little hairs on his neck rising. "Why?"

"Because we think she's in trouble. Come with me."

Ham glanced around, caught Jake's eye, then turned to follow

Logan. He led him out, past the arched entrances, past Secret Service, into a side hallway.

Logan opened a door and Ham stepped inside. A bank of screens lined the walls. "Over here."

Leaning over a tech was Ruby Jane Marshall. She wore a black dress, heels, her dark hair held back with a clip. She looked over her shoulder and stood up straight.

"Hey, Ham."

"Hey. What's going on?"

"We've had eyes on your wife all night, and . . . suddenly, she's gone off the grid."

"What?"

"She's here—see you two talking?"

The tech had stilled the screen and he saw himself kissing Signe before leaving. More of a profile view, probably taken from one of the dozens of cameras around the room.

"Now watch."

As he walked away, Signe turned to face the dance floor.

A waiter walked up to her and delivered a plate to her. He walked away before she could stop him.

"What's on the—"

"Just wait."

She picked up a piece of paper. Opened it. He couldn't read it from this angle, but by the look on her face, something wasn't right.

Then she looked around, as if for him, and disappeared into the crowd.

"We picked her up leaving the hall, then again ducking into a bathroom."

"Please tell me you don't have cameras in the bathroom."

"No, of course not. But we just dispatched a team there, and she's not there."

"Maybe she went back to the table."

"Ham," Logan said quietly. "Your wife has been receiving payments from her husband's account for the past five months."

Ham stared at Logan. "I'm her husband."

"Right. So, from the terrorist Pavel Tsarnaev."

"He's dead."

"Maybe. But someone has access to his account. And has been depositing money into Signe's account."

"That proves nothing—"

"And then there's this," Ruby Jane said. She handed him a list of websites. "These are all the places she's visited, using your computer, since you were given the inaugural invitation. Coffee shops, hotels, and most specifically, schematics of the Patriot Hotel."

"How do you know it was her?"

Ruby Jane raised an eyebrow. "Are you saying you downloaded blueprints of the basement of the Patriot Hotel?"

Ham looked at the lists, pages and pages. "Is this a satellite photo?"

"Yes. We're not sure how she got in, but she's been watching the small island of Lipari, north of Sicily, Italy."

"What's on that island?"

"The estate of Pavel Tsarnaev."

Ham handed RJ back the documents. "What are you saying?"

"Just hear me, Ham. What if Signe is playing a long game, with Tsarnaev?"

"To do *what*?"

She raised a shoulder. "She's providentially here, at an inaugural ball. How many people get invites to that?"

"Because she's my wife!"

Ruby Jane said nothing.

"Seriously. You think she's a terrorist. What—that she's here to kill White." His shook his head. "This is rich, coming from you. You were accused of assassinating a Russian general."

"Ham—" she started, but he put up a hand.

"What about Jackson?"

Ruby Jane looked at Logan, then back to Ham. "We've been running with that theory for a long time. But we just can't find the connection. Nothing to corroborate Signe's story, except for our own circumstantial evidence. We have nothing except Signe's word—"

"Which is true!" He didn't mean to raise his voice and schooled it. "She's not lying. I'd know."

"Ham. She embedded with a terrorist for a decade. She's a master at lying," Logan said quietly.

"No."

"Signe and Tsarnaev faked his death, then used you to get into the country. And now to get to the inaugural ball. She was with a terrorist organization, Ham. You can't actually believe that she held out that long. That she wasn't turned."

He stared at Logan and Ruby Jane. "No. She wouldn't do this. She . . ." He held up his hand. "Let me find her."

"We're already looking for her."

"Please—let me find her!"

Ruby Jane took a breath, shot a look at Logan.

"You find her, you detain her. Okay?" Logan said.

"You tell your men not to scare her."

Ruby Jane looked at the guard by the door. "Let him go."

Ham headed back into the ballroom, his heart banging. On-stage, he heard his sister begin to announce the song Glo had written for her mother, Vice President Reba Jackson.

Moments were starting to click together. Like every time he entered the office, Signe shut down her search. But what about the bank ledger from Tsarnaev? Was she checking on her deposits, lying to him about her so-called research?

He was a stupid fool.

Or not, because he simply couldn't wrap his mind around the rest. The true night terrors, attributed to Tsarnaev. And Aggie's fear too. That hadn't been pretend.

So maybe she was being coerced.

Or maybe she'd simply gone to the restroom—

"Boss!"

Ham nearly rounded on Jake when he grabbed his arm. "We got a problem."

"Another one?"

Jake frowned. "Uh, I don't know. But Orion says he saw Martin in the crowd, and he freaked out and took off after him."

"Martin?"

"The rogue CIA guy who nearly killed them in Italy—"

"Right. *Yes.*" And if Martin was one of the good guys, of course he'd been here to stop Signe.

But Martin had tried to kill Orion. "Help him get Martin. Detain him. I'm trying to find Signe."

"I saw her talking with Scarlett earlier."

"You did? Where?"

Jake looked around. "Maybe back by the band? Ford was with them, talking with his brother, I think."

Yeah, those Marshalls were everywhere.

Jake took off in the direction Orion had gone.

Ham headed toward the stage.

Please, Signe, where are you?

■ ■ ■

Just when Signe thought it was safe to stop looking over her shoulder, to move on, to believe what Ham said to her—that they could start over, that he loved her, that Tsarnaev was dead—her past showed up to mock her.

She'd stared at the picture the waiter had dropped in front of her, and her world imploded.

Ruslan.

It was a recent picture, his hair falling over his dark brown eyes, a smattering of freckles over his nose. He wore a hoodie under his jean jacket and stood like a tourist in front of the White House, decorated for Christmas.

What?

She turned the picture over and read the script on the back, in Chechen.

1102. Now.

She couldn't move, her stomach turning over.

No. It couldn't be. She'd spent hours watching Pavel's estate in Italy, sure he'd hide there if he'd survived. Nothing. No movement at all.

She'd actually started to believe Ham.

Breathe.

But Ruslan . . . She tucked the picture into her dress and got up, looked around for Ham, then headed out of the room.

But not before she spotted Scarlett. She walked right up to her and nodded.

And Scarlett, bless her, delivered to her exactly the package she needed, the one that she'd asked her about in the bathroom at the coffee shop.

Signe ducked into a nearby bathroom, stared in the mirror, and blew out a breath—tucking herself back into the persona that could save her, and exited quickly.

A waiter walked by, probably from the nearby prep kitchen. She kept her head down, found an elevator, and punched the button. Got on and rode it up to the eleventh floor.

She spotted the security officer standing outside a door, tracked the numbers, and yes. The Roosevelt Suite.

The officer stopped her, but a voice behind her said, "Let her pass."

She glanced over her shoulder and spotted the waiter. He had followed her up the elevator and now came up behind her. Dark hair, a scar over his eye.

Oh . . . *no*—

"Walk," Martin said. He nodded to the officer, who let them pass.

Think, Signe.

She knocked on the door and someone opened it.

This couldn't be happening.

"Come in," Vice President Jackson said. She wore a white, beaded dress and her reddish-blonde hair up in a neat coif, and looked absolutely regal. "Nice to see you again, Signe."

Signe couldn't move.

Jackson raised a manicured eyebrow. "Do you need assistance?"

Yes. Maybe. But Signe found herself and walked into the room. It was ornate, with blue carpet and rich red draperies, a white brocade sofa, and an adjoining door to another room. Two uniformed officers stood near the sliding glass door to the balcony.

Jackson opened the other door. "Please."

"I don't understand what I'm doing here—"

And then she did. Because standing with his back to her, staring out the window, was the man she knew—really, she *knew*—was alive.

She should have listened to herself, her gut instincts.

"And you thought you could kill me."

She refused to shake. To allow Tsarnaev to know what his voice did to her.

Then he turned. His face had been scarred, bright red patches of skin crisscrossed over one side of his puckered face. And his hands, too, bore red patchwork.

Burns.

In fact, if she hadn't heard his voice, she might not recognize him.

Maybe that's how he'd gotten into the building, his face unrecognizable to anyone looking.

Then again, he was standing here with the vice president, so . . .

"How did you find me?"

"Please. You tried to get it burned off, but I told you that you'd always belong to me."

Burned—what? "The *tattoo*?"

"The microwave tracker we had inserted while he was marking you."

She could be ill. No wonder they found her all over Europe.

"Besides, even with that, I knew you'd return to him," Pavel said, his accent nearly gone. Another charade. "I knew as soon as I saw that video on your phone."

That video . . . oh. The one she'd downloaded from YouTube after seeing it play on CNN.

A video of Hamilton Jones on a subway, months ago, taking down an attacker.

Precise, calm, the man had put the subway attacker in a sleeper hold, brought him to the ground, and put a foot on him. He'd saved what looked like a college kid, but more importantly . . . she'd found him.

And that day knew she had a way to save their daughter.

She met Pavel's obsidian eyes. "Ham has nothing to do with this."

"Oh, sweetheart, he has *everything* to do with this. It's because of Ham that you're here to help us."

"Help . . ."

"Listen, we understand the game," Pavel said. He wore a suit, his body leaner, probably from time in a hospital. "We understand why you took the list, why you tried to return it. We were counting on it, actually." He came over to her. "But I feel I owe you an apology."

She frowned, but refused to step away from him, despite the way her body tensed at just his smell.

Maybe she had changed, because she didn't have a chance of compartmentalizing how she felt about him. "Yes, you do, you filthy pig."

His eyes darkened. "Really."

She braced herself, this time ready to fight back.

"Pavel. She needs to return to the ball unmarked," Jackson said.

The sentence so confused her that Signe didn't notice Pavel slipping a bracelet around her wrist and snapping it shut.

"Hey!"

It was pretty, a thick ring of diamonds secured in white gold. "What's this?"

"A gift." Then Pavel leaned in and kissed her cheek.

She pushed him away. "Get off me!"

He chuckled but didn't move. Touched her cheek. "You know you will always belong to me."

"No, no I won't—"

"Yes, you will. Because you know that you don't deserve better. You would have never surrendered to me in the first place if you didn't believe that you deserved it."

"You *raped* me."

"Did I, though?" He raised an eyebrow and ran the back of his knuckles down her face.

She refused to flinch. "What is this?" She held up her arm. "I don't want it." She turned it to find the clasp but couldn't unlatch it.

"It's locked. And now that it's active, if you try to remove it, it will detonate."

She stilled. "What?"

Jackson just smiled at her. "I have to go make my appearance. I'm afraid this is the last time we'll see each other, darling. Thank you for your service." She winked and headed out the door.

"Wait—what?" She headed after her, but Pavel grabbed her arm.

She swung around and sent her fist into his face.

He jerked back, let her go.

"You—" And the epithet that followed was in Chechen, but she understood it clearly. He looked like he might come at her, so she stepped behind a table.

"I'm not your wife. I never was. And I'm not going back into that ballroom to let you kill people."

"Then he dies." He pulled out his cell phone.

A live stream. Ruslan, playing a computer game in a hotel room. The Washington Monument gleamed through the window behind him.

"You wouldn't. He's your son too."

"He's the son of an American spy, a witch and an infidel. Of course I would kill him."

His words turned her cold.

"But I won't stop there. If you don't return, he's next."

He scrolled to a picture of Ham, dressed in his tux, talking with a woman, clearly taken tonight.

"I'm so glad you didn't let me kill him. He's been ever so useful."

She looked at Pavel. "You planted the NOC list, knowing I'd find it, knowing I'd get it home."

"Knowing you'd be declared a hero of your beloved country. And find your way back to your true love, Hamilton Jones, a known associate of presidential candidate Isaac White." He said it with a smile.

She went cold. "You used my marriage to Ham to get me to the Inaugural Ball. To . . . what. Blow up a party?"

"Oh sweetheart, think. Not *any* party."

The party with the president. "He's not due here for an hour, maybe more."

"If you think you can leave before he gets here, that bracelet will detonate around any metal detectors. Or, any time I want it to." He held up his cell phone. "There's a GPS attached, so I'll know if you leave the hotel. No, you'll stick around until White arrives and then . . ." He lifted a shoulder. "Boom."

She fought the rise of her breaths, a hyperventilation. *No, no, calm down* . . . "I'll inform Secret Service."

"They already think you're a terrorist, sweetheart. They won't listen to you."

She frowned.

"I filled your bank account with enough evidence to land you in a black site for the rest of your life. You'll wish for execution. Trust me, this is the better way."

Clearly a bank account she'd never seen before. "I'll pull the fire alarm."

He lifted a shoulder. "Boom."

"I'll get on a table and shout it—"

"The bracelet is like a cell phone. It's Bluetooth connected and it has a speaker. I can hear everything you're saying. You tell anyone . . . and well—"

Yeah, she knew. *Boom.*

She pressed her hands on the table. "What about Ruslan?"

"It's simple. You do this, and he lives. You don't and, well, we already know what kind of mother you are. The kind who sacrifices her children for her own agenda."

She stared at him, his words a stone in her heart.

He took a step toward her, but she jerked back.

He held up his hand. "I always told you that you were special to me. Now you know why."

No, *no*—

"You wanted to be important, honey? You will be. You're going to assassinate the president of the United States."

He held up the cell phone and walked out of the room.

She just tried to breathe.

Ham. She might have to stay, but Ham didn't. Ham and his team could leave. And maybe she could figure out a way to evacuate the building.

Before, well, *boom*.

She looked at the jewelry on her wrist, the way it sparkled.

Fake, probably, just like her entire life.

She walked out of the room, but the Secret Service was gone.

Fine. Okay. Breathe.

Because yes, she'd seen this coming. She hadn't been a spy for ten years without learning a few things.

She just had to find Ham.

And figure out a way to keep him safe.

CHAPTER FIFTEEN

HAVE YOU SEEN SIGNE?"

Ham found Scarlett staring at her cell phone. She looked up at Ham. "What?"

"Signe, have you seen her?"

She nodded. "She went upstairs—I think she's on the eleventh floor—"

That's all he heard before he took off out of the hall. Scarlett might have called after him, but he didn't have time.

He had to find Signe before the Secret Service did. Before they arrested her, before they did exactly what he feared—took her away to a undisclosed location and she spent years trying to untangle herself.

Behind him, in the hall, Jackson was coming on stage with her entourage.

The relative quiet of the hallway shook him for a moment, just Secret Service agents milling around.

Eleventh floor.

He slammed his thumb into the button. *C'mon!*

The elevator opened and he got in, banged the eleventh-floor button.

Glued his gaze to the numbers as it rose.

When it opened, he wasn't sure where to turn.

Then, like a miracle, he spotted her. She came out of a room, stood at the door, as if catching her breath. "Signe!"

She turned, and her eyes widened. She shook her head.

What?

He headed down the hall toward her and she backed into the room she'd just come out of.

He followed her inside.

She was standing in the middle of the room, her hand wrapped around her waist.

"What is going on?" He walked over to her, took her by the shoulders. "Where were you? Are you okay?"

She just looked at him.

"Do you know that the Secret Service is looking for you right now? They think you're a terrorist, Sig! They showed me evidence of websites pulled off my computer. And bank deposits and—"

She had started to hyperventilate. Quick breaths that made her hunch over.

He took her in his arms and pulled her down to the sofa. "Breathe. Slow down. Just breathe . . ."

She grabbed his arms, met his eyes.

And he saw it. Fear. Something unhinged inside Signe he'd never—not once—seen before.

No, wait. He had. The night her grandfather died. The night he'd found her in the barn, completely unraveling.

The first time she'd hyperventilated.

"Signe, it's okay. You're going to be okay. I'm not going to let anything happen to you. Just breathe with me, okay?"

She nodded, and he began to slow her down, to breathe with her. "In, out, in . . . out . . . thatta girl."

Her breaths evened out, her hands on his arms.

It was then he noticed the bracelet. Pretty. But he hadn't seen it on her earlier, had he?

"What's—"

"I need some fresh air. Open a window."

He tried the window behind the sofa. It didn't budge, so he opened the sliding door.

She got up and came over to the door. He stepped outside, turned.

She closed the door behind him.

What?

"Sig?"

Her gaze met his through the glass, her palm pressed flat.

"You just keep coming after me. And you shouldn't, Ham. You shouldn't!"

Tears creased down her cheeks, but a muscle pulsed in her jaw. "You're too much. You get in the way and . . . I don't want you in my life. Just stay there and leave me alone!"

The words arrowed right through him, found his soul.

Then she turned and left.

Left.

He stood there in the cold night, unable to move.

What had just happened?

"Signe!" His voice cracked through the air and he slammed his hand on the massive pane, but it only shook.

Shatterproof.

No. This couldn't be right. She couldn't have played him this entire time.

"I love you, Hamilton Jones." She'd said it tonight, looking straight into his eyes, no guile in sight.

She couldn't, just *couldn't* be lying.

"I don't want you in my life."

He pressed his hands on the cold glass. "Signe!"

His voice reverberated through the darkness.

Fine. He reached for his cell phone and let out a yell.

He'd checked it in with his coat.

Which meant he was up here alone.

He sank down on the balcony, his face in his hands. *Okay, think.*

But all he could hear were her words. *"You get in the way."*

The past breezed in, darkened his soul. He pressed his hand to his chest, to the pain there.

He might be having a heart attack.

God, what . . . I don't understand.

And in the chill of the night, he heard nothing. No words of wisdom, no profound truths from deep in his soul.

Simply silence.

No, simply quiet.

Just his heart beating. Him, alone.

Him, alone, in the cellar.

And his mother's hymns.

"No power of hell . . . no scheme of man . . . can ever pluck me from his hand."

He didn't need a voice.

Because he had the truth. *"It sounds like you're being sifted, Ham. The enemy wants to win this one. Don't let him. God calls you to be a warrior. To train, to wait for his command. And that's why you have to lean hard into him. Fill your mind with prayer, with Scripture, with truth."*

He fisted his hands, then pressed his forehead down on them, breathing hard. "I don't know what's going on, Lord, but I know I have you. Fix this, please. I'm here, whatever you need me to do."

He looked up at the stars, barely visible against the lights of the city, but there, named, winking down at him. *And if he knows the stars, he knows us too.*

"What if this is about you, Ham?" Orion's words from the cabin came back to him.

No . . . *what?* Except, Signe had to know he'd try to find her.

Which meant, so did everyone else. Like Isaac White. And by proxy Jackson, who knew who Ham was to White.

"I'm nobody."

"Not to me." Oh boy.

He didn't know what they had on her, but in his gut, he knew Signe's worst fears were somehow playing out—that Jackson was using her.

She had to be. He refused to believe the alternative.

His eyes had adjusted to the darkness, lights from the street below illuminating the building.

He got up. Stared down.

Yeah, his hands got a little slick at the thought of trying to climb down. But he might be able to get to the next balcony. All he had to do was find an open door.

He stood at the edge of the metal balcony and measured the distance to the next one. In the darkness, he couldn't be sure, but it looked about six feet.

Ho-*kay.*

He climbed up on the metal railing, holding on to the building, digging his fingers into the chips in the granite.

This wasn't all that different from climbing Mount Huntington. He just had to hold on.

No, he had to jump. Leap six little feet. The length of his body. Not a problem.

The wind whipped at his legs and his fingers were starting to numb.

Now. Go—

"What are you doing? Have you lost your mind?"

The voice jerked him, his foot slipped, and just like that, he was falling—

"Whoa!" Hands grabbed him and he somehow caught the railing, his feet kicking midair. The man pulled him up and over the balcony. "Holy cow, you're heavy."

Holy cow? Ham set his feet on solid ground, then looked up.

Ford Marshall stood there looking at him like he'd lost his mind. "It's not that bad, dude. Life is worth—"

"I wasn't jumping."

"Looked like it."

"You—okay, what are you doing here?"

"Scarlett said you were in trouble. She sent me up here."

"What—how?"

"She's got the entire thing on video. Just come with me. Signe is on the run."

"Yeah she is. She trapped me—"

"I know. C'mon!" Ford took off out of the room, and Ham followed him, trying to wrap his brain around what was happening. "How did you find me?"

Ford was jamming his thumb into the elevator button. "Signe is wearing one of those contact cameras. Scarlett got it for her."

"Contact cameras?"

The doors opened. "I don't know, man. It's for a dog?"

Ham had nothing as they got in.

"Signe came to Scarlett today after the ceremony and asked her to get one of them. Apparently, they have a camera and are used with K9 SAR dogs."

Right. "Yes. We got trained in that before Italy."

"So, Signe is wearing one. Scarlett got the entire thing on video. Apparently, she met with VP Jackson, and then this other guy— Scarlett said he's Middle Eastern."

"Chechen?" Ham looked at the floor numbers. Must go faster.

"Maybe. He's disfigured. And he gave Signe a gift."

Disfigured.

The man at the Ferris wheel. Ham couldn't breathe. Aggie

had been right and the fact that Tsarnaev had been that close to her . . .

He wanted his hands around the man's throat.

But then, "Wait, a gift? Was it a bracelet?"

"Yeah. We're not sure what it is, but when she locked you on the balcony, we figured it wasn't good."

"Where is she now?"

"A storage closet on the main floor."

"A *storage* closet?"

The doors dinged open and Ford led them out into the hallway.

Logan Thorne stood in the center of the lobby, his back to Ham.

Ham grabbed Ford and slipped down the hall. "Don't tell anyone where she is. We can't let the Secret Service find her."

Ford frowned but nodded. "Down this hall." He took off in a run to a quiet hallway behind the ballroom, now rocking with songs by country singer Benjamin King.

"Down here." Ford turned another corner, and Ham spotted them—Jenny, Aria, and Scarlett standing around a door.

Scarlett looked up. "She's not saying anything."

"Maybe she can't," Jenny said quietly.

Ham frowned at her. "Why?"

"Because, if she could, why didn't she tell you what was going on?"

Because she's a terrorist? The thought pinged through him, but he pushed it away.

No. No she wasn't.

"Signe. Open the door."

Nothing.

"Okay." He turned to Ford. "Find Logan Thorne and tell him I told you to evacuate the building. I don't know what's going down, but we don't need to take any chances with this many people here. And that's an order."

"He's not under your command anymore, Senior Chief."

"No. But he'll understand."

Ford took off.

"What are you thinking?" Jenny said.

"I think Signe has been right this entire time and now she's in trouble. And I've got to figure out a way to help her."

Jenny looked at Ham. "For whatever it's worth, Signe loves you. I know she does."

Ham drew in her words like a fresh wind. "Yeah. Now, you three . . . get out of here. But don't go out the front. Go out through the kitchen—maybe the loading docks." He looked at Scarlett. "Especially you. I need you to keep that video footage safe, okay?"

She nodded. Jenny and Aria followed her down the hall to the stairwell.

Then he sat down beside the door.

"Shorty, it's just you and me now. And I'm not going anywhere. I'm staying right here until you come out."

She said nothing.

"Signe."

"Go away, Ham. I have to do this. Alone."

"Do what?" Oh Signe. "Do *what*?"

Again, she said nothing.

So, he stuck his fingers under the door.

And when she wound hers through his, he just about started to weep.

■ ■ ■

This time, evil would not win.

Orion had stalked down the hallway outside the ballroom, that one thought pinging through his head. He'd seen Martin, dressed like a waiter, head toward the elevators, and now he stood, watching the numbers flicker on to the eleventh floor.

What went up had to come down.

He'd thought he'd seen a ghost, really, when he spotted the man, and for a second, he couldn't move, the recognition was so strong. Then, just like that, it came back to him. *"Take them in the back and kill them."* Martin had said it in Russian, to his thugs, but Orion understood it, or most of it, words he'd picked up while in the service.

And sure, maybe he'd gotten that wrong, but as he stared at the waiter, he knew in his bones it was his second chance.

He'd grabbed Jake, his gaze on his prey as he left the room. "I see Martin, the guy from Italy. Tell Ham."

Then he'd taken off after the guy.

Just missed him as he stepped onto the elevator.

Orion debated taking all eleven flights up, but maybe he'd just park here and wait for the next elevator.

Shoot—no, he hated waiting.

He hit the elevator button. *C'mon!*

The other elevator opened, and he got in.

But a man and woman got in with him, and then held the doors for two more people, and he tried to push out, but they blocked the doors and they closed on him.

He leaned back, folding his arms, staring at the numbers, calling himself all sorts of stupid.

One couple got off on the third floor. Really, they couldn't have walked up?

Worse, they held the door as they chatted with their friends, making plans to meet up in the bar later.

Orion nearly kicked them out, unfolding his arms, taking a breath.

They laughed at a joke and then the other couple came back

inside and let the door go. The man wore a suit, the woman was in a thick wool coat over a dress and boots. She turned to the man and said something in his ear. The man smiled.

For a second, Orion was back in the car, kissing Jenny, his heart breaking for her terrible secret.

Once he took care of business with Martin, he wouldn't mind hunting down this Brendan fellow . . . But he knew about mistakes and regret and maybe the guy hadn't walked away intact.

So instead, Orion would just help Jenny heal, show her every day that she wasn't the sum of her mistakes. *"We're in this together."*

The other couple got off at eight and Orion's nerves buzzed under his skin as he stepped up to the door, watching the numbers light up.

Ten . . . eleven.

Please, let Martin be here, somewhere—how he was going to find him, Orion didn't have a clue, but—

The doors opened. And, as if God had heard him, Martin stood right there.

For a second, they simply stared at each other, Martin still dressed in his waiter disguise.

Orion smiled. "Miss me?"

Then he launched at Martin.

Martin sidestepped him, sent a punch at his head, but Orion ducked and grabbed his hand, twisted, turned, and slammed his fist into Martin's ribs.

Martin bounced away, grunting, and turned. "I see we're still angry about Italy."

Orion drew in a breath just as Martin came at him.

He deflected his punch, trapped his other arm and slapped away the cross punch. Then he swung Martin's arm back into a bar, locking his elbow. He chopped his other hand into the back of Martin's neck, bending him over into submission.

And that's how it's done.

Except Martin slammed his fist into Orion's bad knee, and of course—*of course*—it had to give out. Just for a second, but long enough for Martin to twist away.

He rounded, kicked Orion in the chest, sent him into the wall, and took off down the hall.

Nice. Pain shot up his leg, but not enough to slow Orion down. He hit the stairwell and spotted Martin already two flights down.

Orion took the stairs three at a time, more, nearly jumping from stairwell to stairwell, and frankly any pain vanished by the time he hit the ground floor.

He'd made up time, Martin just ahead of him.

And that's when he spotted Jake. Blessed Jake who was wandering in the hallway outside the ballroom.

"Jake!"

Martin took off toward the other stairwell at the end of the hall.

"Don't let him leave the hotel!"

Jake sprinted for the stairwell.

A security officer came out of the ballroom, took a look at Orion, disheveled and sweaty, and tried to step in front of him.

Orion shoved him out of the way, kept running.

It slowed him down enough for him to hear a shout when he reached the stairwell.

Way to go, Jake.

Except, when he opened the door, he found Jake on the middle landing, on his knees, bleeding hard from a cut in the head. A fire extinguisher lay nearby.

"Jake—get up!" Orion ran past him. "Get help!"

He landed on the service floor and threw open the door. Housekeeping carts, linen baskets, a long supply closet. He slowed, Jake's trauma echoing in his mind. Martin could be hiding. Or he could be long gone, heading for the loading docks.

"Yeah, I'm still hot about Italy. C'mon, Martin. Don't run away."

He crept down the hallway, out into the next room.

The catering kitchen. The place was a hum of activity, shouts from chefs, the clank of utensils, the smell of baked goods and sense of chaos.

A massive vent hung from the center of the room, over a long stainless steel oven-and-stove workspace. Along the wall, giant walk-in refrigerators and freezers gleamed, reflecting the hanging lights.

And, throughout the space, line cooks and chefs worked on plating hors d'oeuvres for the party upstairs.

Orion walked in, looked around.

The kitchen led to another hallway, more stairs, and by the sign posted, the loading dock.

Martin was gone.

Orion stood there, his jaw tight, and a female waitstaff looked over at him as she carried in an empty tray from upstairs.

It was her widened eyes, her shout, that saved his life.

He turned just as Martin's knife came down at him. Orion threw up an arm, and the blade sliced through the flesh of his forearm.

He didn't even feel the pain as he grabbed Martin's wrist and sent a punch across his jaw.

Martin ripped himself away, breathing hard.

Orion ignored the blood from his arm.

Around him, the room had stilled.

Run. Orion heard his instructor—and that of every other hand-to-hand combat class he'd taken—in his head. First rule of knife fighting—someone was going to get hurt.

Yeah, well, today it was Martin.

"You're not getting out of here," Orion said, using his peripheral vision to look for a weapon. Or defense.

"And you think you're going to stop me?" Martin lunged again at Orion.

Orion jumped away, kicked at his hand.

"Run!" Orion shouted to the crowd but kept his eyes on Martin's hand. He came at him again, and this time Orion grabbed his wrist and brought it down to his hip, trapping it.

Martin hit him in the face.

The world blacked, but he held onto his wrist, twisting with Martin as they banged around the room.

They scuffled down the galley.

"Ry!"

The voice shot a chill through him.

No—*no*—how had Jenny gotten here? But he couldn't take his eyes off the knife. Orion headbutted him, and Martin's nose exploded. They'd already bloodied the serving carts, the floor—

Martin broke free, wiped his wrist across his bloodied face.

He couldn't look for Jenny.

The butcher's knife dripped.

"Whoever is left in here needs to get out, right now," Orion said. He just needed to buy time until Jake showed up.

Gun against knife—he hoped Jake arrived armed.

Martin shook his head. "I know you're weak. I saw you go down in Italy. I studied you, Orion Starr. I know one good shot to the knee, and this is over. I don't even need the knife."

He set it down on the counter, held up his hands. "See?"

Orion watched his hands, saw the twitch.

Braced himself because any second Martin was going to sweep up the knife and maybe even throw it—

Bam! The sound was so loud it reverberated into Orion's bones. He stood there, wordless, as Martin dropped, hard, onto the red tile floor.

Jenny stood behind him holding a cast-iron pan, her hair out of its pinnings, her heels off, breathing hard. "I'm done negotiating."

Orion put his hands down and in a second was on Martin, his knee in his back, Martin's wrist bent back in a submission hold.

Right then, Jake showed up. "Dude—sorry." Blood covered his face, a giant welt over his eye getting bigger. He grasped the side of the counter, as if the world was spinning. But he had a gun— where he'd gotten it, Orion didn't want to guess.

Aria rushed in, past Jenny. "Jake!" She grabbed him around the waist and helped him to the floor. "I need some ice, and a bandage."

"It looks worse than it is—"

"Right, that's a serious head wound," Aria said.

Jenny knelt next to Orion. "You're bleeding too."

"Good job with that pan, babe." He looked over at her.

"Teamwork," Jenny said, grinning.

Martin came to, shaking, and Orion held him down. "Somebody get help," he said, because yes, now he was starting to hurt.

"You got it," said a voice, and he looked up to see Ford Marshall, Ruby Jane, and York entering the kitchen.

And behind them—what?

Royal Benjamin.

Orion just looked at him, frozen. The man had leaned out, his face hard, but he smiled as he spotted Orion. "Hey there, PJ."

"What are you doing here?" And that was the least of his questions, but . . . "You're okay?"

Royal knelt next to Orion. "Yeah. I'm good. Especially now that you got this guy. We've been trying to pin him down for a while. All those missives sent by Signe to the CIA? Martin intercepted them. Redirected them."

York came over too. Bent over in front of Martin. "Hey there, pal, remember me?" York looked up at Orion. "I'm getting a little tired of people I trusted betraying me."

"Yeah. Game over," Orion said, a strange, deep sense of satisfaction sweeping through him.

"Is Martin running the rogue CIA group?" Jenny said.

York shook his head. "Oh no. That honor goes to Vice President Reba Jackson, just like Signe said."

Martin's jaw tightened.

"Search him. Make sure he doesn't have anything lethal on him," Roy said.

Ford patted him down and came up with a cell phone and a hotel key card. The phone was locked. He handed the key card to York.

Ford passed the phone to Scarlett. "See if you can unlock the phone."

"It doesn't matter. You're all too late anyway," Martin said.

"No, we're not." Scarlett came up and looked at Roy. "We need to warn the president that he shouldn't come here. That he's in danger."

Royal looked at her, and even Orion went cold at his expression. "The president is already here."

■ ■ ■

Signe chose the closet because, well, she hadn't a clue where else to go.

She was fresh out of places to run.

She couldn't go into the ballroom, not without threatening all those people.

And sure, as long as White wasn't in the building yet, she was safe, but . . .

But there was no getting out of this. She couldn't leave the building, she couldn't call for help.

344

What she could do was keep Ham safe.

Give Aggie a father.

Even if she broke his heart.

She put her head into her knees, hearing her voice shouting at him through the glass. *"You get in the way and . . . I don't want you in my life. Just stay there and leave me alone."*

She was sick to her stomach at her words, but she needed him to stay put.

And then she found a place the farthest away from Ham and locked herself inside.

Scarlett had found her easily, probably because Scarlett had been watching her the entire time.

Smart woman. She'd caught on to Signe's request without the need for explanation, had contacted a friend who brought the device in via her K9 dog kit.

Signe put it on in the bathroom before her meeting, not sure what to expect.

At least . . . well, at least her daughter would know she wasn't a traitor.

And Ruslan would live.

"Talk to me, Signe."

She wanted to weep when she heard Ham's voice outside the door. When he ordered the team away.

When he sat down and said, his voice so calm, so in control—and yes, she desperately needed that right now—"Shorty, it's just you and me now. And I'm not going anywhere. I'm staying right here until you come out."

Shoot. No! Inside her head she was screaming.

And Tsarnaev was probably listening.

So, she kept quiet.

"Signe."

She couldn't stand it. "Go away, Ham. I have to do this. Alone."

And, of course he didn't understand. "Do what?"

Nothing.

"Do *what?*"

Please, Ham. Because if Ham gave away her position, then Tsarnaev would know she wasn't in the ballroom. At least with this position, she looked close to the ballroom, on the main floor.

Aw, he wasn't easily fooled, clearly.

She'd been such an idiot to think that she could be someone amazing. Save lives. Be a hero.

She could choke on her own stupid aspirations.

Then, she felt fingers against her leg, stuck under the door just like she'd done to Ham so many years ago. Under the door, under their desks, across a dark closet.

She couldn't stop herself from reaching down and weaving hers through his.

Oh, she didn't deserve him.

Ever.

And Tsarnaev picked then to roar back into her brain. *"You would have never surrendered to me in the first place if you didn't believe that you deserved it."*

No. That wasn't true.

"At some point in your life, someone told you that you weren't worth protecting. Weren't really worth loving. And you believed them."

Not anymore.

"Start listening to the truth. Ham, your friends, and, if you want, God. Because clearly he brought you back to the starting place."

The starting place.

And suddenly, she was thirteen years old, in a thin dress, hiding in her barn. The smell of stale hay and old manure drifted up through the slats of the haymow and the cool wind whisked over her. She pulled up her dress and hid her knees in it, touched her forehead to her knees.

"I thought I'd find you here."

Signe nearly lifted her head, the voice felt so real, but it was just Ham, tiptoeing into the haymow in her mind. In her heart.

"I'm sorry about your grandfather." He came over to her. He wore his dirty orange-and-brown jacket and a pair of jeans, his hair long and scraggly. "You look cold."

She didn't say anything, and he shucked off his jacket and put it over her shoulders.

Then he moved in around her, his legs and arms embracing her. "It's okay, Shorty. I'm not going anywhere."

She'd held on to him, refusing to cry. Because why did it matter, anyway? God wasn't on her side. And crying wouldn't bring her grandfather back.

"He's the only one who ever wanted me," she said quietly, her voice small.

"That's not true," Ham said. "I want you. You're my best friend."

Huh. She'd sort of forgotten that memory. But sitting here, her fingers touching his, it stirred from the dust of her heart.

That, and, "Why?" she'd asked.

"I don't know. Maybe because you want me, too?"

He'd meant it honestly, and back then, she hadn't assigned anything but friendship to it.

Maybe it was just that simple. Maybe there wasn't a reason to love someone. Maybe you just did. And that was enough.

Nothing to prove. And if she didn't have to prove it, then she didn't have to fear losing it either, by screwing it up.

She simply was loved.

By Ham.

It just took the feel of Ham's fingers, entwined with hers, to realize . . . yes, God had brought her back to the beginning.

To the one her heart loved.

Because . . . maybe the Almighty loved her too.

Her core wasn't shame.

Her core was love.

And love was power.

Love was hope.

Love was happy endings.

Her fingers wove around Ham's.

No more hiding in the closet.

She let go and got up, easing the broom handle away from where she'd lodged it into the door, and opened it.

Ham had also gotten up, and now she pressed her finger to her mouth.

His tuxedo was a mess, untucked, his hair undone by the running of his hand through it.

She pointed to the bracelet, and then her ear. Held up her fingers, like it might be a phone. He nodded.

She exploded her hands out, and his eyes widened.

Then he took her hand. *Trust me*, his mouth said, but she heard it with her heart.

Yes. Always.

Ham headed down the hallway, toward the stairwell.

He took it down, two flights, all the way to the basement, then walked out into the corridor. Signe could see the light on the bracelet still blinking. This wasn't going to work, and she almost said it when he came to a secure door.

He keyed in a code on the keypad.

It opened.

He took her down three more flights to another secure entrance. Ham keyed in another code, and he pulled her into a corridor. The place reeked of age, the lighting dismal but, as he took her hand and began to walk down the tunnel, the light flicked off.

She stopped. "Ham. The bracelet—it stopped transmitting."

He turned. Looked at the bracelet, then, "No."

Huh?

"I'm not going to leave you alone. Ever. If you run, I'll find you. If you push me away, I'll stick around. I love you, Signe. You and I belong together. You're my wife and—"

"Yes." She pressed her hands to his chest. "Yes, I am."

He kissed her. And it wasn't one of those tentative kisses he'd been giving her for the past month, but the kind that reminded her of exactly the man she'd married. A man of honor, yes, but a warrior, a man of purpose and power, and the kind of man she could hang on to. He backed her up to the wall, leaned against it with one hand, and pulled her to himself with the other.

She wrapped her arms around his neck and let him storm into every compartment of her heart. It all belonged to him, anyway.

She was safe. She was wanted.

And, she still wore a bomb on her wrist. She pushed on his good shoulder.

He lifted his head. "I know."

"What?"

"That you're wearing a bomb."

How did he *do* that?

"But down here, the signal won't reach, so for now, we're safe."

Oh, she wished. "No, Ham . . . we're not. I mean, yes, the president is, but . . . Ham, Tsarnaev has my son."

Ham just blinked at her, frowned. "Ruslan?"

He remembered his name. And that shook her to her core . . . except it was Ham.

And he loved her.

Of course he'd remember her son.

"Tsarnaev showed me a live video of him, playing a video game, here in DC. The Washington Monument was in the background."

"Right. Okay, so we get this thing off you and then we track down your son—"

"And how are we going to get this off me? The latch is locked."

"Maybe we can help."

The voice stilled her, and Ham drew in a breath. Stood up. "Sir."

Isaac White—er, *President* Isaac White—came walking down the hallway toward them. "Orion caught Martin. It was quite the spectacle, but he was able to get a message to me. I was already on premises, so your quick thinking saved my life."

He was looking at both of them.

"Sir, I am to blame," Signe said.

"No. You're not. You were doing what your country asked of you. You were protecting the lives of its citizens. And you paid a steep price for it. In my book, you're a hero, Signe."

Oh. His words could hollow her out, except, well . . . She held up the bracelet. "Except for this."

"Yeah, about that." He looked over at a man standing in the shadows. He stepped forward, past the president. "This is my friend Roy—"

"You stay back!" Signe took a running start, and before Ham could stop her, she'd launched herself at Roy, vaulted up his leg, twisted around his body, slung her leg around his neck, and clasped her legs together in a rear triangle choke hold.

And just like that, the man was down.

Apparently, she'd forgotten she was wearing a dress, or perhaps she didn't care. Somewhere in there, however, she'd lost her fancy shoes.

"Signe! Stop!" White said.

Roy had his hands up, clasping her legs. "Let me go!"

"He tried to kill me in Germany!"

"I didn't!" He looked up. "Ham?"

Ham stepped up to him. "Signe, this is Royal Benjamin. He used to be on my team."

"I cut him. Check his knuckles."

"It's true, but I was trying to help you. I was your contact."

She went silent.

"My tag. It's a bonefrog, Signe. See?" Royal lifted his arm, pulling back his sleeve, his air clearly cutting out.

"You can trust him, Signe. But thanks for the save," the president said.

She released her legs, scooted away. "Where were you, in Germany?"

Roy sat up, catching his breath. "Sheesh."

Ham was grinning at her. But he held out a hand to Roy.

Roy got up. "I know I let everything go south. It's my fault. I got there early and I saw Martin, and I needed to know what he was up to, so I hung back."

"And left me to hang."

"I was there—I followed you. But I needed to know what his game was, so—"

"So you let him try and kill me. Kill my friends." She found her feet.

"I'm sorry about that. Really. I shot him in Germany when he tried to take you, but clearly I underestimated him."

"I think we all underestimated this entire conspiracy," White said.

"I didn't," Signe said.

Ham looked at her, his mouth hiding a smile.

She shrugged, but her mouth was a tight bud of anger, her eyes hard on Roy.

"When this is over, clearly you'll still have a job with the CIA," White said.

"Not unless I can serve down here." She held up the bracelet. "Bomb, anyone?"

"I got this," Roy said.

"Without cutting my arm off?"

"Maybe we should evacuate you, sir, just in case," Ham said.

White headed down the tunnel but turned. "Thank you, Ham. For everything. You're a good man and a credit to your country."

Signe watched Ham, the way White's words hit him. The look on his face found her heart.

He was a good man, and she'd spend the rest of her life reminding him of that.

Roy had her arm out, was looking at the clasp. "I've seen this before. It's like a shoe bomb, except it has a firing pin meant to ignite the TATP in the bracelet. I'm not sure how much explosive is in here, but it would have definitely caused damage. I just need to separate the pin from the ignition chamber." He pulled out his Ka-Bar. "Better look away," he said to Signe.

"What?"

He was laughing as he stuck the end into the lock and twisted.

The lock broke and she caught it before it fell onto the cement floor.

"Good nab," Roy said. He held out his hand.

She noticed his scarred knuckles. "Sorry."

"My bad. I shouldn't have let you get in trouble."

She rubbed her wrist. Looked at Ham. "I'm going to find Tsarnaev."

He held out his hand. "Not without me you're not."

CHAPTER SIXTEEN

THIS IS HOW it should have been from the beginning.

Signe and Ham, working together, hunting down a terrorist. Saving lives.

Just like they had poor, sweet Caesar from the storm drain.

"Security has Tsarnaev leaving shortly after Jackson. It looks like he's headed the other direction." Ham braced one hand on the back of the security officer's chair.

"See if you can pick him up outside," Signe said. She had changed clothes into cargo pants, a flannel shirt over her T-shirt, and her Cons.

In the security room, Scarlett and Ruby Jane were trying to unlock the cell phone. Logan and York had taken Martin into another room, probably for interrogation.

Jake had gone to the hospital with Aria. Apparently, he'd taken a good blow to the noggin. Orion, too, needed stitches, and Jenny had ridden with him in the ambulance.

The ball hadn't been evacuated—the news of the bomb threat diminished before Logan could galvanize his team.

Which meant that no one in Washington knew that Jackson and her alliances planned on dismantling the world order.

Or, at least, putting her in power after the untimely death of the president.

But she wasn't going anywhere—not with her face on the world screen as she prepared to make yet another appearance at the Liberty Ball at the Washington Convention Center, this time with the president in attendance.

Surprise, surprise—he wasn't assassinated by a rogue CIA bomber.

"There," Signe said, looking over the shoulder of another security officer, badge name Erredge. "He's headed down 14th, away from the Patriot."

"Get me a map," Ham said, but the first officer had already brought it up.

"If he's headed down 14th, he might be going to the Marriott," Ham said.

The door closed behind him and Ford had come in. "The JW Marriott?" He reached into his pocket. "Sorry. We took this off Martin." He handed him a key card. "It's from the Marriott."

And bingo, Ham knew in his bones, it wasn't a coincidence.

Signe looked at him, the same expression in her eyes. "Let's go."

He turned to Ford. "Get ahold of Logan and ask the Secret Service to meet us there."

"Yes, sir."

Yes, someday he wanted Ford on his team.

Ham followed Signe through the door.

They didn't even bother to get an Uber, the air crisp and bright as they ran down the street, coatless. Just two blocks, and he wasn't even breathing hard when they hit the lobby of the Marriott.

He grabbed Signe's arm, however, before they reached the desk. "We have no weapons, no identification. How are we going to get in?"

"Who says we have no identification?" She pulled a dark red passport out of her pocket. "I brought it along, just in case."

He looked at her. "Research."

"Hunch. Stay here. And give me the key."

He handed it to her, and she walked up to the desk, to a young woman.

"Hello. My husband asked me to meet him here. I have a key but no room number. Can you direct me?" She affected a slight accent, pulled out the key card, and opened her identification.

The woman swiped her card, checked her passport, and put the key in a new envelope, writing the number on the cover. "It's a suite, but this card will get you into both rooms."

"Can I get a copy? You know how it is—they're so easy to lose."

The woman coded another card and slipped it into the envelope.

"Thank you."

She headed toward the elevator bank.

Ham followed her, stood behind her, and said nothing until they got inside.

She pushed the button for the eighth floor. Stood back. Breathed.

He faced her. "We should wait for the Secret Service, Sig."

"No. We need to surprise him. If we wait, he could take Ruslan hostage and hurt him." She flexed a muscle in her jaw.

Well, she knew this man better than he did. And no, Ham didn't want to think about that, but in this case— "What's the best way to do this?"

"I'm going to just go in."

What? "Sig. What if he has an army in there?"

"He doesn't. It's just him. He never lets his men stay in the room with him. Just in case he wants company."

Ham's mouth tightened. "No. Have you lost your mind? No way am I letting you near this monster."

"I'll go in, distract him, and you get Ruslan."

"Ho-kay, listen, I know you took down Orion, but this man—"

"Hurt me, attacked me, and terrorized me for years." Her eyes darkened. "It's my turn."

She scared him a little.

No, a lot.

The elevator dinged and she shot him a look. "My way."

"What if he has a gun?"

"Yeah, well, me too." She reached behind her and pulled a gun from her belt, under her shirt.

And maybe he should have seen that, but it was dark and she was wearing a bulky, flannel shirt and—

No, he just didn't expect it. Again. "Where did you get that?"

"Erredge. The security officer."

"Signe—"

"Ham. Listen. I'm not going to shoot him. I'm just going to keep him away from Ruslan." She touched Ham's chest, put a foot in the door of the elevator to keep it from closing. "Let's rescue my son."

And what was he going to do with that?

He nodded and they headed down the hall.

She handed him a key card. "Go into the other room a second after me."

How he hated it when he wasn't in charge.

He positioned himself at the far door.

She slid the card into the door, hid the gun behind her back.

The door clicked, opened.

He dropped the key card into his door.

She disappeared inside.

His door clicked.

He opened it.

Tsarnaev—or who he assumed was the terrorist—sat on the bed staring at the television. He banged to his feet.

Ham crossed the room in two steps, grabbed him by the throat, and threw him onto the floor.

Apparently, he'd gotten the lucky room.

Tsarnaev swore at him but Ham had him down, his arm across his neck, his other in an arm bar.

Well, that was easy—

"Ham, back away from him."

Signe stood near the door, the gun aimed at Tsarnaev.

"Shorty, what are you doing?"

She wasn't shaking, her breaths were even, and she didn't look in the least rattled.

Oh no, *no*—

"Signe—"

"I'm not going to let him go to trial, sit in prison, let him stir up more hate in our American prisons. He needs to die—"

"Sig, listen." Ham got up, pinning Tsarnaev down with a foot in his neck, still holding his arm. "I get it. I do. But this isn't you. You're a mom. And a patriot. And a warrior. And smart and beautiful. But you're not a killer."

"Yes, she is," Tsarnaev said, smiling. "She tried to kill me."

"Too bad I didn't succeed."

"No, she's not," Ham said. "I should know." He met her eyes. "Because I'm her husband."

She drew in a shaky breath, and her eyes glistened.

"Mama?"

The voice came from behind her, and Signe turned to follow it. Put the gun down.

A little boy had emerged from the bathroom and now stood in the room in a pair of pajamas, a Thor T-shirt. Brown hair, slight build.

Ruslan.

With a roar, Tsarnaev turned, grabbed Ham's ankle, and kicked him in the knee.

Ham caught himself on the dresser, but Tsarnaev had scrambled to his feet.

Tsarnaev picked up the lamp and threw it at Ham.

And that was just it.

Ham deflected the lamp, took two steps, and slammed his fist into Tsarnaev's distorted face. He howled, and Ham sent him to the ground with a cross punch.

Tsarnaev hit his knees and Ham grabbed him around the neck, threw him down, slammed his foot into his spine, and held him there.

"Toss me that gun, Sig," he said.

Her eyes widened, but she obeyed. He caught it, made sure a round was chambered, and pointed it at Tsarnaev's head. "Maybe I should have let her shoot you, but I promise, you get up and I will."

Signe had her arms around Ruslan, holding him to herself. His eyes were wide as he looked at Ham.

Cute kid. Reminded him of Aggie a little.

Of course he did. He was Signe's son.

And maybe in time, his son too.

On the television, the Yankee Belles had just finished their song, the cameras panning to the stage wings for Vice President Jackson's entrance.

Instead, Ham caught sight of President White. And behind him, Royal Benjamin.

He sure hoped Orion was watching.

The door banged open and Logan Thorne and a cadre of Secret Service agents charged into the room.

Ham let them have Tsarnaev and walked over to Signe. Put his arms around her.

"Would you really have shot him?" she asked.

"Would you?"

She smiled at him. "A girl has to have her secrets."

Epilogue

THE PERFECT DAY FOR A WEDDING. The clouds hung high, the air crisp, and a flock of birds had just returned to the budding maple and oak trees around the Marshall family winery. The late-afternoon sun poured through the eyelet curtains of the second-floor double bedroom.

Okay, not quite a wedding, but a *re*-wedding. The kind of wedding that Ham had always wanted.

After fifteen years, Signe called it a vow renewal. But she felt like a bride the way Mama J—as Jenny Calhoun called her—had fixed her hair.

Signe wore a white dress, which she wanted to protest, but maybe they were starting over. Besides, she was giving him a brand-new heart. One without the scars and wounds.

One that God had healed when Ham asked her if he could adopt her son.

God had brought her back to the beginning, to her silly dreams of belonging to Ham.

And he belonged to her, right back.

"You're gorgeous," Jenny said. "Ham is going to flip."

It wasn't a fancy dress, just to her ankles, and she wore a pair of white Uggs, thanks to the snow still patchy in the yard. The dress had long lacy sleeves, and she wore her hair down, curled, just the way Ham liked it.

Jenny had put her hands on her shoulders and looked at her through the mirror, and now Signe noticed the ring.

She took Jenny's hand, sizing up the diamond in the simple setting. "He proposed?"

"Again, yes. Last night at the same pizza joint. You'd think he wouldn't want to be seen there again, but Orion likes to fix the past, so . . . yeah."

"Fancy."

"He's just trying to keep up with your boy," Jenny said.

"And then some," Signe said. She liked Jenny. They shared similar experiences.

Similar PTSD.

In fact, she liked his entire team.

They'd stood beside her over the past two months as she testified before Congress about her experiences with former vice president Jackson.

Orion and Ham had joined her in the Oval Office when Isaac White presented her with the National Intelligence Medal for Valor.

Ham and Orion each received the Presidential Medal of Freedom.

Pavel Tsarnaev's trial was still months ahead, but she'd given her sworn testimony.

The time for mourning was over. It was time for joy.

And when Ham suggested heading out to the Marshall winery to renew their vows . . . well, she'd do anything for the crazy romantic in Ham.

"I think he's ready for you," Mama J said, poking her head into the room. "Your daughter and son are adorable."

Yes, they were. Aggie was the perfect older sister to a brother who needed time and attention. She'd given him almost all of her zoo—keeping back the unicorn and the fuzzy rabbit—and Ham had converted the third bedroom into a room for a little boy, complete with superheroes on the wall, too many Lego sets, and enough sports equipment to turn the kid into a running back for the Minnesota Vikings.

More, Ham was the perfect father, making up for every moment his stepmother had wounded him.

She couldn't wait to re-marry this man.

Jenny handed her a bouquet of lilies, and Signe followed her down the stairs.

The winery hosted tastings and weddings in a small portico area, and now, despite the chill in the air and the twilight hour, twinkle lights lit up the area. Massive heaters lined the outside of the portico. Their friends stood around Ham—Jake and Aria, Orion, his teammate North, who she remembered from Chechnya, Scarlett, and Mr. and Mrs. Marshall.

Ham wore a gray suit, slicked up and handsome, his hair freshly cut. Oh, the man did every look well.

He had one hand on Aggie's shoulder, the other on Ruslan's. Her son wore a matching suit, his dark hair wet and combed back. Aggie wore a pretty pink dress, a girlie-girl down to her bones. Signe hadn't a clue where she got that, but Ham pampered his daughter like a man smitten.

Signe walked into the center of the circle and it closed around her, Jenny taking Orion's hand.

Ham held out his hands, his eyes in hers. "Hey, Shorty. Thanks for coming."

"Thanks for the invite, Hamburglar."

A chuckle went through the circle. Signe handed her bouquet of lilies to Aggie, who beamed at her.

Ham ran his thumbs over the tops of her hands. "Signe, I can't remember when I started loving you. You were just always there, in my heart. The fabric of my life. Every good memory I have of my childhood includes you."

A few of those memories rushed through her, and her body heated.

"When we were apart, I think my heart simply couldn't beat. I tried to move on, tried to make peace with the fact that you were, um, gone . . ." He glanced at Aggie, back to Signe. Right. No need to make their children relive the dark years.

"But I couldn't. You were imprinted on my heart. And when I found you, I finally understood the great love God has for me. For you. For us. The idea that we cannot be erased from his mind. I love you, Signe. I will never stop loving you. You are my yesterday, my today, and my tomorrow. And I will cherish and honor you the rest of the days of my life."

Oh Ham. Sheesh, he could make a former spy cry.

The sun was sinking behind him, a glorious display of gold, amber, magenta, and copper spilling across the horizon. A flock of geese honked overhead, returning to the north. Buds dotted the apple trees in the fields nearby.

"Ham, you were my hero from the first day you walked into my life. My heart always knew it, but my head couldn't believe it. Thank you for not giving up on me. For not letting go. For sacrificing and believing in us. I believe God loves me because he gave me you." She looked at her children. "And Aggie and Ruslan."

Ruslan had lost a tooth, and when he grinned up at her she could barely speak.

She looked back at her husband. "Ham, you showed me love. You showed me hope. You showed me God. And I am never leaving your side again. I am yours, for the rest of my life."

He grinned and moved to kiss her but she backed away. "Not

quite yet, number three." She turned to Jenny and held out her hand. Jenny put the black titanium wedding band in her hand.

Signe held it out to Ham. "Just in case people wonder if you're taken."

He put it on. "Very, very taken."

Then he kissed her, sliding his hand behind her neck, and she laughed while their friends clapped.

"That was beautiful," Aria said, wiping her cheeks, and she hugged Signe.

Ham clapped Jake on the shoulder as Jake shook his hand. Ham whispered in his ear and Jake laughed. "I know."

Aggie tugged on his jacket, and Ham looked down at her.

"Now do we get to roast marshmallows?"

"Anything for you, Aggie."

"Ham, you're so going to spoil her," Signe said.

He looked at Signe and grinned. "Oh, Shorty, that's the point of being a father. To delight in your children. I'm just getting started."

She pressed her hand to her stomach. Smiled. "Yes, Ham, you are."

His eyes widened.

She winked, grabbed Aggie's hand, and went to roast marshmallows.

Susan May Warren is the *USA Today* bestselling author of over eighty novels with more than 1.5 million books sold, including the Montana Rescue series. Winner of a RITA Award and multiple Christy and Carol Awards, as well as the HOLT Medallion and numerous Readers' Choice Awards, Susan has written contemporary and historical romances, romantic suspense, thrillers, romantic comedy, and novellas. She makes her home in Minnesota. Find her online at www.susanmaywarren.com, on Facebook at Susan May Warren Fiction, and on Twitter @susanmaywarren.

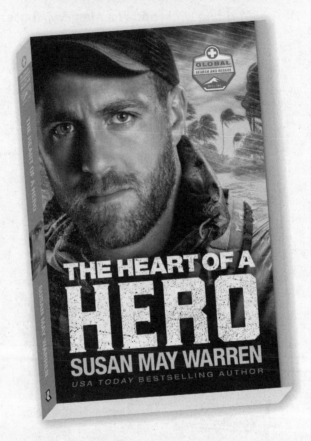

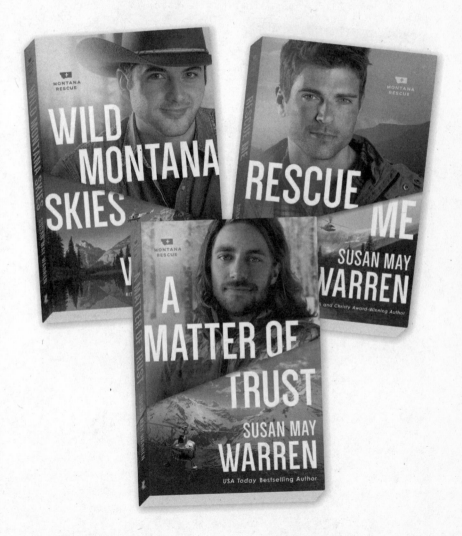

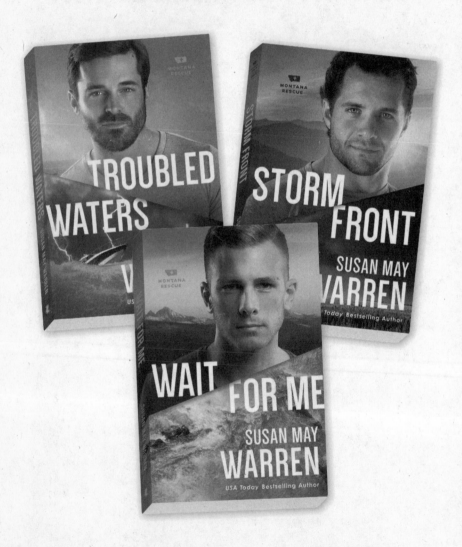